Hungarian
Folktales

Hungarian Folktales

Introduction by Boglárka Klitsie-Szabad

General Editor: Jake Jackson

FLAME TREE
PUBLISHING

This is a FLAME TREE Book

FLAME TREE PUBLISHING
6 Melbray Mews
Fulham, London SW6 3NS
United Kingdom
www.flametreepublishing.com

First published 2023
Copyright © 2023 Flame Tree Publishing Ltd

23 25 27 26 24
1 3 5 7 9 8 6 4 2

ISBN: 978-1-80417-581-1

The cover image is © copyright 2023 Flame Tree Publishing Ltd, based
on artwork courtesy of Shutterstock.com/Andrea Molnar.

All inside images courtesy of Shutterstock.com and the
following: Skaska_I, Imre Sandor, Andrea Molnar.

The stories 'Mezőszárnyasi', 'Cibere' and 'The Priest and Believers' are
© copyright and printed with permission from Maja Bumberák.

The stories in this book derive from the following sources: *The Folk-Tales of
the Magyars, Collected by Kriza, Erdélyi, Pap, and Others*, translated and
edited by Rev. W. Henry Jones and Lewis L. Kropf (1889, The Folk-Lore Society,
published by Elliot Stock); *Old Hungarian Fairy Tales* by Baroness Orczy (1895,
published by Dean & Son/Wolf & Co.); and as re-told by Maja Bumberák.

Printed and bound in the UK by Clays Ltd, Elcograf S.p.A

Contents

Series Foreword

STRETCHING BACK to the oral traditions of thousands of years ago, tales of heroes and disaster, creation and conquest have been told by many different civilizations in many different ways. Their impact sits deep within our culture even though the detail in the tales themselves are a loose mix of historical record, transformed narrative and the distortions of hundreds of storytellers.

Today the language of mythology lives with us: our mood is jovial, our countenance is saturnine, we are narcissistic and our modern life is hermetically sealed from others. The nuances of myths and legends form part of our daily routines and help us navigate the world around us, with its half truths and biased reported facts.

The nature of a myth is that its story is already known by most of those who hear it, or read it. Every generation brings a new emphasis, but the fundamentals remain the same: a desire to understand and describe the events and relationships of the world. Many of the great stories are archetypes that help us find our own place, equipping us with tools for self-understanding, both individually and as part of a broader culture.

For Western societies it is Greek mythology that speaks to us most clearly. It greatly influenced the mythological heritage of the ancient Roman civilization and is the lens through which we still see the Celts, the Norse and many of the other great peoples and religions. The Greeks themselves learned much from their neighbours, the Egyptians, an older culture that became weak with age and incestuous leadership.

It is important to understand that what we perceive now as mythology had its own origins in perceptions of the divine and the rituals of the sacred. The earliest civilizations, in the crucible of the Middle East, in the Sumer of the third millennium BC, are the source to which many of the mythic archetypes can be traced. As humankind collected together in cities for the first time, developed writing and industrial scale agriculture, started to irrigate the rivers and attempted to control rather than be at the mercy of its environment, humanity began to write down its tentative explanations of natural events, of floods and plagues, of disease.

Early stories tell of Gods (or god-like animals in the case of tribal societies such as African, Native American or Aboriginal cultures) who are crafty and use their wits to survive, and it is reasonable to suggest that these were the first rulers of the gathering peoples of the earth, later elevated to god-like status with the distance of time. Such tales became more political as cities vied with each other for supremacy, creating new Gods, new hierarchies for their pantheons. The older Gods took on primordial roles and became the preserve of creation and destruction, leaving the new gods to deal with more current, everyday affairs. Empires rose and fell, with Babylon assuming the mantle from Sumeria in the 1800s BC, then in turn to be swept away by the Assyrians of the 1200s BC; then the Assyrians and the Egyptians were subjugated by the Greeks, the Greeks by the Romans and so on, leading to the spread and assimilation of common themes, ideas and stories throughout the world.

The survival of history is dependent on the telling of good tales, but each one must have the 'feeling' of truth, otherwise it will be ignored. Around the firesides, or embedded in a book or a computer, the myths and legends of the past are still the living materials of retold myth, not restricted to an exploration of origins. Now we have devices and global communications that give us unparalleled access to a diversity of traditions. We can find out about Native American, Indian, Chinese and tribal African mythology in a way that was denied to our ancestors, we can find connections, match the archaeology, religion and the mythologies of the world to build a comprehensive image of the human experience that is endlessly fascinating.

The stories in this book provide an introduction to the themes and concerns of the myths and legends of their respective cultures, with a short introduction to provide a linguistic, geographic and political context. This is where the myths have arrived today, but undoubtedly over the next millennia, they will transform again whilst retaining their essential truths and signs.

Jake Jackson
General Editor

Introduction to Hungarian Folktales

D ear Reader, you are now holding a very special and varied selection of folktales in your hands. In this volume, you will find many interesting old or indeed completely new pieces of Hungarian epic folklore from different areas. In addition to geographical diversity (Transylvania, Palócland or north-eastern Hungary), diverse fairy tale genres and a varied palette of different folktales are also presented. Discoveries of mostly nineteenth-century collections (materials by János Kriza – John Kriza; János Erdélyi – John Erdélyi; and Gyula Pap – Julius Pap) can be found here, but individual creativity and writing talent is also shown through the tales of Baroness Orczy, which may also be rooted in folklore. Another special feature of this volume is that one of today's mindful and thorough contemporary Hungarian storytellers, Maja Bumberák, who tells stories in several languages, shares three of her tales, which she compiled from previous collections and finally shaped into her own retellings.

Tradition and Purpose

What is a folktale? What do we know about the tradition of storytelling, and in particular Hungarian storytelling? Hundreds of books deal with this subject, many of them specifically with stories by Hungarian storytellers or the stories of the different ethnicities found here (for example, the Hungarian-speaking region was very rich in Roma storytellers, but there are also Hungarian collections from Slovak or German-speaking storytellers).

The folktale is often referred to as one of the most beautiful genres of epic oral storytelling, and it is also a fact that Hungarians lack the genre of the heroic epic. A heroic epic is a work centred on one or more of a hero's important acts. It consists of several parts, like a series of stories, but can still be considered a unified work. The hero performs significant acts for the community. There were attempts to find or rewrite the 'lost Hungarian heroic epic', but this was not really successful in Hungary, so we can say that the folktale is our longest epic folklore genre. In the old world, the primary purpose of folktales was to entertain and delight. But many researchers have drawn attention to the fact that the folktale was not only entertainment to make monotonous work more bearable, but it also 'promoted' certain forms of behaviour and offered solutions to problematic situations. Indirectly, therefore, it had an educational and instructive function, although it is almost certain that the function of being fun and helping to pass the time was much more prevalent. Indeed, one of my mentors was Vilmos Csipkés, a traditional Roma storyteller from north-eastern Hungary (the village of Arló). When asked what a story is for, on two different occasions he gave two different answers. According to him, 'Well, you know, folktales are mostly entertainment', but I am still quoting him when I say that 'folktales educate the people, they develop their brain, they develop their ability to speak.'

In Hungary, it was standard that manual work was accompanied by storytelling almost everywhere, be that working on the land, doing agricultural work related to harvesting, or any other communal labour. Most of this was not independent 'leisure' activity. Free time as such did not exist in the peasant culture, usually all the time spent awake was spent being useful (husking beans, weaving baskets, embroidering, etc.). Most of the time when they were 'resting', their hands were still busy with something.

Autumn and winter work and monotonous activity favoured storytelling. The community's more talented storytellers were invited to tell stories during these work occasions, to be there and keep the others talking, in exchange for money, crops or a bottle of brandy. The people smoothed the tobacco faster, stayed longer to pluck feathers, or crumbled more corn if they invited a well-spoken and talented storyteller to the *kaláka* (community labour). Storytelling also had an economic benefit. Among the winter storytelling occasions, the disznótor (pig-slaying feast) is the most important: at this time, so-called 'fatter tales' with an erotic tone often came to the foreground. At other times storytelling was associated with leisure or 'festive' occasions.

Thanks to the work of József Faragó (1922–2004), we know that in Transylvania, which is part of today's Romania, woodcutters working in the mountains listened to tales as a way to relax before falling asleep.

The vigil, for example when someone is dying, and thus an occasion related to the turning point of human life, was a very common storytelling occasion among the Roma living in Hungarian-speaking areas. At such occasions, they often played cards as well.

It's interesting when talking about storytelling occasions that we can also talk about pub-storytelling. There was a storyteller who bankrupted a pub, because out of the two village pubs people would only go to where he was telling stories.

Situations arising out of necessity could also present opportunities for storytelling. Such was the case, for example, during hospital stays, or in labour camps, and in the military. It was special that soldiers, merchants, students or even peasants, who travelled to different places, would share their own communities' stories. In the old times, this was how stories were exchanged and, thanks to bilingual storytellers, languages and tales migrated, from Budapest to the country, or even across national borders to more distant places.

It is interesting that even the first publication containing Hungarian folktales was based on soldiers' storytelling. This was the 1822 work by György Gaál (1783–1855), *Märchen der Magyaren* (*Tales of the Magyars*).

The Storyteller

In the old days, in a village community, everyone danced and sang. While in the Hungarian-speaking areas women excelled at embroidery and weaving, men mostly excelled in wood carving or other areas of handicraft. However, there are some branches of folk art that were cultivated by specialists. Musicians and storytellers alike belonged to this group. Not everyone told stories – more precisely, not just anyone – but only those people in the community who had abilities possessed by only a few. Specialist storytellers were distinctive figures within the village's communal society; their environment valued and recognized their talent. Most often, there were one, two or three good or excellent storytellers in a community (meaning a village or a village district, or even a city district). Of course, there are exceptions. For example, in the village of Ketesd, currently located in Romania, folklorist Ágnes Kovács (1919–90) found a community where almost everyone could tell stories, even the children. (In the old world, storytelling was mainly adult entertainment.)

Every community is different, and it was like that even in the past. In relation to storytelling, researchers who decided to collect stories in past centuries could encounter a variety of unwritten rules and traditions. There were communities where audience participation was a direct requirement (for example, we have data on this from the Roma storytellers in Nagyecsed), but we also have data, mainly from Palóc regions, where interrupting the tale incurred sanctions: here people were not allowed to speak or ask questions until the end of the story. The tale was probably more or less present in all social strata. Thanks to the excellent Hungarian historical folklorists, we know that, for example, stories were told in the family of János Arany (1817–72, a famous nineteenth-century Hungarian poet and writer). Oral sharing of tales was not only part of peasant culture, but also that of more educated people who could read and write.

While today in many parts of Europe there are many more active female storytellers than men, this would not have been true in the nineteenth or twentieth century. We can only infer anything about this from data where the storyteller's name or at least their gender has been recorded. We know that (at least in Hungary) we are familiar with many more male storytellers than famous female storytellers. We can ask ourselves, however, in a fundamentally patriarchal society, where the role of women most often consisted of being the 'silent supporter' who managed the household or raised the children, how appropriate would it have been for them to tell warlike, scary or romantic stories within the larger community? It is likely that the different normative and moral system of the time, and indeed the lack of research interest, were reasons why we do not have as much data on female storytellers as we do on men. From my own fieldwork experience, I know that female storytellers often only told stories to each other in the family circle, or to children, or while spinning or doing something else in a women's circle.

A folktale can never be independent of its teller, since the re-creation, the telling, gives life to these folklore text variations. It is also true for folktales that the person who collects or records them (this is especially true of the nineteenth-century collections) can greatly influence the quality and character of the texts that finally end up on the page. Folklorist Vilmos Keszeg emphasizes, in relation to the reading experiences of Transylvanian storytellers, that storytelling and reading are not opposed to each other, on the contrary, they are two forms of the same cultural behaviour. The two different traditions, the two different registers offer the same experience for those who enjoy stories.

So, in relation to orality and writing, we can look at folktales like the water cycle. The rain falls and later re-enters the atmosphere with the help of the sun's energy. Moisture collects and collects in the clouds until the water condenses again. A folktale is also like this; it appears on paper, then migrates to people's heads through reading, and later it is formed into words and exists as a spoken story. Then someone records them, writes them down again, it enters into a book, and so the cycle is repeated again and again. Whether folktales are told orally or recorded in writing, one thing is certain: they represent great cultural and emotional value. Just as life-giving water is uniform – its formula (H^2O) is the same everywhere in the world – folktales also carry a kind of common knowledge; and yet, just as precipitation can be snow, hail or even a light spring shower, every folktale is unique and unrepeatable.

On the Sources of Folktales

Interest in folktales, and storytelling itself, could be as old as humanity. In Europe and beyond, we have written evidence of people entertaining each other with stories since ancient times. In later periods, we also find collections of folktales all over Europe and the rest of the world (*One Thousand and One Nights* has been present since the ninth century; Straparola Giovanni Francesco's *The Facetious Nights* from 1550–53; or Charles Perrault's *Tales of Mother Goose* from 1697, etc.) but the largest wave of interest in folktales happened during the nineteenth century. We have all heard of the work of Jacob and Wilhelm Grimm from Germany. Their tales have been published in more than 250 editions and have been translated into more than 160 languages. With their first major work, the volume *Kinder und Hausmärchen*, published in 1812, they gave a new direction to the examination of folktales, since before the Grimms' work, such an interest in folktales was not typical. This happened in Hungary as well, where the nineteenth century was the era of awakening national self-awareness. In this age, almost everything that was 'ethnic' was seen as valued, to be saved. Dialects, folk customs, folk music, and folk dance became areas of keen interest. Literary masters, writers, collectors, intellectuals, and even politicians of the time saw 'the People' in a romanticized way as a homogeneous unit, blessed with a collective poetic talent. It is no coincidence that the Grimm brothers' seminal idea, about the nature and importance of collectivity, according to which 'the People create' ('Das Volk dichtet') found such good breeding ground throughout Europe. This strong romantic exaggeration was, of course, viewed critically by later ages, and in the twentieth century it became clear that the individual has at least as much of a role in the process of creating various pieces of folk art as the community. Tradition provides a framework and the community a natural filter or control, but the creative individual – the storyteller – is also an important factor in the creation of each work.

John Erdélyi

Let us now return to Hungary in the first half of the nineteenth century. At this time, ethnography as a scientific discipline did not even officially exist. It is likely that the first university lectures on folk poetry and folklore were given in Budapest by John Erdélyi (1814–68), whose name (as editor, collector and publisher) is connected to many of the folktales published in this volume. At that time there were no departments of folklore or ethnography at Hungarian universities. And although it was possible to listen to lectures of an ethnographic or folkloristic nature at various Hungarian universities from the middle of the nineteenth century, the first Department of Ethnography in Hungary was established only in 1934 at Eötvös Loránd University. The Hungarian Ethnological Society was officially founded in 1889, modelled after the English Folklore Society founded in 1878.

However, there was a group in Hungary which greatly influenced the literary taste of its time as well as the scientific trends related to the topic (literature, linguistics). The Kisfaludy Society was established in 1836, in Pest (at that time Buda and Pest were not yet one united city.) Although the society had many projects and different goals (such as publishing books and magazines), it is important to note that they encouraged the collection of folk stories. The secretary of the Kisfaludy Society at the time was John Erdélyi. He was a Hungarian lawyer, poet, critic, aesthete, folklore collector, teacher, and a regular member of the Hungarian Academy of Sciences.

Based on John Erdélyi's idea, the company published an appeal in the press in 1844. People were encouraged to submit works of folklore, following which

Erdélyi would compile his own work from these submitted materials. The appeal was successful, as letters were received from many parts of the Hungarian-speaking regions. Works from a variety of genres were submitted, originating from various sources. John Erdélyi's material can be considered special, since it was the first collection of this type of folklore in Hungary. Of course, let us not forget that from the submitted texts it's absolutely impossible to know who actually told these stories (if at all they were ever spoken). Thanks to one of the great historical fact-finding studies of academician folklorist Judit Gulyás, we do know on whose correspondence and materials Erdélyi actually based the tales included in his *Népdalok és mondák* (Folksongs and Legends). The book's three volumes contained a total of 33 folktales, one legend and one other text (and many folk songs in addition). In this selection, we present 20 tales from the three volumes, edited by John Erdélyi, and also many tales from another nineteenth-century collection.

John Kriza

It might not be too bold to call John Kriza a polymath, since he was also a nineteenth-century ethnographer, literary translator, poet, and even a Unitarian minister and bishop. He was born in 1811 in Nagyajta (Aita Mare) and died in 1875 in Kolozsvár (Cluj).

Wild Roses: A Collection of Szekler Folk Poetry was published in January 1863. Many folklore genres appear in this collection, such as ballads, folk songs or folktales. John Kriza dates his preface December 27, 1862. This is what he says about the tales: 'Only a handful of folktales can be published this time, as a demonstration of our people's imaginative power, which is still gushing up from a rich source...'

Many famous folklorists have written useful and important works about what Kriza's collecting network was like, who its members were, where the songs, ballads and tales came from, how he edited or perhaps 'improved' the texts. Other researchers such as Ágnes Kovács, Katalin Olosz, Anna Szakál or Mariann Domokos will greatly help readers interested in this important nineteenth-century collection to get a more detailed and thorough picture of the folktales, literary taste, and the ideas about folklore in those days.

In short, it can be said that Kriza worked with an entire network of collectors. Folklorist Anna Szakál, in a 2012 work, identifies a total of 37 people who can be assumed or are definitely stated to have been John Kriza's fellow collectors. Names of storytellers were not recorded in that era. As I mentioned earlier, they viewed 'the People' as a collective creative unit. Nevertheless, we know of three people by name, who were storytellers who contributed to *Wild Roses*. There is even a biography of one of them, Gergely Gotthard, better known as Geczi Puczok (that was his 'mock name' or nickname), about whom Marianna Domokos concludes in her doctoral dissertation that he was probably an extremely popular storyteller of his time. In a nineteenth-century biographical source, it is mentioned that he was a Szekler storyteller, who was first a postman, but later became a beggar. He travelled through Szeklerland (Székelyföld), reciting folktales and folk songs. That was his livelihood. Our selection includes the two folktales attributed to him by researchers. According to the records, Megölő Istefán ('Stephen the Murderer') and Józsi Halász ('Fisher Joe') originate from him.

The two other storytellers, who were also mentioned in the notes by one of Kriza's fellow collectors, Gergely Marosi, were Miska Fa and Tamás Róka (Puskás). Both were from Székelykeresztúr. In this selection, we present the tale of 'Prince Csihan' by Tamás Róka.

Julius Pap

This book also contains tales with nineteenth-century sources. Specifically, the work by Julius Pap (1813–70) entitled *Palóc Folk Poems*, which was published in Sárospatak in 1865. Julius Pap compiled a collection of tales from the Palóc area. In this selection, we present four stories from him.

Baroness Orczy

In terms of nineteenth-century sources, we have an outlier. This is Baroness Orczy (Emma Orczy, 1865–1947), her creative imagination, and her 'Hungarian folk tales'. Emma Orczy came from a rich aristocratic, landowning family. She was born in Tarnaörs and was three years old when her parents set off to try their luck first in Brussels and then in London. She didn't speak a word of English until she was 15 years old, and later, as an adult, she became one of the best-known writers in England. Her adventure novel *The Scarlet Pimpernel* has sold more than 17 million copies worldwide, and they even named a crater on the planet Venus after her.

However, there were still a couple of stops before world fame. She published her first book in 1895, which was a collection of tales entitled *Old Hungarian Fairy Tales*. In the preface of the book, the baroness writes that the tales are from an old, small book, which was already dirty and torn, with a worn-out binding, and the title is: *Népmesék* (Folk Tales), which was written out in Hungarian in the English text. Irrespective of whether the baroness was telling the truth or not, based on the texts, we can say that one of the stories is a variant of a well-known Hungarian tale type. That is the tale entitled 'That's Not True', which is also published in this selection. In her other tales, there is a lot of individual invention and writer's fantasy, so though they often have the feel and spirit of folk and fairy tales, they are arguably not folktales in the strictest sense of the word.

The Twentieth Century

Before I write about the final, twenty-first-century sources of our compilation, we need to jump back in time a little! With her oeuvre, Baroness Orczy already took us to the beginning of the twentieth century, but it wasn't until around 1940 that we arrived at a turning point, which had a great impact on the manner of researching, collecting and recording folktales. Within folkloristics the performer-centred study of narration, focusing on the creative individual, had its roots in the nineteenth century, but developed only in the middle of the twentieth century. Gyula Ortutay (1910–78) produced a programmatic work under the auspices of the Institute of Ethnography at Eötvös Loránd University, which was preceded by very thorough fieldwork. This work was the publication entitled *Mihály Fedics Tells Stories* (*Fedics Mihály mesél*), which was published in 1940. In international folkloristics, the trend of the performer-centred study of narration, often referred to as the Budapest School or the Hungarian School, differs in its essence and purpose from the approach of earlier folklorists, in that it moves from the text to the context. Its focus is therefore on the person who creates the folklore work, in this case the storyteller and their environment. (Compared to previous collections, it was also a new phenomenon that folktales were written down word by word, and in more fortunate cases, the audience reactions were also recorded.)

Ortutay and his students, such as Linda Dégh (1918–2014), Sándor Erdész (1929–2006) or Ágnes Kovács, were also curious about the storyteller's education, their place and status in the community, whether the person had lived elsewhere earlier, whether they spoke any foreign languages, and from whom they learnt their stories. They were also interested in the place, time and occasions for storytelling, the process of learning to tell stories, and, to a lesser extent, the performative phenomena, dialect, gestures, pronunciation, improvisation skills, and the tendency or lack thereof to alter the tale. They wanted to know whether they were dealing with a reproductive storyteller (i.e. storytellers who perform their stories in the same manner, almost word for word) or creative storytellers (who try to incorporate new and different motifs, swap episodes, combine different types of stories, etc.). I have already mentioned that, prior to this, folktale researchers were mostly concerned with the examination of folktale texts. Previously, all over the world, research revolved around defining types, finding new texts, new versions, the systematization and the historical and geographical distribution of folktales. All in all, the focus was on the text rather than the context or the individual who created it. The focus of the new trend, however, was on the storyteller, on the telling of the story, on the rules of the spoken word. Their predecessors, the folktale researchers of the nineteenth century and the turn of the century, had thus not yet understood the importance of the language (and the individual variations) of storytelling. Although, if I want to be thorough in regard to the activities of the generation prior to the performer-centred school of folktale research, I must mention Lajos Kálmány (1852–1919), who – at the beginning of the twentieth century – had already embarked on a path in relation to his storyteller, Mihály Borbély (1882–1953). In the publication of his stories, in addition to the text itself, researching the storyteller and the storytelling community were also seen as important and necessary. Incidentally, Borbély was the first Hungarian storyteller whose tales were recorded and published by Lajos Kálmány as a freestanding volume.

Revival and Folklorism

So far, we have only addressed the areas of scientific research. However, there was a phenomenon appearing in the second half of the twentieth century, which put communities and tradition in focus, and proved to be a community building force, affecting the whole of Hungarian society. And – although only later, in the last decades of the twentieth century – it also influenced the folklorism of storytelling.

Folklorism is when certain folk elements are taken out of their original context and appear in a different context, e.g. a tombstone-shaped keyring, a nativity scene played in a nursery school, a folk-song singing competition, folk dancing at a factory opening.

The 1970s saw the launch of the so-called 'Dance-house Movement' in Hungary, which is now on UNESCO's Intangible Cultural Heritage Best Safeguarding Practices Register. The basic idea of the Dance-house Movement was that since cultural goods – primarily folk music and folk dance, but also crafts and folktales – are no longer inherited instinctively, they are consciously selected, compared and summarized using the results of scientific research and then re-used in new communities (e.g. in cities, not only in rural areas).

The modern or contemporary storytelling movement began to come to life and function actively only later than in, say, Great Britain, and there are social reasons for this. In relation to the phenomenon of folklorism in Hungary, it is only from the mid-2000s that we can talk about conscious storytelling activities connected to the Dance-house Movement. What is important to mention is that the Hungarian Heritage House has been organizing a storytelling training course under the title 'Hungarian Folk Tale – Traditional Storytelling' since 2007. Vilmos Voigt, internationally renowned folklorist and folktale scholar, was teaching in this course for more than 10 years. Since the start of the first year, more than 300 students have completed this accredited course. The course's methodology has become part of UNESCO's National Register of Best Safeguarding Practices. Trends related to twenty-first-century Hungarian folktale and storytelling, as well as applied storytelling (story therapy, folktale pedagogy, etc.) were summarized by Maja Bumberák in her study published in *British Facts and Fiction Storytelling Magazine* (November 2018). We can say that today Hungary is experiencing a renaissance of folktales and folktale-telling.

The Art of Storytelling in Performance

Folktale-telling is first and foremost an art, which has its own unwritten – and nowadays written – rules. Currently, the so-called revival of professional storytellers, brought up in the framework of folklorism, consciously polish their tales and develop their individual style during their years of practice, usually striving to maintain a harmonious balance between the oral folklore tradition and the ever-changing factors of the here and now (audience, storytelling settings, etc.).

The conscious folktale-tellers (I am not talking about applied storytellers, but about performing artists) select their material from authentic collections, reading or listening to several versions before creating their own. They are familiar with the laws of the spoken word, and are in living contact with their audiences. They improvise, and are not afraid of innovation, but are nevertheless aware of the limits which stop them going beyond the boundaries of this folklore genre. They live the tradition and do not put it in a glass showcase. They use the tale, they tell it, live it, and handle it with wisdom, awareness, but also instinct. They serve the community and indeed create community through storytelling. Through storytelling, they connect past and present, known and unknown paths.

Maja Bumberák

Maja Bumberák is an art therapist, storyteller and singer. Her three tales published in this volume are all retellings based on ethnographically authentic collections from the twentieth century (in which every breath and every word uttered was written down and recorded by researchers just as it was spoken by the storyteller at the time of recording).

The story entitled 'The Priest and the Believers', is a version developed from a story by Mihály Fedics (1851–1938) and variations found in two other Hungarian collections. The tale of 'Mezőszárnyasi' is one of the most beautiful pieces in the volume. Maja adapted it mostly from the story by Palkó Józsefné (Mrs. József Palkó, 1880–1962), a Szekler woman from Bukovina, but the formulas of the Transylvanian Roma storyteller János Cifra were also an inspiration for Maja's own version. The tale entitled 'Cibere' is a humorous story that gives a little insight into linguistic ingenuity and humour (the most important element of the tale itself is the name of a dish), and we hope that the readers will enjoy and retell the tale!

On the Structure of Folktales

Judit Raffai, a folklorist living in Serbia, and an instructor at the Hungarian Folktale – Traditional Storytelling course at the Hungarian Heritage House, when speaking about folktales often compares storytelling to a type of creative building process with the use of building blocks. According to this metaphor, the storyteller is the architect who knows that not all the elements fit everywhere, so the storyteller needs to know the structure in order to tell a folktale smoothly and authentically.

Genre

Now let us briefly review the structure of folktales, using the examples in this volume to illustrate and explain each part. If we want to understand the units of a folktale's structure, we must start with the largest unit, the notion of the folktale *genre*, as well as its various subgenres.

Fairy tales or magical tales, for example, are one such large unit, but anecdotes, jokes and religious tales also make up separate groups. Each have different features and characteristics. The most 'exciting' and perhaps the best known are the fairy tales, which include adventures, magical places and objects, magical characters, but also fighting, love, courage and heroes. These protagonists with extraordinary abilities often fight supernatural creatures (often dragons in Hungarian folktales) and they are often aided by magical objects and miraculous helpers so that they can achieve their goals. Our selection mostly includes magical tales, but we can also find anecdotes, jokes and realistic tales. Humour is dominant in the anecdotes and jokes, and the characters are often simple genre characters, priests, spinsters, simple-minded people. Here there is no fairy-tale wonder. In realistic tales, as in 'The Count's Daughter', the hero is not led to success by fairy-tale miracles or miraculous objects and helpers, but by wit, luck or ingenuity. Emotions, and a romantic, often sentimental style is evident in many of these tales. The subgenre is considered by many to have its roots in the Renaissance. Our selection even includes religious tales.

Religious tales are rooted in Christian beliefs and culture, and are mainly about serious and humorous events related to Jesus. In addition to Lord Jesus and Lord God, they also feature St. Peter, other saints, and even angels and the devil. Miracles can be a feature, indeed a determining factor in religious tales, but while in fairy tales miracles are obvious and natural, here they are always seen as an ethical or moral reward, a sign or the result of some good deed. For example, in our selection, 'The Baa-lambs' is a religious tale.

Type

Let's now turn to the concept of tale types. Each tale subgenre has several *types*. For example, within the subgenre of magical tales there are several types of tales. A given type is the tale's short, generalized content frame. There are several variations of a story type, which means that there is not only one 'valid' version of a given type, but many interesting, valuable and unique 'solutions'.

Many readers will be familiar with the story of the 'Three Oranges'. In this type, girls often jump out of oranges, looking for water, but in other Hungarian versions, thirsty maidens come out of reeds, water plants or even cucumbers. In the academic world, this type is classified by Antti Aarne and Stith Thompson, in the folktale catalogue, as Aath 408, 'The Three Oranges'. Another well-known and especially popular type in Hungarian-speaking regions is the story of 'Shepherd Paul'. This heroic tale is usually the story of a hero with great power, who was born or raised in miraculous circumstances by a beast for a mother, and who walks in the world of the three realms, descending to the underworld to fight the evil dragons who kidnap princesses. In our present version, the motif of the birth from an animal, the miraculous coming into the world has been lost, but the fact that the sheep suckles the child for seven years can be seen as a remnant of this motif. In other versions, the child is born of a white horse or a beautiful cow, and is so strong that he can twist trees by hand. This story type is recorded by researchers as Aath 301B 'The Strong Man and his Companions'. A particularly beautiful so-called song-insert story type is the 'My Father Killed Me my Mother Ate Me', Aath 420 type, listed in our present selection as 'The Crow's Nest'. A small number of Hungarian folktales, like some of those of other European peoples, contain verse interludes sung by storytellers. Our selection also includes a sad tale, bizarre at first sight to many, with traces of symbolic rebirth and atonement. There is repetition of a verse within the tale which goes as follows: 'My mother killed me, My father ate me, My sister gathered up my bones, She wrapped them in clean white linen, She placed them in a hollow tree, And now, behold, I am a young crow.'

Many of the tales in the volume could be identified and typified in this way, but we will not go into so much detail here.

Episode

The next building block is the *episode*. In a story, episodes are logically built upon each other, forming a unified, self-contained story within the whole story. An episode is larger than a motif, but smaller than a stand-alone type. For example, in 'The Travels of Truth and Falsehood', the first section of the story up until Falsehood leads Truth to the gallows is an episode. An episode in 'Fairy Elizabeth' is when the lad goes to the lake and is slapped by the fairy girls, has his clothes stolen from him, and returns home sad.

Formula

A unit smaller than the episode is the so-called *formula*. These are the constant elements that the active storyteller uses as a 'crutch'. Many storytellers have a usable 'stock' of such formulas for, for example, describing beauty, for showing hunger, for expressing sadness, for greeting someone (when the protagonist is greeted in a faraway place) or for describing other plots or general situations that frequently recur in many tales. There are almost always formulas at the beginning and the end of a tale, called introductory and closing formulas. These usually bring the listener into and out of the tale. The main purpose of the introductory formula is to lead the listener (in this case the reader) away from reality into the world of fantasy. It is characterized by a formula of impossibility, content that is removed from reality in both place and time. In this case, the tale does not 'lie about itself', since it has already indicated in the introductory formula that what is going to happen is not real, but a fantasy or work of imagination. Let's look at some of the introductory formulas from our volume!

The tale of 'Fairy Elizabeth' opens with this beautiful formula: 'There was once somewhere, I don't know where, beyond seven times seven countries, and even beyond them...'

In 'Prince Csihan', humour is already present in the idea that you should listen carefully to the tale. This too is a long, beautiful introductory formula: 'There was once – I don't know where, at the other side of seven times seven countries, or even beyond them, on the tumbledown side of a tumbledown stove – a poplar tree, and this poplar tree had sixty-five branches, and on every branch sat sixty-six crows; and may those who don't listen to my story have their eyes picked out by those crows!'

Closing formulas are used to conclude folktales, heroic tales, animal tales and anecdotes and jokes. But what is the purpose of the closing formula? Closing formulas are meant to bring the listener (in this case the reader) back to reality. With humour, with exaggerations of the 'mundane', but often with fun, with a dance or a wedding, we are jolted back and understand that we have arrived: the story is over.

In the tale entitled 'The Lamb with the Golden Fleece', a snapping violin string (humour) brings an end to the festivities: 'The wedding lasted from one Monday to the other Tuesday, and the whole land was in great joy, and if the strings of the fiddle hadn't broken, they would have been dancing yet!'

In the story 'Knight Rose', an absurd but funny sentence relating to the main heroes closes the tale: 'May they curl themselves into an eggshell and be your guests tomorrow.'

In one of Maja Bumberák's tales (borrowed from the storyteller Mihály Fedics), the local landscape, the Danube and the Tisza River also appear in the closing formula. The impossible image of the rivers tied in sacks and the water gushing out of the sacks is a fitting conclusion to the beautiful fairy tale, 'Mezőszárnyasi'.

Element

I would like to talk briefly about two more concepts related to structure. The first of these is the *element*, which is the smallest unit of the folktale. Folktale elements are characters, objects and concepts that typically occur only in tales. They may be fictional or unfeasible, or even objects from earlier times. For example, the dragon, the poor man or the táltos horse (*táltos paripa*), which often appear in Hungarian tales, are such folktale elements. The water of youth, or a magical human skull or even 'the little bag which never gets full' can be an element of a tale.

Motif

Finally, a folktale *motif* consists of several folktale elements that are connected together and combined with an action. This is the case, for example, when the girls who jump out of the magical orange die of thirst without water ('The Three Oranges'), and also when an old witch weaves the enemy formations on a loom ('Prince Mirkó').

On the World of Tales

The world of tales, i.e. the images, places, people and landscapes, objects and events in folktales, on the one hand transport the listener or reader to the high realms of fantasy, but on the other hand, also reflect the reality of everyday life, the storyteller's environment. For example, the part in the story of 'Mezőszárnyasi' where a henhouse is found behind the royal palace shows the mindset and world of peasant storytellers. This was probably not intended as a joke or a pun by the Bukovina Szekler storyteller Palkó Józsefné (Mrs József Palkó, from whom Maja's original story comes), but rather to project the reality of her own life on to a king's living conditions. As we wander around the world, we will see the many different forms that these stories (which have the same framework) appear in.

It is possible that while in one part of Europe, the ogre or the troll is the stupid monster who is being fooled, in another part (for example in Hungarian folktales) these follies most often happen to the devil, who becomes the dummy. In the same way, what the heroes of a tale eat, wear or live in will depend on the geographical location and the culture of specific places.

Hungarian folklore is European folklore and the Hungarian folktale is a European folktale, but there are also some interesting features and characteristics that give our small 'island' – which stands out from the neighbouring sea of Slavic and Latin peoples – a slightly different character. Furthermore, the characters and places in our folktales are sometimes similar, but sometimes very different from the characters or geographical locations of our historical legends and those of belief. For example, 'Beyond the Endless Sea', as we know from our introductory formula, is a typical magical tale place, but so is the 'glass mountain' or 'the mountain of porridge'. These places are only found in tales.

In our volume's tales, and thus in Hungarian folktales, there are many characters and folktale figures. And although rarer characters occur (such as giants or fairies, for example), in our current selection we have included a good number of examples containing these not-so-common characters. (For example, 'The Invisible Shepherd Lad', which mentions fairy youths, and also 'The Three Princesses', which deals with giants.)

Dragons

The dragon, however, is one of the most frequent villains of Hungarian fairy tales. A common feature of these figures is that the dragon is considered a malicious demon. In our current selection, five tales contain dragons ('The Hunting Princes', 'Shepherd Paul', 'Fisher Joe', 'The Three Princes, The Three Dragons, and The Woman with The Iron Nose' and 'Mezőszárnyasi'), but in one tale the dragon does not appear as a classic enemy, but as a helpful figure (indeed, figures). This helpful dragon is a real rarity in Hungarian folktales, but we have an example here with 'Fisher Joe'.

The Hungarian folktale's dragon has completely different external and internal characteristics from, for example, the scaly, lizard-like dragon of the Western world, which loves money or treasure and often guards them. The dragon of the Hungarian folktale is an anthropomorphic figure, but at the same time it also has animal characteristics. He sits on horseback, eats at the table with a knife and fork, eats from a plate and drinks from a glass, uses tools, and can even wear a shirt (this happens, for example, in 'Shepherd Paul'). In certain tales, the dragon calls the hero or the hero calls the dragon brother-in-law, thus indicating his human-like nature. At the same time, his sense of smell is well-developed (almost animal-like) and he also has superhuman strength, e.g., throwing his mace a great distance. The dragon kidnaps women, including princesses, as wives (so he doesn't kill or eat them, but marries them). In certain types of tales, dragons appear with a single head, but more often with three, or even with an ever-increasing number of heads. Dragons with 3, 7 and 24, but also 3, 9 and 12 heads are common. In our selection dragons have the following numbers of heads: 3, 5, 6, 7, 8, 14, 18, 24. The 'multi-headed dragon' took a special form in the Hungarian language area; our storytellers imagine him to be a monster in his shape and a malicious person in his qualities. Dragons can live on high, in the upper world, or on the same level as humans, i.e., in our world. They can also live in the underworld (this, in the world of Hungarian folktales, is not the same as hell). The upper-world dragon is the same as the underworld dragon, each with multiple heads, living in a castle and living with a kidnapped earthly woman, like a human. The difference is that the upper-world dragon can also fly. All three types of dragons appear in our selection. Let's start from top to bottom! It is in the tale 'Mezőszárnyasi', where we first meet dragons who steal celestial bodies and also steal princesses:

> 'A *huge black cloud appeared in the sky, it was coming closer and closer, growing and growing, finally covering the sky, and there came a storm, lightning bolts were scraping the ground, and from the middle of that big black cloud, a dragon's tail appeared, it swooped down, grabbed the princesses.*'

The dragons closest to our world are in 'The Hunting Princes' and 'The Three Princes, The Three Dragons, and The Woman with The Iron Nose'. Although there is a hint in the former that these are aquatic dragons, they do not abduct princesses or celestial bodies. In other tales, such earthly dragons living near water often block the city's water supply, and women and girls must be sacrificed by the community so that they can get water again. In the tale 'The Three Princes, The Three Dragons, and The Woman with The Iron Nose', the dragons clearly only feed on bachelor-meat. '…Every Friday he had to send ninety-nine men to the dragons, who were the pest of the place, and who slew and devoured the ninety-nine human beings sent to them.'

'Shepherd Paul' is one of our most popular and beautiful folktale types. Certain researchers believe that this, as well as the 'Three Brothers Steal Back the Sun, Moon and Stars' type (for example 'Mezőszárnyasi' in this volume), is characteristically Hungarian, and occurs almost exclusively in Hungarian culture. But let's go back to 'Shepherd Paul'! The powerful hero, born from an animal mother, finds strong helpers, and then, following a small dwarf, reaches a hole in the ground. However, as I mentioned earlier, the underworld does not mean hell. Here the grass is green, the landscapes are pleasant and beautiful. This is how the descent is mentioned in 'Shepherd Paul': 'So they lowered Paul, and deep below in the earth, among beautiful valleys he found a splendid castle, which he at once entered...' It is in this landscape that the powerful dragons who steal beautiful women from our world can be found.

Helpers

In Hungarian folktales we often not only meet dragons and enemies, but also helpers. One of the most frequent hero-helpers in Hungarian fairy tales is the *táltos paripa* (this is also translated as little magic pony or stallion). The hero has to choose the colt, despite what it looks like. So, our hero – the later owner of the colt – recognizes its hidden strength, pulls it out of the mess it is in, feels sorry for it, feeds it – thus he disregards the prejudices of his environment, and either chooses the colt as his own, or helps it. It is an important fact that you don't just receive the táltos and his aid as a gift – you have to do something for it first, you have to 'serve' it, such as show yourself to be humane, or in some way different from the others; someone who recognizes the strength that will later emerge from its weakness or a not-so-attractive appearance. Another way to earn its help is by cleaning it or feeding it with embers.

The táltos horse, which at first appears to be a rickety, weak, sick horse, turns into a creature of miraculous strength after the first communication and contact with the hero. Such a horse can usually fly – it flies as fast as the wind or thought itself. It can also speak, and often saves the hero and helps him on his way with wonderful gifts. In many of the tales in our volume, we can encounter the táltos horse or *táltos paripa*. In 'Prince Mirkó', for example, the old witch beautifully describes for the protagonist what kind of horse he must choose from the golden herd of his father, the king: '...but at the very last moment there will come a mare with crooked legs and a shaggy coat; you will know her by the fact that when the herd passes through the gates of the royal fortress the mare will come last...'

Witches

The character of the witch appears in several tales in our volume, even though in 'Prince Csihan' she is called *Vasfogu Bába* (Iron-toothed Hag), or in 'The Little Magic Pony' she only appears with the epithet 'woman with iron nose', but we know that these characters are actually witches within the Hungarian folktale world. The witch of folktales is a female figure, a creature with magical powers who, most of the time, lives far away from other people. Some of the witches in Hungarian folktales are benevolent, others are malicious demons. The witch appearing in legends of belief has different qualities. She is no longer mystical, but a real being (could be someone from the village), a person with supernatural abilities. They can be either a man or a woman (although more often a woman) who lives in the community and keeps her science a secret. A flesh-and-blood figure whom the community could usually name. This witch can be an oppressive creature (she drives people out at night, saddles them and harasses them), rarely (only in northern areas, where there is a trace of Slavic influence) she can also suck blood, but most of the time she casts evil spells, damages animals, makes the cows unwell, she can change into animal form and is malevolent. From my fieldwork experience, I know that the name-taboo, the taboo regarding speaking the witch's name aloud, existed even in the twenty-first century in some places where there was a belief in witches. So the members of the community would not say who the witch was out loud or identify her (even when she was dead), because they feared her power. Rather, they would write it down on a piece of paper or just describe the given person. The witch appearing in the tale 'The Lover's Ghost' is the witch of folk beliefs. She is someone's relative, she helps people, gives advice and knows magic.

In our folktales, the evil witch usually doesn't live in the community, but in the forest, and turns the hero into stone, for example. Hungarian folktales have another, benevolent type of witch character, who is a kind old woman, who generously provides accommodation and directions to the hero who knocks on her door. In the tale of 'The Three Oranges', the hero receives the oranges from such a 'good witch'. And although she is not called a witch, based on her attributes – a helpful, kind old woman – in this version of this tale, she can clearly be identified as the good witch of folktales.

Heroes and Secondary Characters

What other characters can we meet in our book's tales? What do we know about heroes or heroines? The main role in our real mythic tales (for example, 'Shepherd Paul' or 'Mezőszárnyasi') is always played by men. The hero fights, stands bravely, goes on adventures, battles the dragons and saves the community or the princesses. Female protagonists are rarer in fairy tales. Even in those fairy tales where the title refers to a female protagonist (for example, 'The Girl with the Golden Hair' or 'Fairy Elizabeth'), we can follow the fate and adventures of the male protagonist, and the famous and beautiful lady turns out to be a less serious, secondary character, whose role is as love interest for the male character. Of course, it would be a mistake if we asked for equal opportunities or equal proportions in the magical tales of olden times. Fortunately, there are also fairy tales in our volume in which gentle and good-natured ('The Wonderful Frog'), lazy but resourceful ('The Lazy Spinning-girl who became a Queen') or brave and reckless ('The Count's Daughter') ladies play the leading role.

To conclude this section, let's take a look at the characters in the anecdotes and jokes which appear in this book! Our funny tales are characterized by the fact that they do not contain any miracles. Miraculous characters, actions and objects cannot be found in this subgenre. However, jokes, simple-minded people, ordinary characters and plain but funny situations are abundantly present. The figures and characters of everyday life – whom we could have met on the street in a village community – are the most frequent characters within such tales. Such figures include the priest, the cantor, the bell ringer, the woman who cheats on her husband, the simpleton husband or the simpleton wife. 'The Children of Two Rich Men' and 'The Hussar and the Servant Girl' are both such stories.

A Bouquet of Stories

In the last part of my introduction, I would like to note that in order to please the readers, the chapters of this volume have been divided in such a way as to provide a bundle of exciting tales of a great variety. The four chapters separate the tales not on the basis of a scholarly division, but in order to fit well with the reader's or audience's imagination. Each chapter contains a magical tale, but the different genres are mixed with religious tales and joke tales or even a beautiful realistic tale bound together in one big unit. It feels like the reader can choose from among many colourful bouquets of flowers. One thing is certain: whoever reads it will not be bored!

Boglárka Klitsie-Szabad
Co-author: Maja Bumberák
Official translation of the introduction by Gábor Csillag

Boglárka Klitsie-Szabad is a Hungarian ethnographer and storyteller. In 2019, she was awarded the 'Young Master of Folk Arts' state prize and in the same year she won the Prima Junior prize in the category of Folk Art and Public Education for her activities in the field of storytelling and achievements for teaching this traditional art. She published a book, with the title *Seven Years and Seven Blinks of an Eye: The Tales of Vilmos Csipkés and Other Storytellers from Arló*. In this work she introduced the traditional art of a Hungarian Roma storyteller. It was published in Hungarian, in 2022, and co-authored by Norbert Varga.

Fairy Folk & Worlds Beyond Our Own

FAIRIES, GIANTS, KINGS, fair maidens and witches: these are the characters that await you in this chapter. We also meet the classic enemy of Hungarian folktales, the dragon, and the heroes who fight them, often accompanied on their journeys by real helpers (such as the táltos horse) and often by treacherous and powerful characters, who at first appear to be friends, but are not.

In this long chapter we can even discover traces of the medieval trial by fire – the false heroes are burned in a hot tub of lead, while the real hero survives immersion in the hot substance without burning. (The false hero is a character appearing near the end of magical tales, claiming to be the hero or heroine, and demanding their position.) Water, life-giving water, plays a central role in many of the tales in this section, as do journeys and adventures to worlds far from our own. The mood of the chapter is lifted and smiles are brought to the reader's face by the actions and antics of various non-mundane creatures (such as fairies).

Uletka and the White Lizard

IN A CERTAIN COUNTRY, there dwelt a prince whose name was Elkàbo. He had a dear little daughter called Uletka, who was a most sweet child. She and her father lived quite alone in an old castle with four towers, that stood in a beautiful glade in the centre of a great forest.

Uletka was a most dainty and lovely little maid, her wings – she had wings, being related to a fairy – had grown quite strong, and glistened in the sunshine, reflecting all the colours of the rainbow. So sweet and graceful was little Uletka, that perhaps you would imagine she had no faults. Unfortunately she had one, which a wicked and revengeful fairy, who was offended with Nastia, her mother, had endowed her with, and this was the dreadful fault of Curiosity.

This wicked fairy, whose name was Mutà, had done even worse than this. She it was who had lured poor Nastia to destruction. In the forest was a great lake, overshadowed by trees, and covered over with water-lilies and lotus, while round its edge grew tall rushes. One day, when Nastia was walking by the shore of this lake, Mutà hid herself in the water, and calling out for help, pretended she was in danger of drowning. Nastia crept out on the great leaves of the water-lilies and grasped Mutà's hands, whereupon the spiteful fairy dragged her down to the bottom. Poor Nastia could not swim, besides which, Mutà held both her hands. She tried to struggle and to call for help, but it was useless, and thus she drowned. Prince Elkàbo, her husband, and all the neighbours, searched for her everywhere, and when they reached the edge of the lake they saw her body floating far off among the lotus flowers. As they watched she slowly changed into a most beautiful snow-white water-lily.

Elkàbo wept bitterly, and even the birds ceased to sing. A kingfisher, who was sitting on a flag-leaf, cried out to him that it was the work of the wicked fairy, Mutà. Then Elkàbo mounted his horse and quickly sought audience of the Queen of the Fairies, who lived at the furthest end of the country in a palace of crystal that had been erected among the mountains. He told her and all her courtiers, wise men and magicians, what misfortune had befallen him. Mutà's evil deed excited general indignation throughout the court, and the Queen ordered that the fairy should be transformed into a white lizard, which her head magician immediately proceeded to do. Then Her Majesty decreed that if Elkàbo could catch the lizard, he might be allowed to retain it captive until his little daughter, Uletka, who was then a baby, should release it with her own hands. In the event of this happening not even the Fairy Queen herself could prevent Mutà from resuming her natural form, together with her evil powers.

So Elkàbo returned home and searched day and night, travelling far and wide, until, at last, far away in Japan, he found the white lizard, hidden away under a cluster of orchids. He captured it and fastened it in a little cage made of silver wire, and every day he fed it himself, and would let no one else come near it. But as time went on Elkàbo grow afraid that Uletka might open the cage, as she was such a very inquisitive little girl. So he built a small tower near the edge of the lake, and there hung the cage, and every day he went down to the tower and fed the lizard with his own hands. The key of the tower he always wore suspended from his neck by a little gold chain, and no one but himself knew the secret of the tower by the lake.

Now Uletka was excessively curious, and often she would wander round the tower and turn the handle of the door, and fret because she always found it locked. She dared not ask her father any more about it, for she had done so once, and then she thought that she never had seen her dear, kind father so angry before.

At last, one day, Elkàbo was obliged to go on a journey, and as Uletka was getting quite a big girl, he felt he could safely entrust her with the key of the tower. He was going to be away two or three days, and told her that in the meanwhile she must go up every day to the tower and take with her a small bowl of bread. Uletka promised to obey her father implicitly, and really meant to keep her promise. Nevertheless, no sooner had Elkàbo departed than Uletka, unable to check her curiosity, started off to see the wonderful lizard in the tower by the lake. She opened the door with a trembling hand, and there, in a cage made entirely of silver wire, was the loveliest lizard she had ever seen. It ran up and down the cage and played with a straw that Uletka held out. She was quite enchanted, and remained a long time watching it play.

"What a lovely fairy you are," the lizard said suddenly.

Uletka was not at all astonished at hearing the lizard talk. It was so very pretty, that she at once knew it must be a fairy in disguise.

"Oh! I am not a fairy," said Uletka, modestly. "I am only a little girl, and am living with my father, Prince Elkàbo, at the palace yonder."

"How funny," said the lizard, "I made sure you were a fairy, you had such pretty wings; I am a fairy you know, my name is Mutà. What is yours?"

"My name is Uletka."

"What a pretty name," said the wily lizard. "I am sure I could easily make you into a fairy if I only had my magic cloak here. I would throw it over your shoulders, and you would become one immediately, and have the power to appear or disappear at will, turn into a tiny mouse, or a monstrous giant, and, in fact, go anywhere, and see everything just as you chose."

"Oh!" said Uletka, excitedly, "tell me where our magic cloak is, I will fetch it for you. I do so long to be a fairy. Do you really think I could become one?"

"There is no doubt about it," said the lizard; "my cloak would soon turn a pretty little girl like you into a fairy. Dear me, dear me, if I only could get out, I know exactly where to find it, together with the necessary wand. Hobo, the king of the gnomes, once hid it in a rose-bush, out of spite, and changed me into a lizard, and locked me up in a cage, so that I should not be able to get at it. But I know where it is, and if you will help me to get out you shall become a great and powerful fairy."

In one moment Uletka quite forgot her promise to her father, and only thought of the delights of becoming a real fairy, and being able to go where she liked, and see and know everything. She opened the cage, and the lizard jumped out. In an instant it changed into a fairy, with raven hair, and great flashing eyes, dressed in a garment of black gauze, all covered over with golden stars. She turned on Uletka, tore her pretty clothes, and broke her dainty wings. Laughing at her for her vanity and curiosity in thinking she could ever become a fairy, she drove her along into the forest, right to the other side of the lake, all among the dark trees, where she had never been before; then the wicked fairy vanished, and left her lying on the ground, weeping bitterly.

After poor little Uletka had been there some time she thought she heard her name softly whispered by the wind; then it sounded more distinctly, breathed in a sweet, sad voice, like a flower sighing. Uletka stalked gently towards the sound, and it grew louder and louder, until it seemed as if the trees murmured her name, one to another, and as she reached again the enchanted lake the voice rose from the waters, calling "Uletka! Uletka!"

As she stood listening, spellbound, the petals of a magnificent water-lily unfolded, and disclosed a fairy form of exquisite beauty, the spirit of her mother – Nastia. She beckoned to Uletka to approach, which the little girl did, stepping on the great flat leaves of the lilies. Nastia then told her to go into the forest, past the silver poplars and the enchanted palm-tree, till she found a great beech standing all alone. There she would find friends, and be safe from the power of the cruel Mutà, who otherwise would be certain to pursue her.

Uletka then knelt on the lily-leaves, and kissed her mother among the silver petals, then slowly saw them fold, hiding her mother from her view.

Away she sped, quickly past the poplars and the enchanted palm tree, till she was so tired and her feet so sore that she could hardly walk, but at last she came up to the tall solitary beech, standing towering above all the other trees of the forest. She went round it, and there in the very centre of the trunk, she discovered a little door. She knocked, but no one came; only the squirrels chattered together and called, "Who is that knocking at the Gnomes' door? whilst a blackbird echoing, said, "Yes; who can that be knocking at the Gnomes' door?"

At last, Uletka, tired of knocking, turned the little handle and went in. There, right in the very heart of the tree was a room with nine little chairs, and a table carved out of the wood of the tree, and on the table were dishes and spoons of wood, and a great feast of nuts, berries and other kinds of fruit, and large bowls full of delicious honey.

So, as Uletka was very hungry, she sat down and ate some honey and nuts, after which, feeling much better, she lay down on the floor and fell asleep...

When she awoke she was surrounded by a number of little men, with funny faces all laughing and looking at her; some of them were pulling her hair and saying, "Yes, yes, we know you; you are Uletka, you have let the wicked fairy, Mutà, escape. If she finds you she will kill you, but you are quite safe with us, therefore with us you must stay."

And the birds outside sang in chorus, "Yes, yes; it is little Uletka, Prince Elkàbo's child!" and then twittered all the more to show their gratification at her safety.

Uletka stayed with the Gnomes in the tree. Mutà could not hurt her there, for it belonged to Hobo, the King of the Gnomes, who reigned supreme in the forest. Every day the little Gnomes gathered nuts and acorns for their dinner. The shells of these they cut into cups and goblets. Sometimes the grass-elves would come and dine with them, and after dinner they all danced round the tree in the moonlight, while the white owl on the tree-top called "te-whit, te-whoo! te-whit, te-whoo!"

The little Gnomes manufactured a chair for Uletka, and carved a plate for her out of the shell of a hazelnut. They made her a spoon of white fir-wood, and wove garments for her out of cobwebs. She lived in the tree with the good little fellows, and made their garments from the fibres of dead leaves, which looked like the finest lace, using the thorn of a wild rose for a needle. Every day she laid the table for their dinner, and did all the house-work. She was kept busy all the day, though sometimes she would lie in the grass and talk to the violets, who smiled and nodded their dainty heads. She was good friends with every one in the forest; even the tall fox-glove nodded to her as she ran past him. The squirrel who lived at the top of the tree would crack nuts for her. A green and gold beetle was her particular friend. He would carry her on his back as he flew about the wood. But the blackbird loved her most of all, and sat and sang to her all day.

The good little Gnomes were continually trying to invent new games and pastimes in order to distract her thoughts. They composed new music, which they played on their funny little instruments made of wood, with fibres for strings, and danced new dances for her all day long. They also built her a most beautiful little summer house, thatched with rose leaves, where she could rest after having seen to the wants of her kind protectors. But poor little Uletka was not happy, for she could not help thinking of her poor mother and father, who would no doubt be so anxious and lonely without her, and she bitterly repented her curiosity which had placed her in this fearful position. She also thought of the wicked old fairy Mutà, who had been so cruel to her and caused her all this pain; and then she would cry bitterly, and wonder whether she would ever see her beautiful home with the four towers.

As her kind protectors did everything they could to make her feel contented, she did not let them see that she was pining for her home, as she knew that if they thought she was not happy, they would be quite miserable.

One day King Hobo called together a lot of his subjects and told them that early in the morning he intended starting on a grand beechnut hunting expedition in a distant part of the wood, where he had never been before, and commanded them to get ready so as to make an early start. Uletka was up betimes to see her little friends start, and promised to have a nice supper ready for them on their return.

King Hobo led his little army deep into the forest, and soon all were busy looking for the nuts. Suddenly one of them called out: "Oh, I have found such a beautiful stone, but it is so large I cannot move it, come and help me!" Some friends ran up to help him and after much digging, puffing and blowing they managed to dig it up. When Hobo saw it he exclaimed, "Why, that is a Diamond, and the largest I have ever seen. We will carry it home and give it to Uletka." But the diamond was so heavy that it took two of the strongest gnomes to carry it.

As it was the largest diamond ever discovered they held a great feast in honour of the event. The tables, covered with the good things prepared by Uletka, were spread all round the pine trees, and invitations were at once sent out to all their friends.

Among the guests who came were the frogs from the pond by the willows, who were accompanied by their fat cousins, old Mr and Mrs. Toad, a lot of grass-elves and little wood goblins; then there also came the large family of mice and the squirrels, all the birds and beetles, to say nothing of all the moths, the butterflies, the bees and the ants.

After every one had satisfied their hunger (and very little was left on the tables) a great concert was held, at which all the birds sang, but Uletka's friend, the blackbird, sang louder than any of the others to try and cheer her up, for he saw she did not feel quite happy. Then King Hobo asked Uletka to dance with him, the Gnomes keeping time by clapping their wooden cymbals. And so they kept up the gaiety until the bats and the white owl came out, when every one hurried off home, especially the mouse family, who were afraid that the owl might take a liking to one of them for supper. So soon everything was quiet in the forest and no one could guess that just before there had been such goings on under the pine trees.

Yet, in spite of all this gaiety, Uletka's sadness daily increased. She seemed to long more intently than ever for her home. At last her friend the blackbird, could not help noticing this, and determined, if possible, to help the little girl to whom he was so attached; so, one day, he flew to the palace of the Fairy Queen, far away beyond the great mountains.

And as Her Majesty was sitting at supper with all her court the blackbird arrived, and humbly begged she would graciously hear his request. Then he told her that he had a very dear little friend, Uletka, the daughter of Prince Elkàbo. She was so sweet, so loving, and so winning that all the birds and beasts in the forest were in love with her, and entirely devoted themselves to making her happy. But Uletka was a dear affectionate little girl, and although she was made so much of, as the guest of Hobo, King of the Gnomes, and was worshipped there almost like a queen, yet she could not manage to be happy, for she loved her father dearly, and knew he was longing for her company again. He (the blackbird) could not bear to see his little friend pining away like this, and had come to beg Her Majesty, the Queen of the Fairies, to help him.

Prince Repto, the Queen's son, heard the blackbird's story with wonder and delight, he thought he never heard anything so beautifully romantic. Immediately he begged his royal mother to allow him to go off with the blackbird, and bring little Uletka home with him, and make her his wife. The queen, who was very kind-hearted, and quite genuinely interested in Uletka, and in frustrating the wicked Mutà's plans, readily gave her consent, and Prince Repto, accompanied by the blackbird, started off for the kingdom of Hobo and his gnomes.

When he arrived it was late at night, the moon was shining brightly, and there, at the foot of the pine-tree he suddenly caught sight of Uletka. She was sitting on a large toadstool, while all the little gnomes were dancing round her, to the tune of harps played by the grass-elves, and the tinkling of the blue bells. Prince Repto had never seen such a beautiful princess before, and at once fell in love with her. Just at that moment Uletka looked up and saw the Prince, she gave a little cry in which fear and admiration were mingled at seeing such a handsome stranger. "Do not be alarmed, Princess," said Prince Repto, advancing and doffing his cap, "I have come to your aid," and then seating himself on a little toadstool at her feet he told her who he was, and how if she would consent he would marry her, when she would be one of the highest in Fairyland, and live with him in a palace of gold, where the wicked Mutà would be powerless to harm her.

This was rather premature for the first meeting, and Uletka was a little startled; but the Prince looked so very handsome, and was dressed so charmingly, the prospect also was so dazzling, that she did not hesitate long, more especially as it was so natural for her to love him, when, in addition to all these good qualities, he had taken so much trouble to win her. She therefore soon consented, much to the delight of the Prince and all the gnomes.

Prince Repto gave Hobo a crown of gold, and made him king of all the woods in the world, to reward him for his kindness to Uletka; all the gnomes clapped their hands, which sounded like twigs crackling, and the elves played a tune of joy, and sang a love song. There never was such rejoicing in the forest. And although it was long after their usual bedtime, all the birds stayed up and sang the most beautiful songs, so glad were they that dear little Uletka would at last be free from trouble; the nightingale and lark had a special duet together, which was the most beautiful music that is possible. But the sweetest song of all and the one that Uletka enjoyed the most, was the one that was sung by her little friend the blackbird, who had been the happy means of bringing her this good fortune. And in after years the blackbird was always a welcome guest in Uletka's home.

The next morning when the sun was shining brightly, the prince brought a beautiful coach made of a seashell; it was drawn by six white doves; he placed Uletka in it, then sat beside her, and all the gnomes gave a loud cheer as the coach rose high in the air, bearing the happy pair to the fairy kingdom beyond the trees. On the way they stopped, so that Uletka might kiss her dear father, who still dwelt in the castle with the four towers. They took him with them to Fairyland, where there were more festivities and rejoicings in honour of the wedding, and Repto and Uletka have lived happily together ever since. Hobo and the gnomes, and the frogs, and the squirrels, and the blackbird often go to see them, but nothing more has been heard of the wicked fairy Mutà.

Forget-me-not

I N THE GOOD OLD DAYS, many many thousands of years ago, you must know that this world was inhabited by various little fairies, gnomes, elves, and such-like funny little creatures; beasts could talk like rational human beings, even better than most human beings can talk now-adays; and in every flower there dwelt a little fairy, who sang sweet songs, and in every tuft of grass little elves played to and fro.

In those days there were no cities, roads, or houses; no big human creatures erected big buildings, drained rivers, or built railroads; everything was peaceful and quiet; wild animals lived happily in the forests, for the little fairies never dreamt of hunting or killing them for mere sport, and the fairy flowers grew in luxurious splendour, for the wild beasts did not pluck or cast them away.

In those days, somewhere in the world – I don't think I can tell you exactly where, for it is such a very long time ago – there stood in the midst of the forest a most beautiful lake, surrounded on all sides by graceful rushes, and covered with water-lilies and lotus. This lake was so clear and beautiful that all the little fairies who dwelt in the rushes and grasses round the lake used to come every morning and sit on the water-lilies, while they looked at themselves in the waters of the lake, which reflected their dainty little forms like a mirror.

It was a very truthful mirror too, for the little goldfishes, who dwelt in the lake, gave their opinion very impartially as to the beauty of the various little faces that peeped down at them from above. Sometimes they would argue down below as to the merits of one or the other beauty; then there was great splashing and disturbance in the waters, which amused the little fairies very much, and they would all shout as loudly as possible:

> *"Goldfish, goldfish, living under the lake,*
> *who will the prize for beauty take?"*

Of course you may imagine that opinions on this point among the little goldfish differed very much, and yet there were some days when they were absolutely unanimous, and those were the days when the beautiful fairy princess, Narcissa, came to the lake, and kneeling on one of the lily leaves, looked down into the clear waters, while she combed her golden hair and sang in the sweetest of voices:

> *"Goldfish, goldfish, tell me where*
> *Is the fairest of the fair?"*

Then all the little fish and all the little sprites would skip out of the water merrily, and sing with one accord:

> *"Of beauteous fairies 'neath the skies,*
> *Princess Narcissa takes the prize."*

And Narcissa would go home happy and proud, with her head held well erect, for all around her the birds and beasts would do her homage. Wherever she walked the little birds would flutter round her to whisper sweet words of praise in her ears; the little frogs and rabbits would stop in their play to watch her pass; and all the little gnomes and grass elves would march before her in state, as if she were a queen.

Now I am sorry to say all this praise and admiration had a very bad effect on Narcissa. She grew haughtier and more conceited every day, and, in consequence idler and more disagreeable at home, so that her father and mother were made quite unhappy by their daughter's vanity, till at last it became almost unendurable. She used to go out morning, noon, and night, and sit for hours on the water-lily leaves, looking at her own reflection in the water, and hearing the waves, the winds, the flowers, the beasts, all murmur in concert: "Princess Narcissa is the most beautiful of all the fairies in the world!"

One day, when her poor fairy mother was thus left sitting all alone in her beautiful palace among the bulrushes, after seeing her daughter go off on her usual journey, she suddenly caught sight, near the edge of the lake, of a lovely little cluster of forget-me-nots. So sweet and modest did they look, and withal so exquisitely lovely in colour, that she sighed regretfully, and said, "Oh, how I wish I had another, a tiny blue-eyed daughter, modest and sweet, who would be a comfort to me."

Now the Fairy Queen, who always hears the wishes of all her subjects, heard the poor mother's cry, and shortly after presented her with a nice little daughter, with lovely golden curls all round her tiny head, and such beautiful blue eyes that looked so sweetly out into the world, that her mother and father were almost beside themselves for joy, and named her "Forget-me-not," because she resembled those dainty little flowers.

The haughty Princess Narcissa did not take very much notice of her baby sister just at first; she was too much occupied with herself and her own beauty, inventing new garments for her little person, and new jewellery for her hair. She used to tease and torment her occasionally, though, especially when Forget-me-not began to grow up, compelling her to dress her hair, fasten her dress, and altogether using her as a sort of servant to help to administer to her own adornment. But Forget-me-not was so modest and unassuming, and really looked upon her older sister as a creature of such exquisite loveliness that she gladly did all that Narcissa wished, and even tried to invent all sorts of pretty new contrivances to further enhance her beauty.

This went on for some time; Forget-me-not was growing up very rapidly, and every day she seemed to grow in beauty, as well as in goodness; her hair was now long and glistened like gold, her skin was fine and transparent, as only fairy skin can be, and her eyes were tenderer and bluer than the little flowers after whom she was named. Her father and mother were now perfectly happy, for their little daughter was all the comfort in the world to them. When Narcissa had finished her toilet in the morning, and gone off to the enchanted lake, followed by her crowd of admirers, little Forget-me-not would go about the house singing merrily, chatting to her father, and helping her mother to spin and sew.

The little creature had never been outside her father's garden, she had never seen any one, except her father, and mother, and sister, so she really did not know how beautiful she was, for the latter had no eyes for any one save herself, and the former had such a dread and horror of vanity creeping up in their darling's heart, that they were particularly careful never to speak on the subject before her.

One day, when Forget-me-not was running about in the garden, she saw a beautiful bright-eyed butterfly lying on the grass. She drew near on tiptoe to have a better look, when the butterfly spread out his wings and flew off to the other end of the garden. Forget-me-not ran after him, for she had never seen such a lovely creature before – all blue and silver, with great dark spots, like eyes. Hardly had she, however, come near enough to him, when the butterfly again flew off; this time far to the other side of the garden gates. Forget-me-not was tempted to follow him, and so she ran on and on till she saw him apparently settle on a water-lily leaf, and then disappear from her view.

Little Forget-me-not, who had now reached the edge of the lake, was determined to see where the beautiful butterfly had disappeared to, so, treading softly on the lotus and lily leaves, she looked round her, and then into the clear waters of the lake, but no butterfly could she see; only as she was looking a whole crowd of little goldfish and water sprites (things she had never seen in all her life before) rose from out of the water, and, forming a circle round the leaf on which she stood, they bowed low before her, and sang in the sweetest chorus she had ever heard:

"Forget-me-not, lovely blue-eyed Forget-me-not,
Fairest far of all the lot."

She could hardly tear herself away from them, so beautifully did they all sing, till finally a little goldfish swam quite close to her, and asked her if she would honour him by getting on his back, and allowing him to swim with her to shore, which she did, as she did not like to wound his feelings by refusing so courteous an offer, but she felt very frightened at this altogether new mode of locomotion, and also very upset and shy at being suddenly so surrounded and admired by a crowd of unknown beings.

When she got to shore she was still so nervous that she quite forgot to thank the goldfish and water sprites for their lovely music, and ran home as fast as her fairy legs could carry her, and into her mother's arms, who was very much upset when she heard the whole story, for she felt that evil would come of this if Narcissa were to know.

The next day Narcissa got up and dressed, or rather made Forget-me-not dress her as usual; she was not yet tired of all the admiration her beauty always roused wherever she passed, and she still loved as dearly as ever to gaze at her own reflection in the lake, and provoke its inhabitants into songs of praise. On this particular morning she had made herself look lovelier than ever, and she stepped out of her mother's garden, anxiously peering round for the squirrels, who always greeted her approach joyfully, and escorted her to the edge of the lake with many a bow of admiration and envy. However, this morning the squirrels were not to be seen, she could hear them in the distance holding an animated discussion, but not one of the little faces peeped down at her, and Narcissa thought it very strange that they should think other matters more interesting than the sight of her.

She ran down to the lake, and stepped on the broad water-lily leaves, then sitting on one of the pink blossoms the little vain fairy peeped down at her dainty image. How pretty she was! with her fairy figure, her milk-white skin and rosy lips, her graceful arms bent over her head, while she combed her golden hair with a pearl comb, while her garments, made of moon-beams, shone like silver, and made her appear like a bright jewel in the heart of the lotus flower.

Very soon a large crowd of gold and silver fish had gathered round her, and funny round eyes and gaping mouths peered at her from the green depths below. But instead of the usual chorus of admiration with which they usually greeted her, she found herself apparently the object of an extraordinary curiosity. The

HUNGARIAN FOLKTALES

fishes appeared to be whispering to each other, then looking at her with their funny wise heads held on one side, till Narcissa could bear the suspense no longer, and she sang in her sweetest tones:

> *"Goldfish, goldfish, tell me where,*
> *Is the fairest of the fair?"*

Then, to her horror and dismay, a mischievous-looking little water sprite rose to the surface and said:

> *"Although Narcissa very beauteous be,*
> *Forget-me-not is fairer far than she."*

Then the whole chorus of fishes echoed:

> *"Yes, Forget-me-not, little blue-eyed Forget-me-not, is fairer far than she."*

Narcissa could hardly believe her own ears. Forget-me-not! ugly little Forget-me-not! Why, she had never been outside her mother's garden! The fishes could never have seen her, and if they had, why, surely there was no comparison between the lovely Narcissa, more beautiful than the Fairy Queen herself, and this tiny, unpretentious little sister of hers.

And yet the goldfish would keep on singing:

> *"Have you seen Forget-me-not,*
> *Fairest far of all the lot?"*

Narcissa went ashore, and in a rage picked up some pebbles and pelted the fishes and water sprites with them, but they did not care; they dived down to the very bottom of the lake and re-appeared again, still singing:

> *"Forgot-me-not, lovely Forget-me-not."*

The enraged little fairy ran off as fast as she could. As she passed the rushes where all the frogs had congregated she heard them croaking:

"Little Forget-me-not with blue eyes grand – Quack, quack, quack.
Is loveliest in Fairyland – Quack, quack, quack."

Through the woods she ran, where her friends, the squirrels, always used to pay her homage; now they were running up and down the trees in a great state of excitement, and shouting to each other:

"Have you seen Forget-me-not, the loveliest of all the lot?"

This was too much for Narcissa altogether. She rushed through her mother's garden, up the steps, to where little Forget-me-not sat spinning a dress of spiders' webs. She was quite startled when she saw her sister rush in in so frantic a manner. Narcissa took hold of her hand, told her to leave her spinning and come with her.

Little Forget-me-not was so accustomed to do as she was told that she obeyed, and followed her sister, though she felt very frightened. On the two fairies ran, Narcissa dragging her little sister after her, till they came to an old dried-up well, which led down to the centre of the earth.

"Now," said Narcissa, "I have dropped my spindle in this well, and cannot finish my spinning; you must jump down and fetch it for me."

"But," said little Forget-me-not, "the well is so deep; mother says it has no bottom. I should not know where to look for your spindle."

"If you don't jump down immediately and do as you are told I will throw you in, for I am stronger than you," said Narcissa, and her eyes glittered with rage so that she looked quite ugly.

What was poor little Forget-me-not to do? She was all alone with her wicked sister, and no chance for any one to come and help her, so she thought of her dear mother as she stood one moment hesitating on the brink of the well; then, suddenly Narcissa gave her a push, and down she fell – down, down, down. It was pitch dark round her; she seemed to be floating in absolute space, and the last thing she remembered as she lost consciousness in her terror, was, high up above, a little speck of light, and Narcissa's wicked little face peering down at her and laughing triumphantly.

And so she fell lower and lower yet, the darkness grew more and more intense, and then all of a sudden a ray of light began to penetrate from a long way down below; this little thin streak of light encroached more and more upon the darkness. Little Forget-me-not re-opened her eyes, and suddenly found herself in full daylight on the edge of another well, with tall, over-hanging trees round her; she clambered up and looked round, she was in a strange part of the world, that was very evident, curiously shaped trees and plants surrounded her, flowers she had never seen before, but still they were trees and flowers, and as such Forget-me-not was not frightened at them, but still she did not dare venture through the thick masses of undergrowth, through which even her fairy-like little form could not have always found a passage. She felt very lonely and miserable, and longed for her dear mother, and her own familiar flowers; this was a very strange country, where perhaps she never would meet a friend who would be kind to her, and take her home. Poor little fairy, she sat down and cried, till the great sobs shook her little form, and her heart ached as if it would break.

Suddenly she heard a shrill voice quite close to her, calling her by her name, "Forget-me-not, Forget-me-not, why do you cry?"

The little fairy, looked up in wonder, and there, standing before her, was the funniest little old woman she ever saw, her face was such a mass of wrinkles that you could not see any of the features, the eyes were hidden by deep furrows and ridges, the mouth appeared like a long narrow slit, only the nose, a very big hook nose, was so prominent and long that it quite frightened poor little Forget-me-not.

Her head was very huge, and seemed much too heavy for the small shrivelled body, all bent as if over-weighted with age. She had large bony hands and feet, with long nails like a bird's claws, and there she stood, blinking at the pretty little fairy, like an old hawk staring at a sparrow.

"Why do you cry?" the old woman repeated impatiently, as poor little Forget-me-not seemed unable to answer, but only stared at her in fear and astonishment.

"Oh," sobbed the poor little fairy, "I am so lonely and so miserable; my sister pushed me down a well, and I have fallen so deep down that now I don't the least bit know where I am, and my poor dear mother at home must be crying after me, and wondering where I am, and I don't remember the way I came here, so I cannot go back. Dear, good, kind fairy, if you are a fairy, take me back to my mother, and I will do anything in the world to serve and help you if I can."

"I don't know that I want to take you back to your mother," the old fairy said, "and I am sure you can be of no possible use to me, so I don't see why I should trouble my head about you at all."

"But l can spin and sew for you," Forget-me-not said eagerly, noticing the funny old green rags in which the old woman was clad, "and I can cook most dainty dishes, and scrub the floors, and dress your hair, in fact, I can make myself most useful about a house, and like doing all kinds of work."

"H'm," said the ugly old fairy, "I have been looking out for a young servant for some time, and you do seem pretty active and willing"… "Well," she said, "if you will come with me and be my maid, attend to my household and look after me, I will undertake to help and protect you. Will you agree to that?"

"But," said little Forget-me-not, "that will never do. I have no other wish but to go back to my dear mother, and go on living my own quiet happy life, and if I go to be your servant, what use is all protection in the world to me, while I know my dear ones at home are mourning for me, and think that I am dead?"

"Well, you can please yourself," said the little old woman, "I have told you under what conditions I will help and protect you, if they don't suit you you can leave them alone, or rather, I will leave you alone, for I am busy, and don't mean to stand here talking with you any longer. If you change your mind, clap your hands three times, and you will see me again. Goodbye."

Saying which, the old fairy hobbled off, leaning on her heavy stick, and laughing maliciously at poor little Forget-me-not, who was left more desolate and lonely than before.

Evening was drawing on rapidly, the forest around grew darker and darker, every moment the poor little fairy began to feel very frightened. She heard strange sounds around her, and great luminous eyes seemed to be staring at her from out the darkness. The moon now rose and shed a soft mysterious light on the strange landscape, and curious little beings, grass-elves and wood-nymphs, came out, skipping and dancing merrily round the now terrified little form. She began to feel that if she spent a whole night here by herself she would die with fright. If only her dear mother could hear her and come to her rescue, or even if the malicious old fairy would be here to keep her company. She felt that anything would be better than stay alone a moment longer, so she clapped her little hands three times, and in a moment, as if she had sprung out of the earth, there stood the funny old woman in her green rags, leaning on her stick. "Oh, take me away from here!" poor Forget-me-not cried. "I will be your servant and do anything you like, but I cannot stay here any longer by myself. I should die of fright."

"Very well," said the old fairy; "you must come with me to my palace, but remember, you are to do everything I tell you, and help me to spin, sew, and cook, and to reward you I will help you and give you shelter."

"Well, then, you must help me now to let my mother know that I am quite safe, and will come back to her as soon as I can."

The old fairy waved her stick three times over her head, and a huge frog came jumping apparently from nowhere, and waited for orders. "Send any message you like," the old fairy said, "and this frog will convey it to your mother before daybreak."

"Please, Mr Frog," said Forget-me-not, "go to my dear mother and tell her that I am still alive. Narcissa pushed me down the well, but a kind fairy has rescued me, and I am going to be her little servant until she releases me."

"Croak, croak," said the frog, and disappeared from view.

"Now," said the old fairy, "you must come home with me at once, and make the beds for the night. My son will be waiting for me, and you must help to make everything comfortable for him at home."

She again waved her stick, and presently two bats came flying along, each carrying a broomstick. The old fairy mounted the one, and told Forget-me-not to get on to the other and follow her.

Away she flew, high up over the trees. Forget-me-not felt very frightened and uncomfortable, as she had never travelled on a broomstick before. However, the journey was not a very long one, and presently the two fairies landed opposite a most gorgeous palace, made entirely of glass. Through the walls one could see the long suites of exquisite rooms, with crystal domes and golden pillars. But not a soul was visible anywhere, neither in the palace nor in the beautiful moonlit grounds, the whole palace glittering in the moonlight, surrounded with gigantic trees and exquisitely-scented flower beds, wore a fearfully deserted look, and Forget-me-not wondered more and more about the curious old fairy who went about in rags, and owned such a magnificent though solitary abode. As she stepped off her broomstick and helped her mistress to alight she caught sight, in one of the gorgeous halls, of a sumptuously-laid-out feast, beautiful gold and silver dishes filled with the rarest fruits, and wine in diamond goblets. And there, alone, having a lonely meal, sat the handsomest fairy prince she could imagine. Little Forget-me-not could not take her eyes off him, he had such a lovely face, though he looked very dejected and melancholy in his loveliness.

"That is my son," said the old fairy. "I am very proud of him, as he is the handsomest prince in all fairyland, but I don't want him to marry, as then, of course, he would have to leave me. That is why I won't allow a living thing to come anywhere near my palace, for fear they should captivate his fancy, and put thoughts of marriage into his head. As for a bird, I won't have one near the place, as they will chirrup of nothing else but love and home. I have had no servant or attendant entirely on that account, and have been obliged to go about in rags, and eat nothing but nuts and fruit, as I had no one to spin, or sew, or cook for me. Bats and frogs are the only creatures I will tolerate, as I don't think there is the faintest chance of my son falling in love with one of them. I have an old bat's skin somewhere up in my room, you will have to wear that all day, while my son is at home, you may only take it off for three hours after midnight, as then he always goes to sleep, and there is no fear of his seeing you."

Little Forget-me-not did not at all relish the idea of going about all day with a horrible old bat's skin on her, but of course she could say nothing, she had to do as her mistress told her.

The old fairy hobbled up the grand glass staircase, and presently returned carrying the skin. She made Forget-me-not put it on, and her own mother would not have recognized in this old grey bat her pretty blue-eyed little daughter.

The old fairy then told her that she might go to bed and rest for the remainder of the night, she would find her room at the top of one of the towers, and little Forget-me-not, now thoroughly tired and worn out, went up a long winding staircase, till she came to a nice little room, with a clean bed of straw, where she lay herself down, and immediately dropped into a long heavy sleep, where she forgot all about the well, the bats, the broomsticks, the little old woman, and even the handsome fairy prince.

The next morning she was up quite early, dressed herself in her bat's skin, and went downstairs. She cooked the breakfast for the prince and his mother, and all day she was kept busy, sewing and spinning new dresses in place of the fairy's old rags. She had to wait at all the meals too, and oh! it made her quite miserable to see the handsome prince sitting at table, looking so dejected and lonely, with no one to talk to, except his ugly old mother; there seemed to be such longing in his eyes when he looked round him, and saw nothing but ugly beings, frogs, bats or spiders; even the new servant was only another old bat, his eyes seemed to quite ache for something beautiful to look at, and his ears for sweet sounds.

Forget-me-not quite longed to tell him of all the lovely things in nature, of the birds, the squirrels, and the butterflies, and also of all the beautiful fairies, of which she herself was one, but she was pledged to the old woman, and was never allowed to take off her disfiguring garment, so she was obliged to hold her peace.

Day after day passed off in solitude for little Forget-me-not, her mistress was very kind to her in her old grim way, but watched over all her movements most rigidly, for fear she should ever speak to the prince. At night only, for three hours after midnight, was the little fairy, allowed to wander freely about the castle and the park, unencumbered by the heavy skin, clad in her pretty dress of cobwebs; she would then run down to the edge of a little neighbouring stream, and gather her little namesakes to weave pretty garlands for her hair, then she would sit on the bank and talk to the frogs and bats, who were her only companions; she had taken a great fancy to them, and loved to hear their quaint talk. They all told her how sorry they were for the poor prince, of whom his mother was so jealous, how they had all hoped when she came to be a little servant, that he would see her, fall in love with her, and marry her, and so change this gloomy, solitary place into one of festivities and gaieties; but, of course, with a badly fitting bat's skin on her, the thing was impossible, and the old fairy, was so watchful all day that it was quite impossible for any one to have a few words with the prince, she only relaxed her vigilance when he was asleep, and then she snored herself.

Forget-me-not listened to all this, and felt more miserable than ever to think that the handsome fairy prince, with whom she was now very much in love, should never have a chance of even knowing there was such a thing as love and beauty in the world; she asked her friend, the chief bat of the establishment, if he could not help her in any way, while her old mistress was asleep.

"Well," said the bat, "if you like to get on my back I can take you into the Prince's room one night, but then he is fast asleep, so I don't know of what use that can be to you."

But Forget-me-not was so desirous of seeing the Prince when his mother was not there, that she told the bat she would not mind his being asleep, would he please take her in at his window and let her see him.

The old bat consented. It was too late then, but on the following night he agreed to wait for Forget-me-not under the old cedar tree. The little fairy could hardly contain her impatience all day. When midnight struck, and the old woman and her son had both gone to sleep, she ran up to her little room and took out her pretty fairy dress, then dressed her beautiful golden hair, and having placed a garland of forget-me-nots on her head, she anxiously awaited her friend, the bat, under the cedar tree.

He was punctual to the minute, and Forget-me-not, having mounted on his back, he deposited her on the sill of the Prince's window. She stepped in, and saw the handsome fairy prince lying asleep, looking, oh! so lonely and dissatisfied. She went up to him and kissed him gently, and a tear fell from her eye on to his pillow, where it changed into a brilliant diamond. Near it she laid the wreath of forget-me-nots from her hair, then stole gently out of the room again and regained her own couch without, fortunately, disturbing her old mistress, who was snoring louder than ever.

The next morning the Prince awoke feeling that he had had a most beautiful dream. He dimly remembered seeing a little form of exquisite beauty fly in at his window, come up close to him and kiss him, and then... But surely it was not a dream, for there, on his pillow, was the wreath of forget-me-nots she wore, and near it glittered the bright tear of love and sympathy which her fair eye had let fall on his forehead, and which had changed into a most brilliant diamond. He took both up and fastened them inside his doublet; then, as it was still very early in the morning, he stole on tiptoe down the stairs, out of the palace, and through the park, into the great world, beyond the crystal gates, which he had never dared to cross before. A new feeling which he could not explain seemed to put an altogether different life into him. Everything around him seemed endowed with unwonted beauty; the great trees waved their majestic branches over his head and whispered words he had never understood before, and when he looked up, there among the boughs, he saw two lovely little beings he had never been allowed to see before, sitting quite close together and chirping sweet words to each other. He seemed to know directly what they were saying: "Love and beauty" was what they were talking of, and that was what the fairy prince was now in quest of – "love and beauty." He was determined to wander until he found the owner of the forget-me-not wreath and the diamond tear. He knew she could not be anywhere within his mother's palace or garden, so he had set off, no matter for how long a distance, until he had once more seen the bright blue eyes which had appeared to him in his dream.

On and on he went; he did not know himself how far he had gone, or how long he had been on the road. He felt no fatigue, all the world was so new to him, and so beautiful. In the forest the nimble squirrels and gaily-coloured birds; in the fields the bright-eyed butterflies, in the grass the tiny elves and fairies, in the waters the jewelled fishes, all were a source of wonder and admiration to him, so beautiful were they all, and yet not one so perfect as the little fairy being whom he had only seen in his dream.

At last, one day, after long, long wanderings, he came to the very lake near which Narcissa and her mother and father still dwelt. As he was beginning to feel very tired, he sat down on the reed-covered bank and looked down with delight at a cluster of forget-me-nots close to him, which so strongly reminded him of the bright blue eyes in his dream. He began to fear that he should never see her; that, perhaps, she did not really exist.

Suddenly he looked up, and coming down the path, he saw a lovely little fairy, walking dejectedly along. She was very beautiful, though not quite so beautiful as his dream. She had golden hair also, and blue eyes, but they were not the same blue eyes he had wandered all this long way to see.

Narcissa, for it was she, had never ceased to come to the edge of the lake, and never ceased to look at herself in the waters and ask the goldfish who was the most beautiful fairy in the land, but the goldfish had never ceased to say:

"Although Princess Narcissa very beauteous be,
Little Forget-me-not, far away, is more beautiful than she."

That is why she looked so dejected, for she was still so vain that she hated the idea that Forget-me-not should still be alive and still be thought more beautiful than she. The Prince looked at the fairy figure in admiration as she trod gracefully on the large lily leaves, then, sitting on a pink lotus, began to comb her golden hair.

Presently a whole row of little goldfish and water sprites put their little heads out of the water, and, looking critically at the fairy, began to sing gaily:

"Although Princess Narcissa very beauteous be,
Little Forget-me-not, far away, is more beautiful than she."

Then the Prince knew that they must mean his own little fairy, the lovely being that he had seen once, and immediately learnt to love, and in search of whom he had wandered from the other end of the world.

He heard Narcissa asking eagerly:

"And tell me, Goldfish, where is Forget-me-not, who you say is a thousand times more beautiful than I?"

"She is there, standing near you! Welcome, Forget-me-not, the most beautiful in all fairy-land."

The Prince looked round in amazement, astonished that this lovely being should have been so near him without his knowing it, but he saw no one, only an ugly old bat, whom he dimly recollected having seen a long time ago in his mother's palace.

Poor little Forget-me-not! When she had perceived the consequences of her midnight adventure, and had seen her dear Prince go forth in quest of her, she resolved to follow him wherever he went. On and on she had wandered, always after him, until she felt so tired and footsore she could hardly walk, till at last she also had arrived near the well-known lake, and had seen her sister, Narcissa, and her old friends, the goldfish, and all the old familiar places; yet she had no eyes for all these, she only thought of her dear prince, and longed to throw off her ugly disguise, and tell him that she was his own little fairy, who had kissed him in the night, and taught him the meaning of love and beauty; yet she dared not, she was pledged to the old fairy not to take off her disguise, and was too frightened of her to break her word. Besides, if Narcissa were to see her now, surely she would throw her into the water and kill her. So she had to stand by, and feel that the Prince was looking at her, and did not recognize her. Narcissa did, however, in one moment; the eyes of envy and vanity are so sharp. She looked round when the goldfish had spoken, and immediately, under the bat's skin, she spied her little blue-eyed sister.

Without a moment's hesitation she rushed at her, and giving her a violent push, threw her into the water.

The Prince, who had learnt to love all living creatures, however mean and humble, could not bear to see even an old bat drown, so he snatched hold of one of its wings to help it swim to shore, when lo! the bat's skin came right off, and in its place he was holding the lovely being from his dream, she was again looking at him with those bright blue eyes, he had never since forgotten. He pulled her to shore, and she at last was happy in his arms.

Now, need I tell my little readers any more? Well! Perhaps they might like to hear that the old fairy mother, though at first sorely vexed at her son's conduct, finally was obliged to give her consent to his marriage with Forget-me-not, so there was a grand wedding in the palace of glass, which henceforth became the abode of mirth and gaiety. As for Narcissa, she was Forget-me-not's bridesmaid, and it was a severe punishment to her for all her wickedness, to hear the whole fairy world, yea even the Queen herself, say joyfully:

"Yes, Forget-me-not, little blue-eyed Forget-me-not, is the most beautiful fairy of the lot!"

The Suitors of the Princess Fire-Fly

FAR, VERY FAR AWAY, and long, very long ago, when all the world was inhabited by the fairies, there lived a great and mighty king called Fire-fly. Now do not run away with the idea that this Fire-fly was in any way like the little glowing insects that are read about in Natural History books. True, he had wings like those flies nowadays, and also a body something like theirs, but he was a fairy fly, and wore a most beautiful crown on his head, which at night shone as brilliantly as the stars. Then this Fire-fly had a most gorgeous palace, which lay right in the middle of a wide river. This palace consisted of one magnificent lotus flower, and a more exquisite dwelling-place it would be impossible to see. His dearest and most precious treasure was his daughter, a most lovely princess. The king was so proud and fond of her that he would not allow any one even to look at her, but kept her hidden inside the pink petals of his beautiful lotus palace, and there the princess grew up more and more lovely every day, till her fame spread far and wide, and all the flies and moths and beetles of the neighbouring kingdoms got out their finest wings in order to go to woo and win this incomparable Fire-fly miss.

But the princess was very proud and very vain of her own beauty, and she said to her mother one day: "It is quite useless for either Dragon-fly or Stag-beetle, or, in fact, any of them to try and woo me, for I will not marry any one unless he perform some perilous task which I will impose upon him. Then if he fails, and dies in the attempt, I shall be thankful to have escaped being married to so foolish and careless a being; or if he should not dare to attempt the task, it will be a proof that he values his life higher than his love, and is therefore not worth having."

As this beautiful princess was very much spoilt at home, her mother and father, King and Queen Fire-fly, both acceded to her whim, and the king issued a proclamation, by which he declared that no suitor should have the hand of his lovely daughter unless he performed the task she imposed upon him.

Forthwith did Prince Gold-beetle start from his kingdom of Gladiola over the grass, and placed his heart and hand at Princess Fire-fly's feet. She listened to all he had to say, and smiled very sweetly. "Yes," she said, "all that you say is very pretty indeed, and I am sure your proposal is exceedingly flattering; but you know the condition, without which I cannot possibly marry you."

"Name the condition, lovely princess," said the Gold-beetle; "no task, be it ever so hard, would be too much to undertake for such a prize."

"You most bring me, from anywhere you like," said the beautiful Fire-fly, "one spark of fire!"

"Is that all you wish for?" said the Gold-beetle. "I fly, and before another night has descended and passed by I will lay this spark at your feet." And away he flew, quite confident that he would be able to obtain so simple a thing as a mere little spark of fire, which the moment night came could be found in every house in the neighbourhood. You will hear presently how he fared in his quest.

In the meantime the beautiful Fire-fly had another suitor. Lord Cockchafer appeared upon the scene, and, obtaining entrance into the Lotus Palace, he boldly asked for the honour of becoming the Princess's husband, but she turned away quite disdainfully from him:

"I don't think I should ever care to marry you at all," she said; "but I am so very, very anxious to possess a spark of fire, and I really would like to know if you would be brave enough to undertake a perilous task in order to please me."

"I will travel night and day," said Lord Cockchafer, "till I bring you what you wish."

Away he went, tripping merrily, and blissfully unconscious of the fact that he was not the only one who was bent on this curious errand.

Presently Fire-fly had another suitor – a beautiful suitor he was too, with his shimmering suit of green and gold, my Lord Dragon-fly. He thought to dazzle her by his beauty and make her forget her foolish fancy about this spark of fire. But the princess would not listen even to him; she only smiled, and said:

"I will only marry him who brings me this spark of fire."

And away he had to go. And thus, day after day, there came a regular crowd of suitors round the beautiful princess; but day after day she sent them off in quest of a spark of fire.

Prince Gold-beetle waited till night set in, then flew off gaily to the nearest city. He came up near a lovely little house, standing in a large garden; he looked in at the window, and there he saw a large table laid out with tea and cakes, sweets and fruit, and twelve little girls and boys sitting round, having their tea; on the table a large lamp was burning very brightly.

"Why, this is just what I want," said Prince Gold-beetle; and as the window was open he flew in. The lamp burnt beautifully, it quite fascinated him; he flew quite close, in order to get a better view of the bright flame.

"Oh, what a lovely beetle," he heard one of the little children say, "Mother, do look! What beautiful wings it has!"

"Oh, dear, it is flying so near the lamp I am sure it will burn its wings," said another.

The Gold-beetle took no notice of what they said, but drew nearer and nearer to the coveted prize; there was a spark of lovely fire, how pleased the beautiful princess would be when he brought it home for her. At last he made a bold dash to catch the flame, when lo! alas! he felt his poor wings all singed and burnt; he could not fly any more, but fell fainting on the tablecloth. He heard the little children say to each other:

"Stupid beetle to go flying into the lamp; now it has burnt its lovely wings."

Then somebody else said, "Throw away the nasty thing, or put it out of its misery."

That was the end of poor Prince Gold-beetle's life.

Another suitor of Fire-fly, a Hawk-moth, while fluttering about one evening, wandered into a room where, at first, he could see nothing, it seemed pitch dark; presently he noticed a large luminous object, which turned out to be long blue flames, apparently emerging from a large bowl, filled with plums; all round he saw eager little laughing faces, and every now and then little fingers would boldly make a dash into the bowl and bring out a flaring sugar plum. Hawk-moth watched them for a time, very much interested; you see, they don't play snap-dragon in the Lotus kingdom. Then he suddenly thought this would be a grand opportunity to steal a lovely spark of blue fire, and with it claim the hand of the proud princess. He fluttered round the bowl for some time, but no one paid any attention to him, they were all so merry pulling out the plums and eating them. It seemed so easy that Hawkmoth determined to try his luck, and boldly flew into the flames. Alas! poor fellow, he was burnt to a cinder, you could hardly tell him from a raisin.

One after another the suitors tried, and one after another they failed. There was a Hornbug who actually, one night, saw a green light in a cat's eye; he tried to snatch that, but you may well imagine how pussy, very much annoyed, made a short meal of my lord Horn-bug.

A venturesome Carrion-beetle having drifted towards the sea-shore, late one night, saw some fish lying there apparently all glowing with fire. He picked off one of the glistening scales, and went away proud and happy, quite convinced that the necessary prize – the much-sought-for spark of fire – was at last in his grasp. He was hurrying to get to Lotus land as fast as his legs could carry him, when he met a Stag-beetle, who apparently was also carrying a luminous object in front of him. The fact of the matter was, that Mr Stag-beetle had also fallen madly in love with the beautiful but capricious princess, and had determined to succeed in bringing her a spark of fire, even if it should cost him his wings!

After several unsuccessful attempts he had found at the foot of a large tree, a funny little bit of old wood, which gave out a beautiful little bright blue light. He approached very carefully (as he had been severely burnt several times), and you may be sure he was delighted when he found that it did not give out any heat, so that he was able to carry it off without burning himself. He was hurrying off with his prize to claim the Princess, when he met Mr Carrion-beetle bent on a similar errand.

They both stopped short, and glared at each other. No explanation was necessary. Each knew where the other one was hurrying to, and each was determined to get there first. They could not both marry Princess Fire-fly, that was very evident, so, after talking matters over for a while, they determined to fight it out till one of them remained dead on the battle-field. It was pitch dark, but the fish-scale and the bit of wood were quite enough light to kill one another by, so they each put down their prize, and began boxing in true beetle-like fashion.

As they both were equally tall, and equally strong, the fight lasted a considerable time. When lo! behold! as the first ray of dawn illumined the eastern sky, and the two combatants turned for a rest, previous to renewing hostilities, there, on the ground, instead of the two tiny sparks of blue flame, lay only a nasty fish's scale and an ugly bit of wood. King Phosphorus had vanished with the dawn. Further fighting was useless. Carrion-beetle and Stagbeetle each went his own way to seek fortune elsewhere.

Meanwhile, the Princess, in her beautiful palace, waited in vain for the return of one of her many suitors. When she heard of the sad fate of Prince Gold-beetle, she wept bitterly, for though she was so proud and vain, she was not wholly devoid of feeling, and of the many who had come wooing her she had preferred Prince Gold-beetle. When the Queen saw her tears, she tried to make her forego her purpose; but all her persuasions were of no avail, for the Princess was very obstinate, and would not own to being in the wrong.

Suitor after suitor came, and they were one and all sent off on the same hopeless errand. One day a most beautiful "Red Admiral" was on the point of committing suicide on the thorn of a rosebush, being so fearfully despondent on account of his non-success, when he caught sight of a luminous object underneath the very branch upon which he meant to end his life. His joy was great; what was it? Would it hurt him? He thought not, it looked so beautiful as it lay and sparkled in the sun. All round it was a hoop of gold. He went closer; no, it did not burn. Then came the question, how was he to convey it to the Princess? It was far too heavy for him to carry. Whilst he was considering how he could possibly convey it, he heard footsteps, and in another second a little child's voice exclaim, "Why, look! here is your diamond ring you lost;... how lucky it is I have found it," and the child picked it up and gave it to a grown-up lady who was a little way off. This was the last straw for the beautiful Red Admiral, and in another minute he had committed suicide.

And thus it was with one and all – some were frightened, and never attempted the task, others were badly singed, some died, none succeeded, and even to this day, in far-off lands, where the lotus grows, we always say when we see a crowd of insects fluttering round a flame: "Ah! Princess Fire-fly has many suitors tonight!"

Fairy Elizabeth

T HERE WAS ONCE SOMEWHERE, I don't know where, beyond
seven times seven countries, and even beyond them, a poor man
who had a wife and three children. They were awfully poor.

One day the eldest son said: "Dear mother, bake me some ash-cake and let me go
into service." His mother at once baked the cake, and the lad started, and went
on and on till he came to a high snow-clad mountain, where he met a grey-haired
man and greeted him: "May the Lord bless you, my good old father." "The Lord
bless you, my son. What are you after?" asked the old man. "I am going out to
service, if the Lord will help me to some place." "Well, then, come to me," said
the old man, "I will engage you." So they went to the house of the grey-haired
old man, and the very next day they went out ploughing but they only ploughed
up some grass-land, and sowed it with seed. Now let me tell you, that the old
man promised him a bushel of seed for sowing. Two days passed, and at dawn
of the third day the old man said: "Well, my son, today you can go out ploughing
for yourself; get the plough ready, yoke the oxen in, and in the meantime I will
get the bushel of wheat I promised." So the lad put the oxen to the plough and
the old man got the bushel of wheat and placed it on the plough. They started,
the old man accompanying him. Just at the end of the village he said to the lad:
"Well, my son, can you see that place yonder covered with shrubs? Go there, and
plough up as much of it for yourself as you think will be enough for the bushel
of wheat." The lad went, but was quite alarmed at the sight of the shrubs, and at
once lost heart. How could he plough there? Why, by the time he had grubbed up
the shrubs alone it would be night. So he ran off home, and left the plough there,
and the oxen then returned of their own accord to the old man's place – if I may
interrupt myself, they were the oxen of a fairy.

When the lad arrived at his father's house, his other brothers asked him:
"What sort of a place have you found?" "What sort of a place!" replied he, "go
yourself, and you will soon find out." The middle son set out, and just as he was
going over the snow-clad mountain he met the old man, who engaged him on
the spot as his servant, and promised him a bushel of wheat, as he had done

before. They went to the old man's home, and he fared just as his elder brother had done. At dawn on the third day, when he had to plough for himself, he got frightened at the sight of the vast number of shrubs, which no human being could have ploughed up in the stated time. So he went home too, and on his way he met his younger brother, who asked him: "What sort of a place have you found, my dear elder brother?" "What sort of a place had I? Get up out of the ashes, and go yourself, and you will soon find out."

Now let me tell you that this boy was continually sitting among the ashes. He was a lazy, ne'er-do-well fellow; but now he got up, and shook the ashes from him and said: "Well, my mother, bake me a cake also: as my brothers have tried their fortune let me try mine." But his brothers said: "Oh! You ash-pan! Supposing you were required to do nothing else but eat, you would not be good enough even for that." But still he insisted, that his mother should bake something for him. So his mother set to work and baked him a cake of some inferior bran, and with this he set out.

As he went over the boundless snow-clad mountain, in the midst of it he met the old man and greeted him: "The Lord bless you, my old father!" "The Lord bless you, my son! Where are you going?" "I am going out to service, if I can find an employer." "Well, you are the very man I want; I am in search of a servant." And he engaged him on the spot, promising to make him a present of a bushel of wheat for sowing. They went home together, and after they had ploughed together for two days, the lad set out on the third day to plough up the land allotted to him for his own use: while the youngster was putting the oxen to the plough the old man got the wheat and placed it on the plough. On the dyke there was a big dog, who always lay there quietly; but this time he got up, and started off in front of him. The old man also accompanied him as far as the end of the village, from whence he showed him where to go ploughing. The youngster went on with the plough, and soon saw that he was not able to plough a single furrow, on account of the thick bushes. After considering what to do, he bethought himself, and took his sharp hatchet and began to cut down a vast quantity of shrubs and thorns, the dog carrying them all into a heap. Seeing that he had cut enough, he began to plough. The two oxen commenced to drag the plough and cut up the roots in a manner never seen before. After he had turned three times, he looked round and said: "Well, I'm not going to plough any more, but will begin to sow, so that I may see how much seed I've got." He sowed the seed, and noticed that it was just sufficient, and therefore he had to plough no more. In great joy he set the plough straight and went home. The old man met him and said: "Well, my son, thanks to the Lord, you have now finished your year, and in God's name I will let you go. I do not intend to engage any more servants." Before I forget to tell you, I may mention it here, that the year had three days then. So the lad went home, and his brothers asked him: "Well, then, what sort of a place have you found?" "Well, I believe I've served my master as well as you did."

One day, a year after, he went into the field to look at his wheat crop. There he saw an old woman reaping some young wheat, so he went home and said to his father: "Well, my father, do you know what we have to do? let's go reaping." "Where, my son?" "Well, father, for my last year's service I had a bushel of wheat given to me for sowing, it has got ripe by this time, so let us go and reap it." So all four (his father, his two brothers, and himself) went; when they came to the spot they saw that it was a magnificent crop, a mass of golden ears from root to top, ready and ripe; so they all started to work and cut down every head.

They made three stacks of it, each stack having twenty-six sheaves. "Well my son," said the father, "there are three stacks here and there are three of you to guard them, so while I go home to hire a cart, guard them well, so that the birds may not carry away a single stem." The father went home, and the three sat down (one at the foot of each stack) to watch them, but the youngest was the most anxious, as it was his own, and ran to and fro continually to prevent his brothers falling asleep. Just as he had awakened them and was going back to his own stack he saw a woodpecker dragging away, by jerks, a golden ear along the ground, so he ran after it in order to get it back, but just as he was on the point of catching it the woodpecker flew off further and further, and enticed him, until at last it got him into the very midst of the boundless snow-clad mountains. All of a sudden the youngster discovered where he was, and that it was getting dusk. Where was he to go? And what was he to do? So he thought he would go back to the stacks, but as he had kept his eye on the woodpecker and the wheat-ear, he had taken no notice of the surroundings, and knew not which way he had come. So he determined to climb the highest tree and look round from there. He looked about and found the highest tree, climbed it, and looked East but saw nought, South and saw nought, North, and far, very far away he saw a light as big as a candle; so he came down, and started off in the direction in which he had seen the light and went straight over ditches, woods, rocks, and fields till at last he came to a large plain, and there he found the fire which he had seen before, and lo! it was such a heap of burning wood that the flames nearly reached heaven. He approached it and when he drew near the burning heap he saw that a man was lying curled round the fire, his head resting on his feet, and that he was covered with a large cloak. Then thought the lad, "Shall I lie down inside or outside of the circle formed by the body of the man?" If he lay outside he would catch cold; if he lay inside he would be scorched, he thought; so he crept into the sleeve of the cloak, and there fell asleep.

In the morning when the sun arose, the big man awoke, he yawned wide, and got up from the fire; as he rose the youngster dropt out of his sleeve on to the ground: the giant looked at him (because I forgot to tell you it wasn't a man, it was a giant), and was very much pleased at the sight; he quickly picked him up, took him into his arms, and carried him into his palace, (and even there put him into the best room) and put him to bed, covered him up well, and crept out of the room on tiptoe lest he should wake him. When he heard that the youngster was awake, he called to him through the open door, "Don't be afraid, my dear son, I am a big man it is true, but notwithstanding I will be to thee like thy father, in thy father's place; like thy mother, in thy mother's place." With this he entered the room, and the poor lad stared into the giant's eyes, as if he were looking up to the sky. Suddenly the giant asked him how he got there, and the lad told him the whole tale. "Well, my dear little son, I will give you everything that your heart can think of, or your mouth name, I will fulfil your every wish, only don't worry yourself;" and he had all sorts of splendid clothes made for him, and kept him on costly food; and this lasted till the lad became twenty years of age, when one day the lad became very sad, and his giant father asked him, "Well, my dear son, tell me why you are so sad, I will do all your heart can think of, or your mouth name; but do tell me what's the matter with you?" So the lad said, after hesitation, "Well! well! well! My dear father, I am so sad because the time has come when I ought to get married, and there's nobody here to get married to." "Oh! My son, don't worry yourself over that, such a lad as you has but to wish and you will find plenty of womankind, the very prettiest of them, ready to have you; you will but have to choose the one your heart loves best." So saying he called the lad before the gate and said: "Well, my son, you can see that great white lake yonder: go there at noon prompt and hide yourself under a tree, for every noon three lovely fairy girls come there who are as handsome as handsome can be: you can look at the sun, but you can't look at them! They will come disguised as pigeons, and when they arrive on the bank they will turn somersaults, and at once become girls: they will then undress, and lay their dresses on the bank: you must then glide up, and steal the dress of the one your heart loves best, and run away home with it, but be careful not to look back, however they may shout: because if you do, believe me, she will catch you, box your ears, and take her clothes from you."

So he went to the lake and hid himself under an oak, and all at once three white pigeons came flying, their wings flapping loudly as they came, they settled down on the bank, and went to take a bath. The lad wasn't slow to leave his hiding-place, and pick up the dress of the eldest fairy girl and run away with it; but she noticed it at once, rushed out of the lake, and ran after him, shouting: "Stop! sweet love of my heart. Look at me; see how beautiful my skin is; how pretty my breasts are. I'm yours, and you're mine!" So he looked round, and the fairy snatched her dress away in a moment, slapped his face, and returned to the others in the lake. Poor lad! he was very sad, and went back and told his giant father all that had happened, and his giant father answered, "Well; wasn't I right? Didn't I tell you not to look back? But don't fret; three in number are the divine truths, and three times also will you have to try. There are two yet left, go again tomorrow at noon. Take care you don't look back, or pick up the same dress that you picked up yesterday, because, believe me, if you do, there will be the mischief to pay." So he went early next day (he couldn't wait till noon) and hid himself under a tree, when all of a sudden the pigeons appeared, turned somersaults, and became three beautiful fairy girls. They undressed, laid their dresses on the bank, and went into the lake; in short, the lad fared with the second as with the first – he couldn't resist the temptation of looking back when the beautiful fairy kept imploring him, as the sweet love of her heart, to gaze at her beautiful skin and breasts. He looked back, was slapped in the face as before, and lost the fairy dress. He went home again, very sad, to his giant father, and told him how he had fared; and the giant said in reply: "Never mind, don't bother yourself, my son, three are the divine truths; there is one more left for you; you can try again tomorrow, but only be very careful not to look back this time." Next day he couldn't wait till noon, but went and hid himself under the oak very early, and had to wait a long, long time. At last the white pigeons arrived, turned somersaults as before, and put their dresses on the bank, whilst they themselves went into the lake. Out he rushed from his hiding-place, snatched up the youngest's dress, and ran away with it. But the fairy noticed that her dress was gone, and rushed out of the lake after him like a hurricane, calling out incessantly: "Stop! sweet love of my heart, look how beautifully white my skin is! See how beautifully white are my breasts. I am yours, and you are mine." But the lad only ran faster than ever, and never looked behind once, but ran straight home to his giant father, and told him that he had got the dress this time. "Well, my dear son," said he, "didn't I tell you not to worry yourself in the least, and that I would do all for you that your heart could desire, or your mouth name?" Once after this the lad was very sad again, so his giant father asked him: "Well, my son, what's the matter this time, that you are so sad?" "Well, my dear father, because we have only got a dress, and that is not enough for a wedding. What's the use of it? What can I do with it?" "Never mind, don't worry about that. Go into the inside closet, and on a shelf you will find a walnut, bring it here." So the lad went and fetched the nut, and the giant split it neatly in two, took out the kernel, folded up the dress (and I may mention it here the dress consisted of only one piece), put it inside the nut-shell, fitted the two halves together, and said to the lad: "Well, my son, let me have your waistcoat, so that I may sew this nut into the pocket; and be careful that no one opens it, neither thy father, nor thy mother, nor any one in this world, because should any one open it your life will be made wretched; you will be an outcast."

With this, the giant sewed the nut into the pocket, and put the waistcoat on him. As they finished this, they heard a great clamping noise, and a chinking (as of coins) outside. So the giant bade him to look out of the window, and what did he see? He saw that in the courtyard there was a lovely girl sitting in a carriage drawn by six horses, and about her beautiful maids and outriders, and the giant said, "You see, it is Fairy Elizabeth, your ladylove." So they went out at once, and helped Fairy Elizabeth out of her carriage, then she ordered the carriage and horses to go back, at once, to where they had come from, and in a moment they disappeared, and there was no trace of them left. They then went into the house, but the giant remained outside, and he drew in the dust figures of a priest, and a cantor, and guests, and they appeared at once. All went into the house, and the young folks got wed, and a great wedding feast was celebrated. There was the bridegroom's best man, and the groom's men, and the bride's duenna, and all her bridesmaids, and the wedding feast lasted three full days. They ate, drank, and enjoyed themselves, and when all was over the young couple lived together in quiet happiness. Once more, however, the lad became very sad, and the giant asked him: "Well, my dear son, why are you sad again? You know that I will do all your heart can desire, or your mouth name." "Well, my dear father," replied he, "how can I help being sad; it is true we live together happily, but who knows how my father and mother and brothers and sisters are at home? I should like to go to see them."

"Well, my dear son," said the giant, "I will let you go; you two go home, and you will find your relations keeping the third anniversary of your death: they have gathered in all the golden corn, and become so rich that they are now the greatest farmers in the village: each of your brothers have their own home and they have become great men (six-ox farmers) and have a whole flock of sheep." So the giant went outside, and drew in the dust the figures of horses and carriage, coachman, footmen, outriders, and court damsels, and they at once appeared; the young couple sat in the carriage, and the giant told the lad if ought happened to him he had only to think of one of these horses, and it would at once bring him back here.

With this they started, and they arrived at home and, saw that the courtyard of his father's house was full of tables, crowded with people sitting round them, but no one spoke a word; they all were speechless so that you could not even hear a whisper. The couple got out of the carriage, in front of the gate, walked into the yard, and met an old man; it happened to be his father. "May the Lord give you a good day, Sir!" said he; and the old man replied, "May the Lord bless you also, my lord!" "Well sir," asked the young man, "what is the meaning of all this feasting that I see, all this eating and drinking, and yet no one speaks a word; is it a marriage or a funeral feast?" "My lord, it is a burial feast," replied the old man; "I had three sons, one was lost, and today we celebrate the third anniversary of his death." "Would you recognize your son if he appeared?" Upon hearing this his mother came forward and said, "To be sure, my dearest and sweetest lord, because there is a mark under his left armpit." With this the lad pulled up his sleeve and showed the mark, and they at once recognized him as their lost son; the funeral feast, thereupon, was at once changed into a grand wedding festival. Then the lad called out to the carriage and horses "Go back where you have come from," and in a moment there was not a trace of them left. His father at once sent for the priest and the verger and they went through all the ceremonies again, and whether the giant had celebrated them or not, certainly the father did: the wedding feast was such a one as had never been seen before! When they rose from the table they began the bride's dance: in the first place they handed the bride to the cleverest dancer, and whether he danced or not, most certainly the bride did: as she danced her feet never touched the ground, and everyone who was there looked at the bride only, and all whispered to each other, that no man had ever seen such a sight in all his life. When the bride heard this she said, "Hum, whether I dance now or whether I don't, I could dance much better if anyone would return to me the dress I wore in my maiden days." Whereupon they whispered to each other, "Where can that dress be?" When the bride heard this she said, "Well, my souls, it is in a nutshell, sewn into my husband's waistcoat pocket, but no one will ever be able to get it." "I can get it for you," said her mother-in-law, "because I will give my son a sleeping-draught in wine and he will go to sleep," and so she did, and the lad fell on the bed fast asleep; his mother then got the nut from his pocket and gave it to her daughter-in-law, who at once opened it, took the dress out, put it on, and danced so beautifully, that, whether she danced the first time or not, she certainly danced this time; you could not imagine anything so graceful.

But, as it was so hot in the house, the windows were left open, and Fairy Elizabeth turned a somersault, became a white pigeon, and flew out of the window. Outside there was a pear tree, and she settled upon the top of it, the people looking on in wonder and astonishment; then she called out that she wanted to see her husband as she wished to say a word or two to him, but the sleeping draught had not yet lost its power, and they could not wake him, so they carried him out in a sheet and put him under the tree and the pigeon dropped a tear on his face; in a minute he awoke. "Can you hear me, sweet love of my heart?" asked the pigeon, "If you ever want to meet me seek for me in the town of Johara, in the country of Black Sorrow," with this she spread her wings and flew away. Her husband gazed after her for a while and then became so grieved that his heart nearly broke. What was he to do now? He took leave of all and went and hid himself. When he got outside of the gate he suddenly remembered what the giant had told him about calling to memory one of the horses; he no sooner did so than it appeared all ready saddled; he jumped upon it and thought he would like to be at the giant's gate. In a moment he was there and the giant came out to meet him. "Well, my dear son, didn't I tell you not to give that nut to anyone?" The poor lad replied, in great sorrow, "Well, my dear father, what am I to do now?" "Well, what did Fairy Elizabeth say when she took leave of you?" "She said that if ever I wished to meet her again I was to go to the town of Johara, in the country of Black Sorrow." "Alas, my son!" said the giant, "I have never even heard the name, so how could I direct you there? Be still, and come and live with me, and get on as well as you can." But the poor lad said that he would go, and he must go, in search of his wife as far as his eye could see. "Well, if you wish to go, there are two more children of my parents left, an elder brother and an elder sister. Take this; here's a mace. We three children couldn't divide it amongst us, so it was left with me. They will know by this that I have sent you; go first to my elder brother, he is the king of all creeping things; perhaps he may be able to help you." With this he drew in the dust the figure of a colt three years old, and bade him sit on it, filled his bag with provisions, and recommended him to the Lord.

The lad went on and on, over seven times seven countries, and even beyond them; he went on till the colt got so old that it lost all its teeth; at last he arrived at the residence of the king of all creeping things, went in, and greeted him, "May the Lord give you a good day, my dear father!" And the old man replied, "The Lord has brought you, my son. What is your errand?" And he replied, "I want to go to the country of Black Sorrow, into the town of Johara if ever I can find it." "Who are you?" asked the old man. With this he showed him the mace, and the king at once recognized it and said, "Ah, my dear son, I never heard the name of that town. I wish you had come last night, because all my animals were here to greet me. But stay, I will call them together again tomorrow morning, and we shall then see whether they can give us any information." Next morning the old man got up very early, took a whistle and blew it three times, and, in the twinkling of an eye all the creeping things that existed in the world came forward. He asked them, one by one, whether they knew aught of the town of Johara in the country of Black Sorrow. But they all answered that they had never seen it, and never even heard its name. So the poor lad was very sad, and did not know what to do. He went outside to saddle his horse, but the poor brute had died of old age. So the old man at once drew another in the dust, and it was again a colt three years old. He saddled it for him, filled his bag with provisions, and gave him directions where to find his elder sister.

With this the lad started off, and went over seven times seven countries, and even beyond them, till at last, very late, he arrived at the elder sister's of the giant and greeted her. She returned it; and asked him, "What is your errand?" he replied that he was going to the town of Johara in the country of Black Sorrow. "Well, my son," said the old woman, "and who has sent you to me?" "Don't you know this mace?" and she recognized it at once, and said, "Alas! my dear son, I am very pleased to see you, but I cannot direct you, because I never even heard of the place. Why did you not come last night, as all the animals were here then. But as my brother has sent you, I will call them all together again tonight, and perhaps they will be able to tell you something." With this, he went out to put his horse in the stable, and found that it had grown so old that it hadn't a single tooth left; he himself, too, was shrivelled up with age, like a piece of bacon rind, and his hair was like snow. At eve the old woman said to him, "Lie down in this bed!" when he lay down she put a heavy millstone upon him; she then took a whip, went outside the door, and cracked it. It boomed like a gun and the poor man inside was so startled that he lifted up the millstone quite a span high. "Don't be afraid, my son," called out the old woman, "I'm only going to crack it twice more," and she cracked it again; whether it sounded the first time or not, it certainly did this time, so that the poor man inside lifted the millstone quite a yard high, and called out to the old woman not to crack that whip again, or he should certainly die on the spot. But she cracked it again, notwithstanding, and it sounded so loud, that whether the first two sounded or not, this time it sounded so loud that the poor man kicked the millstone right up to the ceiling. After that the old woman went in and said to him, "You can get up now, as I am not going to crack my whip any more." So he got up at once, and she went and opened the window, and left the door wide open too. At once it became quite dark, the animals came in such clouds that they quite obscured the sunlight; she let them in one by one through the window, and read out the name of each one of them from a list, and asked them if they knew where the country of Black Sorrow was, but nobody knew it; so she dismissed them and shut the window and door. The poor man was very sad now; he didn't know what to do next or where he was to go. "There is nothing more to be done," said the old woman; "but I will give you a colt, and fill your bag full of provisions, and in heaven's name go back where you have come from."

They were still consulting when somebody knocked at the window and the old woman called out, "Who's that?" "It is I, my dear queen," replied a bird; and she began to scold it for being so late; but still she let it in, hoping that it might tell them something. Lo! it was a lame woodpecker. "Why are you so late?" she demanded, and the bird replied that it was because it had such a bad foot. "Where did you get your leg broken?" inquired the old woman. "In Johara, in the country of Black Sorrow." "You are just the one we want," said the old woman;

"I command you to take this man on your back without delay and to carry him to the very town where you have come from." The woodpecker began to make excuses and said that it would rather not go there lest they should break the other leg also; but the old woman stamped with her foot, and so it was obliged to obey and at once set off with the man on its back, whose third horse had already died; on they went over seven times seven countries, and even beyond them, till they came to a very high mountain, so high that it reached to heaven.

"Now then," said the woodpecker, "you had better get down here, as we cannot get over this." "Well, but," said the poor man, "how did you get over it?" "I? Through a hole." "Well then, take me also through a hole." Then the woodpecker began to make excuses, that it could not take him, first urging this reason and then that; so the poor man got angry with the woodpecker, and began to dig his spurs into the bird's ribs saying, "Go on, you must take me, and don't talk so much; it was you who stole the golden wheat-ear from my stack." So what could the poor woodpecker do but carry him. They arrived in the country of Black Sorrow, and stopped in the very town of Johara. Then he sent the woodpecker away, and went straight into the palace where Fairy Elizabeth lived. As he entered Fairy Elizabeth sat on a golden sofa; he greeted her, and told her he had come to claim her as his wife. "Is that why you have come?" replied she. "Surely you don't expect me to be your wife; an old bent, shrivelled-up man like you. I will give you meat and drink, and then in heaven's name go back to where you have come from." Hearing this the poor man became very sad and didn't know what to do, and began to cry bitterly; but in the meantime (not letting him know) Fairy Elizabeth had ordered her maids to go out at once and gather all sorts of rejuvenating plants, and to bring some youth-giving water, and to prepare a bath for him as quickly as possible. Then she turned to the old man again, and, in order to chaff him, said, "How can you wish a beautiful young girl like me to marry such an ugly old man as you? Be quick, eat, drink, and go back to where you have come from." In his sorrow the poor man's heart was nearly broken, when all at once Fairy Elizabeth said to him, "Well, dearest love of my youth, so that you may not say that I am ungrateful to you for having taken the trouble to come to me, and made all this long journey for me, I will give you a bath." She motioned to the maids, they at once seized him, undressed him, and put him into the tub; in a moment he was a young man again a hundred times handsomer than he was in his youth; and while they were bathing him they brought from a shop numerous costly dresses and clothed him with them and took him to Fairy Elizabeth; man and wife embraced and kissed each other again and again, and once more celebrated a grand marriage festival, going through all the ceremonies again; after all this was over they got into a carriage drawn by six horses, and went to live with the giant, their father, but they never went again, not even once, to the place where he had been betrayed. The giant received them with great joy, and they are still alive to this day, if they haven't died since. May they be your guests tomorrow!

The Three Oranges

THERE WAS ONCE, I don't know where, a king, who had three sons. They had reached a marriageable age, but could not find any one who suited them, or who pleased their father. "Go, my sons, and look round in the world," said the king, "and try to find wives somewhere else."

The three sons went away, and at bed-time they came to a small cottage, in which a very, very old woman lived. She asked them about the object of their journey, which the princes readily communicated to her. The old woman provided them with the necessaries for the journey as well as she could, and before taking leave of her guests, gave them an orange each, with instructions to cut them open only in the neighbourhood of water, else they would suffer great, very great damage. The three princes started on their way again, and the eldest not being able to restrain his curiosity as to what sort of fruit it could be, or to conceive what harm could possibly happen if he cut it open in a place where there was no water near: cut into the orange; and lo! a beautiful girl, such as he had never seen before, came out of it, and exclaimed, "Water! let me have some water, or I shall die on the spot." The prince ran in every direction to get water, but could not find any, and the beautiful girl died in a short time, as the old woman had said. The princes went on, and now the younger one began to be inquisitive as to what could be in his orange.

They had just sat down to luncheon on a plain, under a tall, leafy tree, when it appeared to them that they could see a lake not very far off. "Supposing there is a girl in the fruit, I can fulfil her wish," he thought to himself, and not being able to restrain his curiosity any longer, as to what sort of girl there could be inside, he cut his orange; and lo! a girl, very much more beautiful than the first, stepped out of it, and called out for water, in order to save her life. He had previously sent his brother to what he thought was a lake; and, as he could not wait for his return with the water, he ran off himself, quite out of breath, but the further he ran the further the lake appeared to be off, because it was only a mirage. He rushed back to the tree nearly beside himself, in order to see whether the girl was yet alive, but only found her body lifeless, and quite cold.

The two elder brothers, seeing that they had lost what they had been searching for, and having given up all hope of finding a prettier one, returned in great sorrow to their father's house, and the youngest continued his journey alone. He wandered about until, after much fatigue, he came to the neighbourhood of some town, where he found a well. He had no doubt that there was a girl in his orange also, so he took courage, and cut it; and, indeed, a girl, who was a hundred times prettier than the first two, came out of it. She called out for water, and the prince gave her some at once, and death had no power over her. The prince now hurried into the town to purchase rich dresses for his love; and that no harm might happen to her during his absence, he made her sit up in a tree with dense foliage, the boughs of which overhung the well.

As soon as the prince left, a gypsy woman came to the well for water. She looked into the well, and saw in the water the beautiful face of the girl in the tree. At first she fancied that she saw the image of her own face, and felt very much flattered; but soon found out her mistake, and looking about discovered the pretty girl in the tree. "What are you waiting for, my pretty maid?" inquired the gypsy woman with a cunning face. The girl told her her story, whereupon the gypsy woman, shamming kindness, climbed up the tree, and pushed the pretty girl into the well, taking her place in the tree, when the pretty girl sank. The next moment a beautiful little gold fish appeared swimming in the water; the gypsy woman recognized it as the girl, and, being afraid that it might be dangerous to her, tried to catch it, when suddenly the prince appeared with the costly dresses, so she at once laid her plans to deceive him: the prince immediately noticed the difference between her and the girl he had left; but she succeeded in making him believe that for a time after having left the fairy world, she had to lose her beauty, but that she would recover it the sooner the more he loved her: so the prince was satisfied and went home to his father's house with the woman he found, and actually loved her in hopes of her regaining her former beauty. The good food and happy life, and also the pretty dresses, improved the sunburnt woman's looks a little: the prince imagining that his wife's prediction was going to be fulfilled, felt still more attached to her, and was anxious to carry out all her wishes.

The woman, however, could not forget the little gold fish, and therefore feigned illness, saying that she would not get better till she had eaten of the liver of a gold fish, which was to be found in such and such a well: the prince had the fish caught at once, and the princess having partaken of the liver, got better, and felt more cheerful than before. It happened, however, that one scale of the fish had been cast out in the courtyard with the water, and from it a beautiful tree began to grow; the princess noticed it and found out the reason, how the tree got there, and again fell ill, and said that she could not get better until they burnt the tree, and cooked her something by the flames. This wish also was fulfilled, and she got better; it happened, however that one of the woodcutters took a square piece of the timber home to his wife, who used it as a lid for a milk jug: these people lived not very far from the royal palace, and were poor, the woman herself keeping the house, and doing all servants' work.

One day she left her house very early, without having put anything in order, and without having done her usual household work; when she came home in the evening, she found all clean, and in the best order; she was very much astonished, and could not imagine how it came to pass; and it happened thus on several days, whenever she had not put her house in order before going out. In order to find out how these things were accomplished, one day she purposely left her home in disorder, but did not go far, but remained outside peeping through the keyhole, to see what would happen. As soon as everything became quiet in the house, the woman saw that the lid of the milk jug which was standing in the window, began to move with gentle noise, and in a few moments a beautiful fairy stepped out of it, who first combed her golden tresses, and performed her toilet, and afterwards put the whole house in order. The woman, in order to trap the fairy before she had time to retransform herself, opened the door abruptly. They both seemed astonished, but the kind and encouraging words of the woman soon dispelled the girl's fear, and now she related her whole story, how she came into the world, how she became a gold fish, and then a tree, and how she used to walk out of the wooden lid of the milk jug to tidy the house; she also enlightened the woman as to who the present queen was. The woman listened to all in great astonishment, and in order to prevent the girl from slipping back into the lid, she had previously picked it up, when she entered, and now threw it into the fire. She at once went to the prince, and told him the whole story.

The prince had already grown suspicious about his wife's beauty, which had been very long in returning, and now he was quite sure that she was a cheat: he sent for the girl and recognized her at once as the pretty fairy whom he had left in the tree. The gypsy woman was put into the pillory, and the prince married the pretty girl, and they lived ever after in happiness.

The Invisible Shepherd Lad

THERE WAS ONCE, I don't know where, a poor man who had a very good son who was a shepherd. One day he was tending his sheep in a rocky neighbourhood, and was sending sighs to Heaven as a man whose heart was throbbing with burning wishes. Hearing a noise as of someone approaching he looked round and saw St. Peter standing in front of him in the guise of a very old grey man. "Why are you sighing, my lad?" inquired he, "and what is your wish?" "Nothing else," replied the lad, respectfully, "but to possess a little bag which never gets full, and a fur cloak which makes me invisible when I put it on." His wish was fulfilled and St. Peter vanished. The lad gave up shepherding now and turned to the capital, where he thought he had a chance of making his fortune. A king lived there who had twelve daughters, and eleven of them wanted at least six pairs of shoes each every night. Their father was very angry about this, because it swallowed up a good deal of his income; he suspected that there was something wrong, but couldn't succeed by any traps to get to the bottom of it. At last he promised the youngest princess to him who would unveil the secret.

The promise enticed many adventurous spirits to the capital, but the girls simply laughed at them, and they were obliged to leave in disgrace. The shepherd lad, relying on his fur cloak, reported himself; but the girls measured him, too, with mocking eyes. Night came, and the shepherd, muffling himself in his fur cloak, stood at the bedroom door where they slept, and stole in amongst them when they went to bed. It was midnight and a ghost walked round the beds and woke the girls. There was now great preparation. They dressed and beautified themselves, and filled a travelling bag with shoes. The youngest knew nothing of all this, but on the present occasion the invisible shepherd woke her – whereupon her sisters got frightened; but as she was let into their secret they thought it best to decoy her with them, to which, after a short resistance, the girl consented. All being ready, the ghost placed a small dish on the table. Everyone anointed their shoulders with the contents, and wings grew to them. The shepherd did the same: and when they all flew through the window, he followed them.

After flying for several hours they came to a huge copper forest, and to a well, the railing round which was of copper, and on this stood twelve copper tumblers. The girls drank here, so as to refresh themselves, when the youngest, who was here for the first time, looked round in fear. The lad, too, had something to drink after the girls had left and put a tumbler, together with a twig that he broke off a tree, in his bag; the tree trembled, and the noise was heard all over the forest. The youngest girl noticed it and warned her sisters that someone was after them, but they felt so safe that they only laughed at her. They continued their journey, and after a short time came to a silver forest, and to a silver well. Here again they drank, and the lad again put a tumbler and a silver twig into his bag. In breaking off the twig the tree shook, and the youngest again warned her sisters, but in vain.

They soon came to the end of the forest and arrived at a golden forest, with a gold well and tumblers. Here again they stopped and drank, and the lad again put a gold tumbler and twig in his bag. The youngest once more warned her sisters of the noise the quivering tree made, but in vain. Having arrived at the end of the forest they came to an immense moss-grown rock, whose awe-inspiring lofty peaks soared up to the very heavens. Here they all stopped. The ghost struck the rock with a golden rod, whereupon it opened, and all entered, the shepherd lad with them. Now they came to a gorgeous room from which several halls opened, which were all furnished in a fairy-like manner. From these twelve fairy youths came forth and greeted them, who were all wonderfully handsome. The number of servants increased from minute to minute who were rushing about getting everything ready for a magnificent dance. Soon after strains of enchanting music were heard, and the doors of a vast dancing hall opened and the dancing went on without interruption. At dawn the girls returned – also the lad – in the same way as they had come, and they lay down as if nothing had happened, which, however, was belied by their worn shoes, and the next morning they got up at the usual hour.

The king was impatiently awaiting the news the shepherd was to bring, who came soon after and told him all that had happened. He sent for his daughters, who denied everything, but the tumblers and the twigs bore witness. What the shepherd told the youngest girl also confirmed, whom the shepherd woke for the purpose. The king fulfilled his promise with regard to the youngest princess and the other eleven were burnt for witchcraft.

The Wishes

THERE WERE 10,000 WAGONS rolling along the turnpike road, in each wagon there were 10,000 casks, in each cask 10,000 bags, in each bag 10,000 poppy seeds, in each poppy seed 10,000 lightnings. May all these thunderous lightnings strike him who won't listen to my tale, which I have brought from beyond the Operencian Sea!

There was once, it doesn't matter where: there was once upon a time, a poor man who had a pretty young wife; they were very fond of each other. The only thing they had to complain of was their poverty, as neither of them owned a farthing; it happened, therefore, sometimes, that they quarrelled a little, and then they always cast it in each other's teeth that they hadn't got anything to bless themselves with. But still they loved each other.

One evening the woman came home much earlier than her husband and went into the kitchen and lighted the fire, although she had nothing to cook. "I think I can cook a little soup, at least, for my husband. It will be ready by the time he comes home." But no sooner had she put the kettle over the fire, and a few logs of wood on the fire in order to make the water boil quicker, than her husband arrived home and took his seat by the side of her on the little bench. They warmed themselves by the fire, as it was late in the autumn and cold. In the neighbouring village, they had commenced the vintage on that very day. "Do you know the news, wife?" inquired he. "No, I don't. I've heard nothing; tell me what it is." "As I was coming from the squire's maize-field, I saw in the dark, in the distance, a black spot on the road. I couldn't make out what it was, so I went nearer, and lo! do you know what it was? – A beautiful little golden carriage, with a pretty little woman inside, and four fine black dogs harnessed to it." "You're joking," interrupted the wife. "I'm not, indeed, it's perfectly true. You know how muddy the roads about here are; it happened that the dogs stuck fast with the carriage and they couldn't move from the spot; the little woman didn't care to get out into the mud, as she was afraid of soiling her golden dress. At first, when I found out what it was, I had a good mind to run away, as I took her for an evil spirit, but she called out after me and implored me to help her out of the mud; she promised that no harm should come to me, but on the contrary she would reward me. So I thought that it would be a good thing for us if she could help us in our poverty; and with my assistance the dogs dragged her carriage out of the mud. The woman asked me whether I was married. I told her I was. And she asked me if I was rich. I replied, not at all; I didn't think, I said, that there were two people in our village who were poorer than we. That can be remedied, replied she. I will fulfil three wishes that your wife may propose. And she left as suddenly as if dragons had kidnapped her: she was a fairy."

"Well, she made a regular fool of you!"

"That remains to be seen; you must try and wish something, my dear wife." Thereupon the woman without much thought said: "Well, I should like to have some sausage, and we could cook it beautifully on this nice fire." No sooner were the words uttered than a frying-pan came down the chimney, and in it a sausage of such length that it was long enough to fence in the whole garden. "This is grand" they both exclaimed together. "But we must be a little more clever with our next two wishes; how well we shall be off! I will at once buy two heifers and two horses, as well as a sucking pig," said the husband. Whereupon he took his pipe from his hatband, took out his tobacco-pouch, and filled his pipe; then he tried to light it with a hot cinder, but was so awkward about it that he upset the frying-pan with the sausage in it. "Good heavens! the sausage; what on earth are you doing! I wish that sausage would grow on to your nose," exclaimed the frightened woman, and tried to snatch the same out of the fire, but it was too late, as it was already dangling from her husband's nose down to his toes. "My Lord Creator help me!" shouted the woman. "You see, you fool, what you've done, there! now the second wish is gone," said her husband, "what can we do with this thing?" "Can't we get it off?" said the woman. "Take off the devil! Don't you see that it has quite grown to my nose; you can't take it off." "Then we must cut it off," said she, "as we can do nothing else." "I shan't permit it: how could I allow my body to be cut about? not for all the treasures on earth; but do you know what we can do, love? there is yet one wish left; you'd better wish that the sausage go back to the pan, and so all will be right." But the woman replied, "How about the heifers and the horses, and how about the sucking pig; how shall we get those?" "Well, I can't walk about with this ornament, and I'm sure you won't kiss me again with this sausage dangling from my nose." And so they quarrelled for a long time, till at last he succeeded in persuading his wife to wish that the sausage go back to the pan. And thus all three wishes were fulfilled; and yet they were as poor as ever.

They, however, made a hearty meal of the sausage; and as they came to the conclusion that it was in consequence of their quarrelling that they had no heifers, nor horses, nor sucking pig, they agreed to live thenceforth in harmony together; and they quarrelled no more after this. They got on much better in the world, and in time they acquired heifers, horses, and a sucking pig into the bargain, because they were industrious and thrifty.

Shepherd Paul

THERE WAS ONCE, I don't know where, a shepherd, who one day found a little boy in a meadow; the boy was not more than two days old, and so the shepherd took him to an old ewe and it nursed the child. The little boy was suckled by it for seven years, his name was Paul; and he grew so strong that he was able to uproot good-sized trees.

The old shepherd kept the boy another seven years on the old ewe's milk, and after that he grew so strong that he could pull up oak trees like weeds. One day Paul betook himself into the world in order to see countries, to get to know something of life, and try his luck. He went on and on, and on the very first day he met a man who was combing huge trees like one does flax. "Good day, my relative," said Paul; "upon my word, you are very strong! my Koma!" "I am Tree-Comber," said the man, "and am very anxious to wrestle with Shepherd Paul." "I'm the man you name; come along and let us wrestle," exclaimed Paul. And thereupon he seized Tree-Comber and threw him to the ground with such force that he sunk into the ground as far as his knees. But he soon recovered, jumped up, seized Paul, and threw him to the ground, so that he went in as far as his waist; and then Paul again caught him, and put him in as far as his neck. "That will do!" called out Tree-Comber; "I can see that you are a smart fellow, and should be glad to become your ally." "Well and good," said Paul, and they continued their journey together.

They went on and soon after found a man who was crushing stones to powder with his hands, as if they were clods. "Good day," said Paul; "you must be a strong chap, my Koma." "I am Stone-Crusher, and should like to wrestle with Shepherd Paul." Thereupon Paul wrestled with him too, and defeated him the same way as he had done Tree-Comber; and he too became an ally, and all three continued their journey. After a short time, they came across a man who was kneading hard iron, as if it were dough. "Good day," said Paul; "you must have the strength of a devil, Koma." "I am Iron-Kneader, and should like to fight Shepherd Paul," answered this man. Paul wrestled with him and defeated him, and they all four became allies, and continued their journey. About noon they settled down in a forest, and Paul thus addressed his mates: "We three are going to look for some game, and you, Koma Tree-Comber, will stop here in the meantime and prepare a good supper for us." The three went hunting, and Tree-Comber in the meantime commenced to boil and roast, until he had nearly got the meal ready, when a little dwarf with a pointed beard came to the place, and said, "What are you cooking, countryman? Give me some of it." "I'll give you some on your back if you like," replied Tree-Comber. The little dwarf made no reply, but waited till the sauerkraut was done, and then, suddenly seizing Tree-Comber by the neck and pulling him on his back, he placed the saucepan on his belly, ate the sauerkraut, and disappeared. Tree-Comber was rather ashamed of this, and in order to hide the real facts from his friends, commenced working afresh; however, the vegetable was not done by the time his mates returned, but he did not tell them the cause of it.

Next day, Stone-Crusher remained behind, while the others went hunting; he fared like Tree-Comber with the dwarf with the pointed beard, and the same thing happened to Iron-Kneader on the third day. Thereupon, Paul spoke thus: "Well, my Komas, there must be something behind all this, I think; none of you have been able to do the work while the rest of us were hunting. I propose that you three go hunting, while I remain and prepare the food." They went in high glee, chuckling that the little dwarf would teach Shepherd Paul a lesson also. Paul hurried on with the cooking, and had nearly finished, when the little fellow with the pointed beard came and asked for something to eat. "Be off," shouted Paul, and picked up the saucepan, so that the little fellow could not get it. The dwarf tried to get hold of his collar, but Paul swiftly seized him by his beard and tied him to a big tree, so that he could not move. The three mates returned early from their hunting, but Paul had the supper ready, and thus spoke to the three astonished men: "You, my Komas, are a fraud, you weren't able even to outwit that little dwarf with the pointed beard. Now let us have our supper at once, and then I will show you what I have done with him." When they finished, Paul took his mates to the place where he had fastened the dwarf, but he was gone, and so was the tree, as he had pulled it up by its roots and run away. The four fellows thereupon decided to give chase to him, and they followed the track made by the tree, and thus arrived at a deep hole, and as the track of the tree stopped here they came to the conclusion that the dwarf must have for a certainty got down into the deep hole. They held a short consultation and came to the resolution that they would lower Paul in a basket, and that they would remain above until Paul should pull the rope, and thus give them a signal to haul him up with all haste. So they lowered Paul, and deep below in the earth among beautiful valleys he found a splendid castle, into which he at once entered. In the castle he found a beautiful girl who at once warned him to run away as fast as possible if he valued his life, because the castle belonged to a dragon with six heads, who had kidnapped her from earth, taken her to this underground place, and made her his wife; but Paul decided to await the dragon's return, as he was desirous of liberating the pretty girl. The monster with six heads soon arrived and angrily gnashed his teeth at the foolhardy Paul, who thus addressed him, "I am the famous Shepherd Paul, and I've come to fight you." "Well done," replied the dragon; "so, at least,

I shall have something for supper, but first, let's have something to whet our appetites." Whereupon he commenced to devour a few hundredweights of huge round boulders, and, after he had satisfied his hunger, offered Paul one. Paul took a wooden knife and cut in two the stone offered to him, which weighed one hundredweight, and took up both halves and launched them with such power at the dragon that two of his heads were smashed to pulp. The dragon thereupon got into an awful rage, and made a furious onslaught on Paul, but he with a clever sword-cut slashed off two more of the monster's heads, and took him round the waist, and dashed him against the rock with such force, that the brains splashed out of the remaining two heads. The pretty girl thereupon with tears in her eyes thanked Paul for his services, for having liberated her from her ugly tormentor, but at the same time informed him, that two younger sisters of hers were languishing in the possession of two more powerful dragons.

Paul thereupon at once made up his mind to liberate the other two, and to take the girl with him. The girl handed him a golden rod, with which he struck the castle; and it became a golden apple, which he put in his pocket and went on. Not far off in a gorgeous castle he found the second girl, whose husband and tormentor was a dragon with twelve heads. This girl gave Paul a silk shirt in order to make him more fit for the struggle with her husband. The shirt made Paul twice as strong. He had dinner with the twelve-headed dragon, and after a long struggle succeeded in defeating him, and took away all his twelve heads; he then transformed the castle with a golden rod into a golden apple, and continued his way with the two girls. Not far off in a castle they found the third girl, who was the youngest and the prettiest, and whose husband was a dragon with eighteen heads, who, however, assumed the shape of a little dwarf with a pointed beard whenever he went on his expeditions on the surface of the earth.

Paul longed more than ever to be at him, and in order the better to fortify him for the struggle with the awful monster, the pretty girl dressed him in a silk shirt which made him ten times stronger, and she also gave him some wine which doubled his power again. When the huge dragon with the eighteen heads arrived, Paul at once accosted him, saying, "Well, my Koma, I'm Shepherd Paul, and I've come to wrestle with you, and to liberate that pretty girl from your claws." "I'm glad I've met you," replied the dragon, "it's you who killed my two brothers, and you'll have to pay for that with your life, for it is only your blood that can repay me for the loss." Thereupon the monster went into the next room, to put on the fortifying shirt, and to drink the strengthening wine; but there was no shirt, and no wine in the cask, because the pretty girl had allowed what Paul could not drink to run out. The dragon became very angry and began to pace up and down, being rather nervous as to the issue. But Paul was not long before he set at him, and with one stroke slashed off six of his heads, and, after a short struggle, either broke or cut off the rest; and having thus liberated the third girl, he transformed the castle, like the previous two, into a golden apple, hid it in his pocket, and started with the three girls towards the opening at the top of which his mates awaited him.

Having got there, as there was no room for all four in the basket, Paul bade the three girls to get in, and pulled the rope, whereupon his three mates hastily drew up the basket. Seeing the three pretty girls, they forgot all about hauling up Paul; each chose a girl and hastily left the forest, and settled down with them beyond the seventh country. Paul seeing that he was deceived by his faithless friends, began to swear in his rage, and vowed by heaven and earth that so soon as he should get out he would take bloody revenge on his deceitful mates, even if they had hidden themselves at the end of the world. Thereupon, he walked about aimlessly underground, and cogitated how to get out. After long wanderings he came to the nest of the huge griffin, in which he found several small griffins, and as the old bird was away, and it was hailing fire, he covered the nest with his cloak, and thus saved the little griffins. The old bird, in order to reward him, took him upon its back to carry him up to the surface. It took with it some provisions for the way, which consisted of a roast bullock hanging on one side, and a cask of wine on the other, and gave Paul directions that whenever it turned its head to the bullock he was to cut off a piece, and put it in its mouth, and whenever it turned its head to the cask, to pour a pint of wine down its throat. The griffin started off with Paul on its back, and flew three days and three nights, and on the morning of the fourth day it alighted with Paul outside the very town where his three faithless mates lived, put him down, and returned to its nest. Paul, as soon as he had rested from his fatigues, started off in search of his three mates, who were dreadfully frightened when they saw Shepherd Paul appear, who they thought was dead long ago. Paul gave them a severe scolding for their faithlessness, and then quietly killed all three. He placed the three apples in the prettiest part of the town, side by side, tapped them with the golden rod, and they became three splendid castles. He placed the three girls in them, married the youngest, and lives with her still in the middle castle, if he hasn't died since!

The Fairies' Well

TALE, TALE, MATE; a black little bird flew on the tree; it broke one of its legs; a new cloak, a shabby old cloak; it put it on.

Well, to commence! There was in the world a king, who was called the "Green King," and who had three daughters. He did not like them at all; he would have very much preferred if they had been boys. He continually scolded and abused them, and one day, in a fit of passion, the words slipped from his lips: "What *is* the good of all these wenches? I wish the devil would come and fetch them all three!" The devil wasn't slow; he took the king at his word and ran away with all three girls at once. The king's fondest wish was hereafter fulfilled; his wife bore him three sons, and he was very fond of them.

But the king grew old; his hair turned quite grey. So his sons set out for the fairies' well to fetch their father some youth-giving water. They wandered along till they came to a small road-side inn, where they had something to eat and drink, and gave their horses hay and corn. They tippled for some time, until the two elder princes got jolly, and commenced to dance in true style. The youngest one every now and then reminded them that it was time to continue the journey, but they would not listen to him. "Don't talk so much," they said, "if you are so very anxious to be off you had better leave us and go alone."

So the youngest saddled his horse and left his two brothers. He travelled along until all of a sudden he discovered that he had lost his way and found himself in a vast forest. In wandering hither and thither, he came to a small hut in which an old hermit dwelt. He at once went to it, knocked and entered, and greeted the old man, saying, "May the Lord grant you a happy good day, my father."

"The Lord bless you, my son! where are you going?"

"Well, old father, I intend to go to the fairies' well for some youth-giving water, if I can the way thither."

"May the Lord help you, my son! I don't believe that you will be able to get there unaided, because it is a difficult journey. But I will tell you something. I have a piebald horse, that will carry you without mishap to the fairies' well. I will let you have it if you promise to bring me back some youth-giving water."

"I will bring you some with pleasure, old father. You are quite welcome to it."

"Very well, my son! Get on the piebald, and be off in the name of Heaven!"

The piebald horse was led out and saddled, the prince mounted, and in another second they were high up in the air, like birds, because the piebald was a magic horse that at all times grazed on the silken meadow, the meadow of the fairies. On they travelled, till all at once the piebald said:

"I say, dear master, I suppose you know that once you had three sisters, and that all three were carried off by the devil. We will go and pay a visit to the eldest. It is true, your brother-in-law is at this moment out rabbiting, but he will be back soon if I go to fetch him. He will ask you to bring him, also, some youth-giving water. I'll tell you what to do. He has a plaid which has the power of making the wearer invisible. If you put it on, nobody on this earth can see you. If he will give you that plaid you can promise him as much water as he likes; a whole tub full, if he wants it."

When they reached the house, the prince walked in; and the piebald horse immediately hurried off to the fields, and began to drive the devil so that his eyes sparkled. As the devil ran homewards, he passed a pair of gallows with a man hanging upon them; he lifted off the corpse, and ran away with it. Having arrived at home, he called from the yard through the window: "Take this, wife! Half of him roasted, the other half boiled, for my meal. Be sure to have him ready by the time I get inside." Thereupon he pitched the dead man through the window; the meal was ready in a minute and the devil walked in, sat down and ate him. Having finished, he happened to look towards the oven and caught sight of the prince.

"Halloo! is it you, brother-in-law? Why did you not speak? What a pity that I did not notice you sooner? You are just too late; you could have had a bit or two of my bonne-bouche."

"Thank you, brother-in-law. I don't care for your dainties."

"Well, then get him some wine, wife! perhaps he will have some of that?"

The wife brought in the wine and placed it on the table, and the two set to drinking.

"May I ask, what are you looking for in this strange part of the world?" inquired the devil.

"I am going to the fairies' well for some youth-giving water."

"Look here, my good man, I am a bit of a smart fellow myself, something better than you, and still I could not accomplish that journey. I can get to within about fourteen miles of the place, but even there the heat is so great that it shrivels me up like bacon rind."

"Well, I will go all the same, if Heaven will help me!"

"And I will give you as much gold and silver as you can carry, if you will bring me back a gourdful of that water."

"I'll bring you back some, but for nothing less than for the plaid hanging on that peg. If you will give that to me you shall have the water."

At first the devil would not part with the plaid on any account; but the prince begged so hard that the devil at last yielded.

"Well, brother-in-law! This is such a plaid, that if you put it on nobody can see you."

The prince was just going when the devil asked him, "Have you any money for the journey, brother?"

"I had a little, but I have spent it all."

"Then you had better have some more." Whereupon he emptied a whole dishful of copper coins into the prince's bag. The prince went out into the yard and shook the bridle; the piebald horse at once appeared, and the prince mounted. The devil no sooner caught sight of the piebald than he exclaimed, addressing the prince, "Oh, you rascally fellow! Then you travel on that villainous creature – the persecutor and murderer of our kinsfolk? Give me back at once my plaid and my gourd, I don't want any of your youth-giving water!"

But the prince was not such a fool as to give him back the plaid. In a minute the piebald was high up in the air and flew off like a bird. They travelled along until the horse again spoke and said, "Well then, dear master, we will now go and look up your second sister. True, your brother-in-law is out rabbiting, but he will soon be back if I go for him. He, too, will offer you all sorts of things in return for getting him some youth-giving water. Don't ask for anything else but for a ring on the window sill, which has this virtue, that it will squeeze your finger and wake you in case of need."

The prince went into the house and the piebald fetched the devil. Everything happened as at the previous house. The devil had his meal, recognized his brother-in-law, sent for wine, and asked the prince:

"Well, what are you doing in this neighbourhood?"

"I am going to the fairies' well for some youth-giving water."

"You don't mean that! You have undertaken a very difficult task. I am as good a man as a hundred of your stamp put together, and still I can't go there. The heat there is so great that it would shrivel me up like bacon rind at a distance of fourteen miles. They boil lead there as we boil water here."

"Still I intend to go, by the help of Heaven."

"Very well, brother-in-law. I will give you so much treasure that you can fill several wagons with it, if you will bring me a gourd full of that youth-giving water."

"I don't want anything, brother-in-law, but that ring in the window yonder."

"Of what use would it be to you?"

"Oh! I don't know; let me have it."

So after a good deal of pressing the devil gave him the ring and said:

"Well, brother-in-law, this is such a ring that it will squeeze your finger and wake you, no matter how sound you may be asleep."

By this time the prince had already reached the courtyard, and was ready to start, when the devil stopped him and said:

"Stop a bit, brother-in-law, have you any money for the journey?"

"I had a little, but it is all gone," replied the prince.

"Then you had better have some." Whereupon the devil emptied a dishful of silver money into the prince's bag. The prince then shook the bridle and the piebald horse at once appeared, which nearly frightened the devil into a fit.

"Oh, you rascally fellow!" he exclaimed. "Then you are in league with the persecutor of our kinsfolk? Stop! Give me back that ring and gourd at once. I don't want any of your youth-giving water!"

But the Green Prince took no notice of the devil's shouting and flew away on his piebald like a bird. They had been travelling for some distance when the horse said: "We shall now go to see your youngest sister. Her husband, too, is out at present rabbiting, but I shall fetch him in, in no time. He, also, will beseech you to get him some youth-giving water, but don't you yield, no matter how much wealth he promises you, until he gives you his sword that hangs on the wall. It is such a weapon that at your command it will slay the populations of seven countries."

In the meantime they reached the house. The Green Prince walked in and the piebald went to look for the third devil. Everything happened as on the two previous occasions, and the devil asked his wife to send him in three casks of wine, and they commenced drinking. All of a sudden the devil asked, "Where are you going?"

"I am going to the fairies' well for some youth-giving water. My father has grown very old and requires some of the water to give him back his youth."

The devil replied that it was impossible to get there on account of the great heat. To which the prince said, that he was determined to go, no matter what might happen.

"Very well," continued the devil. "I will give you as much gold and silver as your heart can wish or your mouth name if you will bring me back a gourd full of the water."

"The gold is of no use to me; I have plenty of it at home; as much as I need. But if you will give me that sword on the wall, I will bring you some water from the fairies' well, with pleasure."

"Of what use would that sword be to you? You can't do anything with it."

"No matter. Let me have it."

The devil, at first, would not part with the sword; but, at last, he gave in. The Green Prince went into the yard, and was about to start, when the devil asked:

"Brother-in-law, have you any money left for the journey?"

"I had some; but it's nearly gone."

"Then you had better have some." And with this the devil put a plateful of gold coins into the prince's bag. The latter shook the bridle and his piebald appeared. The devil was very much alarmed at the sight, and exclaimed: "You rascal, then you associate with our arch-persecutor. Let me have back my sword and the gourd, I don't want any of your water." But the prince did not listen to him; in fact he had no time to heed the devil's words even if he had any intention of doing so, as he was already high up in the air, and the piebald now questioned him: "How shall we go, dear master? shall we fly as fast as the whirlwind, or like a flash of thought?" "Just as you please, my dear horse."

And the piebald flew away, with the prince on its back, in the direction of the fairies' well. Soon they reached their goal, and alighted on the ground, whereupon the horse said: "Well, my dear master, we have reached our destination. Put on the plaid that the first devil gave you and walk into the fairy queen's palace. The queen has just sat down to supper. Eat, drink, and enjoy yourself. Don't be afraid, nobody will know that you are there. In the meantime I will go into the silken meadow and graze with the horses of the fairy over night. I shall return in the morning and we will then fill our gourd."

And so it happened. The Green Prince put on the plaid and walked into the fairy queen's dining-room, sat down and supped, and for every glass of wine consumed by the fairy he drank two. The supper over they enjoyed themselves. Suddenly the fairy queen felt a sensation as if she were touched by a man, although she could not see anybody. She thereupon exclaimed to her fairies: "Fairies, fairies, keep the bellows going under the boiling lead. Some calamity will befall us tonight."

In the morning the piebald appeared before the castle; the Green Prince was still fast asleep, but luckily the ring squeezed his finger and he awoke and so was saved. He lost no time in going down to his horse.

"I am glad to tell you, my dear master, that all is well. They have not yet been able to see you. Let us go and get the water at once. This is how you must proceed. Stick the gourd on the point of your sword and then dip it under. But, be careful; the gourd must touch the water before my feet get wet, or else we must pay with our lives for our audacity."

The Green Prince did as he was told. He stuck the gourd on the point of the sword and dipped it into the well, before the piebald's hoofs touched the surface of the water.

"Well, my dear master, this has gone off without mishap. Let us at once go and liberate your sisters." First they visited the youngest. The Green Prince put on the plaid, and brought her away unnoticed. Then he rescued the second princess; and at last the eldest, by the aid of his plaid. And their diabolic husbands never noticed that they had been stolen. Having thus liberated his three sisters, he returned without delay to the hermit's hut.

"Well done, my son! Have you brought back any youth-giving water?" exclaimed the hermit, as he saw the prince approaching in the distance.

"To be sure, old father; I have brought plenty."

With these words the Green Prince approached the hermit, and allowed just one drop of the magic water drop on to the old man's hand; and oh, wonder! immediately a change came over him, and the old man instantly became young, and looked like a lad of sixteen.

"Well, my son; you have not made your journey in vain. You have secured the prize that you have striven for; and I shall always be deeply grateful to you until the end of my days. I won't take back the piebald from you, as I have another one exactly like it hidden away somewhere. True, it is only a little foal; but it will grow, and will then be good enough for me."

Then they parted, and the prince bent his way homewards. Having arrived at home he allowed a drop of the magic water drop on to his father's hand, and the old king immediately became a youth of sixteen. And he not only got younger, but also grew handsomer; and a hundred times better looking than he ever was before.

But the Green Prince had been away for such a length of time on his journey to the fairies' well that not even his father could remember him. The king had completely forgotten that the prince was ever born. What was he to do? Nobody knew him at his father's palace, or would recognize him as his father's son; so he conceived the strange idea of accepting a situation as swineherd in his father's service. He found stables for the piebald in a cellar at the end of the town.

While he tended his father's pigs, and went through his duties as swineherd, the fairies travelled all over the world and searched every nook and corner for the father of the child of their queen. Among other places they also came to the town of the Green King, and declared that it was their intention to examine every prince, as the person for whom they searched could only be a prince. The Green King then suddenly remembered that he had once another son but did not know his whereabouts. Something or other, however, recalled to his mind the swineherd, so he at once took pen and paper and wrote a note to the swineherd. The purport of the writing was that the king was the real father of the swineherd, and that the prince should come home with the least possible delay. The Green King sealed the letter and handed it to a gypsy with strict instructions to at once deliver it to the swineherd. The gypsy went, and the swineherd read the note and handed it back to the messenger, saying:

"My good man, take the note back. They have sent you on a fool's errand. I am not the son of the Green King."

The gypsy took the letter back in great anger. The swineherd, again, ran as fast as his legs would carry him to the stables in the cellar at the outskirts of the town, saddled his piebald, and rode *ventre à terre* to the centre of the town, and pulled up in front of the king's palace. There was such a sight to be seen. A great number of wonderfully pretty fairies had congregated, and were fanning the fire under a huge cauldron of boiling lead, which emitted such a heat that nobody could approach. The eldest prince came out and was about to try his fortune; he was gorgeously dressed, his garments glittering like a mass of gold. As he approached the cauldron full of boiling lead, a pretty fairy called out to him:

"Son of the Green King! are you the father of the child of the queen of fairies?"

"I am."

"Then jump into this seething mass of boiling lead."

He jumped in and was burnt, shrivelling up to the size of a crab-apple.

"You won't do," said the fairy.

Then the second prince stepped forth; his dress, too, was one mass of sparkling gold. As he approached the cauldron a fairy exclaimed:

"Son of the Green King! are you the father of the child of the queen of fairies?"

"I am."

"Then jump into this seething mass of boiling lead."

He jumped in and fared no better than his elder brother.

Now the swineherd rode forth on his piebald horse. His clothes were one mass of dirt and grease. To him, too, the fairy called out:

"Are you the father of the child of the queen of fairies?"

"I am."

"Then jump into this seething mass of boiling lead like the rest."

And, behold! he spurred the piebald horse, pulled tight the bridle, and again slackened it. The piebald shot up into the air like an arrow; and, having reached a good height, it came down with the swineherd on its back in one bold swoop, and jumped into the cauldron full of boiling lead without a single hair of him getting hurt. Seeing this, the fairies at once lifted him out, tore his dirty clothes from him, and dressed him up in garments becoming a king.

He married the queen of fairies and a sumptuous wedding feast was celebrated.

This is the end of my tale.

Mezőszárnyasi

WHAT I'M GOING TO TELL YOU NOW happened a long time ago, over the seventy-seven countries, and over the endless ocean, where the sky touched the earth, and even the swallows had to kneel down, drinking from the cold water of the meadows. There was a kingdom, and in this kingdom there reigned a king. The king and the queen had three beautiful daughters. They were so beautiful, that

the sun stopped every day in the sky for two hours to take pleasure in gazing upon them.

Once the king held a large ball in the courtyard. There came princes, earls, barons, younger and older noblemen. And they danced, and danced with the princesses, clanking their beautiful, freshly-cobbled and polished boots. They moved around, swirling. Oh what a dance it was. And as they danced, oh, Good Lord, what happened! Suddenly they see that the world is getting darker. A huge black cloud appeared in the sky, it was coming closer and closer, growing and growing, finally covering the whole sky, and there came a storm, lightning was scraping the ground, and from the middle of that big black cloud, a dragon's tail appeared, it swooped down, and grabbed the princesses. Everyone's jaws dropped as the girls all disappeared into thin air, as if they had never been there at all. The people were looking at each other – how did all this happen? – there was great wailing and crying. But, alas, as if this was not enough, something else went foul. That dragon didn't only kidnap the three princesses, but stole the Sun, the Moon and the stars from the sky. Pitch-black darkness descended upon the courtyard, indeed upon the entire city, upon the entire kingdom.

Tears rolled down the queen's face, and the king proclaimed to all in the land that whoever could bring back their daughters could choose one of them as their bride, as well as receive half of the kingdom.

Indeed, as you can imagine, there came princes and earls, counts, and a selection of noblemen and poor lads, oh they were queuing at the palace gate, full of hope. But none could bring them back, for they did not know where to search for them. Oh, how the king and the queen grieved and wailed, not knowing where to go, what to do.

There lived an old woman near the castle, and she had three sons. One day this old woman went to the king and said to him:

"Your Majesty! I have three sons; they can bring the princesses back."

"Woman, send your sons here immediately! I want to speak to them!"

The old woman went home and told her sons to prepare to set off for the palace. But, you know, these boys had an old nanny, and before they left, she went up to the youngest one, and whispered to him:

"Whatever the king says, do not do it! He will offer you splendid garments, golden and silver, and shiny swords. But tell him: 'Your Majesty, I only want the ones in which you got married, those old garments.' And when he tells you to tie a new sword on your side, say that 'I only want that rusty sword with which you won your battles.' When he offers you his best stallions from his stable, don't go in there. Behind the stable there is a heap of dung, and there in the middle of the dung you will find a lame, scrawny, three-legged horse, a little colt actually. Get that out of the dung, for that will be your horse!"

So the three sons set off and went up to the king. And he said to them:

"I heard you are skilful lads, and you could bring back my daughters. I will give you everything you need. Go to the treasury, choose from the most beautiful garments, there are gold and silver garbs, shiny swords, everything you need, then go to the stable. There you will find my strongest, most beautiful stallions, and choose from among them."

The two older brothers, dressed in golden corded garbs, tied a bright sword on their sides and went to the stable, and chose two beautiful stallions, but the youngest lad bowed to the king:

"Your Majesty, I only want the garments in which you got married!"

"Oh, my boy, well, if you really want those, you must go out to the yard. You will find them, somewhere, behind the henhouse, probably covered with turkey dung. But if that's what you want, go and find it!" And the boy went on:

"Your majesty, I don't need any shiny swords, either. I only want the rusty one with which you won your battles."

"Oh, my boy, you'll find it there as well, probably near those garments."

So, the boy went out. He found the garments and the king's sword behind the hen house. He cleaned off the turkey dung, put on the garments and tied the rusty old sword to his waist.

Then he didn't go to the stable, like his brothers, but went behind the stall. There in the middle of the dung he found that scrawny, three-legged, ill little colt. He grabbed it and tried to get the horse on its feet, but it was so thin and weak that it fell back to the ground. It was trembling. He pulled it up, but it fell down again.

At this moment, his brothers came out from the stable. When they caught sight of him, they started laughing and mocking him. "Hey, you! Who do you think you are? Look at yourself, you look ridiculous, we won't go with you. Everyone will just laugh at us!" They even spat on him!

But the boy didn't listen to them. He somehow managed to get the horse on its feet and dragged him out to the gate. And behold what happened?! You have not seen or heard anything like this. For as soon as they reached the gate, this scrawny little colt shook itself and turned into a bright, golden beautiful táltos horse. A beautiful magic stallion. And it was so bright and shiny that they had to cover their eyes with their arms so as not to become blinded by the sudden brightness. And you know, it even grew two beautiful wings, and a fourth leg. And in that same minute, the rusty sword turned into a silver sword, and his garb started shining like the sun.

His two brothers stared, their souls were filled with awe, for they had never ever seen anything like this before. At this, the youngest boy quickly jumped up onto the back of his táltos horse, and they started to gallop, and gallop, and then to fly. Yes, they flew up and up and up into the sky, until they reached the blacksmith of the sky. He was just hammering a horseshoe so big, that you could not see from one end of it to the other, and the blacksmith's hand was so huge that the boy could easily fit inside it. Sooty sweat streamed down from blacksmith's neck, like a giant overflowing river.

He greeted the blacksmith:

"Good day, and God bless you, master blacksmith!"

"God be with you, my son. Why did you come here?"

"I came to you, master blacksmith, so you would forge a ton-heavy metal ball for me. Put it in the furnace and make it red hot."

"What is your name, my dear boy?"

"Well, call me whatever you want, master blacksmith!" said the lad.

"Well, then from now on your name will be Mezőszárnyasi, which means 'wing of the meadows'."

The boy shrugged his shoulders.

"Fine, you can call me whatever you want!" And with this, he galloped down from the sky.

He caught up with his brothers. They rode and rode, for seven days and seven nights and seven blinks of an eye, until they reached the edge of the kingdom, where they were facing the land of the dragons. But ay, there, a sulphurous steam hit their noses with an unbearable stench! And as they went more and more into the dragon-land, their hearts were more and more filled with fear. They saw such huge trees growing there, that they could have covered themselves with their leaves, just like with a blanket. They were quivering from fear so much that if they hadn't been riding, you could have seen how their knees trembled. To strengthen their hearts, they started to pray and reminded themselves that they set off to bring back the princesses.

They were surrounded by such ancient forests that had never been cut, never been cleared, and it was getting darker and darker. Finally, they reached a copper bridge.

Here the brothers turned to each other:

"Well, this looks like a good place to rest. Let's sleep here! But one of us needs to be on watch. Lest someone may want to steal our horses or do something to us."

The oldest lad said:

"I'll be on watch, the rest of you can lie down!"

Mezőszárnyasi and his other brothers lay down, but Mezőszárnyasi only pretended to sleep.

And he was right in doing so, because the brother who was supposed to be on guard soon dropped his eyes, and was soon sleeping like a log.

Then Mezőszárnyasi got up, took his silver sword and hid under the bridge. There he stuck his sword up through a crack in between the decks of the bridge, so that the tip of the sword was sticking out, and he waited.

When the bells of dragon-land sounded nine o'clock, he suddenly heard singing from afar, singing in seven different languages.

"Oh, my Lord!", he thought, "My Creator! Seven of them are coming for me. Two or three I could handle, but seven will surround me, and they will put an end to my life!" Then he heard this strange sound, this thumping, coming closer and closer. Suddenly, from the thick of the forest a colossal dragon came forth on horseback. Oh, the boy's heartbeat almost stopped. For indeed it was a seven-headed dragon, spitting fire like a volcano. All of the sudden. with a great thump, he reached the bridge with his horse. And when they arrived at the middle of the bridge, the horse stumbled in the sword sticking through the planks. The dragon gave out a roar.

"Just you wait, you dog, come out at once Mezőszárnyasi! You weren't even born when I already knew you would be trouble and I would have to fight you! Come and let me tear you into pieces!" The boy jumped out from under the bridge, pulled out his sword and shouted:

"My sweet little sword: Get him! Cut off all seven heads, cut him into tiny little bits, bring the pieces and pile them up here in front of me!" And the sword started cutting away all the heads, and it was running and spinning around so quickly that he could hardly hold on to it. But finally, all the seven heads were cut off. The dragon was in front of him in a pile. Mezőszárnyasi cut off and collected the dragon's fingernails, and put them into his pouch.

That's when the brothers began to wake up. They saw the slaughtered dragon, they did not even dare ask what happened. They mounted their horses and crossed the bridge. And at the other side of the copper bridge, what do they see? There was a copper meadow in front of them. Next to the copper meadow, there was a copper castle. And in the copper castle, they found the eldest princess in a copper dress. When she saw them, she shouted: "Oh, Good Lord, how did you get here, to this place in the middle of nowhere? Didn't you know that my husband is the seven-headed dragon? When he comes home and finds you here, he will slice you to shreds! He will come home soon, please go away!"

"My Dear Princess, do not worry about the dragon! Just look out the window, you'll see its pieces in a pile. Stay here, I say, we'll go fetch your two sisters – just wait for us here."

And that is what happened. The three boys set off, they rode for seven days and seven nights and seven blinks of an eye until they reached a silver bridge. Well, there the two older ones again said: "We've come a long way, we're tired. Let's rest here, let's sleep." And they agreed that the middle one will be on watch during the night. But as you may have already guessed, it didn't take long for the middle brother to fall asleep. He tilted over like a sack, his eyes dropping. But Mezőszárnyasi did not fall asleep, he was on guard all night. He took that beautiful shiny silver sword, hid under the bridge, and stuck the tip of the sword through the crack in the bridge and waited. When the great bell of dragon-land struck nine, he heard singing from afar, in fourteen different languages. Now, he clasped his hands and looked up to the sky:

"Oh, this time my life is surely at an end. How on earth will I defeat this one?"

But there wasn't much time to think or grieve. He said another prayer, and not long after, the dragon appeared from the trees of the forest, coming on the back of his horse. It was even bigger than the first one. It had fourteen heads, and was shooting flames everywhere like a furnace. When he reached the middle of the bridge, his horse stumbled and the dragon roared:

"Oh, you dog, come out! You weren't even born, Mezőszárnyasi, when I already knew that I would have to fight you, come out, and let me slaughter you!"

The boy jumped out from under the bridge.

"Sweet little sword, out of the sheath! Cut off all the fourteen heads, and the tips of the nails and bring them here to me. Cut him into small pieces, and put them in a pile in front of me." The sword began its work so quickly, he could barely hold on to it. It didn't take long, and the fourteen heads were cut off. And the dragon was laying in front of him in a pile. So, he cut off its fingernails and put them in his pouch.

That is when his brothers began to wake. They dared not even ask a question, instead just jumped on their horses and together they crossed over the silver bridge, to find a silver meadow, and a silver castle next to it. They crossed the silver meadow and went inside the silver castle. There they found the middle princess in a silver dress. When she saw them, she cried out:

"How on earth did you come here, where not even a bird flies? Didn't you know that my husband is the fourteen-headed dragon? You're all finished. When he comes home, he will slice you to pieces!"

"Oh, dear princess, you don't have to worry about him any more. Look out of the window. He's lying there, slaughtered. We won't have to deal with him any more." And indeed, as she looked out, she saw the dragon lying there, just a pile of meat. Mezőszárnyasi turned to her:

"I say, stay here, dear princess, wait for us here. We're leaving for your youngest sister and will bring her back."

So they jumped on their horses, and rode for seven days, seven nights and seven blinks of an eye, until they reached a golden bridge, but this time they chose Mezőszárnyasi to be on watch. And sure enough, the two older brothers fell asleep. Mezőszárnyasi took his sword, hid under the golden bridge, put out the tip of his sword, and waited. But he was already shaking, his knees trembling, while he prayed. Because when the great bell of dragon-land struck nine, he could hear the singing, coming closer and closer, in twenty-four, yes, twenty-four different languages. He thought to himself:

"Now I'm really done for. I don't know what could possibly help me. Now comes the twenty-four-headed dragon and it will surely tear me into tiny pieces."

He didn't have to wait for long. Out of the trees of the forest, a dragon appeared, so huge that Mezőszárnyasi could hardly breathe. This was the eldest, the strongest, the most powerful of all the brothers. It commanded the other two as well. It scorched everything. It was pure fire. When it reached the middle of the bridge, his horse stumbled, and the dragon roared:

"Oh, you weren't even as big as a thousandth of a millet in your mother's womb, but I already knew then that I would have to fight you. Come out, Mezőszárnyasi, let me tear you to pieces."

The boy jumped out, facing the dragon.

"My sweet little sword, out of the sheath, cut him into small pieces, cut off all twenty-four heads." And the sword began its work, and it continued on and on, so quickly that the boy could hardly hold onto it. And they fought, and fought, but for how long? If the sun had been up in the sky, it would have risen and fallen three times, but they were still struggling, for they couldn't best one another. The heads were rolling down nice enough. The dragon was tired, Mezőszárnyasi was tired. And this great struggle went on until that dragon had only one head left. And with that one head, it began to plead:

"Mezőszárnyasi, leave me this one head, I am begging you! I don't mind that you cut off all the others, but leave me this one, leave me my life. I'll give you anything you ask for. I'll give back the Sun, the Moon, and the stars. I will give you as much treasure as you want. And I will show you the way to your father's land!"

Hearing this Mezőszárnyasi raised his sword and shouted:

"Of course I will leave it!" And, with one swing, he immediately cut off that last head. And then the pitch-black darkness started to slowly disappear. There was brightness everywhere. The Sun, the Moon and the stars rose in the sky. Well, in this great brightness, they jumped on their horses and crossed to the other side of the golden bridge. There the golden meadow lay, next to it the golden trees, with golden birds singing on their branches. On the other side of the golden meadow, in a golden castle, there was the youngest princess, dressed in gold. When Mezőszárnyasi saw the princess, he could barely speak. He thought to himself: "She is the most beautiful, she is noblest, she is the dearest. Either she will be my wife or no one else." But the princess, too, was looking at Mezőszárnyasi, unable to take her eyes off him. She said to him:

"Mezőszárnyasi, did you come for me? You know, when you were born, then I was born. When your star ascended to the sky, so did mine. They are there in the sky next to each other. Were I buried in the land of the seventh kingdom, you would still have come for me and you still would have saved me. But now, let's go to my father's land. In sickness and in health, may we never part."

They hugged and kissed each other. And the golden birds on the golden trees began singing even more beautifully. He planted her on the stallion and they were off. First, they rode back to the silver castle, then, of course, to the copper castle. They collected the princesses, and headed for home, nearing more and more to the edge of dragon-land.

Everything would have been all right, the brightness shined, but these dragons, oh, they had an old mother. And when she found out what Mezőszárnyasi had done to her sons, she started forging their flesh back together. One by one, she was putting all three of her sons back together. And since she had magical powers, she would have been able to breathe their soul back into them. The only trouble was that she needed all the pieces. But the nails were missing. So, the old witch set off and went after them. And as they are on their way on their horse, Mezőszárnyasi said:

"My sweet táltos horse, the spine of my neck is burning so!"

"Then, my sweet master, just turn around! What can you see?"

Mezőszárnyasi turned around and looked back. The forest roared, the fields roared, and he saw the old witch coming forth – she was blowing heat, and blowing cold with her mouth.

"Now what, my sweet horse?!"

"Do not worry for a second, my sweet master, now we will go up to the blacksmith of the sky!" And this is what they did. They galloped and then flew up and up into the high sky, until they reached the blacksmith. Once up there, Mezőszárnyasi shouted:

"Master blacksmith, do you still have that ton-heavy metal ball? Is it red hot now? "

"Yes, my boy!"

"Then look down! What can you see?"

"I see a woman with a strong mouth. She is blowing hot, she is blowing cold. Her mouth is so big that even a cart could turn around in it. "

"Well, take that ton-heavy metal ball, and throw it right into the mouth of that witch!"

The blacksmith took the ball out of the fire – because it was still there in the furnace, hot and red – and when the old woman opened her mouth, to blow hot and cold, he threw the ball right into her mouth. And she burned away immediately.

Now, they rode on, finally leaving dragon-land behind. They rode for seven days and seven nights and seven blinks of an eye, until they reached the king's castle.

The king and the queen had almost cried their eyes out, they were so filled with sorrow. But when they saw the lads with the princesses, they were so happy, they did not know whether to kiss the girls or hug the lads first. They were beyond themselves with joy. They immediately married off the three daughters to the three lads. The lads brought their mother to the palace, and they had a big wedding. Oh what a wedding it was! They danced for seven days and seven nights, and even the cats were drinking coffee with cream, and the dogs were lapping red wine. For sure, they all rejoiced. I was also there. And I danced too. You know, there was a big sack at the wall, and the water of river Tisza and the Danube was kept in it. As I was dancing and swirling, I accidentally tore that sack with the heel of my boot. And the Tisza river and the Danube started to flow out from the sack. As it was flowing, the water grabbed me up and brought me here. And that is why I could tell you how all this happened.

Adventure & Adversity

ADVENTURE, TRAVEL, COMBAT and intrigue dominate the next chapter. While reading the various tales, the reader can experience thrills such as racing against time to trap dawn and midnight, trying to keep the secret of a dream at all costs, or marrying the wicked iron-nosed witch to destroy her.

In this great chapter, we meet the devil in two tales (who is not easily fooled). The devil appearing in our magical tales – as opposed to the stupid devil subgenre – is not silly, but a powerful, often prescient figure with magical powers. Hungarian folktales do not abound in adventures of abstract concepts (e.g., Fortune, Blessing, Truth, Falsehood), but our selection includes one such tale with Truth and Falsehood in the main roles.

Stephen the Murderer

THERE WAS ONCE, I don't know where, over seven times seven countries, or even beyond that, a very, very rich farmer, and opposite to him lived another farmer just as rich. One had a son and the other a daughter. These two farmers often talked over family matters together at their gates, and at last arranged that their children should marry each other, so that in case the old people died the young people would be able to take possession of the farms. But the young girl could not bear the young man, although he was very fond of her. Then her parents threatened to disinherit her if she did not marry as she was bid, as they were very wishful for the marriage to take place.

On the wedding morning, when they arrived at church, and were standing before the altar, the bride took the wedding ring and dashed it on the floor before the clergyman, saying, "Here, Satan, take this ring; and, if ever I bear a child to this man, take it too!" In a moment the devil appeared, snatched up the ring, and vanished. The priest, seeing and hearing all that was done, declined to proceed with the ceremony, whereupon the fathers remonstrated with him, and declared that if he did not proceed he would lose his living. The wedding thereupon was duly celebrated."

As time went by the farmers both died; and the young folks, who couldn't bear each other before, at last grew very fond of each other, and a handsome boy was born. When he was old enough he went to school, where he got on so well that before long his master could teach him no more. He then went to college, where he did the same as at school, so that his parents began to think of him taking holy orders. About this time his father died; and he noticed that every night when he came home from the college that his mother was weeping: so he asked her why she wept. "Never mind me, my son," said she; "I am grieving over your father." "But you never cared much for him," said he; "cheer up, for I shall soon be a priest." "That's the very thing I'm weeping over," said his mother; "for just when you will be doing well the devils will come for you, because when I was married to your father I dashed the wedding ring on the ground, saying, 'Here,

Satan, take this ring; and if ever I bear a child to this man take it too.' One fine day, then, you will be carried off by the devil in the same way as the ring." "Is this indeed true, mother?" said the student. "It is indeed, my son." With that he went off to the priest, and said, "Godfather, are these things which my mother tells me concerning her wedding true?" "My dear godson," replied the priest, "they are true; for I saw and heard all myself." "Dear godfather, give me then at once holy candles, holy water, and incense." "Why do you want them, my son?" asked the priest. "Because," replied the student, "I mean to go to hell at once, after that lost ring and the deed of agreement." "Don't rush into their hands," said the priest; "they will come for you soon enough." But the more the priest talked the more determined was the student to set off at once for the infernal regions.

So off he went, and travelled over seven times seven countries. One evening he arrived at a large forest, and, as darkness set in, he lost his way and roamed about hither and thither looking for some place to rest; at last he found a small cottage where an old woman lived. "Good evening, mother," said he. "Good luck has brought you here, my son," said she. "What are you doing out here so late?" "I have lost my way," replied the student, "and have come here to ask for a night's lodging." "I can give you lodging, my son, but I have a murderous heathen son, who has destroyed three hundred and sixty-six lives, and even now is out robbing. He might return at any moment, and he would kill you; so you had better go somewhere else and continue your way in peace, and mind you take care not to meet him."

"Whether he kill me or not," said the student, "I shall not stir an inch." As the old woman could not persuade him to go he stayed. After midnight the son returned, and shouted out loudly under the window, "Have you got my supper ready?" He then crept in on his knees, for he was so tall that he could not enter otherwise. As they sat at table he suddenly saw the student. "Mother, what sort of a guest is that?" said he. "He's a poor tramp, my son, and very tired." "Has he had anything to eat?" "No; I offered him food, but he was too tired to eat." "Go and wake him, and say, 'Come and eat'; because whether he eat or whether he let the food alone he will repent it."

"Hello!" said the student, "what is the matter?"

"Don't ask any questions," replied the old woman; "but come and eat." The student obeyed, and they sat down to supper. "Don't eat much," said the old woman's son, "because you will repent it if you do eat and you will repent it if you don't." While they were eating the old woman's son said, "Where are you going, mate – what is your destination?" "Straight to hell, among the devils," quoth the student.

"It was my intention to kill you with a blow; but now that I know where you are going I will not touch you. Find out for me what sort of a bed they have prepared for me in that place."

"What is your name?"

"My name," said he, "is Stephen the Murderer."

In the morning, when they awoke, Stephen gave the student a good breakfast, and showed him which way to go. On he travelled till at length he approached the gates of hell. He then lighted his incense, sprinkled the holy water, and lighted the holy candles. In a very short time the devils began to smell the incense, and ran out, crying, "What sort of an animal are you? Don't come here! Don't approach this place; or we will leave it at once!"

"Wherever you go," said the student, "I tell you I will follow you; for, on such and such a date, you carried off from the church floor my mother's wedding ring; and if you don't return it and cancel the agreement, and promise me that I will have no more trouble from you, I will follow you wherever you go." "Don't come here," cried they, "stop where you are, and we will get them for you at once."

They then blew a whistle and the devils came hastily out from all directions, so many you could not count them, but they could not find the ring anywhere. They sounded the whistle again, and twice as many came as before, but still the ring was not to be found. They then whistled a third time, and twice as many more came. One fellow came limping up, very late. "Why don't you hurry?" cried the others, "don't you see that a great calamity has happened? The ring can't be found. Turn out everybody's pockets, and on who ever it is found throw him into the bed of Stephen the Murderer." "Wait a moment," cried the lame one, "before you throw me into Stephen the Murderer's bed. I would rather produce three hundred wedding rings than be thrown into that place." Whereupon he at once produced the ring, which they threw over the wall to the student, together with the agreement, crying out that it was cancelled.

One evening the student arrived back at Stephen the Murderer's. The latter was out robbing. After midnight, as usual, he returned, and when he saw the student he woke him, saying, "Get up, let's have something to eat! And have you been to hell?"

"I have." "What have you heard of my bed?" "We should never have got the ring," said the student, "if the devils had not been threatened with your bed." "Well," said Stephen, "that must be a bad bed if the devils are afraid of it."

They got up the next morning, and the student started for home. Suddenly it struck Stephen the Murderer that as the student had made himself happy he ought to do as much for him. So he started after the student, who, when he saw him coming, was very much afraid lest he should be killed. In a stride or two Stephen overtook the student. "Stop, my friend; as you have bettered your lot, better mine, so that I may not go to that awful bed in hell."

"Well then," said the student, "did you kill your first man with a club or a knife?" "I never killed anybody with a knife," said Stephen, "they have all been killed with a club." "Have you got the club you killed the first man with? Go back and fetch it."

Stephen took one or two strides and was at home. He then took the club from the shelf and brought it to the student; it was so worm-eaten that you could not put a needle-point on it between the holes. "What sort of wood is this made of?" asked the student. "Wild apple tree," replied Stephen. "Take it and come with me," said the student, "to the top of the rock." On the top of the rock there was a small hill; into this he bade him plant the club. "Now, uncle Stephen, go down under the rock, and there you will find a small spring trickling down the face of the stone. Go on your knees to this spring and pray, and, creeping on your knees, carry water in your mouth to this club, and continue to do so till it buds; it will then bear apples, and when it does you will be free from that bed."

Stephen the Murderer began to carry the water to the club, and the student left him, and went home. He was at once made a priest on account of his courage in going to hell; and after he had been a priest for twenty-five years they made him pope, and this he was for many years.

In those days it was the rule – according to an old custom – for the pope to make a tour of his country, and it so happened that this pope came to his journey's end, on the very rock upon which the club had been planted. He stopped there with his suite, in order to rest. Suddenly one of the servants saw a low tree on the top of the rock, covered with beautiful red apples. "Your holiness," said he to the pope, "I have seen most beautiful red apples, and if you will permit me I will go and gather some." "Go," said the pope, "and if they are so very beautiful bring some to me." The servant approached the tree; as he drew near he heard a voice that frightened him terribly saying, "No one is allowed to pluck this fruit except him who planted the tree." Off rushed the servant to the pope, who asked him if he had brought any apples.

"Your holiness, I did not even get any for myself," gasped the servant, "because someone shouted to me so loudly that I nearly dropped; I saw no one, but only heard a voice that said, 'No one is allowed to pluck this fruit but the man who planted the tree.'"

The pope began to think, and all at once he remembered that he had planted the tree when he was a lad. He ordered the horses to be taken out of his carriage, and, with his servant and his coachman, he set off to the red apple tree. When they arrived, the pope cried out, "Stephen the Murderer, where are you?" A dried-up skull rolled out, and said, "Here I am, your holiness; all the limbs of my body dropped off whilst I was carrying water, and are scattered all around; every nerve and muscle lies strewn here; but, if the pope commands, they will all come together." The pope did so, and the scattered members came together into a heap.

The servant and the coachman were then ordered to open a large, deep hole, and to put the bones into it, and then cover all up, which they did. The pope then said mass, and gave the absolution, and at that moment Stephen the Murderer was delivered from the dreadful bed in hell. The pope then went back to his own country, where he still lives, if he has not died since.

Prince Csihan (Nettles)

THERE WAS ONCE – I don't know where, at the other side of seven times seven countries, or even beyond them, on the tumbledown side of a tumbledown stove – a poplar tree, and this poplar tree had sixty-five branches, and on every branch sat sixty-six crows; and may those who don't listen to my story have their eyes picked out by those crows!

There was a miller who was so proud that had he stepped on an egg he would not have broken it. There was a time when the mill was in full work, but once as he was tired of his mill-work he said, "May God take me out of this mill!" Now, this miller had an auger, a saw, and an adze, and he set off over seven times seven countries, and never found a mill. So his wish was fulfilled. On he went, roaming about, till at last he found on the bank of the Gagy, below Martonos, a tumbledown mill, which was covered with nettles. Here he began to build, and he worked, and by the time the mill was finished all his stockings were worn into holes and his garments all tattered and torn. He then stood expecting people to come and have their flour ground; but no one ever came.

One day the twelve huntsmen of the king were chasing a fox; and it came to where the miller was, and said to him: "Hide me, miller, and you shall be rewarded for your kindness." "Where shall I hide you?" said the miller, "seeing that I possess nothing but the clothes I stand in?" "There is an old torn sack lying beside that trough," replied the fox; "throw it over me, and, when the dogs come, drive them away with your broom." When the huntsmen came they asked the miller if he had seen a fox pass that way. "How could I have seen it; for, behold, I have nothing but the clothes I stand in?" With that the huntsmen left, and in a little while the fox came out and said, "Miller, I thank you for your kindness; for you have preserved me, and saved my life. I am anxious to do you a good turn if I can. Tell me, do you want to get married?" "My dear little fox," said the miller, "if I could get a wife, who would come here of her own free will, I don't say that I would not – indeed, there is no other way of my getting one; for I can't go among the spinning-girls in these clothes." The fox took leave of the miller, and, in less than a quarter of an hour, he returned with a piece of copper in his mouth. "Here you are, miller," said he; "put this away, you will want it ere long." The miller put it away, and the fox departed; but, before long, he came back with a lump of gold in his mouth. "Put this away, also," said he to the miller, "as you will need it before long." "And now," said the fox, "wouldn't you like to get married?" "Well, my dear little fox," said the miller, "I am quite willing to do so at any moment, as that is my special desire." The fox vanished again, but soon returned with a lump of diamond in his mouth. "Well, miller," said the fox, "I will not ask you any more to get married; I will get you a wife myself. And now give me that piece of copper I gave you." Then, taking it in his mouth, the fox started off over seven times seven countries, and travelled till he came to King Yellow Hammer's. "Good day, most gracious King Yellow Hammer," said the fox; "my life and death are in your majesty's hands. I have heard that you have an unmarried daughter.

I am a messenger from Prince Csihan, who has sent me to ask for your daughter as his wife." "I will give her with pleasure, my dear little fox," replied King Yellow Hammer; "I will not refuse her; on the contrary, I give her with great pleasure; but I would do so more willingly if I saw to whom she is to be married – even as it is, I will not refuse her."

The fox accepted the king's proposal, and they fixed a day upon which they would fetch the lady. "Very well," said the fox; and, taking leave of the king, set off with the ring to the miller.

"Now then, miller," said the fox, "you are no longer a miller, but Prince Csihan, and on a certain day and hour you must be ready to start; but, first of all, give me that lump of gold I gave you that I may take it to His Majesty King Yellow Hammer, so that he may not think you are a nobody."

The fox then started off to the king. "Good day, most gracious king, my father. Prince Csihan has sent this lump of gold to my father the king that he may spend it in preparing for the wedding, and that he might change it, as Prince Csihan has no smaller change, his gold all being in lumps like this."

"Well," reasoned King Yellow Hammer, "I am not sending my daughter to a bad sort of place, for although I am a king I have no such lumps of gold lying about in my palace."

The fox then returned home to Prince Csihan. "Now then, Prince Csihan," said he, "I have arrived safely, you see; prepare yourself to start tomorrow."

Next morning he appeared before Prince Csihan. "Are you ready?" asked he. "Oh! yes, I am ready; I can start at any moment, as I got ready long ago."

With this they started over seven times seven lands. As they passed a hedge the fox said, "Prince Csihan, do you see that splendid castle?" "How could I help seeing it, my dear little fox." "Well," replied the fox, "in that castle dwells your wife." On they went, when suddenly the fox said, "Take off the clothes you have on, let us put them into this hollow tree, and then burn them, so that we may get rid of them." "You are right, we won't have them, nor any like them."

Then said the fox, "Prince Csihan, go into the river and take a bath." Having done so the prince said, "Now I've done." "All right," said the fox; "go and sit in the forest until I go into the king's presence." The fox set off and arrived at King Yellow Hammer's castle. "Alas! my gracious king, my life and my death are in thy hands. I started with Prince Csihan with three loaded wagons and a carriage and six horses, and I've just managed to get the prince naked out of the water." The king raised his hands in despair, exclaiming, "Where hast thou left my dear son-in-law, little fox?" "Most gracious king, I left him in such-and-such a place in the forest." The king at once ordered four horses to be put to a carriage, and then looked up the robes he wore in his younger days and ordered them to be put in the carriage; the coachman and footman to take their places, the fox sitting on the box.

When they arrived at the forest the fox got down, and the footman, carrying the clothes upon his arm, took them to Prince Csihan. Then said the fox to the servant, "Don't you dress the prince, he will do it more becomingly himself." He then made Prince Csihan arise, and said, "Come here, Prince Csihan, don't stare at yourself too much when you get dressed in these clothes, else the king might think you were not used to such robes." Prince Csihan got dressed, and drove off to the king. When they arrived, King Yellow Hammer took his son-in-law in his arms and said, "Thanks be to God, my dear future son-in-law, for that He has preserved thee from the great waters; and now let us send for the clergyman and let the marriage take place."

The grand ceremony over, they remained at the court of the king. One day, a month or so after they were married, the princess said to Prince Csihan, "My dear treasure, don't you think it would be as well to go and see your realm?" Prince Csihan left the room in great sorrow, and went towards the stables in great trouble to get ready for the journey he could no longer postpone. Here he met the fox lolling about. As the prince came his tears rolled down upon the straw. "Hello! Prince Csihan, what's the matter?" cried the fox. "Quite enough," was the reply, "my dear wife insists upon going to see my home." "All right," said the fox, "prepare yourself, Prince Csihan, and we will go."

The prince went off to his castle and said, "Dear wife, get ready; we will start at once." The king ordered out a carriage and six, and three waggons loaded with treasure and money, so that they might have all they needed. So they started off. Then said the fox, "Now, Prince Csihan, wherever I go you must follow." So they went over seven times seven countries. As they travelled they met a herd of oxen. "Now, herdsmen," said the fox, "if you won't say that this herd belongs to the Vasfogu Bába, but to Prince Csihan, you shall have a handsome present." With this the fox left them, and ran straight to the Vasfogu Bába. "Good day, my mother," said he. "Welcome, my son," replied she, "it's a good thing for you that you called me your mother, else I would have crushed your bones smaller than poppy seed." "Alas! My mother," said the fox, "don't let us waste our time talking such nonsense, the French are coming!" "Oh! My dear son, hide me away somewhere!" cried the old woman. "I know of a bottomless lake," thought the fox; and he took her and left her on the bank, saying, "Now, my dear old mother, wash your feet here until I return." The fox then left the Vasfogu Bába, and went to Prince Csihan, whom he found standing in the same place where he left him. He began to swear and rave at him fearfully. "Why didn't you drive on after me? come along at once." They arrived at the Vasfogu's great castle, and took possession of a suite of apartments. Here they found everything the heart could wish for, and at night all went to bed in peace.

Suddenly the fox remembered that the Vasfogu Bába had no proper abode yet, and set off to her. "I hear, my dear son," said she, "that the horses with their bells have arrived; take me away to another place." The fox crept up behind her, gave her a push, and she fell into the bottomless lake, and was drowned, leaving all her vast property to Prince Csihan. "You were born under a lucky star, my prince," said the fox, when he returned; "for see I have placed you in possession of all this great wealth." In his joy the prince gave a great feast to celebrate his coming into his property, so that the people from Bánczida to Zsukhajna were feasted royally, but he gave them no drink. "Now," said the fox to himself, "after all this feasting I will sham illness, and see what treatment I shall receive at his hands in return for all my kindness to him." So Mr Fox became dreadfully ill, he moaned and groaned so fearfully that the neighbours made complaint to the prince. "Seize him," said the prince, "and pitch him out on the dunghill." So the poor fox was thrown out on the dunghill. One day Prince Csihan was passing that way. "You a prince!" muttered the fox; "you are nothing else but a miller; would you like to be a house-holder such as you were at the nettle-mill?" The prince was terrified by this speech of the fox, so terrified that he nearly fainted. "Oh! Dear little fox, do not do that," cried the prince, "and I promise you on my royal word that I will give you the same food as I have, and that so long as I live you shall be my dearest friend and you shall be honoured as my greatest benefactor."

He then ordered the fox to be taken to the castle, and to sit at the royal table, nor did he ever forget him again.

So they lived happily ever after, and do yet, if they are not dead. May they be your guests tomorrow!

The Travels of Truth and Falsehood

A LONG TIME AGO – I don't exactly remember the day – Truth started, with her bag well filled, on a journey to see the world. On she went over hill and dale, and through village and town, till one day she met Falsehood.

"Good day, countrywoman," said Truth; "where are you bound for? Where do you intend going?" "I'm going to travel all over the world," said Falsehood. "That's right," said Truth; "and as I'm bound in the same direction let's travel together." "All right," replied Falsehood; "but you know that fellow travellers must live in harmony, so let's divide our provisions and finish yours first." Truth handed over her provisions, upon which the two lived till every morsel was consumed; then it was Falsehood's turn to provide. "Let me gouge out one of your eyes," said Falsehood to Truth, "and then I'll let you have some food." Poor Truth couldn't help herself; for she was very hungry and didn't know what to do. So she had one of her eyes gouged out, and she got some food. Next time she wanted food she had the other eye gouged out, and then both her arms cut off. After all this Falsehood told her to go away. Truth implored not to be left thus helpless in the wilds, and asked that she might be taken to the gate of the next town and left there to get her living by begging. Falsehood led her, not to where she wanted to go, but near a pair of gallows and left her there. Truth was very much surprised that she heard no one pass, and thought that all the folks in that town must be dead. As she was thus reasoning with herself and trembling with fear she fell asleep. When she awoke she heard some people talking above her head, and soon discovered that they were devils. The eldest of them said to the rest, "Tell me what you have heard and what you have been doing." One said, "I have today killed a learned physician, who has discovered a medicine with which he cured all crippled, maimed, or blind." "Well, you're a smart fellow!" said the old devil; "what may the medicine be?" "It consists simply of this," replied the other, "that tonight is Friday night, and there will be a new moon: the cripples have to roll about and the blind to wash their eyes in the dew that has fallen during the night; the cripples will be healed of their infirmities and the blind will see." "That is very good," said the old devil. "And now what have you done, and what do you know?" he asked the others.

"I," said another, "have just finished a little job of mine; I have cut off the water supply and will thus kill the whole of the population of the country town not far from here." "What is your secret?" asked the old devil. "It is this," replied he; "I have placed a stone on the spring which is situated at the eastern corner of the town at a depth of three fathoms. By this means the spring will be blocked up, and not one drop of water will flow; as for me I can go everywhere without fear, because no one will ever find out my secret, and all will happen just as I planned it."

The poor crippled Truth listened attentively to all these things. Several other devils spoke; but poor Truth either did not understand them or did not listen to what they said, as it did not concern her.

Having finished all, the devils disappeared as the cock crowed announcing the break of day.

Truth thought she would try the remedies she had heard, and at night rolled about on the dewy ground, when to her great relief her arms grew again. Wishing to be completely cured, she groped about and plucked every weed she could find, and rubbed the dew into the cavities of her eyes. As day broke she saw light once more. She then gave hearty thanks to the God of Truth that he had not left her, his faithful follower, to perish. Being hungry she set off in search of food. So she hurried off to the nearest town, not only for food, but also because she remembered what she had heard the devils say about cutting off the water supply. She hurried on, so as not to be longer than she could help in giving them her aid in their distress. She soon got there, and found every one in mourning. Off she went straight to the king, and told him all she knew; he was delighted when he was told that the thirst of the people might be quenched. She also told the king how she had been maimed and blinded, and the king believed all she said. They commenced at once with great energy to dig up the stone that blocked the spring. The work was soon done; the stone reached, lifted out, and the spring flowed once more. The king was full of joy and so was the whole town, and there were great festivities and a general holiday was held. The king would not allow Truth to leave, but gave her all she needed, and treated her as his most confidential friend, placing her in a position of great wealth and happiness. In the meantime Falsehood's provisions came to an end, and she was obliged to beg for food. As only very few houses gave her anything she was almost starving when she met her old travelling companion again. She cried to Truth for a piece of bread. "Yes, you can have it," said Truth, "but you must have an eye gouged out;" and Falsehood was in such a fix that she had either to submit or starve. Then the other eye was taken out, and after that her arms were cut off, in exchange for dry crusts of bread. Nor could she help it, for no one else would give her anything.

Having lost her eyes and her arms she asked Truth to lead her under the same gallows as she had been led to. At night the devils came; and, as the eldest began questioning the others as to what they had been doing and what they knew, one of them proposed that search be made, just to see whether there were any listeners to their conversation, as someone must have been eavesdropping the other night, else it would never have been found out how the springs of the town were plugged up. To this they all agreed, and search was made; and soon they found Falsehood, whom they instantly tore to pieces, coiled up her bowels into knots, burnt her, and dispersed her ashes to the winds. But even her dust was so malignant that it was carried all over the world; and that is the reason that wherever men exist there Falsehood must be.

The Hunting Princes

ONCE THERE WAS A KING whose only thought and only pleasure was hunting; he brought up his sons to the same ideas, and so they were called the Hunting Princes. They had hunted all over the six snow-capped mountains in their father's realm; there was a seventh, however, called the Black Mountain, and, although they were continually asking their father to allow them to hunt there, he would not give them permission.

In the course of time the king died, and his sons could scarcely wait till the end of the funeral ceremonies before they rushed off to hunt in the Black Mountain, leaving the government in the hands of an old duke. They wandered about several days on the mountain, but could not find so much as a single bird, so they decided to separate, and that each of them should go to one of the three great clefts in the mountain, thinking that perhaps luck would serve them better in this way. They also agreed that whoever shot an arrow uselessly should be slapped in the face. They started off, each on his way. Suddenly the youngest one saw a raven and something shining in its beak, that, he thought, was in all probability a rich jewel. He shot, and a piece of steel fell from the raven's beak, while the bird flew away unhurt. The twang of the bow was heard all over the mountain, and the two elder brothers came forward to see what he had done; when they saw that he had shot uselessly they slapped his face and went back to their places. When they had gone the youngest suddenly saw a falcon sitting on the top of the rock. This he thought was of value, so he shot, but the arrow stuck in a piece of pointed rock which projected under the falcon's feet, and the bird flew away; as it flew a piece of rock fell to the ground which he discovered to be real flint. His elder brothers came, and slapped his face for again shooting in so foolish a manner. No sooner had they gone and the day was drawing to an end than he discovered a squirrel just as it was running into its hole in a tree; so he thought its flesh would be good to eat; he shot, but the squirrel escaped into a hollow of the tree, and the arrow struck what appeared to be a large fungus, knocking a piece off, which he found to be a fine piece of tinder. The elder brothers came and gave him a sound thrashing which he took very quietly, and after this they did not separate.

As it was getting dark and they were wandering on together a fine roebuck darted across their path; all three shot, and it fell. On they went till they came to a beautiful meadow by the side of a spring, where they found a copper trough all ready for them. They sat down, skinned and washed the roebuck, got all ready for a good supper, but they had no fire. "You slapped my face three times because I was wasting my arrows," said the youngest; "if you will allow me to return those slaps I will make you a good fire." The elder brothers consented, but the younger waived his claim and said to them, "You see, when you don't need a thing you think it valueless; see now, the steel, flint, and tinder you despised will make us the fire you need." With that he made the fire. They spitted a large piece of venison and had an excellent huntsman's supper. After supper they held a consultation as to who was to be the guard, as they had decided not to sleep without a guard. It was arranged that they should take the duty in turns, and that death was to be the punishment of any negligence of duty. The first night the elder brother watched and the two youngest slept. All passed well till midnight, when all at once in the direction of the town of the Black Sorrow, which lay behind the Black Mountain, a dragon came with three heads, a flame three yards long protruding from its mouth. The dragon lived in the Black Lake, which lay beyond the town of the Black Sorrow, with two of his brothers, one with five heads and the other with seven, and they were sworn enemies to the town of the Black Sorrow. These dragons always used to come to this spring to drink at midnight, and for that reason no man or beast could walk there, because whatever the dragons found there they slew. As soon as the dragon caught sight of the princes he rushed at them to devour them, but he who was keeping guard stood up against him and slew him, and dragged his body into a copse near. The blood streamed forth in such torrents that it put the fire out, all save a single spark, which the guarding prince fanned up, and by the next morning there was a fire such as it did one good to see. They hunted all day, returning at night, when the middle prince was guard. At midnight the dragon with the five heads came; the prince slew him, and his blood as it rushed out put the fire entirely out save one tiny spark, which the prince managed to fan into a good fire by the morning.

On the third night the youngest prince had to wrestle with the dragon with seven heads. He vanquished it and killed it. This time there was so much blood that the fire was completely extinguished. When he was about to relight it he found that he had lost his flint. What was to be done? He began to look about him, and see if he could find any means of relighting the fire. He climbed up into a very high tree, and from it he saw in a country three days' journey off, on a hill, a fire of some sort glimmering: so off he went; and as he was going he met Midnight, who tried to pass him unseen; but the prince saw him, and cried out, "Here! stop; wait for me on this spot till I return." But Midnight would not stop; so the prince caught him, and fastened him with a stout strap to a thick oak tree, remarking, "Now, I know you will wait for me!" He went on some four or five hours longer, when he met Dawn: he asked him, too, to wait for him, and as he would not he tied him to a tree like Midnight, and went further and further. Time did not go on, for it was stopped. At last he arrived at the fire, and found there were twenty-four robbers round a huge wood fire roasting a bullock. But he was afraid to go near, so he stuck a piece of tinder on the end of his arrow, and shot it through the flames. Fortunately the tinder caught fire, but as he went to look for it the dry leaves crackled under his feet, and the robbers seized him. Some of the robbers belonged to his father's kingdom, and, as they had a grudge against the father, they decided to kill the prince. One said, "Let's roast him on a spit"; another proposed to dig a hole and bury him; but the chief of the robbers said, "Don't let us kill the lad, let's take him with us as he may be very useful to us. You all know that we are about to kidnap the daughter of the king of the town of the Black Sorrow, and we intend to sack his palace, but we have no means of getting at the iron cock at the top of the spire because when we go near it begins at once to crow, and the watchman sees us; let us take this lad with us, and let him shoot off the iron cock, for we all know what a capital marksman he is; and if he succeeds we will let him go." To this the robbers kindly consented, as they saw they would by this means gain more than if they killed him. So they started off, taking the prince with them, till they came close to the fortress guarding the town of the Black Sorrow. They then sent the prince in advance that he might shoot off the iron cock; this he did. Then said the chief of the robbers, "Let's help him up to the battlements, and then he will pull us up, let us down on the other side, and keep guard for us while we are at work, and he shall have part of the spoil, and then we will let him go." But the dog-soul of the chief was false, for his plan was, that, having finished all, he would hand the prince over to the robbers. This the prince had discovered from some whisperings he had heard among them. He soon found a way out of the difficulty. As he was letting them down one by one, he cut off their heads, and sent them headless into the fortress, together with their chief. Finding himself all alone, and no one to fear, he went to the king's palace: in the first apartment he found the king asleep; in the second the queen; in the third the three princesses. At the head of each one there was a candle burning; that the prince moved in each case to their feet, and none of them noticed him, except the youngest princess, who awoke, and was greatly frightened at finding a man in her bedroom; but when the prince told her who he was, and what he had done, she got up, dressed, and took the young prince into a side chamber and gave him plenty to eat and drink, treated him kindly, and accepted him as her lover, and gave him a ring and a handkerchief as a sign of their betrothal. The prince then took leave of his love, and went to where the robbers lay, cut off the tips of their noses and ears, and bound them up in the handkerchief, left the fortress, got the fire, released Midnight and Dawn, arrived at their resting place, made a good fire by morning, so that all the blood was dried up.

At daybreak in the town of the Black Sorrow, Knight Red, as he was inspecting the sentries, came across the headless robbers. As soon as he saw them he cut bits off their mutilated noses and ears, and started for the town, walking up and down, and telling everybody with great pride what a hero he was, and how that last night he had killed the twenty-four robbers who for such a length of time had been the terror of the town of the Black Sorrow. His valour soon came to the ears of the king, who ordered the Red Knight to appear before him: here he boasted of his valour, and produced his handkerchief and the pieces cut from the robbers. The king believed all that he said, and was so overjoyed at the good news that he gave him permission to choose which of the princesses he pleased for his wife, adding that he would also give him a share of the kingdom. The Red Knight, however, made a mistake, for he chose the youngest daughter, who knew all about the whole affair, and was already engaged to the youngest prince. The king told his daughter he was going to give her as a wife.

To this she said, "Very well, father, but to whomsoever you intend to give me he must be a worthy man, and he must give proofs that he has rendered great service to our town." To this the king replied, "Who could be able or who has been able to render greater services to the town than this man, who has killed the twenty-four robbers?" The girl answered, "You are right, father; whoever did that I will be his wife." "Well done, my daughter, you are quite right in carrying out my wish; prepare for your marriage, because I have found the man who saved our town from this great danger." The young girl began to get ready with great joy, for she knew nothing of the doings of the Red Knight, and only saw what was going to happen when all was ready, the altar-table laid, and the priest called, when lo! in walked the Red Knight as her bridegroom, a man whom she had always detested, so that she could not bear even to look at him. She rushed out and ran to her room, where she fell weeping on her pillow. Everyone was there, and all was ready, but she would not come; her father went in search of her, and she told him how she had met the youngest of the Hunting Princes the night before, and requested her father to send a royal messenger into the deserted meadow, where the dragons of the Black Lake went to drink at the copper trough, and to invite to the wedding the three princes who were staying there; and asked her father not to press her to marry the Red Knight till their arrival; on such conditions she would go among the guests. Her father promised this, and sent the messenger in great haste to the copper trough, and the young girl went among the guests. The feast was going on in as sumptuous a manner as possible. The messenger came to the copper trough, and hid himself behind a bush at the skirts of an open place, and as he listened to the conversation of the princes he knew that he had come to the right place; he hastened to give them the invitation from the king of the town of the Black Sorrow to the wedding of his youngest daughter.

The princes soon got ready, especially the youngest one, who, when he heard that his fiancée was to be married, would have been there in the twinkling of an eye if he had been able. When the princes arrived in the courtyard the twelve pillows under the Red Knight began to move, as he sat on them at the head of the table. When the youngest prince stepped upon the first step of the stairs, one pillow slipped out from under the Red Knight, and as he mounted each step another pillow fled, till as they crossed the threshold even the chair upon which he sat fell, and down dropped the Red Knight upon the floor.

The youngest Hunting Prince told them the whole story, how his elder brothers had slain the dragons with three and five heads, and he the one with seven heads; he also told them especially all about the robbers, and how he met the king's daughter, how he had walked through all their bedrooms and changed the candles from their head to their feet; he also produced the ring and the handkerchief, and placed upon the table the nose and ear-tips he had cut off the robbers.

They tallied with those the Red Knight had shown, and it was apparent to everybody which had been cut off first.

Everyone believed the prince and saw that the Red Knight was false. For his trickery he was sentenced to be tied to a horse's tail and dragged through the streets of the whole town, then quartered and nailed to the four corners of the town.

The three Hunting Princes married the three daughters of the king of the town of the Black Sorrow. The youngest prince married the youngest princess, to whom he was engaged before, and he became the heir-apparent in the town of Black Sorrow, and the other two divided their father's realm.

May they be your guests tomorrow!

Prince Mirkó

THERE WAS ONCE, I don't know where, a king who had three sons. This king had great delight in his three sons, and decided to give them a sound education, and after that to give them a place in the government, so that he might leave them as fit and willing heirs to his throne; so he sent these sons to college to study, and they did well for

a while; but all of a sudden they left college, came home, and would not return. The king was very much annoyed at their conduct, and prohibited them from ever entering his presence. He himself retired, and lived in an eastern room of the royal residence, where he spent his time sitting in a window that looked eastward, as if he expected someone to come in that direction. One of his eyes was continually weeping, while the other was continually laughing.

One day, when the princes were grown up, they held a consultation, and decided to ascertain from their royal father the reason why he always sat in the east room, and why one eye was continually weeping while the other never ceased laughing. The eldest son tried his fortune first, and thus questioned the king: "Most gracious majesty, my father. I have come to ask you, my royal sire, the reason why one of your eyes is always weeping while the other never ceases laughing, and why you always sit in this east room." The king measured his son from top to toe, and never spoke a word, but seized his long straight sword which leant against the window and threw it at him: it struck the door, and entered into it up to the hilt. The prince jumped through the door and escaped the blow that was meant for him. As he went he met his two brothers, who inquired how he had fared. "You'd better try yourself and you will soon know," replied he. So the second prince tried, but with no better result than his brother. At last the third brother, whose name was Mirkó, went in, and, like his brother, informed the king of the reason of his coming. The king uttered not a word, but seized the sword with even greater fury, and threw it with such vehemence that it entered up to the hilt in the wall of the room: yet Mirkó did not run away, but only dodged the sword, and then pulled it out of the wall and took it back to his royal father, placing it on the table in front of him. Seeing this the king began to speak and said to Prince Mirkó, "My son, I can see that you know more about honour than your two brothers. So I will answer your question. One of my eyes weeps continually because I fret about you that you are such good-for-nothings and not fit to rule; the other laughs continually because in my younger days I had a good comrade, Knight Mezey, with whom I fought in many battles, and he promised me that if he succeeded in vanquishing his enemy he would come and live with me, and we should spend our old age together. I sit at the east window because I expect him to come in that direction; but Knight Mezey, who lives in the Silk Meadow, has so many enemies rising against him every day as there are blades of grass, and he has to cut them down all by himself every day; and until the enemies be extirpated he cannot come and stay with me." With this, Prince Mirkó left his father's room, went back to his brothers, and told them what he had heard from the king. So they held council again, and decided to ask permission from their father to go and try their fortunes. First the eldest prince went and told the king that he was anxious to go and try his fortune, to which the king consented: so the eldest prince went into the royal stables and chose a fine charger, had it saddled, his bag filled, and started on his journey the next morning. He was away for a whole year, and then suddenly turned up one morning, carrying on his shoulder a piece of bridge-flooring made of copper; throwing it down in front of the royal residence, he walked into the king's presence, told him where he had been, and what he had brought back with him. The king listened to the end of his tale and said, "Well, my son, when I was as young as you are I went that way, and it only took me two hours from the place where you brought this copper from. You are a very weak knight: you won't do; you can go." With this the eldest prince left his father's room. The second prince then came in and asked the king to permit him to try his fortune, and the king gave him permission. So he went to the royal stables, had a fine charger saddled, his bag filled, and set off. At the end of a year he returned home, bringing with him a piece of bridge-flooring made of silver; this he threw down in front of the royal residence, and went in unto the king, told him all about his journey and about his spoil. "Alas!" said the king, "when I was as young as you I went that way, and it did not take me more than three hours; you are a very weak knight, my son: you will not do."

With this he dismissed his second son also. At last Prince Mirkó went in and asked permission to go and try his fortune, and the king granted him permission, so he also went into the royal stables in order to choose a horse for the journey; but he did not find one to suit him, so he went to the royal stud farm to choose one there. As he was examining the young horses, and could not settle which to have, there suddenly appeared an old witch, who asked him what he wanted. Prince Mirkó told her his intention, and that he wanted a horse to go on the journey. "Alas! my lord," said the old witch, "you can't get a horse here to suit you, but I will tell you how to obtain one: go to your father, and ask him to let you have the horn which in his younger days he used to call together his stud with golden hair, blow into it, and the golden stud will at once appear. But don't choose any of those with the golden hair; but at the very last there will come a mare with crooked legs and shaggy coat; you will know her by the fact that when the stud passes through the gates of the royal fortress the mare will come last, and she will whisk her tail and strike the heel-post of the fortress gate with such force that the whole fort will quiver with the shock. Choose her, and try your fortune." Prince Mirkó followed the witch's advice most carefully. Going to the king he said, "My royal father, I come to ask you to give me the horn with which in your younger days you used to call together your stud with the golden hair." "Who told you of this?" inquired the king. "Nobody," replied Prince Mirkó. "Well, my dear son, if no one has informed you of this, and if it be your own conception, you are a very clever fellow; but if anyone has told you to do this they mean no good to you. I will tell you where the horn is, but by this time, I daresay, it is all rust-eaten. In the seventh cellar there is a recess in the wall; in this recess lies the horn, bricked up; try to find it, take it out, and use it if you think you can." Prince Mirkó sent for the bricklayer on the spot, and went with him to the cellar indicated, found the recess, took the horn, and carried it off with him. He then stood in the hall of the royal residence and blew it, facing east, west, south, and north. In a short time he heard the tingle of golden bells begin to sound, increasing till the whole town rang with the noise; and lo! through the gates of the royal residence beautiful golden-haired horses came trooping in. Then he saw, even at the distance, the mare with the crooked legs and shaggy coat, and as she came, the last, great Heavens! as she came through the gates she whisked the heel-post with her tail with such force that the whole building shook to its very foundation. The moment the stud had got into the royal courtyard he went to the crooked-legged shaggy-coated mare, caught her, had her taken to the royal stables, and made it known that he intended to try his fortune with her. The mare said, "Quite right, my prince; but first you will have to give me plenty of oats, because it would be difficult to go a long journey without food." "What sort of food do you wish? Because whatever my father possesses I will willingly give to you," said the prince. "Very well, my prince," said the mare; "but it is not usual to feed a horse just before you start on a journey, but some time beforehand." "Well, I can't do much at present," said the prince; "but whatever I've got you shall have with pleasure." "Well, then, bring me a bushel of barley at once, and have it emptied into my manger." Mirkó did this; and when she had eaten the barley she made him fetch a bushel of millet; and when she had eaten that she said, "And now bring me half a bushel of burning cinders, and empty them into my manger." When she had eaten these she turned to a beautiful golden-haired animal like to the morning star. "Now, my prince," said she, "go to the king and ask him to give you the saddle he used when he rode me in his younger days." Prince Mirkó went to the old king and asked him for the saddle. "It cannot be used now," said he, "as it has been lying about so long in the coach house, and it's all torn by this, but if you can find it you can have it." Prince Mirkó went to the coach house and found the saddle, but it was very dirty, as the fowls and turkeys had for many years roosted on it, and torn it; still he took it to the mare in order to put it on her, but she said that it was not becoming a prince to sit upon such a thing, wherefore he was going to have it altered and repaired; but the mare told him to hold it in front of her, and she breathed on it, and in a moment it was changed into a beautiful gold saddle, such as had not an equal over seven countries; with this he saddled the táltos (mythical horse). "Now, my prince," said she, "you had better go to your father and ask him for the brace of pistols and the sword with which he used to set out when he rode me in former days." So the prince went and asked these from his father, but the old king replied "that they were all rusty by this time, and of no use," but, if he really wanted them, he could have them, and pointed out the rack where they were. Prince Mirkó took them and carried them to the mare, who breathed upon them, and changed them into gold; he then girded on his sword, placed the pistols in the holsters, and got ready for a start. "Well, my dear master," said the mare, "where now is my bridle?" Whereupon, the prince fetched from the coach house an old bridle, which she blew upon and it changed into gold; this the prince threw over her head, and led her out of the stable, and was about to mount her when the mare said, "Wait a minute, lead me outside the town first, and then mount me;" so he led her outside the town, and then mounted her. At this moment the mare said, "Well, my dear master, how shall I carry you? Shall I carry you with a speed like the quick hurricane, or like a flash of thought?" "I don't mind, my dear mare, how you carry me, only take care that you run so that I can bear it."

To this the mare replied, "Shut your eyes and hold fast." Prince Mirkó shut his eyes, and the mare darted off like a hurricane. After a short time she stamped upon the ground and said to the prince, "Open your eyes! What can you see?" "I can see a great river," said Prince Mirkó, "and over it a copper bridge." "Well, my dear master," said the mare, "that's the bridge from which your eldest brother carried off part of the flooring: can't you see the vacant place?" "Yes, I can see it," said the prince, "and where shall we go now?" "Shut your eyes and I will carry you;" with this, she started off like a flash of lightning, and in a few moments again stamped upon the ground and said, "Open your eyes! Now what do you see?" "I see," said Prince Mirkó, "a great river, and over it a silver bridge." "Well, my dear master, that's the bridge from which your second brother took the silver flooring; can't you see the place?" "Yes," said he, "I can, and now where shall we go?"

"Shut your eyes and I will carry you," said the mare, and off she darted like lightning, and in a moment she again stamped upon the ground and stopped and said to Prince Mirkó, "Open your eyes! What can you see?" "I see," replied he, "a vast, broad, and deep river, and over it a golden bridge, and at each end, on this side and that, four immense and fierce lions. How are we to get over this?" "Don't take any notice of them," said the mare, "I will settle with them, you shut your eyes." Prince Mirkó shut his eyes, the mare darted off like a swift falcon, and flew over the bridge; in a short time she stopped, stamped, and said, "Open your eyes! Now what do you see?" "I see," said the prince, "an immense, high glass rock, with sides as steep as the side of a house." "Well, my dear master," said the mare, "We have to get over that too."

"But that is impossible," said the prince; but the mare cheered him, and said, "Don't worry yourself, dear master, as I still have the very shoes on my hooves which your father put on them with diamond nails six hundred years ago. Shut your eyes and hold fast."

At this moment the mare darted off, and in a twinkling of the eye she reached the summit of the glass rock, where she stopped, stamped, and said to the prince, "Open your eyes! What can you see?" "I can see, below me," said Prince Mirkó, "on looking back, something black, the size of a fair-sized dish." "Well, my dear master, that is the orb of the earth; but what can you see in front of you?" "I can see," said Prince Mirkó, "a narrow round-backed glass path, and by the side of it, this side as well as on the other side, a deep bottomless abyss." "Well, my dear master," said the mare, "we have to get over that, but the passage is so difficult that if my foot slips the least bit either way we shall perish, but rely on me. Shut your eyes and grasp hold of me, and I will do it." With this the mare started and in another moment she again stamped on the ground and said, "Open your eyes! What can you see?" "I can see," said Prince Mirkó, "behind me, in the distance, some faint light and in front of me such a thick darkness that I cannot even see my finger before me." "Well, my dear master, we have to get through this also. Shut your eyes, and grasp me." Again she started and again she stamped. "Open your eyes! What can you see now?" "I can see," said Prince Mirkó, "a beautiful light, a beautiful snow-clad mountain, in the midst of the mountain a meadow like silk, and in the midst of the meadow something black." "Well, my dear master, that meadow which looks like silk belongs to Knight Mezey, and the black something in the middle of it is his tent, woven of black silk; it does not matter now whether you shut your eyes or not, we will go there." With this Prince Mirkó spurred the mare, and at once reached the tent.

Prince Mirkó jumped from his mare and tied her to the tent by the side of Knight Mezey's horse, and he himself walked into the tent, and lo! Inside, a knight was laid at full length on the silken grass, fast asleep, but a sword over him was slashing in all directions, so that not even a fly could settle on him. "Well," thought Prince Mirkó to himself, "this fellow must be a brave knight, but I could kill him while he sleeps; however, it would not be an honourable act to kill a sleeping knight, and I will wait till he wakes." With this he walked out of the tent, tied his mare faster to the tent-post, and he also lay down full length upon the silken grass, and said to his sword, "Sword, come out of thy scabbard," and his sword began to slash about over him, just like Knight Mezey's, so that not even a fly could settle on him.

All of a sudden Knight Mezey woke, and to his astonishment he saw another horse tied by the side of his, and said, "Great Heavens! What's the meaning of this? It's six hundred years since I saw a strange horse by the side of mine! Whom can it belong to?" He got up, went out of the tent, and saw Prince Mirkó asleep outside, and his sword slashing about over him. "Well," said he, "this must be a brave knight, and as he has not killed me while I was asleep, it would not be honourable to kill him," with this he kicked the sleeping knight's foot and woke him. He jumped up, and Knight Mezey thus questioned him: "Who are you? What is your business?" Prince Mirkó told him whose son he was and why he had come. "Welcome, my dear brother," said Knight Mezey, "your father is a dear friend of mine, and I can see that you are as brave a knight as your father, and I shall want you, because the large silken meadow that you see is covered with enemies every day, and I have to daily cut them down, but now that you are here to help me I shall be in no hurry about them; let's go inside and have something to eat and drink, and let them gather into a crowd, two of us will soon finish them."

They went into the tent and had something to eat and drink; but all at once his enemies came up in such numbers that they came almost as far as the tent, when Knight Mezey jumped to his feet and said, "Jump up, comrade, or else we are done for." They sprang to their horses, darted among the enemy, and both called out, "Sword, out of thy scabbard!" and in a moment the two swords began to slash about, and cut off the heads of the enemy, so that they had the greatest difficulty in advancing on account of the piles of dead bodies, till at last, at the rear of the enemy, twelve knights took to flight, and Knight Mezey and Prince Mirkó rode in pursuit of them, till they reached a glass rock, to which they followed the twelve knights, Prince Mirkó being the nearest to them. On the top of the rock there was a beautiful open space, towards which the knights rode and Prince Mirkó after them on his mare, when all at once they all disappeared, as if the earth had swallowed them; seeing this, Prince Mirkó rode to the spot where they disappeared, where he found a trapdoor, and under the door a deep hole and a spiral staircase. The mare without hesitation jumped into the hole, which was the entrance to the infernal regions. Prince Mirkó, looking round in Hades, suddenly discerned a glittering diamond castle, which served the lower regions instead of the sun, and saw that the twelve knights were riding towards it; so he darted after them, and, calling out "Sword, come out of thy scabbard," he slashed off the twelve knights' heads in a moment, and, riding to the castle, he heard such a hubbub and clattering that the whole place resounded with it: he jumped off his horse, and walked into the castle, when lo! there was an old diabolical-looking witch, who was weaving and making the clattering noise, and the whole building was now full of soldiers, whom the devilish witch produced by weaving. When she threw the shuttle to the right, each time two hussars on horseback jumped out from the shuttle, and when she threw it to the left, each time two foot soldiers jumped from it fully equipped. When he saw this, he ordered his sword out of its scabbard, and cut down all the soldiers present. But the old witch wove others again, so Prince Mirkó thought to himself, if this goes on, I shall never get out of this place, so he ordered his sword to cut up into little pieces the old witch, and then he carried out the whole bleeding mass into the courtyard, where he found a heap of wood: he placed the mass on it, put a light to it, and burnt it. But when it was fully alight a small piece of a rib of the witch flew out of the fire and began to spin around in the dust, and lo! another witch grew out of it. Prince Mirkó thereupon was about to order his sword to cut her up too, when the old witch addressed him thus: "Spare my life, Mirkó, and I will help you in return for your kindness; if you destroy me you can't get out of this place; here! I will give you four diamond horseshoe nails, put them away and you will find them useful." Prince Mirkó took the nails and put them away, thinking to himself, "If I spare the old witch she will start weaving again, and Knight Mezey will never get rid of his enemies," so he again ordered his sword to cut up the witch, and threw her into the fire and burnt her to cinders. She never came to life again. He then got on his mare and rode all over the lower regions, but could not find a living soul anywhere, whereupon he spurred his mare, galloped to the foot of the spiral staircase, and in another moment he reached the upper world. When he arrived at the brink of the glass rock he was about to alight from his mare: and stopped her for this purpose, but the mare questioned him thus, "What are you going to do, Prince Mirkó?" "I was going to get down, because the road is very steep and it's impossible to go down on horseback." "Well then, dear master, if you do that you can't get below, because you couldn't walk on the steep road, but if you stop on my back, take hold of my mane, and shut your eyes, I will take you down." Whereupon the mare started down the side of the rock, and, like a good mountaineer, climbed down from the top to the bottom, and having arrived at the foot of the steep rock, spoke to Prince Mirkó thus: "You can open your eyes now." Mirkó having opened his eyes, saw that they had arrived in the silken meadow.

They started in the direction of Knight Mezey's tent, but Knight Mezey thought that Mirkó had already perished, when suddenly he saw that Mirkó was alive, so he came in great joy to meet him, and leading him into his tent, as he had no heir, he offered him the silk meadow and his whole realm, but Mirkó replied thus: "My dear brother, now that I have destroyed all your enemies, you need not fear that the enemy will occupy your country, therefore I should like you to come with me to my royal father, who has been expecting you for a very long time." With this they got on their horses, and started off in the direction of the old king's realm, and arrived safely at the very spot on the glass rock where Mirkó had jumped down. Knight Mezey stopped here, and said to Prince Mirkó: "My dear brother, I cannot go further than this, because the diamond nails of my horse's shoes have been worn out long ago, and the horse's feet no longer grip the ground." But Mirkó remembered that the old witch had given him some diamond nails, and said: "Don't worry yourself, brother. I have got some nails with me, and I will shoe thy horse." And taking out the diamond nails, he shod Knight Mezey's horse with them. They mounted once more, and like two good mountaineers descended the glass rock, and as swift as thought were on the way home.

The old king was also then sitting in the eastern window, awaiting Knight Mezey, when suddenly he saw two horsemen approaching, and, looking at them with his telescope, recognized them as his dear old comrade Knight Mezey, together with his son, Prince Mirkó, coming towards him; so he ran down at once, and out of the hall. He ordered the bailiff to slaughter twelve heifers, and by the time that Knight Mezey and Mirkó arrived, a grand dinner was ready waiting for them; and on their arrival he received them with great joy, embraced them and kissed them, and laughed with both his eyes. Then they sat down to dinner, and ate and drank in great joy. During dinner Knight Mezey related Mirkó's brave deeds, and, amongst other things, said to the old king: "Well, comrade, your son Mirkó is even a greater hero than we were. He is a brave fellow, and you ought to be well pleased with him." The old king said: "Well, when I come to think of it, I begin to be satisfied with him, especially because he has brought you with him; but still I don't believe that he would have courage to fight Doghead also." Prince Mirkó was listening to their talk but did not speak. After dinner, however, he called Knight Mezey aside, and asked him who Doghead was, and where he lived. Knight Mezey informed him that he lived in the north, and that he was such a hero that there was no other to equal him under the sun. Prince Mirkó at once gave orders for the journey, filled his bag, and next day started on his mare to Doghead's place; according to his custom, he sat upon the mare, grasped her firmly, and shut his eyes. The mare darted off, and flew like a swift cyclone, then suddenly stopped, stamped on the ground, and said, "Prince Mirkó, open your eyes. What do you see?" "I see," said the Prince, "a diamond castle, six storeys high, that glitters so that one can't look at it, although one could look at the sun." "Well, Doghead lives there," said the mare, "and that is his royal castle." Prince Mirkó rode close under the window and shouted loudly: "Doghead! Are you at home? Come out, because I have to reckon with you." Doghead himself was not at home, but his daughter was there – such a beautiful royal princess, whose like one could not find in the whole world. As she sat in the window doing some needlework, and heard the high, shrill voice, she looked through the window in a great rage, and gave him such a look with her beautiful flashing black eyes, that Prince Mirkó and his mare at once turned into a stone statue. However, she began to think that perhaps the young gentleman might be some prince who had come to see her; so she repented that she had transformed him into a stone statue so quickly; and ran down to him, took out a golden rod, and began to walk round the stone statue, and tapped its sides with her gold rod, and lo! the stone crust began to crack, and fell off, and all at once Prince Mirkó and his mare stood alive in front of her. Then the princess asked; "Who are you? and what is your business?" And Mirkó told her that he was a prince, and had come to see the Princess of Doghead. The princess slightly scolded him for shouting for her father so roughly through the window, but at the same time fell in love with Prince Mirkó on the spot, and asked him to come into her diamond castle, which was six stories high, and received him well. However, while feasting, Prince Mirkó during the conversation confessed what his true errand was, viz., to fight Doghead; but the princess advised him to desist from this, because there was no man in the whole world who could match her father. But when she found that Mirkó could not be dissuaded, she took pity on him, and, fearing that lest he should be vanquished, let him into the secret how to conquer her father. "Go down," she said, "into the seventh cellar of the castle; there you will find a cask which is not sealed. In that cask is kept my father's strength. I hand you here a silver bottle, which you have to fill from the cask; but do not cork the bottle, but always take care that it shall hang uncorked from your neck; and when your strength begins to fail, dip your little finger into it, and each time your strength will be increased by that of five thousand men; also drink of it, because each drop of wine will give you the strength of five thousand men." Prince Mirkó listened attentively to her counsel, hung the silver bottle round his neck, and went down into the cellar, where he found the wine in question, and from it he first drank a good deal, and then filled his flask, and, thinking that he had enough in his bottle, he let the rest run out to the last drop, so that Doghead could use it no more. There were in the cellar six bushels of wheat flour, with this he soaked it up, so that no moisture was left, whereupon he went upstairs to the princess, and reported that he was ready and also thanked her for her directions, and promised that for all her kindness he would marry her, and vowed eternal faith to her. The beautiful princess consented to all, and only made one condition, viz., that in case Prince Mirkó conquered her father he would not kill him.

Prince Mirkó then inquired of the beautiful princess when she expected her father home, and in what direction, to which the princess replied that at present he was away in his western provinces, visiting their capitals, but that he would be home soon, because he was due, and that it was easy to predict his coming, because when he was two hundred miles from home, he would throw home a mace weighing forty hundredweight, thus announcing his arrival, and wherever the mace dropped a spring would suddenly burst from the ground. Prince Mirkó thereupon went with the royal princess into the portico of the royal castle, to await there Doghead's arrival, when suddenly, good Heavens! the air became dark, and a mace, forty hundredweight, came down with a thud into the courtyard of the royal fortress, and, striking the ground, water burst forth immediately in the shape of a rainbow. Prince Mirkó at once ran into the courtyard in order to try how much his strength had increased. He picked up the mace swung it over his head, and threw it back so that it dropped just in front of Doghead. Doghead's horse stumbled over the mace; whereupon Doghead got angry. "Gee up! I wish the wolves and dogs would devour you," shouted Doghead to the horse. "I have ridden you for the last six hundred years, and up to this time you have never stumbled once. What's the reason that you begin to stumble now?" "Alas! my dear master," said his horse, "there must be something serious the matter at home, because someone has thrown back your mace that you threw home, and I stumbled over it." "There's nothing the matter," said Doghead; "I dreamt six hundred years ago that I would have to fight Prince Mirkó, and it is he who is at my castle; but what is he to me? I have more strength in my little finger than he in his whole body." With this he darted off at a great speed and appeared at the castle. Prince Mirkó was awaiting Doghead in the courtyard of the fortress. The latter, seeing Prince Mirkó, galloped straight to him and said, "Well, Mirkó. I know that you are waiting for me. Here I am. How do you wish me to fight you? With swords? or shall we wrestle?" "I don't care how; just as you please," said Mirkó. "Then let us try swords first," said Doghead, and, getting off his horse, they stood up, and both ordered out their swords. "Swords, come out of the scabbards." The two swords flew out of the scabbards and began to fence over the heads of the combatants. The whole place rung with their clashing, and in their vehemence they sent forth sparks in such quantity that the whole ground was covered with fire, so that no one could stand the heat. Whereupon Doghead said to Mirkó, "Don't let us spoil our swords, but let us put them back into their scabbards, and let us wrestle." So they sheathed their swords and began to wrestle. When suddenly Doghead grasped Mirkó round the waist, lifted him up, and dashed him to the ground with such force that Mirkó sank to his belt. Mirkó was frightened, and quickly dipped his little finger into the bottle. Whereupon he regained his strength, and, jumping out of the ground, made a desperate dash at Doghead, and threw him to the ground with such force, that he lay full length on the ground like a green frog; then he seized him by his hair and dragged him behind the royal residence, where a golden bridge stood over a bottomless lake. He dragged him on to the bridge, and, holding his head over the water, ordered his sword out of the scabbard and cut off his head, so that it dropped into the bottomless lake, and then he pushed the headless trunk after it.

Doghead's daughter saw all this, and grew very angry with Prince Mirkó, and as he approached her she turned her face away, and would not even speak to him; but Prince Mirkó explained to her that he could not do otherwise, for if he had spared Doghead's life he would have destroyed his; and that he was willing to redeem his promise, and keep his faith to the princess and take her for his wife. Whereupon the royal princess became reconciled, and they decided to get ready to go to Prince Mirkó's realm. They ordered the horses – Doghead's charger was got ready for the beautiful princess – and, mounting them, were about to start, when all at once deep sorrow seized Prince Mirkó, and the beautiful royal princess thus questioned him: "Why are you so downcast, Mirkó?" "Well, because," said Mirkó, "I'm anxious to go back to my country, but I am also extremely sorry to leave behind this sumptuous diamond castle, six storeys high, which belonged to your father, for there is nothing like it in my country." "Well, my love," said the princess, "don't trouble about that. I will transform the castle into a golden apple at once, and sit in the middle of it, and all you will have to do is to put the apple into your pocket, and then you can take me with you and the castle too, and when you arrive at home you can re-transform me wherever you like." Thereupon the pretty princess jumped down from her horse, handed the reins to Mirkó, took out a diamond rod, and commenced to walk round the diamond castle, gently beating the sides of it with the diamond rod, and the castle began to shrink and shrunk as small as a sentry box, and then the princess jumped inside of it, and the whole shrivelled up into a golden apple, the diamond rod lying by the side of it. Prince Mirkó picked up the golden apple and the diamond rod, and put them into his pocket, and then got on horseback, and, taking Doghead's horse by the bridle, he rode quietly home. Having arrived at home, Mirkó had the horses put in the stables, and then walked into the royal palace, where he found the old king and Knight Mezey quite content and enjoying themselves. He reported to them that he had conquered even Doghead, and that he had killed him; but the old king and Knight Mezey doubted his words. Therefore Prince Mirkó took them both by their arms, and said to them, "Come along with me, and you can satisfy yourselves, with your own eyes, that I have conquered Doghead, because I have brought away with me, not only his diamond castle, six storeys high, but also his beautiful daughter, inside it, as a trophy of my victory." The old king and Knight Mezey were astonished at his words, and, still doubting, followed Mirkó, who took them into the flower garden of the king, in the middle of which Prince Mirkó selected a nice roomy place for the diamond castle, and placed the golden apple there, and commenced walking round, and, patting its sides with the diamond rod, the golden apple began to swell. It took a quadrangular shape, growing and growing, higher and higher, till it became a magnificent six-storey diamond castle; and then he took the old king and Knight Mezey by their arms, and led them up the diamond staircase into the rooms of the castle, where the princess, who was world-wide known for her beauty, met them, and received them most cordially. She bade them sit down, and sent lackeys to call the other sons of the old king and also the higher dignitaries of the court. In the dining hall there was a big table, which could be opened out. She gave orders, and the table was laid of itself, and on it appeared all sorts of costly dishes and drinks, and the assembled guests feasted in joy. The old king was highly satisfied with his son's doings, and handed over to Mirkó the royal power and the whole realm: he himself and Knight Mezey retired into quiet secluded life, and lived long in great happiness. The young royal couple who got married had beautiful children, and they are alive still, to this very day, if they have not died since. May they be your guests tomorrow!

The Three Dreams

THERE WAS ONCE, I don't know where, even beyond the Operencziás Sea, a poor man, who had three sons. Having got up one morning, the father asked the eldest one, "What have you dreamt, my son?" "Well, my dear father," said he, "I sat at a table covered with many dishes, and I ate so much that when I patted my belly all the sparrows in the whole village were startled by the sound." "Well, my son," said the father, "if you had so much to eat, you ought to be satisfied; and, as we are rather short of bread, you shall not have anything to eat today." Then he asked the second one, "What have you dreamt, my son?" "Well, my dear father, I bought such splendid boots with spurs, that when I put them on and knocked my heels together I could be heard over seven countries." "Well, my good son," answered the father, "you have got good boots at last, and you won't want any for the winter." At last he asked the youngest as to what he had dreamt, but this one was reticent, and did not care to tell; his father ordered him to tell what it was he had dreamt, but he was silent.

As fair words were of no avail the old man tried threats, but without success. Then he began to beat the lad. "To flee is shameful, but very useful," they say. The lad followed this good advice, and ran away, his father after him with a stick. As they reached the street the king was just passing down the high road, in a carriage drawn by six horses with golden hair and diamond shoes. The king stopped, and asked the father why he was ill-treating the lad. "Your Majesty, because he won't tell me his dream." "Don't hurt him, my good man," said the monarch; "I'll tell you what, let the lad go with me, and take this purse; I am anxious to know his dream, and will take him with me." The father consented, and the king continued his journey, taking the lad with him. Arriving at home, he commanded the lad to appear before him, and questioned him about his dream, but the lad would not tell him. No imploring, nor threatening, would induce him to disclose his dream. The king grew angry with the lad's obstinacy, and said, in a great rage, "You good-for-nothing fellow, to disobey your king, you must know, is punishable by death! You shall die such a lingering death that you will have time to think over what disobedience to the king means." He ordered the warders to come, and gave them orders to take the lad into the tower of the fortress, and to immure him alive in the wall. The lad listened to the command in silence, and only the king's pretty daughter seemed pale, who was quite taken by the young fellow's appearance, and gazed upon him in silent joy. The lad was tall, with snow-white complexion, and had dark eyes and rich raven locks. He was carried away, but the princess was determined to save the handsome lad's life, with whom she had fallen in love at first sight; and she bribed one of the workmen to leave a stone loose, without its being noticed, so that it could be easily taken out and replaced; and so it was done!

And the pretty girl fed her sweetheart in his cell in secret. One day after this, it happened that the powerful ruler of the dog-headed Tartars gave orders that seven white horses should be led into the other king's courtyard; the animals were so much alike that there was not a hair to choose between them, and each of the horses was one year older than another; at the same time the despot commanded that he should choose the youngest from among them, and the others in the order of their ages, including the oldest; if he could not do this, his country should be filled with as many Tartars as there were blades of grass in the land; that he should be impaled; and his daughter become the Tartar chief's wife. The king on hearing this news was very much alarmed, held a council of all the wise men in his realm, but all in vain: and the whole court was in sorrow and mourning. The princess, too, was sad, and when she took the food to her sweetheart she did not smile as usual, but her eyes were filled with tears: he seeing this inquired the cause; the princess told him the reason of her grief, but he consoled her, and asked her to tell her father that he was to get seven different kinds of oats put into seven different dishes, the oats to be the growths of seven different years; the horses were to be let in and they would go and eat the oats according to their different ages, and while they were feeding they must put a mark on each of the horses. And so it was done, The horses were sent back and the ages of them given, and the Tartar monarch found the solution to be right.

But then it happened again that a rod was sent by him both ends of which were of equal thickness; the same threat was again repeated in case the king should not find out which end had grown nearest the trunk of the tree. The king was downcast and the princess told her grief to the lad, but he said, "Don't worry yourself, princess, but tell your father to measure carefully the middle of the rod and to hang it up by the middle on a piece of twine, the heavier end of it will swing downwards, that end will be the one required." The king did so and sent the rod back with the end marked as ordered. The Tartar monarch shook his head but was obliged to admit that it was right. "I will give them another trial," said he in a great rage; "and, as I see that there must be someone at the king's court who wishes to defy me, we will see who is the stronger." Not long after this, an arrow struck the wall of the royal palace, which shook it to its very foundation, like an earthquake; and great was the terror of the people, which was still more increased when they found that the Tartar monarch's previous threats were written on the feathers of the arrow, which threats were to be carried out if the king had nobody who could draw out the arrow and shoot it back. The king was more downcast than ever, and never slept a wink: he called together all the heroes of his realm, and every child born under a lucky star, who was born either with a caul or with a tooth, or with a grey lock; he promised to the successful one, half of his realm and his daughter, if he fulfilled the Tartar king's wish. The princess told the lad, in sad distress, the cause of her latest grief, and he asked her to have the secret opening closed, so that their love might not be found out, and that no trace be left; and then she was to say, that she dreamt that the lad was still alive, and that he would be able to do what was needed, and that they were to have the wall opened. The princess did as she was told; the king was very much astonished, but at the same time treated the matter as an idle dream in the beginning. He had almost entirely forgotten the lad, and thought that he had gone to dust behind the walls long ago. But in times of perplexity, when there is no help to be found in reality, one is apt to believe dreams, and in his fear about his daughter's safety, the king at last came to the conclusion that the dream was not altogether impossible. He had the wall opened; and a gallant knight stepped from the hole. "You have nothing more to fear, my king," said the lad, who was filled with hope, and, dragging out the arrow with his right hand, he shot it towards Tartary with such force that all the finials of the royal palace dropped down with the force of the shock.

Seeing this, the Tartar monarch was not only anxious to see, but also to make the acquaintance of him who did all these things. The lad at once offered to go, and started on the journey with twelve other knights, disguising himself so that he could not be distinguished from his followers; his weapons, his armour, and everything on him was exactly like those around him. This was done in order to test the magic power of the Tartar chief. The lad and his knights were received with great pomp by the monarch, who, seeing that all were attired alike, at once discovered the ruse; but, in order that he might not betray his ignorance, did not dare to inquire who the wise and powerful knight was, but trusted to his mother, who had magic power, to find him out. For this reason the magic mother put them all in the same bedroom for the night, she concealing herself in the room. The guests lay down, when one of them remarked, with great satisfaction, "By Jove! What a good cellar the monarch has!" "His wine is good, indeed," said another, "because there is human blood mixed with it." The magic mother noted from which bed the sound had come; and, when all were asleep, she cut off a lock from the knight in question, and crept out of the room unnoticed, and informed her son how he could recognize the true hero. The guests got up next morning, but our man soon noticed that he was marked, and in order to thwart the design, every one of the knights cut off a lock. They sat down to dinner, and the monarch was not able to recognize the hero.

The next night the monarch's mother again stole into the bedroom, and this time a knight exclaimed, "By Jove! what good bread the Tartar monarch has!" "It's very good, indeed," said another, "because there is woman's milk in it." When they went to sleep, she cut off the end of the moustache from the knight who slept in the bed where the voice came from, and made this sign known to her son; but the knights were more on their guard than before, and having discovered what the sign was, each of them cut off as much from their moustache as the knight's who was marked; and so once more the monarch could not distinguish between them.

The third night the old woman again secreted herself, when one of the knights remarked, "By Jove! what a handsome man the monarch is!" "He is handsome, indeed, because he is a love child," said another. When they went to sleep, she made a scratch on the visor of the knight who spoke last, and told her son. Next morn the monarch saw that all visors were marked alike. At last the monarch took courage and spoke thus: "I can see there is a cleverer man amongst you than I; and this is why I am so much more anxious to know him. I pray, therefore, that he make himself known, so that I may see him, and make the acquaintance of the only living man who wishes to be wiser and more powerful than myself." The lad stepped forward and said, "I do not wish to be wiser or more powerful than you; but I have only carried out what you bade me do; and I am the one who has been marked for the last three nights." "Very well, my lad, now I wish you to prove your words. Tell me, then, how is it possible there can be human blood in my wine?" "Call your cupbearer, your majesty, and he will explain it to you," said the lad. The official appeared hastily, and told the king how, when filling the tankards with the wine in question, he cut his finger with his knife, and thus the blood got into the wine. "Then how is it that there is woman's milk in my bread?" asked the monarch. "Call the woman who baked the bread, and she will tell," said the lad. The woman was questioned, and narrated that she was nursing a baby, and that milk had collected in her breasts; and as she was kneading the dough, the breast began to run, and some milk dropped into it. The magic mother had previously informed her son, when telling him what happened the three nights, and now confirmed her previous confession that it was true that the monarch was a love-child. The monarch was not able to keep his temper any longer, and spoke in a great rage and very haughtily, "I cannot tolerate the presence of a man who is my equal: either he or I will die. Defend yourself, lad!" and with these words he flashed his sword, and dashed at the lad. But in doing so, he accidentally slipped and fell, and the lad's life was saved. Before the former had time to get on his feet, the lad pierced him through, cut off his head, and presented it on the point of his sword to the king at home. "These things that have happened to me are what I dreamt," said the victorious lad; "but I could not divulge my secret beforehand, or else it would not have been fulfilled." The king embraced the lad, and presented to him his daughter and half his realm; and they perhaps still live in happiness today, if they have not died since.

The Three Princesses

THERE WAS ONCE, I shan't tell you where, it is enough if I tell you that there was somewhere a tumbledown oven, which was in first-rate condition barring the sides, and there were some cakes baking in it; this person (the narrator points to someone present) has eaten some of them. Well then, on the mountains of Komárom, on the glass bridges, on the beautiful golden chandelier, there was once a Debreczen cloak which had ninety-nine tucks, and in the ninety-ninth I found the following tale.

There was once a king with three daughters, but the king was so poor that he could hardly keep his family; his wife, who was the girls' stepmother, therefore told her husband one night, that in the morning she would take the girls into the wood and leave them in the thicket so that they might not find again their way home. The youngest overheard this, and as soon as the king and queen fell asleep she hurried off to her godmother, who was a magic woman, to ask her advice: her godmother's little pony (táltos) was waiting at the front gate, and taking her on its back ran straight to the magic woman. She knew well what the girl needed and gave her at once a reel of cotton which she could unwind in the wood and so find her way back, but she gave it to her on the condition that she would not take her two elder sisters home with her, because they were very bad and proud. As arranged next morning the girls were led out by their stepmother into the wood to gather chips as she said, and, having wandered about a long time, she told them to rest; so they sat down under a tree and soon all three went to sleep; seeing this, the stepmother hurried home.

On waking up, two of the girls, not being able to find their mother, began to cry, but the youngest was quiet, saying that she knew her way home, and that she would go, but could not take them with her; whereupon the two elder girls began to flatter her, and implored her so much that she gave in at last. Arriving at home their father received them with open arms; their stepmother feigned delight. Next night she again told the king that she would lead them deeper still into the wood: the youngest again overheard the conversation, and, as on the night before, went on her little pony to her godmother, who scolded her for having taken home her bad sisters, and on condition that this time she would not do so, she gave her a bag full of ashes, which she had to strew over the road as they went on, in order to know her way back; so the girls were led into the wood again and left there, but the youngest again took her sisters home, finding her way by the ashes, having been talked over by many promises and implorings. At home, they were received, as on the first occasion; on the third night their stepmother once more undertook to lead them away; the youngest overheard them as before, but this time, she had not courage to go to her godmother, moreover she thought that she could help herself, and for this purpose she took a bag full of peas with her, which she strewed about as they went. Left by their mother, the two again began to cry, whereas the youngest said laughing, that she was able to go home on this occasion also; and having again yielded to her sisters she started on her way back, but to her astonishment could not find a single pea, as the birds had eaten them all. Now there was a general cry, and the three outcasts wandered about the whole day in the wood, and did not find a spring till sunset, to quench their thirst; they also found an acorn under an oak under which they had lain down to rest; they set the acorn, and carried water in their mouths to water it; by next morning it had grown into a tree as tall as a tower, and the youngest climbed up it to see whether she could not discover some habitation in the neighbourhood; not being able to see anything, they spent the whole day crying and wandering about. The following morning, the tree was as big as two towers, but on this occasion too the youngest girl looked in vain from its summit: but at last, by the end of the third day, the tree was as tall as three towers, and this time the youngest girl was more successful, because she discovered far away a lighted window, and, having come down, she led her sisters in the direction of the light. Her sisters, however, treated her most shamefully, they took away all her best clothes, which she thoughtfully had brought with her, tied up in a bundle, and she had to be satisfied with the shabbiest; whenever she dared to contradict them they at once began to beat her; they gave her orders that wherever they came she had to represent them as daughters of rich people, she being their servant. Thus, they went on for three days and three nights until at last they came to an immense, beautiful castle.

They felt now in safety, and entered the beautiful palace with great hopes, but how frightened were they when they discovered a giantess inside who was as tall as a tower, and who had an eye in the middle of her forehead as big as a dish, and who gnashed her teeth, which were a span long. "Welcome, girls!" thus spoke the giantess, "What a splendid roast you will make!" They all three were terrified at these words, but the youngest shewed herself amiable, and promised the giantess that they would make all kind of beautiful millinery for her if she did them no harm; the woman with the big teeth listened, and agreed, and hid the girls in a cupboard so that her husband might not see them when he came home; the giant, who was even taller than his wife, however, at once began to sniff about, and demanded human flesh of his wife, threatening to swallow her if she did not produce it. The girls were fetched out, but were again spared, having promised to cook very savoury food for the grumbling husband.

The chief reason of their life having been spared, however, was because the husband wanted to eat them himself during the absence of his wife, and the woman had a similar plan in her mind. The girls now commenced to bake and roast, the two eldest kneaded the dough, the youngest making the fire in the oven, which was as big as hell, and when it got red hot, the cunning young girl called the giant, and having placed a pot full of lard into the oven, asked him to taste it with his tongue to see whether the lard was hot enough, and if the oven had reached its proper heat. The tower of flesh tried it, but the moment he put his head inside the oven, the girl gave him a push and he was a dead man in the fiery oven; seeing this, the giantess got in a rage, and was about to swallow them up, but, before doing so, the youngest induced her to let herself be beautified, to which she consented; a ladder was brought, so that the young girl might get on to her head to comb the monster's hair; instead of combing, however, the nimble little girl knocked the giantess on the head with the huge iron comb, so that she dropped down dead on the spot. The girls had the bodies carted away with twenty-four pair of oxen, and became the sole owners of the immense castle. Next Sunday, the two eldest dressed up in their best, and went for a walk, and to a dance in the royal town.

After their departure their youngest sister, who remained at home to do servants' work, examined all the rooms, passages, and closets in the castle. During her search she accidentally found something shining in a flue. She knocked it off with a stone, and found that it was a most beautiful golden key. She tried it in every door and cupboard, but only succeeded, after a long search, in opening a small wardrobe with it; and, how great was her surprise to find that it was full of ladies' dresses and millinery, and that every thing seemed made to fit her. She put on a silver dress in great haste, and went to the dance. The well-known little pony was outside waiting for her, and galloped away with her like a hurricane. The moment she entered the dancing hall all eyes were fixed on her, and the men and youths of the highest dignity vied with each other as to who should dance with her. Her sisters who, till her arrival, were the heroines of the evening and the belles of the ball, were quite set aside now. After a few hours' enjoyment the young lady suddenly disappeared; and, later on, received her sisters on their return in her servant's clothes. They told her that they had enjoyed themselves very well at first, but that later on some impudent female put them in the background. The little girl laughed and said, "Supposing that I was that lady," and she was beaten by her sisters, and called some not very polite names for her remark. Next Sunday the same thing happened again, only this time the young girl was dressed in gold. Everything happened the same, and she was again beaten at home.

The third Sunday the little girl appeared in a diamond dress. At the dance, again, she was the soul of the evening; but this time the young men wanted her to stay to the end of the ball, and watched her very closely, so that she might not escape. When, therefore, she tried to get away, she was in such a hurry that she had no time to pick up a shoe she accidentally dropped in the corridor; she was just in time to receive her sisters. The shoe came into the possession of the prince, who hid it carefully. After a few days the prince fell very ill, and the best physicians could not find a cure for him; his father was very nearly in despair about his only son's health, when a foreign doctor maintained that the patient could only be cured by marrying, because he was lovesick. His father, therefore, implored him to make him a full confession of his love, and, whoever the person whom he wished might be, he should have her. The prince produced the shoe, and declared that he wanted the young lady to whom the shoe belonged. So it was announced throughout the whole realm, that all the ladies of the country should appear next Sunday to try on the shoe, and whosoever's foot it fitted she should become the prince's wife. On Sunday the ladies swarmed in crowds to the capital. Nor were the two eldest of the three sisters missing, who had had their feet previously scraped with a knife by their youngest sister, so that they might be smaller. The youngest sister also got ready after their departure, and, having wrapped the mate of the lost shoe in a handkerchief, she jumped on the pony's back in her best dress, and rode to the appointed place. She overtook her sisters on the road, and, jumping the pony into a puddle, splashed them all over with mud. The moment she was seen approaching 100 cannons were fired off, and all the bells were rung; but she wouldn't acknowledge the shoe as her own without a trial, and, therefore, tried it on. The shoe fitted her exactly, and when she produced its mate, 300 cannons greeted her as the future queen. She accepted the honour upon one condition, namely, that the king should restore her father's conquered realm. Her wish was granted, and she became the prince's wife. Her sisters were conducted back to their royal father, who was now rich and powerful once more; where they live still, if they have not died since.

The Three Valuable Things

THERE WERE ONCE TWO KINGS who lived in great friendship; one had three sons, the other a daughter. The two fathers made an agreement, that in case of either of them dying, the other should become guardian of the orphans; and that if one of the boys married the girl he should inherit her property. Very soon after the girl's father

died, and she went to live with her guardian. After a little time the eldest boy went to his father and asked the girl's hand, threatening to commit suicide if his request was refused; his father promised to give him a reply in three weeks. At the end of the first week the second son asked the girl's hand, and threatened to blow out his brains if he could not wed her; the king promised to reply to him in a fortnight. At the end of the second week, the youngest asked for the girl, and his father bade him wait a week for his answer.

The day arrived when all three had to receive their reply, and their father addressed them thus: "My sons, you all three love the girl, but you know too well that only one can have her. I will, therefore, give her to the one who will show himself the most worthy of her. You had better go, wherever you please, and see the world, and return in one year from this day, and the girl shall be his who will bring the most valuable thing from his journey." The princes consented to this, and started on their journey, travelling together till they came to a tall oak in the nearest wood; the road here divided into three branches; the eldest chose the one leading west, the second selected the one running south, and the third son the branch turning off to the east. Before separating, they decided to return to the same place after the lapse of exactly one year, and to make the homeward journey together.

The eldest looked at everything that he found worthy of note during his travels, and spared no expense to get something excellent: after a long journey hither and thither, he at last succeeded in getting a telescope by the aid of which he could see to the end of the world; so he decided to take it back to his father, as the most valuable thing he had found. The second son also endeavoured to find something so valuable that the possession of it should make him an easy winner in the competition for the girl's hand: after a long search he found a cloak by means of which, when he put it on and thought of a place, he was immediately transported there. The youngest, after long wandering, bought an orange which had power to restore to life the dead when put under the corpse's nose, provided death had not taken place more than twenty-four hours before. These were the three valuable things that were to be brought home; and, as the year was nearly up, the eldest and the youngest were already on their way back to the oak: the second son only was still enjoying himself in various places, as one second was enough for him to get to the meeting place. The two having arrived at the oak, the middle one appeared after a little while, and they then shewed each other the valuables acquired; next they looked through the telescope, and to their horror they saw that the lady for the possession of whom they had been working hard for a whole year, was lying dead; so they all three slipped hurriedly into the cloak, and as quick as thought arrived at home; the father told them in great grief that the girl could belong to no one as she was dead: they inquired when she died, and receiving an answer that she had been dead not quite twenty-four hours, the youngest rushed up to her, and restored her to life with his magic orange. Now there was a good deal of litigation and quarrelling among the three lads: the eldest claimed the greatest merit for himself, because, he said, had they not seen through his telescope that the girl was dead they would have been still lingering at the oak, and the orange would have been of no avail; the second maintained that if they had not got home so quickly with his cloak the orange would have been of no use; the third claimed his orange as the best, for restoring the girl to life, without which the other two would have been useless. In order to settle the dispute, they called all the learned and old people of the realm together, and these awarded the girl to the youngest, and all three were satisfied with the award, and the two others gave up all idea about suicide. The eldest, by the aid of his telescope, found himself a wife who was the prettiest royal princess on earth, and married her: the second heard of one who was known for her virtue and beauty, and got into his cloak, and went to her, and so all three to their great satisfaction led their brides to the altar, and became as happy as men can be.

The Three Princes, the Three Dragons, and the Woman with the Iron Nose

ON THE SHORES OF THE BLUE SEA there was a land in which dragons grew. This land had a king whose court was draped in black, and whose eye never ceased to weep, because every Friday he had to send ninety-nine men to the dragons, who were the pest of the place, and who slew and devoured the ninety-nine human beings

sent to them. The king had three sons, each of whom was handsomer and more clever than the other. The king was very fond of his sons, and guarded them most carefully. The eldest was called Andrew, the next Emerich, and the youngest Ambrose. There were no other lads left in the land, for the dragons fed on lads' flesh only.

One day Andrew and Emerich went to their father and begged him to allow them to go and fight the dragons, as they were sure they could conquer them, and that the dragons would not want any more human flesh after they had been there. But the father would not even listen to his sons' request. As for Ambrose, he did not even dare so much as to submit such a request to his father. Andrew and Emerich, at length, by dint of much talking, prevailed upon their father to allow them to go and fight the dragons. Now, there were only three dragons left in the land: one had seven heads, another eight, and the third nine; and these three had devoured all the other dragons, when they found that there were no more lads to be had. Andrew and Emerich joyfully galloped off towards the copper, silver, and golden bridges in the neighbourhood of which the dragons lived, and Ambrose was left alone to console his royal father, who bewailed his other sons.

Ambrose's godmother was a fairy, and as it is the custom for godmothers to give presents to their godchildren, Ambrose received a present from his fairy godmother, which consisted of a black egg with five corners, which she placed under Ambrose's left armpit. Ambrose carried his egg about with him under his left armpit for seven winters and seven summers, and on Ash Wednesday, in the eighth year, a horse with five legs and three heads jumped out of the egg; this horse was a Táltos and could speak.

At the time when the brothers went out to fight the dragons, Ambrose was thirteen years and thirteen days old, and his horse was exactly five years old. The two elder brothers had been gone some time, when he went into the stable to his little horse, and, laying his head upon its neck, began to weep bitterly. The little horse neighed loudly and said, "Why are you crying, my dear master?" "Because," replied Ambrose, "I dare not ask my father to let me go away, although I should like to do so very much." "Go to your royal father, my dear master, for he has a very bad attack of toothache just now, and tell him that the king of herbs sends word to him through the Táltos-horse with three heads, that his toothache will not cease until he gives you permission to go and fight the dragons; and you can also tell him that if you go, there will be no more dragons left on this earth; but if you do not go his two elder boys will perish in the stomachs of the dragons. Tell him, also, that I have assured you that you will be able to make the dragons vomit out, at once, all the lads whomsoever they have swallowed; and that his land will become so powerful when the lads, who have grown strong in the stomachs of the dragons, return, that, while the world lasts, no nation will ever be able to vanquish him." Thus spoke the Táltos colt, and neighed so loudly that the whole world rang with the sound. The little boy told his father what the Táltos colt had told him; but the king objected for a long time, and no wonder, as he was afraid lest evil might happen to his only son: but at last his sufferings got the better of him, and, after objecting for three hours, he promised his son that if the Táltos were able to carry out its promise he would give him permission to go and fight the dragons.

As soon as he had uttered these words his toothache left him. The little lad ran off and told the message to his little horse, which capered and neighed with delight. "I heard you when you were bargaining," said the horse to its little master, who in his delight didn't know what to do with himself, "and I should have heard you even if you had been a hundred miles away. Don't fear anything, my little master; our ride, it is true, will be a long one, but in the end it will turn out a lucky one. Go, my great-great-grandmother's great-great-grandmother's saddle is there on that crooked willow; put it on me, it will fit me exactly!"

The prince ran, in fact he rushed like a madman, fetched the ragged old saddle, put it on his horse, and tied it to a gate-post. Before leaving his father's home, the little horse asked its little master to plug up one of its nostrils; the prince did so, and the little horse blew upon him with the other nostril which he had left open, when, oh, horror! the little boy became mangy like a diseased sucking pig. The little horse, however, turned into a horse with golden hair, and glistened like a mirror. When the little boy caught sight of his ugly face amidst the hair of his shining horse, he became very sad. "Plug up my other nostril, too!" said the horse with the golden hair. At first the little master would not do it, until the horse neighed very loudly and bade him do it at once, as it was very unwise to delay obeying the commands of a Táltos. So what could the poor lad do but plug up the other nostril of the horse. The horse then opened wide its mouth, and breathed upon the lad, who at once became a most handsome prince, worthy to be a fairy king. "Now sit on my back, my little master, my great king, we are worthy of each other; and there is no thing in the world that we cannot overcome. Rejoice! You will conquer the dragons, and restore the young men to your father's realm; only do as I bid you, and listen to no one else."

In an hour's time they arrived on the shore of the Red Sea, which flows into the Blue Sea. There they found an inn, and close to the inn, within earshot, stood the copper bridge, on the other side of which the dragon with seven heads roamed about. Andrew and Emerich were already at the inn, and as they were very tired, they sat down and began to eat and drink: when the new guest arrived the knives and forks dropped from the two princes' hands; but when they learned that he, too, had come to fight the dragons they made friends with him. They could not, however, recognize him for all the world. Night set in, and Andrew and Emerich had eaten and drunk too much, and became decidedly drunk, and so slept very deeply. Ambrose ate little, drank nothing, and slept lightly. At dawn the Táltos horse pulled his master's hair, in order to wake him; because it knew that the dragon had least strength at dawn, and that the sun increased his strength. Ambrose at once jumped on horseback and arrived at the copper bridge: the dragon heard the clattering of the horse's hooves, and at once flew to meet him. "Pooh!" cried the dragon and snorted, "I smell a strange smell! Ambrose, is it you? I know you; may you perish, you and your horse! Come on!" They fought for one hour and three quarters. Ambrose, with two strokes, slashed six of the dragon's heads off, but could not, for a long time succeed in cutting off the seventh, for in it lay the dragon's magic power. But, at last, the seventh head came off too.

The dragon had seven horses, these Ambrose fastened together, and took them to the inn, where he tied them by the side of Emerich's horse. Andrew and Emerich did not awake till nine o'clock, when Emerich asked Andrew if he had killed the dragon, and Andrew asked Emerich if he had done so; at last Ambrose told them that he had killed the dragon with seven heads and taken away his seven horses, which he gave to Emerich, who thanked him for them. The three then continued their journey together as far as the silver bridge: here again they found an inn, which stood close to the bridge. Emerich and Andrew ate and drank and went to sleep as before; the Táltos horse, as soon as day began to break, awoke his master, who cheerfully jumped up, dressed neatly, and left the princes asleep. The Táltos scented the dragon quite ten miles off, and growled like a dog, and the dragon in his rage began to throw his sparks at them when four German miles off; they rushed upon each other and met with a tremendous clash on the bridge; it was a very difficult task for Ambrose to conquer this huge monster, but at last, through the skilful manœuvring of his horse, he deprived the dragon of all his eight heads: the eight horses belonging to the dragon he tied to a post near the head of the eldest prince, Andrew. Andrew and Emerich did not awake till noon, and were astonished at the sight of the splendid horses, questioning each other as to who could have brought them there at such an early hour, and then came to the conclusion that the prince must have killed the dragon, and that these horses had belonged to the monster, for no such horses ever neighed under a man before. Ambrose again confessed that he had killed the dragon, and brought away his horses for them. He also urged his two companions to hurry on to kill the third dragon, or they would be too late. They all got on horseback, but in their joy two of them had had to eat and drink, till they had more than enough, but Ambrose, according to his custom, took but little; the two elder brothers again went to sleep and slept like tops; but again the little Táltos pulled Ambrose's hair, so soon as the morning star began to glimmer.

Ambrose got up at once, and dressed even more quickly than before; for the journey he took a small flask of wine, which he secured upon his saddle. The horse warned its master to approach the dragon with great caution, because it was a very excitable one, and if he got frightened the least it would be very difficult to conquer the monster. Soon the monster with nine heads arrived, thumped once on the golden bridge, so that it trembled under the thump; Ambrose dashed at the dragon and fought with it, but they could not conquer each other, although they fought fiercely and long. At the last hug, especially, Ambrose grew so weak that, if he had not taken a long draught from his flask he would have been done for on the spot; the draught, however, renewed his strength, and they dashed at each other again, but still neither could conquer the other.

So the dragon asked Ambrose to change himself into a steel hoop and he, the dragon, would become a flint hoop, and that they should both climb to the top of yon rock, which was so high that the sun was only a good span above it; and that they should roll down together, and if, while running, the flint hoop left the rut, and, striking the steel hoop, drew sparks therefrom, that Ambrose's head should fall off; but if on the other hand, the steel hoop left the rut and struck the flint hoop so as to draw sparks, then all the dragon's heads should fall off. But they were both wise and stuck to their own ruts, rolling down in a straight course till they reached the foot of the mountain without touching each other, and lay down when they got to the bottom. As they could not manage in this way, the dragon proposed: "I will become a red flame and you will become a white one, and which ever flame reaches highest he shall be victor." Ambrose agreed to this also; while they were contending, they both noticed an old crow, which croaked at them from a hollow tree; the dragon was an old acquaintance of the aged crow, and requested it to bring in its beak as much water as would extinguish the white flame, and promised that if he won, he would give his foe's flesh to the crow, every bit of it.

Ambrose asked for a single drop of water, and promised the crow all the flesh of the big-bodied dragon. The crow helped Ambrose: it soaked its crop full of water and spat it over the red flame; thus Ambrose conquered his last foe. He got on his horse, tied together the nine horses of the dragon with nine heads and took them to his brothers, who were still snoring loudly, although the sun had reached its zenith and was hot enough to make a roast. At last the two lazy people got up, and Ambrose divided the nine horses between them and took leave of them, saying, "Go in peace, I myself am obliged to run wherever my eyes can see." The two good-for-nothing brothers were secretly delighted, and galloped off homewards. Ambrose turned himself into a small rabbit, and as it ran over hill and dale it ran into a small hut where the three wives of the three dragons were seated. The wife of the dragon with seven heads took it into her lap and stroked it for a long time, and thus addressed it: "I don't know whether Ambrose has killed my husband; if he has, there will be a plague in the world, because I will turn into a great pear tree, and the odour of its fruit will be smelt seven miles off, and will be sweet to the taste but deadly poison. The tree which thus grows from me will not dry up till Ambrose plunge his sword into its root, then both it and myself will die." Then the wife of the dragon with eight heads also took the little rabbit in her lap, and spoke thus: "If Ambrose has killed my husband there will be a plague in the world, I can tell you! because in my sorrow I will change into a spring; there will be eight streams flowing out of this spring, each one of which will run eight miles, where it again will subdivide into eight more branches. And whoever drinks of the water will die; but if Ambrose wash his sword in my blood – which is the water of the spring – all the water will at once dry up and I shall die." Then the wife of the dragon with nine heads spoke to the rabbit, saying, "If Ambrose has killed my husband, in my sorrow I will change into a huge bramble, and will stretch all over the world, all along the highroads. And whoever trips over me, will die; but if Ambrose cut my stalk in two anywhere the bramble will dry up everywhere and I shall die."

Having listened to all this, the little rabbit scampered off out of the hut; but an old woman with an iron nose, the mother of the three dragons, chased him, and chased him over hill and dale: he ran, and rushed about, till at length he overtook his brothers; jumping on his little horse's back, he continued his journey at his leisure. As they travelled on, his eldest brother longed for some good fruit; just then they saw a fine pear tree, whereupon Ambrose jumped from his horse, and plunged his sword into the roots of the tree, and drew blood, and a moaning voice was heard. They travelled on for a few miles, when Emerich all of a sudden became very thirsty: he discovered a spring, and jumped off his horse in order to drink, but Ambrose was first to arrive at the water; when, plunging his sword into it, it became blood, and fearful screams were heard, and in one moment the whole of the water dried up. From this point Ambrose galloped on in front till he left his brothers two miles behind, because he knew that the bramble was stretching far along the country road; he cut it in two, blood oozed out, and the bramble at once dried up. Having thus cleared away all dangers from his brothers' way, he blest them and separated from them.

The brothers went home, but the old woman with the iron nose persecuted Ambrose more than ever, being in a great rage at his having killed her sons and her daughters-in-law. Ambrose ran as hard as he could, for he had left his horse with his brothers; but when he was quite exhausted and had lost all confidence in himself, he ran into a smithy, and promised the smith that he would serve him for two years for nothing if he would hide him safely and well. The bargain was soon struck, and no sooner had the smith hidden him than the old woman appeared on the spot and inquired after a youth: she described his figure, the shape of his eyes and mouth, height, colour of his moustache and hair, dress, and general appearance. But the smith was not such a fool as to betray the lad who had engaged to work at his anvil for him for two years for nothing. So the old witch with the iron nose got to know nothing and left the place growling. One day Ambrose was perspiring heavily by the side of the anvil, so at eventide he went for a short walk in the road in order to get a mouthful of fresh air. When he had nearly reached the edge of the wood, which was only at a dog's trot from the smithy, he met a very old woman with wizened face, whose carriage was drawn by two small cats: the old woman began to ogle little Ambrose, making sheep's eyes at him, like fast young women do. "May hell swallow you, you old hag," said Ambrose to her angrily, "I see you have still such foolish ideas in your head, although you have grown so old!" Having said this he gave the carriage in which the witch sat, a kick, but poor Ambrose's right foot stuck fast to the axle, and the two cats scampered off over hill and dale with him until he suddenly discovered that he was trotting in hell, and saw old Pilate staring at him. The old witch with the iron nose – because it was she who had the carriage and pair of cats – fell over head and ears in love with the young lad, and at once asked him to marry her.

Ambrose shuddered when he heard this repulsive, unnatural request. "Very well," said the woman with the iron nose, "as you don't intend to marry me, into jail you go! Twelve hundredweight of iron on your feet!" Nine black servants seized hold of poor Ambrose, at once, and took him nine miles down into the bowels of the earth, and fastened a piece of iron weighing twelve hundredweight on his feet and secured it with a lock. The poor lad wept and groaned, but no one had admission to where he was, with the exception of the old witch and one of her maids. The maid of the witch with the iron nose was not quite such an ugly fright as her wizened old mistress, in fact she was such a pretty girl that one would have to search far for a prettier lass. She commenced to visit Ambrose in his prison rather often, sometimes even when the old witch did not dream of it – to tell the truth, she fell head over ears in love with the lad, nor did Ambrose dislike the pretty girl; on the contrary, he promised to marry her if she were able to effect his escape from his deep prison. The girl did not require any further coaxing, but commenced plotting at once. At last she hit upon a scheme, and thus spoke to her darling Ambrose: "You cannot get out of this place, unless you marry the old woman with the iron nose. She having once become your wife will reveal to you all her secrets; she will also tell you how she manages to keep alive so long, and by what ways and means she may be got rid of." Ambrose followed her instructions and was married to the old witch by a clergyman – there are clergy even in hell, as many as you want. The first night Ambrose, after having for a long time been kissing and making love to the old iron nose, asked her: "What keeps you alive for so long, and when do you think you will die? I don't ask these questions, my dearest love," he added, flatteringly, "as if I wished for your death, but because I should like to use those means myself which prolong your life and keep away everything from me which would shorten life, and thus preserve me, living long and happily with you." The old woman at first was half inclined to believe his words, but while meditating over what she had just heard, she suddenly kicked out in bed, and Ambrose flew three miles into hell in his fright.

But the result of all the questioning and flattering in the end was that the old woman confessed. She confided to him that she kept a wild boar in the silken meadow, and if it were killed, they would find a hare inside, inside the hare a pigeon, inside the pigeon a small box, inside the little box one black and one shining beetle: the shining beetle held her life, the black one her power; if those two beetles died then her life would come to an end, too. As soon as the old woman went out for a drive – which she had to do every day – Ambrose killed the wild boar, took out the hare, from the hare the pigeon, from the pigeon the box, and from the box the two beetles: he killed the black one at once, but kept the shining one alive. The old witch's power left her immediately. When she returned home her bed had to be made for her. Ambrose sat by her bedside and looked very sad, and asked her with tears if she, who was the other half of his soul, died what would become of him, who was a man from earth and a good soul, who had no business there. "In case I die, my dear husband," said the doomed woman, in a mild voice, "open with the key which I keep in my bosom yon black closet in the wall. But you can't remove the key from my bosom until I am dead. In the closet you will find a small golden rod; with this rod you must strike the side of the castle in which we are, and it will become a golden apple. You, then, can get into the upper world by harnessing my two cats in my carriage, and by whipping them with the golden rod." Hereupon Ambrose killed the shining beetle too, and her pára (animal soul) left the old witch at once.

He then struck the castle side with the golden rod, and it turned into an apple; having harnessed the two cats and patted them with the golden rod, he bade the maid sit by him, and in a wink they reached the upper world. The maid had been kidnapped by the old witch with the iron nose from the king of the country in the upper world, in whose land the mouth of hell was situated. Ambrose placed the golden apple in the prettiest part of the country and tapped its side with the rod and it became a beautiful castle of gold, in which he married his sweetheart and lived with her happily. Some time after he returned to his father's land, where an immense number of strong soldiers had grown up since Ambrose had killed the dragons. The old king distributed his realm among his three sons, giving the most beautiful empires to Ambrose, who took his father to him and kept him in great honour. His wife bore pretty children who rode out every day on the Táltos.

The Devil and the Red Cap

THERE WAS ONCE, I know not where, a soldier who was flogged many times, and who one night had to stand on sentry. As he paced up and down, a man with a red cap stopped in front of him and stared hard into his eyes. The soldier said not a word, but the stranger began: "My dear son, I know what happens in your heart, you don't like this soldier's life, and your thoughts are at this very minute wandering to your sweetheart."

The soldier at once concluded that he had to do with the devil, and so made his acquaintance. "Well, my dear son," said the devil, "undress quickly, and let's change our clothes; I will stand here on guard for you if you promise me that in a year hence, on this very day, at this very hour, to the very minute, you will be back here. In the meantime, go home to your native place, and don this red cap, as you can freely walk about and no one will see you as long as you have it on your head." The soldier went home to his native land, over seven times seven countries, and no one saw him as he reached his village. He walked into the garden and opened the door leading into his father's house and stood there listening. His friends were just then speaking of him. He was delighted to hear it, and gradually took the red cap from his head and suddenly appeared before them, who were very pleased to see him back. His sweetheart was also there; but no one would believe their own eyes, and thought that some sprite played them a trick. But the soldier explained it all; and, in order to prove the truth, he disappeared, and the next minute reappeared. All went well with the poor soldier until the time came when he had to start back. At the appointed hour and minute he took leave of his friends and sweetheart amid tears.

He put on his red cap and walked back unseen by any. "Bravo, my son," said the devil. "I see now that you are an honest man. A Magyar always keeps his word. You've returned to the very hour and minute. I've received a good many floggings, though, during your absence; but don't be afraid, we shall alter all this. You needn't be particular about your good conduct; nobody will touch you henceforth, as I've cast a spell and whenever they flog you the captain will feel the pain." The devil then changed his uniform, took back the red cap, and disappeared. The poor soldier – he couldn't help it, as he was tired of soldiering – again committed something wrong, the punishment for which was one hundred strokes. All the preparations to carry out the sentence had already been made, but before he was even touched the captain began to yell as he felt quite sure that he would suffer under it. Therefore he deemed it more wise to recommend the dismissal of the useless fellow, instead of worrying about him. And so it happened, the soldier was dismissed and arrived home safely: but since this happened even the devil will not take pity on a poor soldier.

The Lover's Ghost

SOMEWHERE, I DON'T KNOW WHERE even beyond the Operencian Seas, there was once a maid. She had lost her father and mother, but she loved the handsomest lad in the village where she lived. They were as happy together as a pair of turtle doves in the wood. They fixed the day of the wedding at a not very distant date, and invited their most intimate friends to it; the girl, her godmother – the lad, a dear old friend of his.

Time went on, and the wedding would have taken place in another week, but in the meantime war broke out in the country. The king called out all his fighting men to march against the enemy. The sabres were sharpened, and gallant fellows, on fine, gaily-caparisoned horses, swarmed to the banners of the king, like bees. John, our hero, too, took leave of his pretty *fiancée*; he led out his grey charger, mounted, and said to his young bride: "I shall be back in three years, my dove; wait until then, and don't be afraid; I promise to bring you back my love and remain faithful to you, even were I tempted by the beauty of a thousand other girls." The lass accompanied him as far as the frontier, and before parting solemnly promised to him, amidst a shower of tears, that all the treasures of the whole world should not tempt her to marry another, even if she had to wait ten years for her John.

The war lasted two years, and then peace was concluded between the belligerents. The girl was highly pleased with the news, because she expected to see her lover return with the others. She grew impatient, and would sally forth on the road by which he was expected to return, to meet him. She would go out often ten times a day, but as yet she had no tidings of her John. Three years elapsed; four years had gone by, and the bridegroom had not yet returned. The girl could not wait any longer, but went to see her godmother, and asked for her advice, who (I must tell you, between ourselves) was a witch. The old hag received her well, and gave her the following direction: "As it will be full moon tomorrow night, go into the cemetery, my dear girl, and ask the gravedigger to give you a human skull. If he should refuse, tell him that it is I who sent you. Then bring the skull home to me, and we shall place it in a huge earthenware pot, and boil it with some millet, for, say, two hours. You may be sure it will let you know whether your lover is alive yet or dead, and perchance it will entice him here." The girl thanked her for her good advice, and went to the cemetery next night. She found the gravedigger enjoying his pipe in front of the gate.

"Good evening to you, dear old father."

"Good evening, my lass! What are you doing here at this hour of the night?"

"I have come to you to ask you to grant me a favour."

"Let me hear what it is; and, if I can, I will comply with your request."

"Well, then, give me a human skull!"

"With pleasure; but what do you intend to do with it?"

"I don't know exactly, myself; my godmother has sent me for it."

"Well and good; here is one, take it."

The girl carefully wrapped up the skull, and ran home with it. Having arrived at home, she put it in a huge earthenware pot with some millet, and at once placed it on the fire. The millet soon began to boil and throw up bubbles as big as two fists. The girl was eagerly watching it and wondering what would happen. When, all of a sudden, a huge bubble formed on the surface of the boiling mass, and went off with a loud report like a musket. The next moment the girl saw the skull balanced on the rim of the pot. "He has started," it said, in a vicious tone. The girl waited a little longer, when two more loud reports came from the pot, and the skull said, "He has got halfway." Another few moments elapsed, when the pot gave three very loud reports, and the skull was heard to say, "He has arrived outside in the yard." The maid thereupon rushed out, and found her lover standing close to the threshold. His charger was snow-white, and he himself was clad entirely in white, including his helmet and boots. As soon as he caught sight of the girl, he asked: "Will you come to the country where I dwell?" "To be sure, my dear Jack; to the very end of the world." "Then come up into my saddle."

The girl mounted into the saddle, and they embraced and kissed one another ever so many times.

"And is the country where you live very far from here?"

"Yes, my love, it is very far; but in spite of the distance it will not take us long to get there."

Then they started on their journey. When they got outside the village, they saw ten mounted men rush past, all clad in spotless white, like to the finest wheat flour. As soon as they vanished, another ten appeared, and could be very well seen in the moonlight, when suddenly John said:

> *"How beautifully shines the moon, the moon;*
> *"How beautifully march past the dead.*
> *"Are you afraid, my love, my little Judith?"*

"I am not afraid while I can see you, my dear Jack."

As they proceeded, the girl saw a hundred mounted men; they rode past in beautiful military order, like soldiers. So soon as the hundred vanished another hundred appeared and followed the others. Again her lover said:

> *"How beautifully shines the moon, the moon;*
> *"How beautifully march past the dead.*
> *"Are you afraid, my love, my little Judith?"*

"I am not afraid while I can see you, my darling Jack."

And as they proceeded the mounted men appeared in fast increasing numbers, so that she could not count them; some rode past so close that they nearly brushed against her. Again her lover said:

> *"How beautifully shines the moon, the moon;*
> *"How beautifully march past the dead.*
> *"Are you afraid, my love, my little Judith?"*

"I am not afraid while I see you, Jack, my darling."

"You are a brave and good girl, my dove; I see that you would do anything for me. As a reward, you shall have everything that your heart can wish when we get to my new country."

They went along till they came to an old burial ground, which was inclosed by a black wall. John stopped here and said to his sweetheart: "This is our country, my little Judith, we shall soon come to our house." The house to which John alluded was an open grave, at the bottom of which an empty coffin could be seen with the lid off. "Go in, my darling," said the lad. "You had better go first, my love Jack," replied the girl, "you know the way." Thereupon the lad descended into the grave and laid down in the coffin; but the lass, instead of following him, ran away as fast as her feet would carry her, and took refuge in a mansion that was situated a couple of miles from the cemetery. When she had reached the mansion she shook every door, but none of them would open to her entreaties, except one that led to a long corridor, at the end of which there was a dead body laid out in state in a coffin. The lass secreted herself in a dark corner of the fire-place.

As soon as John discovered that his bride had run away he jumped out of the grave and pursued the lass, but in spite of all his exertions could not overtake her. When he reached the door at the end of the corridor he knocked and exclaimed: "Dead man, open the door to a fellow dead man." The corpse inside began to tremble at the sound of these words. Again said Jack, "Dead man, open the door to a fellow dead man." Now the corpse sat up in the coffin, and as Jack repeated a third time the words "Dead man, open the door to a fellow dead man," the corpse walked to the door and opened it.

"Is my bride here?"

"Yes, there she is, hiding in the corner of the fireplace."

"Come and let us tear her in pieces." And with this intention they both approached the girl, but just as they were about to lay hands upon her the cock in the loft began to crow, and announced daybreak, and the two dead men disappeared.

The next moment a most richly attired gentleman entered from one of the neighbouring rooms. Judging by his appearance one would have believed it was the king himself, who at once approached the girl and overwhelmed her with his embraces and kisses.

"Thank you so much. The corpse that you saw here laid out in state was my brother. I have already had him buried three hundred and sixty-five times with the greatest pomp, but he has returned each time. As you have relieved me of him, my sweet, pretty darling, you shall become mine and I yours; not even the hoe and the spade shall separate us from one another!"

The girl consented to the proposal of the rich gentleman, and they got married and celebrated their wedding feast during the same winter.

This is how far the tale goes. This is the end of it.

Human Foibles, Folly & Everyday Life

THIS SECTION is full of joke tales, but you can also find magical tales and realistic tales. What happens when two rich, but totally dim-witted people get married? A series of everyday disasters and bad decisions. Is it true that 'one fool makes a hundred'? The tale of 'The Hussar and the Servant Girl' demonstrates exactly this saying: an entire village becomes foolish because of one silly thought. It is not only everyday characters or events that await us here: wonderful gifts from a beggar make a poor man a king, but we can also read about a severed finger as evidence of a murder, or about a ghost wandering into a cellar, and there is even talk about people who have been hanged.

One of the oldest Hungarian 'Snow-white' versions is also hidden in this chapter. Although 'The World's Beautiful Woman' is slightly different from the versions best known in Europe, it is an interesting example of how the characters in tales can change, even if the frame of the tale remains the same. Here, for example, the dwarfs become robbers. One of the special features of the chapter is Baroness Orczy's tale 'That's Not True'. Although I pointed out in the introduction that the baroness's tales are excellent works, but from a folkloristic point of view they cannot be called folktales, it is certain that this is one Orczy tale that can confidently be said to be rooted in folklore.

The Twin Hunchbacks

ONCE UPON A TIME, long, very long ago, in the midst of Fairyland, there stood an extensive forest, so large that it would take many, many days to walk across it; in fact, it was an enchanted forest, for all night it was the haunt of all the little fairies in the neighbourhood. They would skip and dance there all night long, and far into the next day; but the moment the noonday sun streamed down upon them, they would all run away and go to bed inside the water lilies and pink lotus, and leave fairy rings on the grass to mark the place of their nightly revels.

There was a lovely glade in this forest, with a large pond in the middle, and tall dark trees around, which was a specially favoured spot with all the fairies and elves of the forest. Three little fairies particularly there were, who used to come here every morning at sunrise and enjoy themselves to their hearts' content. They were especially fond of a dance they had invented, which consisted in holding hands and twirling round, singing all the while, "Humpty Dumpty! Humpty Dumpty!"

Well, one day a little hunchback woodcutter, who was out very early in the morning gathering chopsticks, suddenly came upon the lovely glade, and there, before him, he saw the three little fairies dancing in a ring, laughing and singing, "Humpty Dumpty! Humpty Dumpty!" so merrily, that he threw down his bundle of faggots, and joined in their dance and their song with great energy. He danced so amazingly, and amused them so much by turning back somersaults, that they thought it the greatest pity in the world that so brisk a little man should be spoilt by having a great hump on his back; so they took some water from the pond in little golden cups, and each fairy emptied her own tiny vessel on the hunchback, singing the while, "Go away, ugly hump!" Then they again joined hands, and danced round him till his hunch had quite disappeared; whereupon he romped more gaily than before, and was so glad and merry he could hardly sing "Humpty Dumpty!" any more for laughing. After that he kissed each of the fairies, and ran home as fast as his little legs would carry him, singing all the way, "Humpty

Dumpty! Humpty Dumpty!" springing in the air, and jumping over every obstacle – so glad was he to have got rid of his ugly hump.

Now this little hunchback had a twin brother just as ugly and deformed as he had been himself, and when the now straightened little man came in at the cottage door his brother was very much astonished to see him skipping about without his hunch, and he naturally asked how he had managed to get rid of his ugly deformity.

"Oh," said the woodcutter, "it happened in a very curious way. I was out chopping sticks very early this morning in the woods, when I suddenly saw three dear little fairies before me, dancing in a ring, and singing, 'Humpty Dumpty! Humpty Dumpty!' They were tripping it so merrily that the desire seized me to join in their dance, so I boldly took them by the hand and joined in the ring, singing with them, 'Humpty, Dumpty! Humpty Dumpty!'

"They seemed to like this very much, for when they got tired of dancing they took some water from the pond, and pouring it over my back, they sang, 'Go away, go away, ugly hunch!' and sure enough my ugly hunch has gone."

The twin brother was very much surprised at the strange story he had just heard. Naturally enough he did not quite care about being known as the "hunchback woodcutter" whilst his brother looked so erect and handsome. In fact, he was not only jealous of his brother, but most anxious to be as good looking. He therefore thought the best plan would be to at once seek out the fairies and get them to be as kind and as useful to him as they had been to his brother. He therefore started off at a run for the enchanted glade, determined to get rid of his hump as his brother had done; unfortunately he was so afraid of being too late, that he ran himself quite out of breath, and was tired out by the time he reached the three little fairies, who were dancing and singing as gaily as ever. The poor little fellow could neither sing nor dance, and had not sufficient breath left to cut a caper or turn a back somersault; this disappointed the little fairies very much. Presently they all joined hands, taking the little hunchback with them, and began their special dance, singing, "Humpty Dumpty! Humpty Dumpty!" but he got so confused and giddy from turning round so fast, that instead of singing, "Humpty Dumpty! Humpty Dumpty!" as the little fairies did, he would add – in his efforts to please them – "Humpty Dumpty sat on a wall!" and kept on saying, "Sat on a wall, sat on a wall!" which so annoyed the fairies, that when they took the water out of the pond in their little golden cups, and poured it over his back, instead of singing, "Go away, ugly hump!" they sang, "Hunch, get twice as big as before!" which it did immediately, and was then such a terrible size that it was frightful to look at, and so heavy that he had to crawl on his hands and knees all the way home.

Mr Cuttlefish's Love Story

THERE WAS A GREAT COMMOTION in the Coral Palace of the Queen of the Sea. It was very plain that something unusual was happening in the otherwise peaceful dwelling at the bottom of the deep blue sea. As a rule, on hot summer evenings, the Queen reclined lazily on a bed of pink sea-shell, while her two mermaids-in-waiting stood near her, fanning her with tall fans, made of sharks' fins, and telling her all the latest news that occurred among the upper ten of the fish kingdom. Everything had to be kept very quiet during that time, as the Queen objected to every kind of noise that might disturb her, if she chose to take a nap, which she usually did.

But on this particular evening the royal palace wore a totally different aspect; the bed of seashell was deserted, the fans of sharks' fins lay idle on the ground, and not a fish was visible in any of the pink coral halls.

Stay, that is not quite correct. When I say not a fish could be seen, I mean not a whole fish, for at every crevice, every window, and every door, there were rows and rows of tails, the heads and bodies of their owners being thrust as far out as possible. Apparently they were intent on watching a most amusing spectacle, for every now and then these tails shook with suppressed laughter, making the water foam and bubble all around.

The Queen herself so far forgot her dignity as to sit at a half-opened window, and gaze out into the blue depths, and clap her hands with glee, and laugh till the tears streamed down her cheeks.

What so evidently excited the mirth of Her Majesty and all her subjects was certainly, to any impartial observer, a most amusing sight. Under the shades of the giant seaweed, in the grounds of the Coral Palace, Mr Cuttlefish was making love to dear little Marina, the Queen's favourite mermaid, whose amorous glances quite equalled his own. He rolled his great goggle eyes at her, and surrounded her graceful little form with five of his long arms.

"My dearest, I am afraid we must part," she was saying to him, "and I don't think I can possibly meet you out here again. I am sure someone will see us; the Palace is so near and the windows of the great hall look out on this part of the grounds, and," she added, kissing his great puffy cheek, "I know the Queen will never consent to our marriage; you have no appointment at court, and your business compels you to live in quite another part of the sea. I must remain near the Queen, or by our laws I should lose the human half of my body and become a fish altogether, probably a sole, or some other nasty flat thing. What a comedown for me, dear. I have always been accounted so sharp."

Mr Cuttlefish did not appreciate jokes which were not his own, and would have administered a severe rebuke to Marina for venturing to make one at so serious a moment. She, however, looked so pretty, and was evidently so much in love with him, poor dear, that he merely withdrew two or three of his arms from round her waist to show his displeasure. This act of unnecessary cruelty brought tears to the eyes of poor little Marina.

"Well, my dear," he said, when harmony was once more restored between them, "you must try and find out whether there is not some good appointment vacant at Court, and I will immediately apply for and obtain it. There were several reasons why I withdrew myself from Court life altogether... Ahem!... I will leave you to guess these reasons, dear Marina... As a matter of fact Her Majesty herself... ahem!... lately intimated to her subjects her desire for a fitting helpmate through the cares of State... ahem!... and when she announced this intention in public... ahem!... ahem!"

"Well! well!"

"Well! ahem!... you won't be jealous, dear Marina?"

"Jealous? Why?"

"Well! the fact is," said Mr Cuttlefish, now blushing to the tips of his fingers, or rather suckers, "that Her Majesty deigned to cast eyes of approval on one of her subjects whom modesty forbids me to name."

"Oh," said Marina, clasping her hands in awed reverence, "then you would be king of us all."

"Well; yes! my dear, I believe that would have been my position," said Mr Cuttlefish, modestly covering his eyes with an arm or two and wiping a humble tear. "What was that?" he added, in sudden alarm, as a loud peal of irrepressible laughter from the hidden spectators of this dainty scene echoed through the grounds.

"Nothing, my dearest, only a difference of opinion, I expect, between two pikes in Her Majesty's kitchen; they never can agree over the way in which a minnow should be sliced, and quarrel over it in a most rowdy manner."

Mr Cuttlefish thought to himself that he would not even slice a pike for that matter, but said nothing. Suddenly little Marina had an idea.

"I'll tell you what, dear Mr Cuttlefish, I believe there is a vacant appointment at Court, it is a very lucrative one I know, and one to which, I think, you are peculiarly suited. Her Majesty's Royal Musician died the other day; one of the choir swallowed him accidentally while singing a bass solo. I know you have great talent for music, and, you see, none of your choir could possibly succeed in swallowing you."

"That is so," said Mr Cuttlefish, "and how do you think I could best succeed in obtaining this appointment?"

"By thoroughly convincing the Queen of your musical capabilities. I should say if you could get an orchestra together, and a few soloists, you might obtain permission to perform before Her Majesty – that is," added little Marina, "if your modesty will allow you to stand once more before her after the forward advances she made to you."

At this point the laughter in the palace became so uproarious, that all the sea around became a wilderness of foam and bubbles. Little Marina ran home in dismay, terrified lest she should have been seen; and Mr Cuttlefish sailed away more rapidly than dignity generally allows. Modesty had now got the better of him and he thought it prudent to retire for the night to his cavern between the rocks.

The next day all was quiet and peaceful in the beautiful kingdom under the sea. The light shone like brilliant emeralds through the water, illuminating the coral grottoes, and lighting their fantastic forms with innumerable points of glittering sparks. The great branches of giant seaweed waved to and fro with slow rhythmic cadence, and the ribbon-weed floated gracefully, forming myriads of little ripples.

There was a general air of festivity pervading the whole of the royal palace. Every little fish seemed to have donned his gayest colours, and all the crabs and the lobsters seemed to have assumed an air of being very busy and pressed for time.

Suddenly a most singular sound echoed through all the neighbouring caverns, and caused a general commotion in the waters. It penetrated as far as the Queen's bedchamber, where Her Majesty was enjoying a quiet rest while reflecting over the events of the night before. She had forbidden all her Court to make the slightest allusion to them before her little mermaid, as it might distress her to feel that she and her lover had been so openly laughed at. She was a dear, kind-hearted sort of queen, and really very fond of little Marina, so she determined to smooth the path of true love as much as lay in her power.

In the meantime the noise was growing louder and louder, and more and more distinct. Now it resembled a grampus blowing through his nose, and now it seemed like a hundred engines letting steam off all at once. At last an unusually discordant note resounded through the royal bedchamber, and Her Majesty, now fully aroused, and not at all pleased at being disturbed in her nap, dispatched an attendant crab to inquire the cause of this extraordinary commotion. He came back with the startling news that Mr Cuttlefish was preparing for a grand concert, which he proposed to give that very afternoon.

"But," said the Queen, addressing no once in particular, "I did not know the gentleman was musical."

"He is not," said an old thornback, spitefully, "but he fancies he is, and likes to be thought a distinguished amateur and musical critic. He wrote a very severe article in the 'Fly Fancier's Gazette' on the subject of Your Majesty's choir."

"In which," said the nautilus, indignantly, "he disapproved of my voice."

"And distinctly hinted that we sang flat," exclaimed the chorus of crabs.

"And," added the oysters, opening their shells, and looking defiantly round, "that we have no notion of time."

A wail of indignation rose at these complaints against Mr Cuttlefish. However, the Queen was determined to try and make matters as pleasant for Marina as possible, and influence public opinion in her lover's favour as far as she could. She wished to hear more about the concert.

"May it please Your Majesty," said a little bony fish, who seemed well posted up in all the news, "Mr Cuttlefish issued cards of invitation early this morning, but the Grand Chamberlain, the Right Honourable Tortoise, who is offended with him about something or other, has evidently withheld Your Majesty's card. As for me, I shall certainly not go, he does not mention the word supper, and I don't believe there will be any." While all this was going on poor little Marina felt on thorns, she grew hot and cold alternately, and hardly knew how to hold herself erect on her tail, while fanning the Queen. The concert was evidently now in full swing, the waters around were continually disturbed by crowds of fishes trooping to join in it, and carrying their cards of invitation under their fins; the Queen was now quite unable to check her curiosity any longer, and announced her gracious intention to honour the concert by her august presence.

Lord Chamberlain Tortoise, who had been simply dying to go himself, but, of course, did not dare show his eagerness before Her Majesty, now stalked off in high glee to order the royal mermen, who always conveyed the Queen, to be in readiness.

Her Majesty mounted one of them while another swam in front, both blowing a shell trumpet; Marina and the other little seamaids brought up the rear, carrying the fans, handkerchiefs and smelling salts. On seeing the Queen approach, Mr Cuttlefish bade the music cease, then rose with great ceremony and bowed three times, as did all the other fishes present, while the oysters, whose absence of legs forbade them to bow, clapped their shells respectfully. Mr Cuttlefish extended one of his arms and, taking the queen's hand, led her to a seat on a large green rock, covered with beautiful anemones. Seating himself, with a look at Marina, which conveyed to her the expression of his endless love, he took a great trumpet in one hand, seized a drumstick in another, a pair of cymbals and a concertina in four more. A large lobster then gravely announced that Mr Cuttlefish would play a grand march, composed by himself, entitled "The good old Sharks," and would be assisted in the performance by a full choir, selected and trained by himself.

The words and music were alike impressive, the orchestration eminently modern, and the chorus written in four parts. Three huge frogs, rolling their goggle eyes, rolled out the bass, the herrings sang alto in sentimental style, the whiting were high treble, and as they sang with their tails in their mouths – as all well-regulated whiting do – their voices had an additional charm. The moonfish, the trunkfish, the gurnard were all tenors, but as they had been unavoidably prevented from attending the rehearsals, their parts did not go very well; however, the swordfish, who sang baritone, and the firefish, who sang contralto, managed to drown their mistakes pretty effectually.

The conductor was a great green crab, who endeavoured to keep time by waving his claws; he found this fairly easy while the slow part of the march was being performed, but in the more rapid movements no one paid any attention to him, which somewhat marred the harmony of the whole effect, but in no way interfered with the enjoyment of the performers. As for Mr Cuttlefish's trumpet and big drum, nothing seemed to drown them, he never ceased blowing the one or beating the other; though he sometimes disengaged an available arm to administer an impressive rebuke to any of the chorus who appeared to slacken energy.

In fact the whole affair was a brilliant success, and when the piece was over, everybody clapped his shell or his fins, and congratulated the composer, who took all these honours with the indifference characteristic of genius.

Her Majesty desired his presence.

Mr Cuttlefish advanced, and bending exceedingly low, humbly waited her gracious pleasure.

"We are very pleased with the extraordinary talent, sir, displayed by you this afternoon; in fact, our royal ears have never been struck by so large a volume of sound. We will therefore appoint you our Royal Musician, with a fitting salary, and give you the hand of our favourite sea-maiden, Marina, in marriage."

Mr Cuttlefish cast a grateful look at his sovereign, who taking a shark's fin fan in her hand and smiting him on top of his bald head, added:

"Rise, Sir Cuttlefish. We confer this honour upon you for your distinguished talents, and for the pleasure you have given us this afternoon."

Sir Cuttlefish wished to raise a modest protest against so much honour, but eventually thought better of it, and accepted it all with the noble resignation of the really great.

The lobster now announced a dance, Sir Cuttlefish opened the ball by standing on his head and whirling all his arms about till the water foamed, while everybody did their best to make the evening lively, by turning over and over and round and round. The shrimps waltzed together, while the eels curled themselves up first one way and then the other.

When they were all tired out the supper was brought in by five and twenty green tortoises. It was the most magnificent repast, consisting of crayfish, minnows, and some deliciously prepared carp; Sir Cuttlefish ate five hundred of these, which proved to be an injudicious quantity. There was a slight stir towards the end of the supper, caused by the sharks, who had not been invited, gobbling up some of the company, but, on the whole, the evening passed off very pleasantly. After supper the gathering broke up, Sir Cuttlefish seeing the Queen home.

Next day the great composer was suffering from a detestable fit of indigestion. The poor Queen had a fearful headache, but, nevertheless, she had never enjoyed herself so much in all her life.

The wedding of Sir Cuttlefish and Marina was fixed for an early date, and the Queen did the bride the great honour of not only being present at the ceremony, but of holding a reception at the Palace. All the Court officials were ordered to be present, and the poor Lord Chamberlain Tortoise had his hands full, what with issuing the invitation cards, settling the order of precedence, and making arrangements for the breakfast. The Queen ordered that everything should be conducted in the best style, and expense should be no obstacle to the success of the entertainment.

Meanwhile, Sir Cuttlefish was busy. He chose the leader of his choir for his "best fish." Then he ordered the lobsters to make the ring of pearl, and it took no little ingenuity on their part to round off and polish it to Sir Cuttlefish's satisfaction. The happy bridegroom also presented his bride with a brooch made of sea diamonds, in shape like a big drum – a perfect work of art – in commemoration of the great concert that had proved such a triumph.

Needless to add, I think, that the deep sea orchestra and choir played and sang the wedding march and hymns, the new R. M. – Royal Musician – having drilled them himself most carefully. On the great day, Sir Cuttlefish got himself up in most sumptuous style; he had ordered four pairs of white gloves – you see he had eight arms; this was looked upon as a piece of most extravagant folly, and the shark (who had not yet got over his annoyance at not being asked to the concert) made some very unpleasant remarks on the subject in his paper, "The Fisherman's Foe."

The gorgeousness of the ceremony and the splendour of the wedding breakfast it were vain to attempt to relate, for they even threw the glories of the Cuttlefish's concert and fête into the shade.

The bridegroom borrowed a most beautiful grotto in which to pass his honeymoon, and also spent much time in having his own house thoroughly done up and repaired, and in that newly decorated house under the sea, dear little readers, we will leave the happy pair, for in it they have lived in joy and prosperity from that day to this.

The Wishing Skin

ONCE UPON A TIME, there lived a woodcutter in a little cottage at the foot of an old gigantic oak tree. He had a wife, but no children, and together they lived humbly, but very contentedly; for in front of his cottage he had a nice little garden in which he grew everything that was necessary for their daily food; fine wheat, with which to bake bread, and rich fruit and vegetables; he also had a cow which gave him abundance of milk, and sheep that yielded him soft wool, which his wife wove into garments for themselves.

One day a pedlar had come wandering past the cottage, with pots and pans and other goods for sale; the wife bought a thing or two from him that she needed, and he again went his way. When he had gone, the woodcutter found an old book of tales lying in the road, which the pedlar had evidently dropped; he took it home to his wife, and, in the evening, when she sat at her spinning, he read some of the stories aloud to her. They were a curious lot of tales, all about fairies and magicians that granted people's wishes and changed woodcutters into kings.

That night the little woodcutter could not sleep a wink, he lay awake thinking of the fairies, and picturing himself having one of those godmothers, whose only duty seemed to consist in waving their wands and fulfilling requests. In the morning he went quite dejectedly to his work, quite different to his usual sprightly, little self. He chopped the wood with a heavy heart for a time, finally he threw down his axe in despair and sat down sullenly on the stump of a tree, wishing at least to see a fairy, and persuade her to take an interest in him. His attention was presently attracted by a bright-eyed rabbit which seemed to have suddenly come from nowhere, and sat opposite to him blinking one eye in a knowing way.

So absorbed was the little woodcutter in the castle he was building in the air, that he never started, even when the rabbit suddenly began talking to him.

"Well, Mr Woodcutter, and what can I do for you? You have been wishing to have a fairy godmother ever since last night; now, though I am not your godmother, I know a thing or two, for instance, I know where the wishing skin lies, which the little fairies have been weaving for three hundred years, and which is now completed, any one wearing the same can have every wish fulfilled the moment he formulates it. Of course, as the skin is made of wishes, every time one is fulfilled it evaporates, and the skin becomes that much smaller, but then what does that matter? The little fairies have hidden the skin under a lightning-struck willow tree, but I have burrowed a hole and I know exactly how to get at it. I will show it you, if you like."

Thereupon the little rabbit darted off, and presently returned dragging a large bundle after it, which he spread out before the woodcutter's eager eyes.

"And is this skin really made of wishes? Oh! Mr Rabbit, please let me put it on just for a few minutes, I would like just to make one wish. I promise I will give it you back directly."

The good-natured little rabbit willingly helped the woodcutter to put the magic skin on, which fitted him somewhat tightly, but still it felt pretty comfortable.

"Oh! How I wish this skin were altogether mine," sighed the woodcutter, "and that I never need part with it."

Hardly had he uttered these words when he felt as if the skin fitted him a shade tighter than before.

"Hallo!" said the rabbit, "what have you been wishing for? Certainly you seem to me to have diminished in size. Here, give me the skin, I must put it back where I found it, or the fairies will be after me."

But the woodcutter knew he need not give up his treasure any more, so looking disdainfully at the rabbit he stalked off in the direction of his cottage, his head full of plans for future grandeur. But Mr Bunny, in a great rage, lopped after him, yelling with all his might, till the woodcutter, losing all patience, turned round and screamed at him, "I wish you'd go to Jericho, and leave me alone." When immediately, the rabbit ran away as hard as he could tear, and he felt the skin again tighten round him. He knew that Mr Bunny had gone to Jericho, and would trouble him no more.

When he got home, he told his wife his wonderful adventure, but she only thought he had been drinking, and advised him to go to bed and sleep it off, when, to convince her, he said, "I wish there was a fine supper table laid all ready here, with roast fowls, roast ducks, and roast turkeys, pies and puddings, and four flunkeys to wait on my wife and me."

Hardly were the words out of his mouth when a most gorgeous table appeared in the centre of the room, heavily laden with the most delicious dishes, fruits and wines, while four servants in gold and silver livery stood waiting to serve the supper.

The wife could hardly believe her eyes, and they both sat down and ate and drank and made merry, for they felt that their future was now likely to be a glorious one. Certainly, the little man felt himself a good bit smaller – his feet, when he sat, no longer reached the ground – but what of that, he would become so rich and proud that his stature would not be of the slightest consequence, so lifting a glass of wine high over his head, he said:

"I wish to be a rich lord, with a castle instead of a cottage, and lands and woods all my own; I wish to wear velvet garments, and my wife to go about in nothing but silk dresses, I wish to eat off nothing but gold plates, and use glasses cut of pure diamonds; I wish…"

But his wife checked him just in time, for at every new wish he uttered he diminished an inch before her very eyes, and, lo! the humble cottage had disappeared, and they were sitting in a grand hall, with marble pillars and soft carpets. They looked out of the window, and, though it was evening, they could see distinctly a lovely garden planted with graceful trees and flowers, and fountains in crystal basins, while soft music filled the air.

The woodcutter looked at his wife and she at him. Poor little man, he was only three feet high now, but he was clad in a sumptuous coat and cloak of velvet lined with ermine; his wife was dressed in a lovely silk gown, with diamonds on her arms and neck. They could hardly contain themselves for joy, and the wife, seizing her little lord in her arms, began dancing round the room to the time of the distant music. The entrance of a number of lackeys and maid-servants asking his lordship for orders for the night, reminded them of the duties of their new position, and they marched off to their bedchamber in solemn state.

The next day they spent in visiting their extensive domains, the stables, coach houses, farms, and dairies, they found that they were indeed considered enormously wealthy, everybody bowed down to them, and listened deferentially to all they had to say. The only thing that was very annoying was that the little lord felt that his three feet of stature were evidently a source of intense amusement to all his retainers and servants.

In the afternoon, they ordered their gilded coach and six white horses to take them to pay calls on their neighbours, whom they hoped to dazzle with their great splendour. They set off in most gorgeous style, with an army of outriders and flunkeys following the carriage; but to their intense astonishment the various neighbouring lords had just as fine houses and gardens as their own, and wore just as fine dresses and magnificent jewels as they did themselves, so they returned home in disgust, Joan especially was intensely annoyed. One lady on whom she called, wore three more bracelets than she did, another had seven more servants, and a third wore a dress embroidered with real pearls, while her own was only embroidered in silver; and one and all had sneered at her diminutive lord, and pointed to their own handsome husbands. She wished she could be richer and grander than they were, so that they should be obliged to bow down before her, even at the cost of another foot off her husband's stature.

So after supper she talked to her lord about her grievances, and pointed out to him, that while he was merely the equal of his neighbours, they would always laugh at him, but once their superiors, say a royal duke or a prince, they would never dare to do so again. At first Jack refused to wish for anything else just yet, he felt himself quite small enough, and did not think that any additional grandeur could compensate him for the loss of another twelve inches. However, at last, his wife prevailed upon him, and just before going to bed he wished to become a royal duke, second only to the king, and equal to any prince in the land; and the next morning Jack and Joan woke to find themselves in a royal palace, with all the servants in royal liveries calling them their Royal Highnesses; and all the lords and ladies in the land came to pay their respects to them. Joan was proud indeed; not one lady wore such fine jewels, or had such a number of servants and palaces as she had, and though her husband was now only two feet high, all the lords stood round him, loudly laughing at his jokes, and the ladies vied with each other as to who should lift him up into his chair. That very day the king was himself coming, with the queen and all his retinue, to pay a visit to the royal duke and duchess, and grand preparations were made for His Majesty's reception.

When the King and Queen arrived, Jack and Joan received them in the grand hall of their palace. Poor little Jack! He felt very nervous when he had to kiss the Queen's hand, Joan had to lift him into a chair, which amused Their Majesties very much, and caused a titter among the other royal dukes, princes and princesses. During the banquet, the diminutive royal duke had to sit on a very tall stool, and had to have his food placed on his plate for him, as he could not reach the dishes; the King was quite convulsed with laughter, and hardly could eat anything; no one else dared to smile, but the Queen made sneering remarks to the duchess about her funny little husband.

That night Joan and Jack had a frightful difference of opinion: she wished to rule supreme over everybody so that even the King and the Queen, who had laughed at them, should have to come and do homage to her and her husband, whatever be his size. In fact she wished to become the greatest empress in the world; whereas Jack felt that another foot off his height would be a trial he could never undergo. However his wife goaded him on till she had gained her point, and before the sun rose next morning, the woodcutter and his wife became the most powerful emperor and empress in the world. There was not a King or a Queen in the world that did not come to do homage before Their Imperial Majesties, no war was declared between any nations or treaty signed without their consent, they exacted tribute from all duchies, principalities, and even kingdoms around; but alas! for the poor little Emperor he was only six inches high, and had to be carried in state on a cushion to all the great functions, and to stand on a gold table when he received the ambassadors from foreign courts. At banquets and state dinners he had to sit on a little golden chair placed on the table, and be fed with a salt spoon out of the Empress's plate.

Very soon he got tired of all this, more especially as, after a little while, Joan, now having reached the height of her ambition, took very little notice of him, she wouldn't allow him to have any voice in any of the affairs of state, and grew tired of seeing her husband carried before her on a cushion. Finally she had a tiny doll's house built in the garden, into which she relegated her lord and master, and only took him out to play with occasionally. Poor little Jack! He thought sorrowfully of the days when he was a fine grown man and cut wood in the forest and was master of his own little home by the old oak tree. He cursed the rabbit, the fairies, the pedlar, and chiefly his own blind stupidity in wishing to change his own contented happy lot, for all this gilded misery.

At last one day, looking out of one of the tiny windows of his doll's house, he saw a woodcutter going along merrily with his bundle of faggots, whistling a lively tune. The poor little Emperor took his jewelled crown, which he always wore, off his head, and throwing it violently on the ground, so that the gems were scattered in all directions, he said, "Oh, how I wish I were a full-grown man, a woodcutter again, with my wife in my own little cottage, not dreaming even of such things as kings and emperors."

When he had spoken, in one moment, the magnificent palace, the exquisite gardens had vanished, and he sat in his big armchair opposite his wife who was knitting, his feet touched the ground, and his arm reached to where Joan was sitting. They fell into each other's arms. Was it all a dream, little readers? I cannot tell you, but all I know is that henceforth Jack and Joan lived humbly in their little cottage contented and happy ever after.

"That's Not True"

ONCE UPON A TIME there was a princess who was very beautiful, but very eccentric. She announced publicly that she would only marry the man who could tell her father, the king, a story which he could not believe. Now, in a village there dwelt a poor young peasant, who, hearing of this proclamation, went up to the king's palace, and loudly knocking at the gates demanded an audience of His Majesty.

The king knew very well what the young fellow wanted, as by that time many princes and knights had come on the same errand, in the hope of winning the beautiful princess, but they had all failed.

So John, the young peasant, was admitted to the royal presence.

"Good morning, Your Majesty," he said.

"Good morning, my lad. Well, what do you want?" asked the king, kindly.

"So please, Your Majesty, I want a wife."

"Very good, lad; but what would you keep her on?"

"Oh! I dare say I could manage to keep her pretty comfortably. My father has a pig."

"Indeed!" said the king.

"A wonderful pig, Your Majesty; he has kept my father, my mother, seven sisters, and myself, for the last twenty years."

"Indeed!" said the king.

"He gives us as good a quart of milk every morning as any cow."

"Indeed!" said the king.

"Yes, Your Majesty, and lays most delicious eggs for our breakfast."

"Indeed!" said the king.

"And every day my mother cuts a nice bit of bacon out of his side, and every night it grows together again."

"Indeed!" said the king.

"The other day this pig disappeared, my mother looked for him high and low, he was nowhere to be seen."

"That was very sad," said the king.

"Finally, she found him in the larder, catching mice."

"A very useful pig!" said the king.

"My father sent him into town every day to do errands for him."

"Very wise of your father," said the king.

"He ordered all my father's clothes, aye, and mine too, of Your Majesty's own tailor."

"They do appear very well made!" said the king.

"Yes, Your Majesty, and he pays all the bills out of the gold he picks up on the road."

"A very precious pig," said the king.

"Latterly he has seemed unruly, and rather out of sorts."

"That's very sad!" said the king.

"He has refused to go where he is told, and won't allow my mother to have any more bacon from his side."

"He should be chastised!" said the king.

"Besides which, Your Majesty, he is growing rather blind, and can't see where he is going."

"He should be led," said the king.

"Yes, Your Majesty, that is why my father has just engaged your father to look after him."

"That's not true," yelled the king... then suddenly he remembered his daughter's promise. So he was obliged to allow the princess to marry the peasant's son, but this he never regretted, for the peasant's son became a most clever and amiable young prince, and lived happily with his bride and his father-in-law for very many years. Years after, when John became the king, all his people declared they had never had so wise a ruler. Then it was that he romanced no longer but was always believed and respected.

The Lazy Spinning-Girl Who Became a Queen

A COMMON WOMAN HAD A DAUGHTER who was a very good worker, but she did not like spinning; for this her mother very often scolded her, and one day got so vexed that she chased her down the road with the distaff. As they were running a prince passed by in his carriage. As the girl was very pretty the prince was very much struck with her, and asked her mother, "What is the matter?" "How can I help it?" said the mother, "for, after she has spun everything that I had, she asked for more flax to spin." "Let her alone, my good woman," said the prince; "don't beat her. Give her to me, let me take her with me, I will give her plenty to spin. My mother has plenty of work that needs to be done, so she can enjoy herself spinning as much as she likes."

The woman gave her daughter away with the greatest pleasure, thinking that what she was unwilling to do at home she might be ashamed to shirk in a strange place, and get used to it, and perhaps even become a good spinster after all. The prince took the girl with him and put her into a large shed full of flax, and said, "If you spin all you find here during the month you shall be my wife." The girl seeing the great place full of flax nearly had a fit, as there was enough to have employed all the girls in the village for the whole of the winter; nor did she begin to work, but sat down and fretted over it, and thus three weeks of the month passed by. In the meantime she always asked the person who took her her food, "What news there was?" Each one told her something or other. At the end of the third week one night, as she was terribly downcast, suddenly a little man half an ell long, with a beard one and a half ells long, slipped in and said, "Why are you worrying yourself, you good, pretty spinning girl?" "That's just what's the matter with me," replied the girl; "I am not a good spinster, and still they will believe that I am a good spinster, and that's the reason why I am locked up here." "Don't trouble about that," said the little man; "I can help you and will spin all the flax during the next week if you agree to my proposal and promise to come with me if you don't find out my name by the time that I finish my spinning." "That's all right," said the girl, "I will go with you," thinking that then the matter would be all right. The little dwarf set to work. It happened during the fourth week that one of the manservants, who brought the girl's food, went out hunting with the prince. One day he was out rather late, and so was very late when he brought the food. The girl said, "What's the news?" The servant told her that that evening as he was coming home very late he saw, in the forest, in a dark ditch, a little man half an ell high, with a beard one and a half ells long, who was jumping from bough to bough, and spinning a thread, and humming to himself, "My name is Dancing Vargaluska. My wife will be good spinster Sue."

Sue, the pretty spinning girl, knew very well what the little man was doing, but she merely said to the servant, "It was all imagination that made you think you saw it in the dark." She brightened up; for she knew that all the stuff would be spun, and that he would not be able to carry her off, as she knew his name. In the evening the little man returned with one-third of the work done and said to her, "Well, do you know my name yet?"

"Perhaps, perhaps," said she; but she would not have told his real name for all the treasures in the world, fearing that he might cease working if she did. Nor did she tell him when he came the next night. On the third night the little man brought the last load; but this time he brought a wheelbarrow with him, with three wheels, to take the girl away with him. When he asked the girl his name she said, "If I'm not mistaken your name is Dancing Vargaluska."

On hearing this the little man rushed off as if somebody had pulled his nose.

The month being up, the prince sent to see if the girl had completed her work; and when the messenger brought back word that all was finished the king was greatly astonished how it could possibly have happened that so much work had been done in so short a time, and went himself, accompanied by a great suite of gentlemen and court dames, and gazed with great admiration upon the vast amount of fine yarn they saw. Nor could they praise the girl enough, and all found her worthy to be queen of the land. Next day the wedding was celebrated, and the girl became queen. After the grand wedding dinner the poor came, and the king distributed alms to them; amongst them were three deformed beggars, who struck the king very much: one was an old woman whose eyelids were so long that they covered her whole face; the second was an old woman whose lower lip was so long that the end of it reached to her knee; the third old woman's posterior was so flat that it was like a pancake.

These three were called into the reception room and asked to explain why they were so deformed. The first said, "In my younger days I was such a good spinster that I had no rival in the whole neighbourhood. I spun till I got so addicted to it that I even used to spin at night: the effect of all this was that my eyelids became so long that the doctors could not get them back to their places."

The second said, "I have spun so much during my life and for such a length of time that with continually biting off the end of the yarn my lips got so soft that one reached my knees."

The third said, "I have sat so much at my spinning that my posterior became flat as it is now."

Hereupon the king, knowing how passionately fond his wife was of spinning, got so frightened that he strictly prohibited her ever spinning again.

The news of the story went out over the whole world, into every royal court and every town; and the women were so frightened at what had happened to the beggars that they broke every distaff, spinning wheel, and spindle, and threw them into the fire!

The Children of Two Rich Men

THERE LIVED, AT THE TWO CORNERS OF A COUNTRY, far away from each other, two rich men; one of them had a son, the other a daughter; these two men asked each other to be godfather to their children, and, during the christening they agreed that the babes should wed. The children grew up, but did no work, and so were spoilt. As soon as they were old enough their parents compelled them to marry. Shortly afterwards their parents died and they were

left alone; they knew nothing of the world and did not understand farming, so the serfs and farm labourers had it all their own way. Soon their fields were all overgrown with weeds and their corn bins empty; in a word they became poor.

One day the master bethought himself that he ought to go to market, as he had seen his father do; so he set off, and drove with him a pair of beautiful young oxen that were still left. On his way he met a wedding party, and greeted them thus, "May the Lord preserve you from such a sorrowful change, and may He give consolation to those who are in trouble," words he had once heard his father use upon the occasion of a funeral. The wedding party got very vexed, and, as they were rather flushed with wine, gave him a good drubbing, and told him that the next time he saw such a ceremony he was to put his hat on the end of his stick, lift it high in the air, and shout for joy. He went on further till he came to the outskirts of a forest, where he met some butcher-like looking people who were driving fat pigs, whereupon he seized his hat, put it on the end of his stick, and began to shout: which so frightened the pigs that they rushed off on all sides into the wood; the butchers got hold of him and gave him a sound beating, and told him that the next time he saw such a party he was to say, "May the Lord bless you with two for every one you have." He went on again and saw a man clearing out the weeds from his field, and greeted him, "My brother, may the Lord bless you with two for every one you have." The man, who was very angry about the weeds, caught him and gave him a sound beating, and told him that the next time he saw such things he had better help to pull out one or two. In another place he met two men fighting, so he went up and began to pull first at one and then at the other, whereupon they left off fighting with each other and pitched into him. Somehow or other he at last arrived at the market, and, looking round, he saw an unpainted cart for sale, whereupon he remembered that his father used to go into the wood in a cart, and so he asked the man who had it for sale whether he would change it for his two oxen – not knowing that having once parted with the oxen he would not get them back again. The man was at first angry, because he thought he was making fun of the cart, but he soon saw that the man with the oxen was not quite right in his head, and so he struck the bargain with the young farmer, who, when he got the cart, went dragging it to and fro in the market. He met a blacksmith and changed the cart for a hatchet; soon the hatchet was changed for a whetstone; then he started off home as if he had settled matters in the most satisfactory manner. Near his village he saw a lake, and on it a flock of wild ducks. He immediately threw his whetstone at them, which sank to the bottom, whilst every one of the ducks flew away.

He undressed and got into the lake, in order to recover his whetstone, but in the meantime his clothes were stolen from the bank, and, having no clothes, he had to walk home as naked as when he was born. His wife was not at home when he arrived. He took a slice of bread from the drawer, and went into the cellar to draw himself some wine; having put the bread on the door sill of the cellar, he went back to get his wine, as he did so he saw a dog come up and run away with his bread; he at once threw the spigot after the thief, so the spigot was lost, the bread was lost, and every drop of wine was lost, for it all ran out. Now there was a sack of flour in the cellar, and in order that his wife might not notice the wine he spread the flour over it. A goose was sitting on eggs in the cellar, and as he worked she hissed at him. Thinking that the bird was saying, that it was going to betray him to his wife, he asked it two or three times, "Will you split?" Going up to the goose, it hissed still more, so he caught hold of it by the neck, and dashed it upon the ground with such force that it died on the spot. He was now more frightened than ever, and in order to amend his error he plucked off the feathers, rolled himself about in the floury mess, then amongst the feathers, and then sat on the nest as if he were sitting. His wife came home, and, as she found the cellar door wide open, she went down stairs, and found her husband sitting in the nest and hissing like a goose; but his wife soon recognized him, and, picking up a log of wood, she attacked him, saying, "Good Heavens, what an animal, let me kill it at once!" Up he jumped from the nest, and cried out in a horrible fright, "Don't touch me, my dear wife, it's I!" His wife then questioned him about his transactions, and he gave a full account of all that had happened; so his wife drove him away and said, "Don't come before my eyes again till you have made good your faults." She then gave him a slice of bread and a small flask of spirit, which he put in his pocket and went on his way, his wife wishing him "a happy journey, if the road is not muddy." On his way he met Our Lord Christ and said to him, "I'm not going to divide my bread with you, because you have not made a rich man of me." Then he met Death, with him he divided his bread and his spirits, therefore Death did not carry him off, and he asked Death to be his child's godfather.

Then said Death, "Now you will see a wonder"; with this he slipped into the spirit flask, and was immediately corked up by the young man. Death implored to be set free, but the young farmer said, "Promise me then that you will make me a rich man, and then I will let you out." Death promised him this, and they agreed that the man was to be a doctor, and whenever Death stood at the patient's feet, he or she was not to die, and could be cured by any sort of medicine whatever: but if Death stood at the patient's head he was to die: with this they parted.

Our man reached a town where the king's daughter was very ill. The doctors had tried all they could, but were not able to cure her, so he said that he was going to cure her, if she could be cured, if not, he would tell them; so thereupon he went into the patient and saw Death standing at her feet. He burnt a stack of hay, and made a bath for her of the ashes, and she recovered so soon as she had bathed in it. The king made him so many presents that he became a very rich man: he removed to the town, brought his wife there, and lived in great style as a doctor. Once however he fell sick, and his koma (his child's godfather) came and stood at his head, and the patient begged hard for him to go and stand at his feet, but his koma replied, "Not if I know it," and then the doctor also departed to the other world.

The Hussar and the Servant Girl

THE WIFE OF A PRIEST IN OLDEN TIMES, it may have been in the antediluvian world, put all the plates, dishes, and milk jugs into a basket and sent the servant to wash them in the brook. While the girl was washing she saw a crayfish crawl out of the water, and, as she had never seen one in her life before, she stood staring at it, and was a little frightened. It so happened that a hussar rode past on horseback, and the girl asked him, "Would you mind telling me, my gallant horseman, what sort of a God's wonder that yonder is?" "Well, my sister," said the soldier, "that is a crayfish." The servant then took courage, and went near the crayfish to look at it, and said, "But it crawls!" "But it's a crayfish," said the soldier again. "But it crawls," said the servant abruptly. "But it's a crayfish," said the soldier a third time. "Well, my gallant horseman, how can you stand there and tell me that, when I can see that it crawls?" said the servant. "But, my sister, how can you stand there and tell me, when I can see that it's a crayfish?" said the soldier. "Well, I'm neither blind nor a fool, and I can see quite well that it's a-crawling," said the servant. "But neither am I blind nor a fool, and I can see that it is a crayfish," said the soldier.

The servant got so angry that she dashed her crockery to the ground and broke it into fragments, crying, in a great rage, "May I perish here if it is not a-crawling!" The hussar jumped off his saddle, drew his sword, and cut off his horse's head, saying, "May the executioner cut off my neck like this if it isn't a crayfish!" The soldier went his way on foot, and the servant went home without her ware, and the priest's wife asked, "Well, where are all the pots?" The servant told her what had happened between the soldier and her about a crayfish and a-crawling. "Is that the reason why you have done all the damage?" said the priest's wife. "Oh, mistress, how could I give in when I saw quite well that it was a-crawling; and still that nasty soldier kept on saying it was a crayfish?" The wife of the priest was heating the oven, as she was going to bake, and she got into such a rage that she seized her new fur jacket, for which she had given a hundred florins, and pitched it into the oven, saying, "May the flames of the fire burn me like this if you were not both great fools!" "What is all this smell of burning?" asked the priest, coming in. Learning what had happened about a crayfish and a-crawling, he took his gown and cut it up on the threshold with a hatchet, saying, "May the executioner cut me into bits like this if the three of you are not fools!" Then came the schoolmaster (his calf had got loose and run into the clergyman's yard, and he had come after it to drive it home): and, hearing what had happened, and why, he caught hold of a stick, and struck his calf such a blow on the head that it fell down dead on the spot, exclaiming, "If God will, may the fiery thunderbolt thus strike me dead if you all four are not fools!"

Then came the churchwarden, and asked what had happened there, and when he was told he got into such a rage that he picked up the church box and dashed it on the ground in the middle of the yard, so that the box was broken to pieces, and the precious altar covers and linen were rolling about on the dirty ground, saying, "May I perish like this, at this very hour, if the whole five of you are not fools!"

In the meantime the sacristan came in, and, seeing the linen on the floor, he threw up his hands and said, "Well, I never! whatever's the matter?" Then they told him what had happened, and why, whereupon he picked up all the covers and linen and tore them into shreds, saying, "May the devil tear me to atoms like this if you six are not a parcel of raving lunatics!"

News of the event soon got abroad, and the whole congregation gathered together and set the priest's house on fire, crying, "May the flames of the fire burn us all like this, every one of us, if all the seven were not fools!"

The Devil and the Three Slovák Lads

THERE WAS ONCE, I don't know where, in Slavonia, a man who had three sons. "Well, my sons," said he one day to them, "go to see the land; to see the world. There is a country where even the yellowhammer bathes in wine, and where even the fence of the yards is made of strings of sausages; but if you wish to get on there you must first learn the language of the country." The three lads were quite delighted with the description of the wonderful country, and were ready to start off at once. The father accompanied them as far as the top of a high mountain; it took them three days to get to the top, and when they reached the summit they were on the border of the happy land: here the father slung an empty bag on every one of the lads' shoulders, and, pointing out to the eldest one the direction, exclaimed, "Ah! Can you see Hungary?" and with this he took leave of them quite as satisfied as if he had then handed them the key of happiness.

The three lads went on and walked into Hungary; and their first desire was to learn Hungarian, in accord with their father's direction. The moment they stepped over the border they met a man, who inquired where they were going? They informed him, "To learn Hungarian." "Don't go any further, my lads," said the man, "the school year consists of three days with me, at the end of which you will have acquired the requisite knowledge." The three lads stayed; and at the end of the three days one of them had happily learned by heart the words "we three"; the other, "for a cheese"; and the third, "that's right." The three Slovák lads were delighted, and wouldn't learn any more; and so they continued on their journey. They walked till they came to a forest, where they found a murdered man by the road side; they looked at him, and to their astonishment they recognized the murdered man as their late master whom they had just left; and while they were sighing, not knowing what to do, the rural policeman arrived on the spot. He began to question them about the murdered man, saying, "Who killed him?" The first, not knowing anything else, answered, "We three." "Why?" asked the policeman. "For a cheese," replied the second. "If this is so," growled the policeman, "I shall have to put you in irons." Whereupon the third said, "That's right." The lads were escorted by the policeman, who also intended to get assistance to carry away the dead man; but the moment they left, the dead man jumped up, shook himself, and regained his ordinary appearance, and became a sooty devil, with long ears and tail, who stood laughing at the lads, being highly amused at their stupidity, which enabled him to deceive them so easily.

The Beggar's Presents

THERE WAS ONCE A VERY POOR MAN, who went into the wood to fell trees for his own use. The sweat ran down his cheeks, from his hard work, when all at once an old beggar appeared and asked for alms. The poor man pitied him very much, and, putting his axe on the ground, felt in his bag, and, with sincere compassion, shared his few bits of bread with the poor old beggar. The latter, having eaten his bread, spoke thus to the woodcutter: "My son, here! for your kindness accept this tablecloth, and whenever hereafter you feel need and are hungry, say to the cloth, 'Spread thyself, little cloth,' and your table will be laid, and covered with the best meats and drinks. I am the rewarder of all good deeds, and I give this to you

for your benevolence." Thereupon the old man disappeared, and the woodcutter turned homewards in great joy.

Having been overtaken by night on his way, he turned into a hostelry, and informed the innkeeper, who was an old acquaintance, of his good fortune; and, in order to give greater weight to his word, he at once made a trial of the tablecloth, and provided a jolly good supper for the innkeeper and his wife, from the dainty dishes that were served up on the cloth. After supper he laid down on the bench to sleep, and, in the meantime, the wicked wife of the innkeeper hemmed a similar cloth, and by the morning exchanged it for that of the woodcutter. He, suspecting nothing, hurried home with the exchanged cloth, and, arriving there, told his wife what had happened; and, to prove his words, at once gave orders to the cloth to spread itself; but all in vain. He repeated at least a hundred times the words "Little cloth, spread thyself," but the cloth never moved; and the simpleton couldn't understand it. Next day he again went to the wood, where he again shared his bread with the old beggar, and received from him a lamb, to which he had only to say, "Give me gold, little lamb," and the gold coins at once began to rain. With this the woodcutter again went to the inn for the night, and showed the present to the innkeeper, as before. Next morning he had another lamb to take home, and was very much surprised that it would not give the gold for which he asked. He went to the wood again, and treated the beggar well, but also told him what had happened to the tablecloth and lamb. The beggar was not at all surprised, and gave him a club, and said to him, "If the innkeeper has changed your cloth and lamb, you can regain them by means of this club: you have only to say, 'Beat away, beat away, my little club,' and it will have enough power to knock down a whole army." So the woodcutter went to the inn a third time, and insisted upon his cloth and lamb being returned; and, as the innkeeper would not do so, he exclaimed, "Beat away, beat away, my little club!" and the club began to beat the innkeeper and his wife, till the missing property was returned.

He then went home and told his wife, with great joy, what had happened; and, in order to give greater consequence to his house, he invited the king to dinner next day. The king was very much surprised, and, about noon, sent a lackey to see what they were cooking for him; the messenger, however, returned with the news that there was not even a fire in the kitchen. His majesty was still more surprised when, at mealtime, he found the table laden with the finest dishes and drinks. Upon inquiry where all came from, the poor woodcutter told him his story, what happened in the wood, about the lamb and cloth, but did not mention a word about the club. The king, who was a regular tyrant, at once claimed the cloth and the lamb; and, as the man would not comply, he sent a few lackeys to him, to take them away; but they were soon knocked down by the club. So the king sent a larger force against him; but they also perished to a man. On hearing this the king got into a great rage, and went in person with his whole army against him; but on this occasion, too, the woodcutter was victorious, because the club knocked down dead every one of the king's soldiers; the king himself died on the battlefield and his throne was occupied by the once poor woodcutter. It was a real blessing to his people; because, in his magnanimity, he delighted to assist all whom he knew to be in want or distress; and so he, also, lived a happy and contented man to the end of his days!

The World's Beautiful Woman

I N THE MOST BEAUTIFUL LAND OF ASIA, where Adam and Eve may have lived, where all animals, including cows, live wild, where the corn grows wild, and even bread grows on trees, there lived a pretty girl, whose palace was built on a low hill, which looked over a pretty, a very pretty valley, from which one could see the whole world. In the same country there lived a young king who decided not to get married till he succeeded in finding the prettiest woman or girl in the world.

The pretty maid lived with her old father, and with only two servant girls. The young king lived and enjoyed himself amongst the finest young aristocrats. One day it struck the young king that it would be a good thing to get married; so he instructed his aristocratic friends to go all over his vast realm, and to search about till they found the prettiest girl in the land: they had not to trouble whether she was poor or rich; but she must be the prettiest. Each of them was to remain in the town where he found the girl that he deemed was the prettiest and to write and let the king know, so that he might go and have a look at all of them and choose for himself the prettiest amongst all the beauties, the one he liked best. After a year he received letters from every one of his seventy-seven friends, and extraordinarily all the seventy-seven letters arrived from the same town, where, on a low hill above a pretty little valley, there stood a golden palace, in which there lived a young lady with a nice old man and two maids, and from the four windows of which palace the whole world could be seen. The young king started with a large retinue of wedding guests to the place where the prettiest girl in the world lived: he found there all his seventy-seven friends, who were all fever-stricken with love, and were lying about on the pavement of the palace, on hay which was of a very fine silk-like grass; there they lay every one of them. The moment the young king saw the beautiful girl he cried: "The Lord has created you expressly for me; you are mine and I am yours! And it is my wish to find my rest in the same grave with you."

The young lady also fell very much in love with the handsome king; in her fond passion she could not utter a word, but only took him round his slender waist and led him to her father. Her old father wept tears of joy, that at last a man was found whom his daughter could love, as she had thought every man ugly hitherto. The ceremony of betrothal and wedding was very short; at his pretty wife's wish, the king came to live on the beautiful spot, than which there was not a prettier one in the whole world! By the side of the palace there was an earth-hut, in which lived an old witch who knew all the young lady's secrets, and who helped her with advice whenever she needed it. The old witch praised the young lady's beauty to all she met, and it was she who had gathered the seventy-seven young aristocrats into the palace. On the evening of the wedding she called upon "the world's beautiful lady" and praised the young king to her, his handsomeness and riches, and after she had praised him for an hour or two she sighed heavily: the pretty young lady asked her what troubled her, as she had this very moment spoken of her husband as being a handsome, rich, and worthy man? "Because, my pretty lady, my beautiful queen, if you two live sometime here, you will not long be the prettiest woman in the world; you are very pretty now, and your husband is the handsomest of all men; but should a daughter be born to you, she will be more beautiful than you; she will be more beautiful than the morning star – this is the reason of my sadness, my beautiful lady." "You are quite right, good old woman, I will follow any advice; if you tell me what to do, I will obey you. I will do anything to remain the most beautiful woman in the world." This was what the old witch said to the beautiful lady: "I will give you a handful of cotton wool; when your husband sleeps with you, put this wool on your lips, but be careful not to make it wet, because there will be poison on it. When your husband arrives at home all in perspiration from the dance, he will come to you and kiss you, and die a sudden death." The young lady did as the witch told her, and the young king was found dead next morning; but the poison was of such a nature that the physicians were not able to find out what the king had died of.

The bride was left a widow, and again went to live with her maid and her old father, and made a solemn vow that she would never marry again. And she kept her word. As it happened, however, by some inexplicable circumstance, or by some miracle, after a few months she discovered that she was with child; so she ran to the old witch and asked her what to do. The witch gave her a looking-glass and the following advice: "Every morning you have to ask this mirror whether there is a more beautiful woman than yourself in existence, and if it says that there is not, there really won't be one for a long time, and your mind may be at ease; but should it say that there is one, there will be one, and I will see to that myself." The beautiful lady snatched the mirror from the witch in great joy, and as soon as she reached her dressing room she placed the little mirror on the window ledge and questioned it thus: "Well, my dear little mirror, is there a more beautiful woman in the world than I?" The mirror replied: "Not yet, but there will be one soon, who will be twice as handsome as you." The beautiful woman nearly lost her wits in her sorrow, and informed the witch what the mirror had replied. "No matter," said the old hag, "let her be born, and we shall soon put her out of the way."

The beautiful lady was confined, and a pretty little daughter was born, and it would have been a sin to look at her with an evil eye. The bad woman did not even look at the pretty little creature, but fetched her mirror and said: "Well, my dear little mirror, is there a more beautiful creature than I?" and the looking-glass replied: "You are very beautiful, but your little daughter is seven times prettier than you." So as soon as she left her bed she sent for the old witch to ask her advice, who, when she took the babe in her arms, exclaimed that she had never seen such a beautiful creature in all her life. While she gazed at the beautiful child she spat in her eyes and covered her face, telling the beautiful woman to look at the child again in three hours, and when she uncovered it she would be surprised to find what a monster it had become. The beautiful lady felt very uneasy, and asked the witch whether she was allowed to question the mirror again? "Certainly," replied the witch, "for I know that at this moment you are the most beautiful woman in existence." But the mirror replied, "You are beautiful, but your daughter is seventy-seven times more beautiful than you." The beautiful woman nearly died of rage, but the old witch only smiled, being confident of her magic power.

The three hours passed, the little girl's face was uncovered, and the old witch fainted away in her rage; for the little girl had become not only seven times, but seventy-seven times more beautiful than ever from the very same thing that usually disfigured other babies: when she recovered she advised the beautiful lady to kill her baby, as not even the devil himself had any power over it. The old father of the beautiful woman had died suddenly, broken-hearted by his daughter's shame! The beautiful woman was nearly killed by sorrow over the loss of her father, and in order to forget her troubles, she spared her daughter till she was thirteen: the little girl grew more beautiful every day, so that the woman could not bear her daughter's beauty any longer, and handed her to the old witch to be killed. The witch was only too glad to avail herself of the opportunity, and took her into a vast forest, where she tied the girl's hands together with a wisp of straw, placed a wreath of straw on her head, and a girdle of straw round her waist, so that by lighting them she would burn to death the most beautiful masterpiece of the Lord. But all of a sudden a loud shouting was heard in the forest, and twelve robbers came running as swift as birds towards the place where the old witch and the pretty girl were standing. One of the robbers seized the girl, another knocked the old witch on the head, and gave her a sound beating. The witch shammed death, and the robbers left the wicked old wretch behind, carrying off the pretty girl (who had fainted in her fright) with them. After half an hour the old witch got up, and rushed to the castle where the beautiful woman lived, and said, "Well, my queen, don't question your mirror any more, for you are now the most beautiful creature in the world, your beautiful daughter lies under ground." The beautiful lady jumped for joy, and kissed the ugly old witch.

The pretty girl upon her recovery found herself in a nice little house, in a clean bed, and guarded by twelve men, who praised her beauty in whispers, which was such as no human eye had seen before. The innocent little thing, not thinking of any harm, looked at the men with their great beards, who stared at her with wide-open eyes. She got up from her soft bed, and thanked the good men for having delivered her from the clutches of the awful old witch, and then inquired where she was, and what they intended to do with her; if they meant to kill her, she begged them do it at once, as she would die with pleasure, and was only afraid of being killed by that horrible old witch, who was going to burn her to death. None of the robbers could utter a word, their hearts were so softened by her sweet words: such words as they had never before heard from human lips, and her innocent look which would have tamed even a wild bull. At last one of the robbers, who was splendidly dressed, said: "You pretty creature of the Lord, you are in the midst of twelve robbers, who are men of good hearts, but bad morals; we saved you from the hands of the ugly old witch whom I knocked down, and killed I believe; we would not kill you, for the whole world; but, on the contrary, would fight the whole world for you! Be the ornament of our house and the feast of our eyes! Whatsoever your eyes or your mouth may desire, be it wherever man exists, we will bring it to you! be our daughter, and we will be everything to you! Your fathers! Brothers! Guardians! And, if you need it, your soldiers!" The little girl smiled, and was very pleased: she found more happiness among the robbers than she ever did in her mother's palace; she shook hands with all, commended herself to their protection, and at once looked after the cooking. The chief of the robbers called three strong maidens, dressed in white, from a cave, and ordered them to carry out without delay the orders of their queen, and if he heard one word of complaint against any of them, they should die the death of a pig. The young girl spoke kindly to the three maids, and called them her companions.

The robbers then went out on to the highway in great joy – to continue their plundering – singing and whistling with delight, because their home and their band had the most beautiful queen in the world. The beautiful woman, the girl's mother, one day felt weary, and listless, because she had not heard anyone praise her beauty for a very long time. So in her ennui she took her mirror and said to it: "My dear, sweet little mirror, is there a more beautiful creature in all the world, than I?" The little mirror replied, "You are very beautiful, but your daughter is a thousand times handsomer!" The woman nearly had a fit, in her rage, for she had not even suspected that her hateful daughter was yet alive: she ran to the old witch like one out of her mind, to tell what the mirror had said. The witch at once disguised herself as a gypsy, and started on her journey, and arrived at the fence of the place where the pretty girl lived; the garden was planted with flowers and large rose bushes; among the flower beds she could see the pretty girl sauntering in a dress fit for a queen. The old witch's heart nearly broke when she saw the young girl, for never, not even in her imagination, had she ever seen anyone so beautiful. She stole into the garden among the flower beds, and on approaching saw that the young girl's fingers were covered with the most precious diamond rings: she kissed the girl's beautiful hand, and begged to be allowed to put on a ring more precious than any she had; the girl consented, and even thanked her for it. When she entered the house, she all at once dropped down as if dead; the witch rushed home, and brought the good news to the beautiful queen, who at once questioned the mirror, whether there was yet any one who was prettier than she, and the mirror replied, that there was not.

The pretty woman was delighted, and nearly went mad with joy on hearing that she was once more the most beautiful creature in existence, and gave the witch a handful of gold.

At noon the robbers dropped in one after another from their plundering, and were thunderstruck when they saw that the glory of their house and the jewel of their band lay dead. They bewailed her with loud cries of grief, and commanded the maidens with threats to tell them who had done it, but they were even more stunned with grief, and bewailed the good lady, and could not utter a single word, till one of them said that she saw the pretty girl talking with a gypsy woman for a while, and that the moment the woman left she suddenly dropped down dead. After much weeping and wailing the robbers made preparations for the laying out of their adored queen; they took off her shoes in order to put more beautiful ones upon her pretty feet: they then took the rings off her fingers in order to clean them, and as at the very last one of the robbers pulled off the most precious ring from her little finger, the young girl sat up and smiled, and informed them that she had slept very well, and had had most beautiful dreams; and also that if they had not taken off that very ring (which the gypsy woman had put on that day) from her little finger she would never have waked again. The robbers smashed the murderous ring to atoms with their hatchet-sticks, and begged their dear queen not to speak to anyone, except themselves, as all others were wicked, and envious of her on account of her beauty, while they adored her. Having partaken of a good supper, the robbers again went out to their plunder singing, and quite at rest in their minds, and for a couple of weeks nothing happened to the young lady; but after a fortnight her mother again felt ennui and questioned her mirror:

"Is there anyone living being on this earth more beautiful than I?" The mirror replied: "You are very beautiful, but your daughter is one thousand times more beautiful." The beautiful lady began to tear her hair in rage, and went to complain to the witch that her daughter was alive still, so the witch again went off and found the young lady, as before, among the flowerbeds. The witch disguised herself as a Jewess this time, and began to praise the gold and diamond pins with which the young lady's shawl was fastened, which she admired very much, and begged the young lady's leave to allow her to stick another pin amongst those which she had already in her bosom, as a keepsake. Among all the pins the prettiest one was the one which the witch disguised as a Jewess stuck in the young lady's bosom. The young lady thanked her for it, and went indoors to look after the cooking, but as soon as she arrived in the house she gave a fearful scream and dropped down dead.

The joy of her mother was great when the witch arrived home in great delight and the mirror again proved that the girl was dead. The robbers were full of joy, in anticipation of the pleasure of seeing again their pretty young girl, whose beauty was apparently increasing daily; but when they heard the cries of sorrow of the three servant maids and saw the beautiful corpse stretched out on the bier, they lost all their cheerfulness and began to weep also. Three of the robbers carried in all the necessaries for the funeral, while the others undressed and washed the corpse, and as they were drawing out from her shawl the numerous pins, they found one amongst them which sparkled most brilliantly, whereupon two of them snatched it away, each being anxious to replace it in the girl's bosom when redressing her for burial, when suddenly the virgin queen sat up and informed them that her death was caused by a Jewess this time. The robbers buried the pin five fathoms deep in the ground, so that no evil spirit might get it. There is no more restless being in the world than a woman; it is a misfortune if she is pretty, and the same if she is not: if she be pretty she likes to be continually told of it, if she be not she would like to be. The evil one again tempted the beautiful lady, and she again questioned her mirror whether any living being was prettier than she: the mirror replied that her daughter was prettier.

Upon this she called the old witch all kinds of bad names in her rage, and threatened her that if she did not kill her daughter outright she would betray her to the world, and accuse her of having led her to all her evil deeds; that it was she who induced her to kill her handsome husband, and that she had given her the mysterious mirror, which was the cause of her not being able to die in peace. The old hag made no reply, but went off in a boisterous manner: she transformed herself into a pretty girl and went straight into the house in which the young lady was dressing herself and falsely told her that she had been engaged by the robbers to wait always upon her while she dressed, because she had already been killed twice, once by a gypsy woman, and another time by a Jewess; and also that the robbers had ordered her not to do anything else but to help her in her toilet. The innocent girl believed all that the she-devil said. She allowed her to undo her hair and to comb it. The witch did her hair in accordance with the latest fashion, and plaited it and fastened it with all sorts of hairpins; while doing so she hid a hairpin which she had brought with her among the girl's hair, so that it could not be noticed by anyone; having finished, the new lady's maid asked permission to leave her mistress for a moment, but never returned, and her young lady died, while all wept and sobbed most bitterly. The men and the maids had again to attend with tears to their painful duty of laying her out for her funeral; they took away all her rings, breastpins, and hairpins; they even opened every one of the folds of her dress, but still they did not succeed in bringing the young girl to life again. Her mother was really delighted this time, because she kept on questioning the mirror for three or four days, and it always replied to her heart's content. The robbers wailed and cried, and did not even enjoy their food; one of them proposed that they should not bury the girl, but that they should come to pray by the side of their dear dead; others again thought that it would be a pity to confide the pretty body to the earth, where it would be destroyed; others spoke of the terrible pang, and said that their hearts would break if they had to look at her dead beauty for any length of time. So they ordered a splendid coffin to be made of wrought gold. They wrapped her in purple and fine linen; they caught an elk and placed the coffin between its antlers, so that the precious body might not decompose underground: the elk quietly carried the precious coffin about, and took the utmost care to prevent it falling from its antlers or its back. This elk happened to graze in Persia just as the son of the Persian king was out hunting all alone. The prince was twenty-three years old; he noticed the elk and also the splendid coffin between its antlers, whereupon he took a pound of sugar from his bag and gave it to the elk to eat. Taking the coffin from its back the Persian king's son opened the gold coffin with fear and trembling, when, unfolding the fine linen, he discovered a corpse, the like of which he had never seen before, not even in his dreams.

He began to shake it to wake her: to kiss her, and at last went down upon his knees by her side to pray to God fervently to restore her to life, but still she didn't move. "I will take her with me into my room," he said, sobbing. "Although it is a corpse that must have been dead for some time, there is no smell. The girl is prettier in her death than all the girls of Persia alive." It was late at night when the prince got home, carrying the golden coffin under his cloak. He bewailed the dead girl for a long time and then went to supper. The king looked anxiously into his son's eyes, but did not dare to question him as to the cause of his grief. Every night the prince locked himself up, and did not go to sleep until he had, for a long time, bemoaned his dead sweetheart; and whenever he awoke in the night he wept again.

The prince had three sisters, and they were very good girls, and very fond of their brother. They watched him every night through the keyhole, but could see nothing. They heard, however, their brother's sobbing and were very much grieved by it. The Persian king had war declared against him by the king of the neighbouring country. The king, being very advanced in age, asked his son to go in his place to fight the enemy. The good son promised this willingly, although he was tortured by the thought of being obliged to leave his beautiful dead girl behind. As, however, he was aware that he would again be able to see and weep over his dear one when once the war was over, he locked himself in his room for two hours, weeping all the time, and kissing his sweetheart. Having finished, he locked his room and put the key in his sabretache. The good-hearted princesses impatiently waited till their brother crossed the border with his army, and so soon as they knew that he had left the country they went to the locksmith of the castle and took away every key he had, and with these tried to unlock their brother's room, till at last one of the keys did fit. They ordered every servant away from the floor on which the room was situated and all three entered. They looked all round, and in all the cupboards, and even took the bed to pieces, and as they were taking out the planks of the bed they suddenly discovered the glittering gold coffin, and in all haste placed it on the table, and having opened it found the sleeping angel. All three kissed her; but when they saw that they were unable to restore life, they wept most bitterly. They rubbed her and held balsam under her nose, but without avail. Then they examined her dress, which was very far superior to their own. They moved her rings and breastpins, and dressed her up like a pretty doll. The youngest princess brought combs and perfumed hair oils in order to do the hair of the dear dead. They pulled out the hairpins and arranged them in nice order, so as to be able to replace them as before. They parted her golden hair, and began to comb it, adorning each lock with a hairpin. As they were combing the hair at the nape of the neck the comb stuck fast, so they looked at once for the cause of it, when they saw that a golden hairpin was entangled in the hair, which the eldest princess moved with the greatest care. Whereupon the beautiful girl opened her eyes and her lips formed themselves into a smile; and, as if awakening from a long, long dream, she slightly stretched herself, and stepped from the coffin. The girls were not afraid at all, as she, who was so beautiful in her death, was still more beautiful in life. The youngest girl ran to the old king and told him what they had done, and that they had found out the cause of their brother's grief, and how happy they were now. The old king wept for joy and hastened after his daughter, and on seeing the beautiful child exclaimed: "You shall be my son's wife, the mother of my grandchildren!" And thereupon he embraced and kissed her, and took her into his room with his daughters. He sent for singing birds so that they might amuse his dear little new daughter. The old king inquired how she made his son's acquaintance and where she first met him. But the pretty princess knew nothing about it, but simply told him what she knew, namely, that she had two enemies who sooner or later would kill and destroy her; and she also told him that she had been living among robbers, to whom she had been handed over by an old witch who would always persecute her till the last moment of her life. The old king encouraged her, and bade her not to fear anyone, but to rest in peace, as neither her mother nor the old witch could get at her, the Persian wise men being quite able to distinguish evil souls from good ones. The girl settled down and partook of meat and drink with the king's daughters, and also inquired after the young prince, asking whether he was handsome or ugly; although, she said, it did not matter to her whether he was handsome or ugly; if he was willing to have her, she would marry him. The princesses brought down the painted portrait of the prince and the young girl fell so deeply in love with it that she continually carried it with her kissing it. One morning the news spread over all the country that the young king had conquered his enemy and was hurrying home to his residential city. The news turned out to be true, and clouds of dust could be seen in the distance as the horsemen approached. The princesses requested their pretty new sister to go with them into the room which adjoined their brother's, where her coffin was kept under the bed.

The moment the prince arrived, he jumped off his horse, and, not even taking time to greet his father, he unlocked his room and began to sob most violently, dragging out the coffin gently from under the bed, placing it on the bed with great care, and then opening the lid with tears; but he could only find a hairpin. He rushed out of the room like a madman, leaving the coffin and the door open, crying aloud, and demanding what sacrilegious hand had robbed his angel from him. But his angel, over whom he had shed so many tears, stood smiling before him. The youth seized her and covered her with as many kisses as there was room for. He took his betrothed, whom Providence had given to him, to his father and told him how he had found the pretty corpse on the back of an elk; and the girl also told the whole story of her life; and the princesses confessed how they had broken into their brother's room, and how they restored his sweetheart to life again. The old king was intoxicated with joy, and the same day sent for a priest, and a great wedding feast was celebrated. The young folks whom Providence had brought together lived very happily, when one day the young queen, who was as beautiful as a fairy, informed her husband that she was being persecuted, and that while her mother lived she could never have any peace. "Don't fear, angel of my heart," said the young king, "as no human or diabolic power can harm you while you are here. Providence is very kind to us. You seem to be a favourite and will be protected from all evil." The young queen was of a pious turn of mind and believed the true words of her husband, as he had only spoken out her own thoughts. About half a year had passed by and the beautiful woman of the world was still happy. Her mirror was covered with dust, as she never dreamt for a moment that her daughter was yet alive; but being one day desirous to repeat her former amusement she dusted her mirror, and, pressing it to her bosom, said: "Is there a prettier living creature in the world than myself?" The mirror replied: "You are very pretty, but your daughter is seventy-seven thousand times more beautiful than you." The beautiful woman, on hearing the mirror's reply, fainted away, and they had to sprinkle cold water over her for two hours before she came round. Off she set, very ill, to the old witch and begged her, by everything that was holy, to save her from that hateful girl, else she would have to go and commit suicide. The old witch cheered her, and promised that she would do all that lay in her power.

After eight months had elapsed the young prince had to go to war again; and, with a heavy heart, took leave of his dear pretty wife, as – if one is obliged to tell it – she was *enceinte*. But the prince had to go, and he went, consoling his wife, who wept bitterly, that he would return soon. The young king left orders that as soon as his wife was confined a confidential messenger was to be sent without delay to inform him of the event. Soon after his departure two beautiful boys with golden hair were born and there was great joy in the royal household. The old king danced about, like a young child, with delight. The princesses wrapped the babies in purple and silk, and showed them to everybody as miracles of beauty.

The old king wrote down the joyful news and sent the letter by a faithful soldier, instructing him that he was not to put up anywhere under any pretence whatever. The old soldier staked his moustache not to call anywhere till he reached the young king.

While angels were rejoicing, devils were racking their brains and planning mischief!

The old witch hid a flask full of spirits under her apron and hurried off on the same road as the soldier, in order to meet him with his letter. She pitched a small tent on the roadside using some dirty sheets she had brought with her, and, placing her flask of spirits in front of her, waited for the passersby. She waited long, but no one came; when all of a sudden a huge cloud gathered in the sky, and the old witch was delighted. A fearful storm set in. As the rain poured down, the old witch saw the soldier running to escape the rain. As he ran past her tent, the wicked old soul shouted to him to come in and sit down in her tent till the rain was over. The soldier, being afraid of the thunder, accepted her invitation, and sat musingly in the tent, when the old woman placed a good dose of spirits in front of him, which the soldier drank; she gave him another drop, and he drank that too. Now there was a sleeping draught in it, and so the soldier fell fast asleep, and slept like a fur cloak. The old woman then looked in his bag for the letter, and, imitating the old king's handwriting to great perfection, informed the young prince that a great sorrow had fallen upon his house, inasmuch as his wife had been delivered of two puppies. She sealed the letter and woke the soldier, who began to run again and did not stop until he reached the camp. The young prince was very much upset by his father's letter, but wrote in reply that no matter what sort of children his wife had borne they were not to touch but to treat them as his own children until he returned. He ordered the messenger to hurry back with his reply, and not to stop anywhere; but the old soldier could not forget the good glass of spirits he had, and so went into the tent again and had some more.

The witch again mixed it with a sleeping-draught and searched the bag while the soldier slept. She stole the letter, and, imitating the young prince's handwriting, wrote back to the old king that he was to have his wife and the young babes killed, because he held a woman who had puppies must be a bad person. The old king was very much surprised at his son's reply but said nothing to anyone. At night he secretly called the old soldier to him and had his daughter-in-law placed in a black carriage. The old soldier sat on the box and had orders to take the woman and her two children into the middle of the forest and brain them there. The carriage stopped in the middle of the forest, the old soldier got down and opened the door, weeping bitterly. He pulled out a big stick from under his seat and requested the young queen to alight. She obeyed his orders and descended holding her babes in her arms.

The old soldier tried three times to raise the stick, but could not do so; he was too much overcome by grief. The young queen implored him not to kill her, and told him she was willing to go away and never see anyone again. The old soldier let her go, and she took her two babes and sheltered in a hollow tree in the forest: there she passed her time living on roots and wild fruit.

The soldier returned home, and was questioned by the old king as to whether he had killed the young queen, as he didn't like to disappoint his son, who was to return from the camp next day. The old soldier declared on his oath that he had killed her and her babes too, and that he had thrown their bodies into the water. The young king arrived at home in great sorrow, and was afraid to catch sight of his unfortunate wife and her ugly babes.

The old king had left his son's letter upon his desk by mistake; the prince picked it up, and was enraged at its contents: "This looks very like my writing," he said, "but I did not write it; it must be the work of some devil." He then produced his father's letter from his pocket, and handed it to him. The old king was horrified at the awful lie which some devil had written in his hand. "No, my dear son," said the old father, weeping, "this is not what I wrote to you; what I really did write was, that two sons with golden hair had been born to you." "And I," replied the young king, "said that whatsoever my wife's offspring was, no harm was to happen to them till I returned. Where is my wife? Where are my golden-haired children?" "My son," said the old king, "I have carried out your orders; I sent them to the wood and had them killed, and the corporal belonging to the royal household had their bodies cast into the water." The old soldier listened, through a crack in the door, to the conversation of the two kings, who both wept bitterly. He entered the room without being summoned, and said: "I could not carry out your orders, my lord and king; I had not the heart to destroy the most beautiful creature in the world; so I let her go free in the forest, and she left, weeping. If they have not been devoured by wild beasts, they are alive still." The young king never touched a bit of supper, but had his horse saddled at once, and ordered his whole bodyguard out. For three days and three nights they searched the wood in every direction, without intermission. On the fourth night, at midnight, the young king thought he heard, issuing from a hollow tree, a baby's cry, which seemed as harmonious to him as the song of a nightingale. He sprang off his horse, and found his beautiful wife, who was more beautiful than ever, and his children, who were joyfully prattling in their mother's arms. He took his recovered family home, amidst the joyous strains of the band, and, indeed, a high festival was celebrated throughout the whole realm.

The young woman again expressed her fears with trembling, that, while her mother and that she-devil were alive, she could not live in peace.

The young king issued a warrant for the capture of the old witch; and the old soldier came, leading behind him, tied to a long rope, an awful creature, whose body was covered all over with frightful prickles, and who had an immense horn in the middle of her forehead. The young queen at once recognized her as the old witch, who had been captured in the act of searching the wood in order to find her, and slay her and her two babes. The young queen had the old witch led into a secret room, where she questioned her as to why she had persecuted her all her life. "Because," said the old witch, "I am the daughter of your grandfather, and the sister of your mother! When I was yet but a suckling babe, your grandmother gave orders that I was to be thrown into the water; a devil coming along the road took me and educated me. I humoured your mother's folly because I thought she would go mad in her sorrow that a prettier creature than herself existed; but the Lord has preserved you, and your mother did not go mad till I covered her with smallpox, and her face became all pitted and scarred. Her mirror was always mocking her, and she became a wandering lunatic, roaming about over the face of the land, and the children pelting her with stones. She continually bewails you."

The young queen informed her husband of all this, and he had the old witch strangled, strung up in a tree, and a fire made of brimstone lighted under her.

When her pára (animal soul) left her wicked body, a horse was tied to each of her hands and feet, and her body torn into four, one quarter of her body being sent to each of the points of the compass, so that the other witches might receive a warning as to their fate.

The "most beautiful woman in the world" was now very ugly, and happened by chance to reach the palace where the pretty queen lived. Her daughter wept over her, and had her kept in a beautiful room, every day showing her through a glass door her beautiful children. The poor lunatic wept and tortured herself till one day she jumped out of the window and broke her neck. The young king loved his beautiful wife as a dove does its mate; he obeyed her slightest wish, and guarded her from every danger.

The two little sons with the golden hair became powerful and valiant heroes, and when the old king died he was carried to his vault by his two golden-haired grandchildren.

The young couple, who had gone through so many sad trials, are alive still, if they have not died since.

The Count's Daughter

THERE WAS ONCE, I don't know where, an old tumbledown oven, there was nothing left of its sides; there was also once a town in which a countess lived, with an immense fortune. This countess had an exceedingly pretty daughter, who was her sole heiress. The fame of her beauty and her riches being very great the marrying magnates swarmed about her. Among others the three sons of a count used to come to the house, whose castle stood outside the town in a pretty wood. These young men appeared to be richer than one would have supposed from their property, but no one knew where and how the money came to them. The three young men were invited almost every day to the house, but the countess and her daughter never visited them in return, although the young lady was continually asked by them.

For a long time the girl did not accept their invitation, till one day she was preparing for a walk into the wood, in which the young counts' castle was supposed to be: her mother was surprised to hear that she intended to go into the wood, but as the young lady didn't say exactly where she was going her mother raised no objection. The girl went, and the prettiness of the wood, and also her curiosity enticed her to go in further and further till at last she discovered the turrets of a splendid castle; being so near to it her curiosity grew stronger, and at last she walked into the courtyard. Everything seemed to show that the castle was inhabited, but still she did not see a living soul; the girl went on till she came to the main entrance, the stairs were of white marble, and the girl, quite dazzled at the splendour she beheld, went up, counting the steps. "One hundred," said the girl, in a half whisper, when she reached the first flight, and tarried on the landing. Here she looked round when her attention fell on a bird in a cage. "Girl, beware!" said the bird. But the girl, dazzled by the glitter, and drawn on by her curiosity, again began to mount the stairs, counting them, without heeding the bird's words. "One hundred," again said the girl, as she tarried on the next landing, but still no one was to be seen, but thinking that she might find someone she opened the first door, which revealed a splendour quite beyond all she had ever imagined, a sight such as she had never seen before, but still no one appeared. She went into another room and there amongst other furniture she also found three bedsteads. "This is the three young men's bedroom," she thought, and went on. The next room into which she stepped was full of weapons of every possible description; the girl stared and went on, and then she came to a large hall which was full of all sorts of garments, clerical, military, civilian, and also women's dresses. She went on still further and in the next room she found a female figure, made up of razors, which, with extended arms as it seemed, was placed above a deep hole. The girl was horror-struck at the sight and her fear drove her back; trembling she went back through the rooms again, but when she came into the bedroom she heard male voices. Her courage fled and she could go no further, but hearing some footsteps approach she crept under one of the beds. The men entered, whom she recognized as the three sons of the count, bringing with them a beautiful girl, whom the trembling girl recognized by her voice as a dear friend. They stripped her of all, and as they could not take off a diamond ring from her little finger, one of the men chopped it off and the finger rolled under the bed where the girl lay concealed. One of the men began to look for the ring when another said, "You will find it some other time," and so he left off looking for it. Having quite undressed the girl they took her to the other room, when after a short lapse of time she heard some faint screaming, and it appeared to her as if the female figure of razors had snapped together, and the mangled remains of the unfortunate victim were heard to drop down into the deep hole. The three brothers came back and one of them began to look for the ring: cold sweat broke out on the poor girl hiding under the bed. "Never mind, it is ours new and you can find it in the morning," said one of the men, and bade the others go to bed; and so it happened: the search for the ring was put off till next day. They went to bed and the girl began to breathe more freely in her hiding place; she began to grope about in silence and found the ring and secreted it in her dress, and hearing that the three brothers were fast asleep, she stole out noiselessly leaving the door half ajar. The next day the three brothers again visited the countess when the daughter told them that she had a dream as if she had been to their castle. She told them how she went up a flight of marble stairs till she counted 100, and up the next flight when she again counted 100. The brothers were charmed and very much surprised at the dream and assured her that it was exactly like their home. Then she told them how she went from one room to another and what she saw, but when she came in her dream as far as the razor-maid they began to feel uneasy and grew suspicious, and when she told them the scene with the girl, and in proof of her tale produced the finger with the ring, the brothers were terrified and exclaiming, "We are betrayed!" took flight; but everything was arranged, and the servants, who were ordered to watch, caught them. After an investigation all their numberless horrible deeds were brought to light and they were beheaded.

Jack Dreadnought

A **POOR WIDOW HAD A SON who was so courageous that not even the devil's mother would have frightened him, and therefore he was named in his childhood Jack Dreadnought. His mother was in continual terror lest something dreadful might happen to her son,**

as he was so plucky, nay foolhardy, and determined to use all possible means to teach him to fear. For this reason she sent him to the clergyman of the village as "mendicant," and requested the minister to use all his knowledge in trying to teach her son to fear. The clergyman left nothing untried to make the boy frightened; he told him all sorts of ghostly and horrible tales, but these, instead of frightening the lad, made him only more anxious to make the acquaintance of ghosts similar to those mentioned in the tales. The clergyman thereupon hit upon the idea of introducing some sham ghosts in order to break Jack Dreadnought's intrepidity.

He fixed upon the three nights before Christmas; on these nights the lad had to go to ring the bells at midnight in the tower that stood at the very end of the village, and the clergyman thought that he could find some opportunity of frightening Jack. He took an old cassock and stuffed it with straw and placed it before the tower door with one hand on the handle. Midnight came and Jack went to ring the bells and discovered the dummy in the cassock. "Who are you?" he called out, but received no reply. "Very well," said the boy, "if you won't answer I will tell you this, that if you don't clear off from that door I'll kick you in the stomach that you will turn twelve somersaults." As there was no reply, Jack in his rage took hold of the dummy's collar and threw him on the ground with such violence that it rolled away three fathoms, and then, as if nothing had happened, went up into the tower, rang the bells, and went home. The clergyman, as his first experiment did not succeed, made two dummies the next day, which were exactly alike; one he placed in the same position as before at the door of the tower, the other near the bell ropes.

At midnight Jack again went to ring the bells and, as before, made short work of the first dummy; as he did not receive any reply he took him by the collar and threw him on the ground. When he went up into the tower and saw that the rope was held by another, he thought it was the first one, and thus addressed him: "Well, my friend, you've come here, have you? You hadn't enough with the first fall? Answer me or I will dash you on the ground so that you will not be able to get up again," and as the dummy did not reply Jack took it by the throat and pitched it from the window of the tower, and it whizzed through the air. The clergyman had had two unsuccessful experiments but he had great confidence in the third. He made three dummies this time, two were placed as before and the third he stood on the bell so that it might prevent it ringing. Jack Dreadnought dealt with the two first dummies as on the previous night, but as he was about to ring, to his astonishment, he discovered the dummy on the bell; he was not frightened, but when he saw that it would not come down, after a polite request, took it angrily by one leg and pitched it through the window like a cat. The clergyman had now come to the conclusion that he was unable to teach Jack fear, and now commenced to plan how he might get rid of him. The next morning he called him, and thus spoke to him: "Jack, you are a fine courageous fellow; go, take my grey horse, and as much provisions as you think will last you three days, and go into the world and follow your nose; do not stop all day, but take up your night quarters wherever darkness finds you. Do this for three days, and settle down where you spend the third night, and you will be prosperous."

The clergyman thought that Jack would perish on the way; but we shall see whether he did. Jack started off the first day, and in the evening came to a narrow, round timber hut, which was rather high, and he decided to sleep there. As he found it empty he made a fire in its centre and commenced to fry some bacon; all of a sudden he felt something dripping, he looked up and saw something like a human form dangling in the air. "Well, upon my word," shouted he, "the devil won't leave me alone even here: get down from there, will you, or do you expect me to take you down?" No reply came, and Jack, with a clever jump, caught hold of one of his legs, and brought it down, but the head was torn off and fell down. Only then he discovered that it was a hanged man, but he did not think much of it, and stayed there all night. He travelled the whole of the next day; in the evening he reached an inn and asked for a room, and received in reply that they had an empty room on the upper floor, the only one vacant; but that no one could sleep there, as the place was haunted. "What!" shouted Jack; "Oh! I know those ghosts; let me have a dish of good food, a mouthful of good wine, and a burning candle in the upper room, and I will sleep there. I swear by Beelzebub that the ghosts will come no more!" The innkeeper tried to dissuade Jack from his foolhardy attempt, but he would not give way.

He was shown into the room; it was a large apartment on the upper floor. Jack placed the lighted candle in the middle, a dishful of food and a jug of wine by the side of it, and settled down in a chair, waiting for the awful ghosts. No sooner had the clock struck midnight than, all of a sudden, a fearful chorus of animal noises was to be heard, like the howling of dogs, neighing of horses, bellowing of cattle, roaring of wild beasts, bleating of sheep and of goats, and also crying, laughing, and clanking of chains. Jack was quite delighted with the nocturnal concert; but, all of a sudden a big skull rolled in through the door and stopped by the side of the dish. Jack stared at it, and, instead of the skull, he saw an old monk standing before him with long heavy chains. "Good evening, brother friar!" shouted Jack, "pray have supper with me." "I'm going from here," said the friar, "and I want you to come too; I will show you something." "With pleasure," replied Jack, "will you lead the way, you devil, or you reverend gentleman?" Thereupon Jack followed the friar with the lighted candle. When they arrived at the stairs the friar insisted upon his going first, but Jack would not; and the friar was obliged to lead the way. Next they came to a narrow landing at the top of the cellar stairs. Here, again, the friar invited him to go first, but he would not; and so the apparition had to go first. But, as soon as he went down a few steps, Jack gave the friar such a push with such dexterity that he went head over heels down the steps and broke his neck. In the morning the innkeeper had the friar buried. He made Jack a handsome present, and the latter continued his journey.

Jack Dreadnought rode the whole next day, and in the evening again came to an inn, where he could not get any room except up stairs, where no one else would sleep, on account of ghostly visitors. Jack took the room and was again enjoying his supper in the centre, when the old clock struck midnight. The same sort of music struck his ear as on the previous night, and, amid a great crash, a human hand dropped from the ceiling to near his dish. Jack, in cold blood, took up the hand and threw it behind the door. Another hand fell and went the same way. Now a leg came, and this, too, went behind the door. Then came its fellow, which was soon despatched to the rest. At last a big skull dropped right into the middle of the dish and broke it. Jack got into a rage, and threw the skull violently behind the door; and, on looking back, he found, instead of the limbs, an immense ghost standing behind the door, whom Jack at once taxed with the damage done to the dish, demanding payment. The ghost replied, "Very well; I will pay for it, if you come with me." Jack consented, and they went off together; as before, he always insisted on the ghost going first. They came to a long winding staircase, and down into a huge cellar. Jack opened his eyes and mouth wide when he found in the cellar three vats full of gold, six vats of silver, and twelve vats of copper coins. Then the ghost said to him, "There, choose a vat full of coins for your dish, and take it whenever you like." But Jack, however, did not touch the money, but replied, "Not I; do you suppose that I will carry that money? Whoever brought it here, let him take it away." "Well done," replied the ghost; "I see I've found my man at last. Had you touched the treasure you would have died a sudden death; but now, since you are such a fine courageous fellow, the like of whom I have never seen before, settle down in this place and use the treasure in peace; nobody will ever disturb or haunt you any more." After these words the ghost disappeared.

Jack became the owner of the immense treasure, and married the innkeeper's only daughter, who was very pretty, and lives with her to this day, if he has not died since, enjoying life and spending the money he found in the vats in the cellar.

Cibere

ONCE, A LONG TIME AGO, some simpletons went to make a visit somewhere in the region of Csík, and there they were offered many kinds of tasty foods. But what they found the most delicious was a kind of thick soup. They liked it so much that when it came time to say goodbye and leave for home, they asked their hosts what this tasty food was called, so that when they went back home, they could tell their wives to prepare it.

The hosts told them, "Oh, this soup is called cibere." They said their farewells, and set off for home. But as they were walking, in order not to forget the name of this wonderful dish, all along the road they kept repeating the word: "cibere, cibere, cibere" at every step. It went very well until, eventually, they reached this huge ditch. The ditch was so wide they had to make a run for it in order to jump to the other side. So they took a go at it and whoosh, jumped. But ay, there was some trouble. When they reached the other side, lo and behold… they forgot the precious word, you know, the name of the soup. "Well", they thought, "there can only be one reason for this. We must have dropped it into the ditch, when we were jumping over it." So what was there left to do? They rolled up their shirts, pulled up their trousers, climbed into the ditch, got on their hands and knees and began looking for it. But the weather wasn't that fine. It had been raining for three whole days, and the bottom of the ditch was filled with water and mud. As they were searching, a much-travelled soldier came walking by and stopped at the side of the ditch. As he looked down upon them, his eyes grew as big as two walnuts, and he asked, "What on earth are you doing there at the bottom of the ditch?" "Oh, don't even ask! We are looking for a sweet, precious word that we accidentally dropped." The soldier kept on looking at them, then he shouted: "Oh you can keep on looking for it till Doomsday! You have stirred up the mud so much, that it looks exactly like cibere!" "Oh, dear sir," they exclaimed. "Oh, you've found it! You have found our precious word!" They all jumped up, and muddy as they were, they went up to embrace the soldier one after the other.

Then they set off again for home. As they walked, they kept on saying, "cibere, cibere cibere cibere," you know, at every step. And believe it or not, they remembered it all the way. When they got home, they told their wives, who prepared it for them. They loved it. It was delicious, but never as delicious as the one they had in Csík.

The Priest and the Believers

WHAT I'M GOING TO TELL YOU ABOUT NOW, well, it happened a long time ago. Once there was a village. For the people of the village, every year was like a great wheel turning, every year filled with joy and sadness, every year the same. They ploughed, they sowed, they pulled the weeds, hoed the crops and when summer came, they harvested. They sang together, worked together and laughed together.

But one year, what happened? They sowed the seeds, and the wheat started to grow beautifully, and then, they waited for the rain, but it did not come. A week passed, two weeks passed, one month, two months, no rain. The people started to panic. If this goes on like this, we will have nothing to harvest! Talk went around the village. What could we have possibly done wrong? And they were praying, but no rain came. Then the people in the village thought, "there can only be one reason for this. The priest, our priest doesn't pray properly! This is why we don't have any rain."

So the following Sunday, after the holy mass, they gathered around the priest in the churchyard, and told him, "Well, Reverend, it cannot go on like this. No matter how much you pray, it seems, your prayers are not well received in heaven. If you do not find a better way to pray, we're all lost. And we will look for another priest for the village, for sure." The priest looked around, scratched his beard and then said:

"Well, people, let me go back to the chapel, all right? Let me pray and find out what God tells me about this." He went in and after half an hour came back saying:

"Well, brethren, I got a message from heaven. You can have rain, you just need to decide which day of the week it should come. So please let me know now!"

So the magistrate of the town stepped forward and said:

"Let it be on Monday!"

"Monday's no good", replied the priest. "I've already hired a group of people to tidy my corn."

"Then Tuesday!" responded the magistrate.

But another answered:

"Haven't you seen how much wheat I have drying in my yard, waiting to be milled?"

"Alright, so let it be Wednesday then!" said the magistrate.

But then an old woman jumped out of the crowd placing her hands on her head:

"Wednesday's not good. I'm celebrating my patron-saint that day, and I will have guests coming over from the other village. It would be terrible if they got all wet."

"Fine, then let's have it on Thursday," said the magistrate.

But then a young farmer spoke out:

"For God's sake, no! One of my comrades is coming over. We will plough with my two oxen. And if he likes them, we'll agree on the deal, and he'll buy them, and we will raise our glasses and say a blessing. But how could we even plough if it's raining?"

"Let it be on Friday then," said the magistrate.

Now the whole crowd roared up:

"Friday? Everyone knows it is an unlucky day. It would be a big mistake to have it on Friday. What if a storm comes, and hail comes and then even what we have on the fields will be destroyed!"

"Well, brothers and sisters, let's have it on Saturday then!"

"Now an old man with unbelievable blue eyes stepped forward and clasped his hand. Oh people, please don't do this to me. How could it be on Sunday? That is the day of my son's wedding."

"Then Sunday it has to be."

"Oh not on Sunday!" some women shouted. "Don't you remember? There will be a fair in town. We have been looking forward to it for so long. The last thing we need that day is rain."

At this point, the priest looked around:

"Well brethren, I think it would be best if you decided among yourselves what the best day would be next week, and when you're done, let me know. I'll be waiting in the chapel."

But the village folk couldn't agree. First they threw words at each other, then some punches arrived. And then it became a free-for-all, some grabbing a scythe, some a pitchfork, and they went at each other. Now even the reverend ran out from the chapel, and started shouting:

"Oh people, let us leave it up to Heaven. God will know which day the rain should come." But by the time he uttered this, he got a big push from behind, so he set off running.

Well, they could not agree on a date for the next week, or the week after that, or any week for that matter.

You could ask now, what about the rain? Well, ever since then, the rain comes when it comes.

Magical Creatures &
Transformations

THIS CHAPTER FOCUSES on transformation, showing the 'true self', as well as beings with fantastic abilities. Here too, we can meet the 'iron-nosed' woman, who is actually the witch, as well as the deservedly popular character of Hungarian folktales, the táltos horse, or dragons, which here appear as helpers. Two tales, 'The Girl with the Golden Hair' and 'The Little Magic Pony', are partially the same tale type. This does not mean that they are 'copies', in fact, I think that these two stories are one of the greatest assets of the chapter, as they can encourage the reader to make comparisons! If you are interested in the world of variations, or, as a storyteller or just someone curious, you would like to see several versions of interesting episodes or dialogues within a particular type of story, I definitely recommend these two tales.

There are two other special tales in this chapter. One of them is the wonderful and moving religious tale called 'The Baa-Lambs', which many twenty-first-century Hungarian storytellers like to tell around Advent or any other quiet, thoughtful time. The tale 'The Crow's Nest' is also about a special transformation, where the bones of a child – who was sent to death by his mother and then eaten by his father – turn into a bird. The wonderful motif of transformation and the return from the afterlife appears here, with a poetic insert added to the tale. This is one of our beautiful examples of tales that have songs in them.

The Lamb with the Golden Fleece

THERE WAS ONCE A POOR MAN who had a son, and as the son grew up his father sent him out to look for work. The son travelled about looking for a place, and at last met with a man who arranged to take him as a shepherd. Next day his master gave him a flute, and sent him out with the sheep to see whether he was fit for his work. The lad never lay down all day, very unlike many lazy fellows. He drove his sheep from place to place and played his flute all day long.

There was among the sheep a lamb with golden fleece, which, whenever he played his flute, began to dance. The lad became very fond of this lamb, and made up his mind not to ask any wages of his master, but only this little lamb. In the evening he returned home; his master waited at the gate; and, when he saw the sheep all there and all well fed, he was very pleased, and began to bargain with the lad, who said he wished for nothing but the lamb with the golden fleece. The farmer was very fond of the lamb himself, and it was with great unwillingness he promised it; but he gave in afterwards when he saw what a good servant the lad made. The year passed away; the lad received the lamb for his wages, and set off home with it. As they journeyed night set in just as he reached a village, so he went to a farmhouse to ask for a night's lodging. There was a daughter in the house who when she saw the lamb with the golden fleece determined to steal it. About midnight she arose, and lo! the moment she touched the lamb she stuck hard and fast to its fleece, so that when the lad got up he found her stuck to the lamb. He could not separate them, and as he could not leave his lamb he took them both. As he passed the third door from the house where he had spent the night he took out his flute and began to play. Then the lamb began to dance, and on the wool the girl. Round the corner a woman was putting bread into the oven; looking up she saw the lamb dancing, and on its wool the girl. Seizing the peel in order to frighten the girl, she rushed out and shouted, "Get away home with you, don't make such a fool of yourself." As the girl continued dancing the woman called out, "What, won't you obey?" and gave her a blow on her back with the peel, which at once stuck to the girl, and the woman to the peel, and the lamb carried them all off. As they went they came to the church. Here the lad began to play again, the lamb began to dance, and on the lamb's fleece the girl, and on the girl's back the peel, and at the end of the peel the woman. Just then the priest was coming out from matins, and seeing what was going on began to scold them, and bid them go home and not to be so foolish. As words were of no avail, he hit the woman a sound whack on her back with his cane, when to his surprise the cane stuck to the woman, and he to the end of his cane. With this nice company the lad went on; and towards dark reached the royal borough and took lodgings at the end of the town for the night with an old woman. "What news is there?" said he. The old woman told him they were in very great sorrow, for the king's daughter was very ill, and that no physician could heal her, but that if she could but be made to laugh she would be better at once; that no one had as yet been able to make her smile; and moreover the king had issued that very day a proclamation stating that whoever made her laugh should have her for his wife, and share the royal power. The lad with the lamb could scarcely wait till daylight, so anxious was he to try his fortune. In the morning he presented himself to the king and stated his business and was very graciously received. The daughter stood in the hall at the front of the house; the lad then began to play the flute, the lamb to dance, on the lamb's fleece the girl, on the girl's back the peel, at the end of the peel the woman, on the woman's back the cane, and at the end of the cane the priest. When the princess saw this sight she burst out laughing, which made the lamb so glad that it shook everything off its back, and the lamb, the girl, the woman, and the priest each danced by themselves for joy.

The king married his daughter to the shepherd; the priest was made court-chaplain; the woman court bakeress; and the girl lady-in-waiting to the princess.

The wedding lasted from one Monday to the other Tuesday, and the whole land was in great joy, and if the strings of the fiddle hadn't broken they would have been dancing yet!

Fisher Joe

THERE WAS ONCE A POOR MAN, who had nothing in the world but his wife and an unhappy son Joe. His continual and his only care was how to keep them: so he determined to go fishing, and

thus to keep them from day to day upon whatever the Lord brought to his net. Suddenly both the old folks died and left the unhappy son by himself; he went behind the oven and did not come out till both father and mother were buried. He sat three days behind the oven, and then remembered that his father had kept them by fishing, so he got up, took his net, and went fishing below the weir: there he fished till the skin began to peel off the palms of his hands, and never caught so much as one fish. At last he said, "I will cast my net once more, and then I will never do so again." So he cast his net for the last time and drew to shore a golden fish.

While he was going home he thought he would give it to the lord of the manor, so that perhaps he might grant a day's wages for it. When he got home he took down a plate from the rack, took the fish from his bag, and laid it upon the plate. But the fish slipped off the plate and changed into a lovely girl, who said, "I am thine, and you are mine, love." The moment after she asked, "Joe, did your father leave you anything?" "We had something," replied her husband, "but my father was poor and he sold everything, but," continued he, "do you see that high mountain yonder? It is not sold yet, for it is too steep and no one would have it." Then said his wife, "Let's go for a walk and look over the mountain." So they went all over it, length and breadth, from furrow to furrow. When they came to a furrow in the middle his wife said, "Let us sit down on a ridge, my love, and rest a little." They sat down, and Joe laid his head on his wife's lap and fell asleep. She then slipped off her cloak, made it into a pillow, drew herself away, and laid Joe upon the pillow without waking him. She rose, went away, uncoiled a large whip and cracked it. The crack was heard over seven times seven countries. In a moment as many dragons as existed came forth. "What are Your Majesty's commands?" said they. "My commands are these," replied she. "You see this place – build a palace here, finer than any that exists in the world; and whatever is needed in it must be there: stables for eight bullocks and the bullocks in them, with two men to tend them; stalls for eight horses and the horses in them, and two grooms to tend them; six stacks in the yard, and twelve threshers in the barn." She was greatly delighted when she saw her order completed, and thanked God that He had given her what He had promised. "I shall now go," said she, "and wake my husband." When she came to him he was still asleep. "Get up, my love," said she, "look after the threshers, the grooms, the oxen, and see that all do their work, and that all the work be done, and give your orders to the labourers. And now, my love, let us go into the house and see that all is right. You give your orders to the manservants, and I will give mine to the maids. We have now enough to live on." And Joe thanked God for His blessings. He then told his wife that he would invite the lord of the manor to dine with him on Whit Sunday. "Don't leave me," replied his wife, "for if he catch sight of me you will lose me. I will see that the table is laid and all is ready, but a maid shall wait on you. I will retire into an inner room lest he should see me."

Joe ordered the carriage and six, seated himself in it, the coachman sat on the box, and away they went to the lord's house. They arrived at the gate, Joe got out, went through the gate, and saw three stonemasons at work in the yard. He greeted them and they returned the greeting. "Just look," remarked one of them, "what Joe has become and how miserable he used to be!" He entered the castle, and went into the lord's room. "Good day, my lord." "God bless you, Joe, what news?" "I have come to ask your lordship to dine with me on Whit Sunday, and we shall be very pleased to see you." "I will come, Joe;" they then said goodbye and parted. After Joe had gone the lord came into the courtyard, and the three masons asked him "What did Joe want?" "He has invited me to dine with him," was the reply, "and I am going." "Of course; you must go," said one of them, "that you may see what sort of a house he keeps."

The lord set out in his carriage and four, with the coachman in front, and arrived at the palace. Joe ran out to meet him, they saluted each other, and entered arm in arm. They dined, and all went well till the lord asked, "Well, Joe, and where is your wife?" "She is busy," said Joe. "But I should like to see her," explained the baron. "She is rather shy when in men's society," said Joe. They enjoyed themselves, lit their pipes and went for a walk over the palace. Then said the baron to his servant, "Order the carriage at once." It arrived, and Joe and he said farewell. As the baron went through the gate he looked back and saw Joe's wife standing at one of the windows, and at once fell so deeply in love with her that he became dangerously ill. When he arrived at home the footmen were obliged to carry him from his carriage and lay him in his bed.

At daybreak the three masons arrived and began to work. They waited for their master. As he did not appear, "I will go and see what's the matter with him," said one of them, "for he always came out at 8 a.m." So the mason went in and saluted the baron, but got no reply. "You are ill, my lord," said he. "I am," said the baron, "for Joe has such a pretty wife, and if I can't get her I shall die." The mason went out and the three consulted together as to what was best to be done. One of them proposed a task for Joe, i.e. that a large stone column which stood before one of the windows should be pulled down, the plot planted with vines, the grapes to ripen overnight, and the next morning a goblet of wine should be made from their juice and be placed on the master's table. If this was not done Joe was to lose his wife. So one of them went in to the baron and told him of their plan, remarking that Joe could not do that, and so he would lose his wife. A groom was sent on horseback for Joe, who came at once, and asked what his lordship desired. The baron then told him the task he had to propose and the penalty. Poor Joe was so downcast that he left without even saying "goodbye," threw himself into his carriage, and went home. "Well, my love," asked his wife, "what does he want?" "Want?" replied her husband. "He ordered me to pull down the stone column in front of his window. Since my father was not a working man, how could I do any work? Nor is that all. I am to plant the place with vines, the grapes have to ripen, and I am to make a goblet of wine, to be placed on his table at daybreak. And if I fail I am to lose you."

"Your smallest trouble ought to be greater than that," said his wife. "Eat and drink, go to bed and have a good rest, and all will be well." When night came she went out into the farmyard, uncoiled her whip, gave a crack, which was heard over seven times seven countries, and immediately all the dragons appeared. "What are Your Majesty's commands?" She then told them what her husband required, and in the morning Joe had the goblet of wine, which he took on horseback lest he should be late; he opened the baron's window, and, as nobody was there, he placed the goblet on the table, closed the window, and returned home.

At daybreak the baron turned in his bed. The bright light reflected by the goblet met his eyes, and had such an effect on him that he fell back in his bed, and got worse and worse.

The three masons arrived and wondered why their master did not appear. Said the tallest to the middle one, "I taught him something yesterday; now you must teach him something else." "Well," said the middle one, "my idea is this, that Joe shall build a silver bridge in front of the gate during the night, plant both ends with all kinds of trees, and that the trees be filled with all kinds of birds singing and twittering in the morning. I'll warrant he won't do that, and so he will lose his wife." When the baron came out they communicated their plan. He at once sent for Joe and told him what he required. Joe went away without even saying goodbye, he was so sad. When he got home he told his wife what the baron wanted this time. "Don't trouble yourself, my love," said his wife, "eat and drink and get a good rest, all shall be well." At night she cracked her whip and ordered the dragons to do all that was required, and so at daybreak all was done. The birds made such a noise that the whole of the village was awakened by them. One nightingale loudly and clearly to the baron sang, "Whatever God has given to someone else that you must not covet; be satisfied with what has been given to you." The baron awoke and turned over, and, hearing the loud singing of the birds, rose and looked out of the window. The glare of the silver bridge opposite the gate blinded him, and he fell back in bed and got worse and worse. When the three masons arrived they could not enter, for the splendour of the silver bridge dazzled them, and they were obliged to enter by another gate.

As they were working, the shortest said to the middle one, "Go and see why his lordship does not come out; perhaps he is worse." He went in and found the baron worse than ever. Then said the shortest, "I thought of something, my lord, which he will never be able to do, and so you will get his wife." "What is that, mason?" demanded the baron. "It is this, my lord," said the mason, "that he shall ask God to dinner on Palm Sunday, and that he can't do, and so he will lose his wife." "If you can get Joe's wife for me you shall have all this property," said the baron. "It's ours, then," said they, "for he can't do that." Joe was sent for, and came at once to know what was required of him. "My orders are these," replied the baron, "that you invite God to dinner on Palm Sunday to my house. If you do not your wife is lost." Poor Joe went out without saying goodbye, jumped into his carriage, and returned home dreadfully miserable. When his wife asked him what was the matter he told her of the baron's commands. "Go on," said his wife; "bring me that foal, the yearling, the most wretched one of all, put upon it an old saddle and silver harness on its head, and then get on its back." He did so, said goodbye, and the wretched yearling darted off at once straight to heaven. By the time it arrived there it had become quite a beautiful horse. When Joe reached the gates of Paradise he tied his horse to a stake, knocked at the door, which opened, and he went in and greeted the Almighty. St. Peter received him, and asked him why he had come. "I've come," said he, "to invite God to dinner at my lord's on Palm Sunday." "Tell him from me," said the deity, "that I will come, and tell him that he is to sow a plot with barley, and that it will ripen, and that I will eat bread made of it at dinner. That a cow is to be taken to the bull today, and that I will eat the flesh of the calf for my dinner."

With this Joe took leave, and the foal flew downward. As they went Joe was like to fall head-foremost off, and called upon the deity. St. Peter told him not to fear, it was all right: he would fall on his feet. When Joe arrived at home the barley was waving in the breeze and the cow was in calf. "Well, wife," said he, "I will go to the baron's and give him the message." So he went, knocked at the door, and entered the room. "Don't come a step further," cried the baron. "I don't intend to," said Joe: "I've come to tell you I have executed your commands, and mind you don't blame me for what will happen. The deity has sent you this message: you are to sow a plot with barley, and of it make bread for His dinner. A cow is to go to the bull, and of the calf's flesh He will eat." The baron became thoughtful. "Don't worry yourself, my lord," said Joe, "you have worried me enough, it is your turn now." And so he said "goodbye," and went off home. When he got there the barley bread was baking and the veal was roasting.

At this moment the deity and St. Peter arrived from heaven and were on their way to the baron's, who the moment he saw them called out to his servant, "Lock the gate, and do not let them in." Then said the deity, "Let us go back to the poor man's home, and have dinner there." When they reached the foot of the mountain St. Peter was told to look back and say what he saw, and lo! the whole of the baron's property was a sheet of water. "Now," said the deity to St. Peter, "let us go on, for the mountain is high, and difficult to ascend." When they arrived at Joe's he rushed out with outspread arms, fell to the ground, and kissed the sole of the deity's foot. He entered and sat down to dinner, so did Joe and his wife and also St. Peter. Then said God to Joe, "Set a table in this world for the poor and miserable, and you shall have one laid for you in the world to come; and now goodbye: you shall live in joy, and in each other's love."

They are living still if they have not died since. May they be your guests tomorrow!

Knight Rose

A KING HAD THREE SONS. When the enemy broke into the land and occupied it, the king himself fell in the war. The young princes were good huntsmen and fled from the danger, all three, taking

three horses with them. They went on together for a long time, till they did not even know where they were. On they journeyed, till at last they came to the top of the very highest snow-covered mountain, where the road branched off. Here they decided to separate and try their luck alone. They agreed that on the summit of the mountain, at the top of a tall tree, they would fix a long pole, and on it a white handkerchief. They were to keep well in sight of this white flag, and whenever the handkerchief was seen full of blood the one who saw it was to start in search of his brothers, as one of them was in danger.

The name of the youngest was Rose; he started off to the left, the other two went to the right. When Rose came to the seventh snow-capped mountain and had got far into it he saw a beautiful castle and went in. As he was tired with travelling and wanted a night's rest, he settled down. When even came the gates of the castle opened with great noise, and seven immense giants rushed into the courtyard and from thence into the tower. Every one of them was as big as a tall tower. Rose, in his fright, crept under the bed; but the moment the giants entered one of them said, "Phuh! What an Adam-like smell there is here!" Looking about they caught Rose, cut him up into small pieces like the stalk of a cabbage and threw him out of the window.

In the morning the giants went out again on their business. From a bush there came forth a snake, which had the head of a pretty girl. She gathered up every morsel of Rose's body, arranged them in order, and said, "This belongs here, that belongs there." She then anointed him with grass that had healing power, and brought water of life and death from a spring that was not far off and sprinkled it over him. Rose suddenly jumped up on his feet and was seven times more beautiful and strong than before. At this moment the girl cast off the snakeskin as far as the armpits. As Rose was now so strong he became braver, and in the evening did not creep under the bed, but waited for the giants coming home, at the gate. They arrived and sent their servants in advance to cut up that wretched heir of Adam, but they could not manage him, it took the giants themselves to cut him up. Next morning the serpent with the girl's head came again and brought Rose to life as before, and she herself cast off her skin as far as her waist. Rose was now twice as strong as a single giant. The same evening the seven giants killed him again, he himself having killed the servants and wounded several of the giants. Next morning the giants were obliged to go without their servants. Then the serpent came and restored Rose once more, who was now stronger than all the seven giants put together, and was so beautiful that though you could look at the sun you could not look at him. The girl now cast off the serpent's skin altogether and became a most beautiful creature. They told each other the story of their lives. The girl said that she was of royal blood, and that the giants had killed her father and seized his land, that the castle belonged to her father, and that the giants went out every day to plunder the people. She herself had become a snake by the aid of a good old quack nurse, and had made a vow that she would remain a serpent until she had been avenged on the giants, and she knew now that although she had cast off the snake's skin she had nothing to fear because Rose was a match for the seven giants. "Now, Rose," said she, "destroy them every one, and I will not be ungrateful." To which he replied, "Dearest one, you have restored me to life these three times. How could I help being grateful to you? My life and my all are yours!" They took an oath to be true to each other till death, and spent the day merrily till evening set in, when the giants came, and Rose addressed them thus: "Is it not true, you pack of scoundrels, that you have killed me three times? Now, I tell you that not one of you shall put his foot within these gates! Don't you believe me? Let's fight!" They charged upon him with great fury, but victory was, this time, on his side; he killed them one after the other and took the keys of the castle out of their pockets. He then searched over every nook in the building, and came to the conclusion that they were safe, as they had now possession of the castle.

The night passed quietly; next morning Rose looked from the courtyard to the top of the snow-covered mountain, in the direction of the white flag, and saw that it was quite bloody. He was exceedingly sorry, and said to his love, "I must go in search of my two elder brothers, as some mischief has befallen them; wait till I return, because if I find them I shall certainly be back."

He then got ready, took his sword, bow and arrow, some healing grass, and water of life and death with him, and went to the very place where they had separated. On the way he shot a hare, and when he came to the place of separation he went on the same road by which his elder brothers had gone. He found there a small hut and a tree beside it; he stopped in front of the tree, and saw that his brothers' two dogs were chained to it. He loosed them, lighted a fire, and began to roast the hare. As he roasted it he heard a voice as if someone were shouting from the tree in a shivering voice, "Oh, how cold I am!" it said. "If you're cold," replied Rose, "get down and warm yourself." "Yes," said the voice, "but I'm afraid of the dogs." "Don't be afraid as they won't hurt an honest person." "I believe you," said the voice in the tree, "but still I want you to throw this hair between them. Let them smell it first, then they will know me by it." Rose took the hair and threw it into the fire. Down came an old witch from the tree and warmed herself. Then she spitted a toad and began to roast it. As she did so she said to Rose, "This is mine, that is yours," and threw it at him. As Rose couldn't stand this he jumped up, drew his sword, and smote the witch. But lo! the sword turned into a log of wood, and the witch flew at him to kill him, crying, "It's all up with you also. I've killed your brothers in revenge because you killed my seven giant sons." But Rose set the dogs at her, and they dragged her about till they drew blood. The blood was spilt on the log of wood and it became a sword again. Rose caught hold of it and chopped the old witch's left arm off. Now the witch showed him the place where she had buried his brothers. Rose smote her once more with his sword and the old witch went to Pluto's. Rose dug out the bodies, put the bits together, anointed them with the healing grass, and sprinkled them with the water of life and death, and they came to life again.

When they opened their eyes and saw Rose, they both exclaimed, "Oh! How long I have been asleep." "Very long indeed," said Rose, "and if I hadn't come you'd have been asleep still." They told him that soon after they had separated they received the news that the enemy had withdrawn from their country, and they decided to return, and that the elder should undertake the government of the land, and the other go in search of Rose. On their way they happened to go into the hut, and the old witch treated them as she was going to treat Rose.

Rose also told them his tale, and spoke to them thus: "You, my eldest brother, go home, and sit on our father's throne. You my other brother come with me, and let us two govern the vast country over which the giants had tyrannized until now." And thus they separated and each went on his own business.

Rose found his pretty love again, who was nearly dead with fretting for him, but who quite recovered on his happy return. They took into their hands the government of the vast country which they had delivered from the sway of the giants. Rose and his love got married with the most splendid wedding feast, and the bride had to dance a great deal; and if they've not died since they're alive still to this very day.

May they curl themselves into an eggshell and be your guests tomorrow.

The Baa-Lambs

THERE WAS ONCE, SOMEWHERE or in some other place, I don't know where, over seven times seven countries, or even beyond them, a poor widow, and she had three unmarried sons who were so poor that one had always to go out to service. First the eldest went, and, as he was going and going over seven times seven countries, and even beyond them, he met an old man, who accosted him, saying, "My younger brother, where are you going?" The lad answered, "My father, I am going to look for work." "And I am in need of a servant," the old man replied. So he engaged the lad on the spot to tend his baa-lambs. In the morning, as the lad went out with them, the old man told him not to drive them and not to guide them, but simply to go after them, as they would graze quietly if left to themselves.

The lad started with the baa-lambs. First they came to a splendid meadow, he went in and trotted after them as his master had told him. Then they came to a swift stream and the baa-lambs went over it, but the lad had not the courage to go into the water, but walked up and down the bank till evening, when the baa-lambs returned of their own accord, recrossed the water, and, as night had set in, he drove them home. "Well, my dear son," said his master, "tell me where you have been with the baa-lambs." "My dear father, I only followed after them. First of all they went into a large plain. After that we came to a great, swift stream. They got over the large sheet of water, but I remained on this side, as I did not dare to go into the deep water." As the poor lad finished his tale the master said, "Well, my dear son, I shall send you away, as I can see very well that you are not fit for service," and he sent him off without any pay. The lad went home, very much cast down. When he got home his two brothers asked him, "Well, dear brother, how did you get on in service?" "Hum, how did I get on, and what did I do? You'd better go yourselves and you will soon know." "Very well," they replied, and the second son went to look for service, met the same old man, and fared the same as his brother, and was sent home without anything. As he arrived home his younger brother met him and asked, "Well, dear brother, what sort of service did you get?" "Hum," replied he, "what sort of a place did I get? You had better go and then you also will know." "Very well," replied the youngest, and he too went to try his luck. As he went along he met the same old man, and was engaged by him to tend his baa-lambs for a year. The old man told him, too, to walk after them, and not to leave them under any circumstances. Next morning the old man prepared the lad's bag, and let the baa-lambs out of the fold. They started off, and the lad followed them, step by step, till they came to a pretty, green plain. They walked over it, quietly grazing along as they went, till they came to the swift stream; the baa-lambs crossed it, and the lad followed them, but the moment he entered the water the swift current swept off his clothes and shrivelled his flesh, so that, when he got to the other side, he was only skin and bones. So soon as he reached the other bank the baa-lambs turned back and began to blow on him, and his body was at once fairer than it ever was before. The baa-lambs started off again till they came to a large meadow where the grass was so high that it was ready for the scythe, and still the cattle grazing on it were so ill-fed that a breath of wind would have blown them away. The baa-lambs went on to another meadow which was quite barren, and the cattle there had nothing to eat, yet they were as fat as butter. Thence the baa-lambs went into a huge forest, and there, on every tree, was such a lamentation and crying and weeping as one could not conceive of. The lad looked to see what the meaning of the loud crying could be, and lo, on every bough there was a young sparrow, quite naked! And all were weeping and crying. From here the baa-lambs went sauntering on till they came to a vast garden. In this garden there were two dogs fighting, so that the foam ran from their mouths; still they could not harm each other. The baa-lambs went on further till they came to a great lake, and there the lad saw a woman in the lake, scooping with a spoon something from the water incessantly, and still she was not able to scoop the thing up. From there the baa-lambs went further, and, as they went, he saw a brook of beautiful, running water, clear like crystal, and, as he was very thirsty, he had half a mind to drink of it, but, thinking that the spring-head was very much better, he went there, and saw that the water was bubbling out of the mouth of a rotting dead dog, which so frightened him that he did not taste a drop. From there the baa-lambs went into another garden, which was so wonderfully pretty that human eye had never seen the like before. Flowers of every kind were blooming, but the baa-lambs left them untouched, only eating the green grass, and, as they ate, he sat down under the shade of a beautiful flowering tree in order to partake of some food, when suddenly he saw that a beautiful white pigeon was fluttering about in front of him. He took his small blunderbuss, which he had with him, and shot at the pigeon, knocking off a feather, but the pigeon flew away. He picked up the feather and put it in his bag. From thence the baa-lambs started off home, the lad following them. When they arrived, the old man asked: "Well, my son, and how did the baa-lambs go?" "They went very well," answered the lad, "I had no trouble with them. I had merely to walk after them." As he said this, the old man asked him: "Well, my son, tell me where you have been with the baa-lambs." Then he told him that the baa-lambs first went into a pretty green plain, then they went through a swift stream. And he told him all – where he had been with them and so on. When he had finished his tale, the old man said: "My dear son, you see that wonderful pretty green plain where you went first with the baa-lambs represents your youth up to this day. The water through which you went is the water of life which washes away sin: that it washed away all your clothes and dried up your flesh means that it washes away all your previous sins: that on the other shore, upon the baa-lambs breathing on you, your body became purer, means that the holy faith, by the water of life, has penetrated all over your soul, and you have become purified from your sins, regenerate in all. The baa-lambs who breathed upon you are angels, and your good and pious teachers. The ill-fed cattle amidst the luxuriant grass means that the avaricious, whilst surrounded by plenty, even begrudge themselves food; they will be misers even in the other world: they will have plenty to eat and drink, they will partake of both, and still will be eternally hungry and thirsty. Those beasts who fed in the barren field, and were so fat, means that those who have given from their little to the poor in this world, and have not chastised their bodies with hunger and thirst, will feed heartily in the other world out of little food, and will never know hunger or thirst. That the young birds cried so mournfully in the woods, my son, means that those mothers in this world who do not have their children baptised, but have them buried without, will, in the other world, eternally weep and cry. The two dogs who fought so in the garden means that those relatives who in this world fight and squabble over property will eternally fight in the other world, and never come to terms. That woman who was fishing in a lake so busily for something with a spoon, and could not catch it, is he who in this world adulterates milk with water and sells it in this state to others; he will in the other world continually be in a lake, and will eternally fish about with a spoon, in order to fish the milk out of the water, and will never succeed. That you saw a pretty clear brook and did not drink of it, but went to the spring where the water flowed out of the mouth of a dead dog, that means, my dear son, the beautiful sermons of the clergy and their holy prayers. The dead dog from whose mouth the clear water flowed represents the priests who preach pious and wise lessons, but never keep them themselves. The garden into which you went is Heaven. Those who live without sin in this world will come into such a beautiful garden in the other world. But now, my dear son, can you show me some proof that you have really been in that garden?"

The lad quickly took from his bag the white pigeon's feather, and handed it to him, saying, "Look here, my old father, I shot this from a white pigeon there." The old man took the pigeon's feather, and said to him, "You see, my son, I was that white pigeon, and I have been following you all the journey through, and always kept watch over you, to see what you did. So God also follows man unknown to him, to see what he does. The feather you shot away was one of my fingers. Look here, I have not got it!" And as he looked he saw that the little finger was missing from the old man's hand. With this, the old man placed the feather there, blew upon it, and the finger was once more all right. In the meantime the year came to an end – for if I may mention it here the year consisted of but three days then – so the old man said to the lad: "Well, my son, the year is now ended; hand me over the bag, and then you can go. But first let me ask you would you rather have heaven, or so much gold as you can carry home?" To this the lad replied that he did not wish for gold, but only desired to be able to go to heaven. Thereupon the old man at once filled a sack with gold for him, lifted it upon the lad's back, and sent him home. The lad thanked the old man for his present, betook himself home with his sack of gold, and became such a rich farmer with six oxen that not in the whole village, nay, not even in the whole neighbourhood, was there such a one who came near him. He also took to himself a suitable girl as his wife, who was as pretty as a flower. He is alive to this very day, if he has not died since. May he be your guest tomorrow!

The Speaking Grapes, The Smiling Apple, and The Tinkling Apricot

THERE WAS ONCE, I don't know where, beyond seven times seven countries, a king who had three daughters. One day the king was going to the market, and thus inquired of his daughters: "What shall I bring you from the market, my dear daughters?" The eldest said, "A golden dress, my dear royal father." The second said, "A silver dress for me." The third said, "Speaking grapes, a smiling apple, and a tinkling apricot for me." "Very well, my daughters," said the king, and went. He bought the dresses for his two elder daughters in the market, as soon as he arrived; but, in spite of all exertions and inquiries, he could not find the speaking grapes, the smiling apple, and tinkling apricot. He was very sad that he could not get what his youngest daughter wished, for she was his favourite, and he went home.

It happened, however, that the royal carriage stuck fast on the way home, although his horses were of the best breed, for they were such high steppers that they kicked the stars. So he at once sent for extra horses to drag out the carriage, but all in vain, for the horses couldn't move either way. He gave up all hope, at last, of getting out of the position, when a dirty, filthy pig came that way, and grunted, "Grumph! grumph! grumph! King, give me your youngest daughter, and I will help you out of the mud." The king, never thinking what he was promising, and over-anxious to get away, consented, and the pig gave the carriage a push with its nose, so that carriage and horses at once moved out of the mud. Having arrived at home the king handed the dresses to his two daughters, and was now sadder than ever that he had brought nothing for his favourite daughter. The thought also troubled him that he had promised her to an unclean animal.

After a short time the pig arrived in the courtyard of the palace dragging a wheelbarrow after it, and grunted, "Grumph! grumph! grumph! King, I've come for your daughter." The king was terrified, and, in order to save his daughter, he had a peasant girl dressed in rich garments, embroidered with gold, sent her down and had her seated in the wheelbarrow. The pig again grunted, "Grumph! grumph! grumph! King, this is not your daughter." And, taking the barrow, it tipped her out. The king, seeing that deceit was of no avail, sent down his daughter, as promised, but dressed in ragged, dirty tatters, thinking that she would not please the pig; but the animal grunted in great joy, seized the girl, and placed her in the wheelbarrow. Her father wept that, through a careless promise, he had brought his favourite daughter to such a fate. The pig went on and on with the sobbing girl, till, after a long journey, it stopped before a dirty pigsty and grunted, "Grumph! grumph! grumph! Girl, get out of the wheelbarrow." The girl did as she was told. "Grumph! grumph! grumph!" grunted the pig again, "go into your new home." The girl, whose tears, now, were streaming like a brook, obeyed. The pig then offered her some Indian corn that it had in a trough, and also its litter which consisted of some old straw, for a resting place. The girl had not a wink of sleep for a long time, till at last, quite worn out with mental torture, she fell asleep.

Being completely exhausted with all her trials, she slept so soundly that she did not wake till next day at noon. On awaking, she looked round, and was very much astonished to find herself in a beautiful fairy-like palace, her bed being of white silk with rich purple curtains and golden fringes. At the first sign of her waking maids appeared all round her, awaiting her orders, and bringing her costly dresses. The girl, quite enchanted with the scene, dressed without a word, and the maids accompanied her to her breakfast in a splendid hall, where a young man received her with great affection. "I am your husband, if you accept me, and whatever you see here belongs to you," said he; and after breakfast led her into a beautiful garden. The girl did not know whether it was a dream she saw or reality, and answered all the questions put to her by the young man with evasive and chaffing replies. At this moment they came to that part of the garden which was laid out as an orchard, and the bunches of grapes began to speak: "Our beautiful queen, pluck some of us." The apples smiled at her continuously, and the apricots tinkled a beautiful silvery tune. "You see, my love," said the handsome youth, "here you have what you wished for – what your father could not obtain. You may know now, that once I was a monarch but I was bewitched into a pig, and I had to remain in that state till a girl wished for speaking grapes, a smiling apple, and a tinkling apricot. You are the girl, and I have been delivered; and if I please you, you can be mine for ever." The girl was enchanted with the handsome youth and the royal splendour, and consented. They went with great joy to carry the news to their father, and to tell him of their happiness.

Cinder Jack

A PEASANT HAD THREE SONS. One morning he sent out the eldest to guard the vineyard. The lad went, and was cheerfully eating a cake he had taken with him, when a frog crept up to him, and asked him to let it have some of his cake. "Anything else?" asked the lad angrily, and picked up a stone to drive the frog away. The frog left without a word, and the lad soon fell asleep, and, on awaking, found the whole vineyard laid waste. The next day the father sent his second son into the vineyard, but he fared like the first.

The father was very angry about it, and did not know what to do, whereupon his youngest son spoke up, who was always sitting in a corner amongst the ashes, and was not thought fit for anything, and whom for this reason they nicknamed Cinder Jack. "My father, send me out, and I will take care of the vineyard." His father and his brothers laughed at him, but they allowed him to have a trial, so Cinder Jack went to the vineyard, and, taking out his cake, began to eat it. The frog again appeared, and asked for a piece of cake, which was given to him at once. Having finished their breakfast, the frog gave the lad a copper, a silver, and a gold rod, and told him that three horses would appear shortly, of copper, silver, and gold, and they would try to trample down the vineyard, but, if he beat them with the rods he had given him they would at once become tame, and be his servants, and could at any time be summoned to carry out his orders. It happened as the frog foretold, and the vineyard produced a rich vintage. But Cinder Jack never told his master or his brothers how he had been able to preserve the vineyard; in fact, he concealed all, and again spent his time as usual, lying about in his favourite corner.

One Sunday the king had a high fir pole erected in front of the church, and a golden rosemary tied to the top, and promised his daughter to him who should be able to take it down in one jump on horseback. All the knights of the realm tried their fortune, but not one of them was able to jump high enough. But all of a sudden a knight clad in copper mail, on a copper horse, appeared with his visor down, and snatched the rosemary with an easy jump, and quickly disappeared. When his two brothers got home they told Cinder Jack what had happened, and he remarked, that he saw the whole proceeding much better, and on being asked "Where from?" his answer was, "From the top of the hoarding." His brothers had the hoarding pulled down at once, so that their younger brother might not look on any more. Next Sunday a still higher pole, with a golden apple at the top, was set up, and whosoever wished to marry the king's daughter had to take the apple down. Again, hundreds upon hundreds tried, but all in vain, till, at last, a knight in silver mail, on a silver horse, took it and disappeared. Cinder Jack again told his brothers that he saw the festivities much better than they did. He saw them, he said, from the pigsty; so this was pulled down also. The third Sunday a silk kerchief interwoven with gold was displayed at the top of a still higher fir pole, and, as nobody succeeded in getting it, a knight in gold mail, on a gold horse, appeared, snatched it down and galloped off. Cinder Jack again told his brothers that he saw all from the top of the house, and his envious brothers had the roof of the house taken off, so that the youngest brother might not look on again.

The king now had it announced that the knight who had shown himself worthy of his daughter should report himself, and should bring with him the gold rosemary, the apple, and the silk kerchief, but no one came. So the king ordered every man in the realm to appear before him, and still the knight in question could not be found, till, at last, he arrived clad in gold mail on a gold charger, whereupon the bells were at once rung, and hundreds and hundreds of cannons fired. The knight, having handed to the princess the golden rosemary, the apple, and the kerchief, respectfully demanded her hand, and, having obtained it, lifted his visor, and the populace, to their great astonishment, recognized Cinder Jack, whom they had even forgotten to ask to the king's presence. The good-hearted lad had his brothers' house rebuilt, and gave them presents as well. He took his father to his house, as the old king died soon after. Cinder Jack is reigning still, and is respected and honoured by all his subjects!

The Little Magic Pony

ONCE A POOR MAN HAD twelve sons, and, not having sufficient means to keep them at home, he sent them into the great world to earn their bread by work and to try their fortunes. The brothers wandered twelve days and nights over hills and dales till at last they came to a wealthy king, who engaged them as grooms, and promised them each three hundred florins a year for their wages. Among the king's horses there was a half-starved looking, decrepit little pony. The eleven eldest boys continually beat and ill-treated this animal on account of its ugliness, but the youngest always took great care of it, he even saved all the bread crumbs and other little dainties for his little invalid pony, for which his brothers very often chaffed him, and in course of time they treated him with silent contempt, believing him to be a lunatic. He bore their insults patiently, and their badgering without a murmur, in the same way as the little pony the bad treatment it received. The year of service having come to an end, the lads received their wages, and as a reward they were also each allowed to choose a horse from the king's stud. The eleven eldest chose the best-looking horses, but the youngest only begged leave to take the poor little decrepit pony with him. His brothers tried to persuade him to give up the foolish idea, but, all in vain: he would have no other horse.

The little pony now confessed to his keeper that it was a magic horse, and that whenever it wanted it could change into the finest charger and could gallop as fast as lightning. The twelve brothers then started homewards. The eleven eldest were proudly jumping and prancing about on their fine horses, whereas the youngest dragged his horse by its halter along the road: at one time they came to a boggy place and the poor little decrepit pony sank into it. The eleven brothers who had gone on before were very angry about it, as they were obliged to return and drag their brother's horse out of the mud. After a short journey the youngest's again stuck in the mud, and his brothers had to drag it out again, swearing at him all the time. When at last it stuck the third time they would not listen any more to their brother's cries for help. "Let them go," said the little pony, and after a short time inquired if they had gone far? "They have," answered the lad. Again, after a short time, the pony inquired whether he could still see them. "They look like flying crows or black spots in the distance," replied his master. "Can you see them now?" asked the pony in a few minutes. "No," was the reply; thereupon the pony jumped out of the mud and, taking the lad on its back, rushed forth like lightning, leaving the others far behind. Having arrived at home the pony became poor and decrepit as before, and crawled on to the dung heap, eating the straw it found there, the lad concealing himself behind the oven. The others having arrived showed their wages and horses to their father, and being asked about their brother they replied that he had become an idiot, and chosen as his reward an ugly pony, just such a one as the one on the dung heap, and that he stuck fast in a bog, and perhaps was now dead. "It is not true," called out the youngest from behind the oven, and stepped forth to the astonishment of all.

Having spent a few days in enjoying themselves at their father's house, the lads again started on a journey to find wives. They had already journeyed over seven countries and seven villages as well, and had not as yet been able to find twelve girls suitable for them, till at last, as the sun was setting, they came across an old woman with an iron nose, who was ploughing her field with twelve mares. She asked of them what they sought, and, having learned the object of their wanderings, she proposed that they should look at her twelve daughters. The lads having consented, the old woman drove her twelve mares home and took the lads into her house and introduced them to her daughters, who were none others than the twelve mares they saw before. In the evening she bade each lad go to bed with one of the girls. The eldest lad got into bed with the eldest girl and so on, her youngest, who was the favourite daughter and had golden hair, becoming the youngest lad's bedfellow.

This girl informed the lad that it was her mother's intention to kill his eleven brothers, and so, in order to save them, on their all falling asleep, the youngest lad got up and laid all his brothers next to the wall, making all the girls lie outside, and having done this, quietly crept back into his bed.

After a little while, the old woman with the iron nose got up and, with a huge sword, cut off the heads of the eleven sleepers who were lying outside, and then she went back to bed to sleep. Thereupon the youngest lad again got up, and, waking his brothers, told them how he had saved them, and urged them to flee as soon as possible. So they hurried off, their brother remaining there till daybreak. At dawn he noticed that the old woman was getting up, and that she was coming to examine the beds, so he, too, got up, and sat on his pony, taking the little girl with the golden hair with him. The old woman with the iron nose, as soon as she found out the fraud, picked up a poker, turned it into a horse, and flew after them. When she had nearly overtaken them, the little pony gave the lad a currycomb, a brush, and a piece of a horse rug, and bade him throw first the currycomb behind him, and in case it did not answer, to throw the brush, and as a last resource the piece of horse rug; the lad threw the currycomb, and in one moment it became a dense forest, with as many trees as there were teeth in the comb. By the time that the old woman had broken her way through the wood, the couple had travelled a long distance. When the old woman came very near again, the lad threw the brush behind him, and it at once became a dense forest, having as many trees as there were bristles in the brush. The old woman had the greatest difficulty in working her way through the wood, but again she drew close to their heels, and very nearly caught them, when the lad threw the horse rug away, and it became such a dense forest between them and the old woman, that it looked like one immense tree. With all her perseverance, the old woman could not penetrate this wood, so she changed into a pigeon to enable her to fly over it, but as soon as the pony noticed this he turned into a vulture, swooped down on the pigeon, and tore it in pieces with his claws, thus saving both the lad and the pretty girl with the golden hair from the fury of the hateful old woman with the iron nose.

While the eleven elder brothers were still out looking after wives, the youngest married the pretty little girl with the golden hair, and they still live merrily together, out of all danger, if they have not died since.

The King and The Devil

IN THE COUNTRY WHERE lions and bearded wolves live there was a king whose favourite sport was hunting and shooting. He had some hundred hounds or more, quite a house full of guns, and a great

many huntsmen. The king had a steady hand, a sharp eye, and the quarry he aimed at never escaped, for the king never missed what he aimed at. His only peculiarity was that he did not care to go out shooting with his own people only, but he would have liked the whole world to witness his skill in killing game, and that every good man in the world should partake of it. Well then, whenever he made a good bag the cook and the cellarer had so much work to do that they were not done till dawn. Such was the king who reigned in the land where lions and bearded wolves live.

Once upon a time this king, according to custom, invited the sovereigns of the neighbouring lands to a great shooting party, and also their chief men. It was in the height of summer, just at the beginning of the dog days. In the early morning, when they were driving out on to the pasture the sheep with the silken fleece, the dogs could already be heard yelping, huntsmen blowing with all their might into the thin end of their horns, and all was noise and bustle, so that the royal courtyard rang out with the noise. Then the king swallowed his breakfast in a soldier-like fashion, and all put on their hunting hats adorned with eagle's feathers, buckled the shining straps under their chins, mounted their horses, and in a short time were off over hedges and ditches, plunging into the vast forest, as the heat was too great for them to hunt in the open country. Each king accompanied by his own men went in his own direction, and game was killed with lightning speed; but the king who owned the forest went by himself in order to show his friends how much game he could kill single handed. But by some strange chance – who can tell how? – no game crossed the king's track. He went hither and thither but found nothing; looking round he discovered that he had got into a part of the wood where not even his grandfather had ever been. He went forward but still was lost; sideways, but still did not know the way; to the right, and found that he was in the same predicament as the man in Telek, namely, that unless he was taken home he would never find it. He called upon God for help, but as he never did that before – for the king didn't like to go to church and never invited the priest, except upon All Souls' Day, to dinner – the Lord would not help him. So he called upon the Devil, who appeared at once, as he will appear anywhere, even where he is not wanted. "You need not tell me what you are doing here, good king," said the evil spirit, "I know that you have been out shooting and have found no game and that you have lost your way. Promise me that you will give me what you have not got in your house and you shall find plenty of game and I will take you home." "You ask very little, poor soul," said the king. "Your request shall be granted. Moreover, I will give you something of what I have, whatever you may wish, if you will but take me home."

Shortly afterwards the king arrived at home, and had so much game with him that his horse could scarcely stand beneath the weight; the other kings were quite impatient with waiting for him, and were highly delighted when he arrived. At last they sat down to supper and ate and drank heartily, but the devil ate nothing but the scrapings from the pots and pans, and drank no wine but the dregs that were left in the bottles. At midnight an old woman appeared before the company of jolly kings and shouted as loud as she could in delight because a beautiful little daughter had been born to the king. The devil jumped up and capered about in his joy: standing on his toes and clapping his bony heels together, he spun the king round like a whirlwind and shouted in his ear, "That girl, king, was not in your house today and I will come for her in ten years." The devil hereupon saddled midnight and darted off like lightning, while the guests stared at each other in amazement, and the king's face turned ghastly pale.

Next morning they counted the heads of game and found that the king had twice as much as all the rest put together: yet he was very sad. He made presents to all his guests, and gave them an escort of soldiers as far as the boundary of his realm.

Ten years passed as swiftly as the bird flies and the devil appeared punctually to the minute. The king tried to put him off, and walked up and down his room greatly agitated; he thought first of one thing and then of another. At last he had the swineherd's daughter dressed up like a princess, and placed her on his wife's arm, and then took her to the devil, both parents weeping most bitterly, and then handed the child over to the black soul. The devil carried her away in high glee, but when the pretty little creature was passing a herd of swine she said, "Well, little sucking pigs, my father won't beat me any more on your account, for I'm leaving you and going to the 77th country, where the angels live." The devil listened to the little girl's words and at last discovered that he had been deceived. In a rage he flew back to the royal fortress, and dashed the poor child with such force against the gate-post that her smallest bone was smashed into a thousand atoms. He roared at the king in such a voice that all the window fittings dropped out and the plaster fell off the walls in great lumps. "Give me your own daughter," he screamed, "for whatever you promise to the devil you must give to him or else he will carry off what you have not promised." The king again tried to collect his wits and had the shepherd's daughter who tended the sheep with the golden fleece, and who was ten years old, dressed in the royal fashion and handed her to the devil amidst great lamentation. He even placed at the devil's disposal a closed carriage, "so that the sun might not tan his daughter's face or the wind blow upon her," as he said, but it was really to prevent the little girl seeing what was passing and so betraying herself. As the carriage passed by the silken meadow and the little girl heard the baaing of the lambs she opened the door and called to the little animals, saying, "Well, little baa-lambs, my father won't beat me any more on your account, and I won't run after you in the heat now, because the king is sending me to the 77th country, where the angels live." The devil was now in a towering passion, and the flame shot out of his nostrils as thick as my arm. He threw the little girl up into the clouds and returned to the royal palace.

The king saw the carriage returning and trembled like an aspen leaf. He dressed up his daughter, weeping bitterly as he did so, and when the devil stepped across the threshold of the palace he went to meet him with the beautiful child, the like of which no other mother ever bore. The devil, in a great rage, pushed the pretty lily into a slit of his shirt, and ran with her over hill and dale. Like a thunderstorm he carried off the little trembling Maria into his dark home, which was lighted up with burning sulphur, and placed her on a pillow stuffed with owl's feathers. He then set a black table before her, and on it mixed two bushels of millet seed with three bushels of ashes, saying, "Now, you little wretch, if you don't clean this millet in two hours, I will kill you with the most horrible tortures." With this he left her, and slammed the door that it shock the whole house. Little innocent Maria wept bitterly, for she knew she could not possibly finish the work in the stated time. While she wept in her loneliness, the devil's son very quietly entered the room. He was a fine handsome lad, and they called him Johnnie. Johnnie's heart was full of pity at seeing the little girl's sorrow, and cheered her up, telling her that if she ceased crying he would do the work for her at once. He felt in his pocket, and took out a whistle; and, going into a side room, he blew it, and in a moment the whole place was filled with devils, whom Johnnie commanded to clean the millet in the twinkling of an eye. By the time little Maria winked three times, the millet was not only cleansed, but every seed was polished and glittered like diamonds. Until the father's return Maria and Johnnie amused themselves in childish games. The old devil upon his return, seeing all the work done, shook his head so vehemently that burning cinders dropped from his hair. He gave the little girl some manna to eat and lay down to sleep.

Next day the ugly old devil mixed twice as much millet and ashes, as he was very anxious to avenge himself on the child whose father had taken him in twice. But, by the help of Johnnie's servants, the millet was again cleaned. The devil in his rage gnawed off the end of his beard and spat it out on the ground, where every hair became a venomous serpent. The little girl screamed, and at the sound of her voice all the serpents stretched themselves on the ground, and wriggled about before the little girl like young eels, for they were charmed, never having heard so sweet a voice before. The devil was very much enraged that all the animals and the devils themselves, with the exception of himself, were so fond of this pretty little girl. "Well, soul of a dog, you little imp," said the devil, gnashing his teeth, "if by tomorrow morning you do not build from nothing, under my window, a church, the ceiling of which will be the sky, and the priest in it the Lord Himself, whom your father does not fear, I will slay you with tortures the like of which are not known even in nethermost hell."

Little Maria was terribly frightened. The old devil, having given his orders, disappeared amidst thunder. The kind-hearted Johnnie here appeared, blew his whistle, and the devils came. They listened to the orders, but replied, that no devil could build a church out of nothing, and that, moreover, they dare not go up to heaven and had no power over the Lord to make him become a priest; that the only advice they could give was, for Johnnie and the little girl to set off at once, before it was too late, and so escape the tortures threatened by the old devil. They listened to the advice of the devils, and Johnnie buried his whistle in a place where his father would not be able to find it, and send the devils after them. They hurried off towards Maria's father's land; when, all of a sudden, Maria felt her left cheek burning very much, and complained of it to Johnnie, who, looking back, found that his mother was galloping after them on the stick of a whitewashing brush. Johnnie at once saw their position, and told Maria to turn herself into a millet field, and he would be the man whose duty it was to scare away the birds. Maria did so at once, and Johnnie kept the sparrows off with a rattle. The old woman soon came up, and asked whether he had not seen a boy and girl running past, a few minutes before. "Well, yes," replied he, "there are a great many sparrows about, my good lady, and I can't guard my millet crop from them. Hush! Hush!" "I didn't ask you," replied she, "whether you had any sparrows on your millet field or not, but whether you saw a boy and girl running past." "I've already broken the wings of two cock sparrows, and hanged them to frighten away the rest," replied the artful boy.

"The fellow's deaf, and crazy too," said the devil's wife, and hurried back to the infernal regions. The boy and girl at once retransformed themselves, and hurried on, when Maria's left cheek began to burn again, more painfully this time than before; and not without reason, for when Johnnie looked back this time, he saw his father, who had saddled the south wind, tearing after them, and great, awe-inspiring, rain-bearing clouds following in his track. Maria at once turned into a tumbledown church, and Johnnie into an aged monk, holding an old clasp Bible in his hand.

"I say, old fool, have you not seen a young fellow and a little wench run past? If you have, say so; if you have not, may you be struck dumb!" yelled the old devil to the monk with the Bible. "Come in," said the pious monk, "come in, into the house of the Lord. If you are a good soul pray to Him and He will help you on your journey, and you will find what you are so anxiously looking for. Put your alms into this bag, for our Lord is pleased with the offerings of the pure in heart." "Perish you, your church, and your book, you old fool. I'm not going to waste any money in such tomfoolery. Answer my question! Have you seen a boy and girl go past?" again inquired the devil, in a fearful rage. "Come back to your Lord, you old cursed soul," replied the holy father, "it's never too late to mend, but it's a sin to put off amending your ways. Offer your alms, and you will find what you seek!" The devil grew purple with rage; and, lifting up his huge mace, he struck like lightning at the monk's head, but the weapon slipped aside and hit the devil on the shin such a blow that made him and all his family limp. They would limp to this very day, if they had not perished since! Jumping on the wind with his lame leg, the devil rode back home. The young couple by this time had nearly reached the land where Maria's father reigned, when, all of a sudden, both the girl's cheeks began to burn as they had never burnt before. Johnnie looked back and saw that both his father and his mother were riding after them on two dragons, who flew faster than even the whirlwind. Maria at once became a silver lake and Johnnie a silver duck. As soon as the two devils arrived they at once scented out that the lake was the girl and the duck the boy, because wherever there are two devils together nothing can be concealed. The woman began to scoop up the water of the lake, and the male devil to throw stones at the duck; but each scoop of water taken out of the lake only caused the water to rise higher and higher, and every stone missed the duck, as he dived to the bottom of the lake and so dodged them. The devil became quite exhausted with throwing stones, and beckoned to his wife to wade with him into the lake, and so catch the duck, as it would be a great pity for their son to be restored to earth. The devils swam in, but the water of the lake rose over their heads so quickly that they were both drowned before they could swim out, and that's the reason why there are no devils now left. The boy and the girl, after all their trials, at last reached the palace of Maria's parents. The girl told them what had happened to her since the devil carried her off, and praised Johnnie very highly, telling them how he had guarded her. She also warned her father, that he who does not love God must perish, and is not worthy of happiness. The king listened to his daughter's advice, and sent for a priest to the next village, and first of all married Maria to the son of the devil, and the young couple lived very happily ever after. The king gave up hunting, and sent messages to the neighbouring kings that he was a happy father, and the poor found protection and justice in his land. The king and his wife both died at the same time, and, after that, Johnnie and his wife became rulers of the land inhabited by lions and bearded wolves.

The Two Orphans

THERE WAS ONCE, I know not where, even beyond the Operencian Land, a village, and at the end of the village a little hovel. Within the tumbledown walls of this hovel a poor old woman was lying on some rotting straw, and two children were crying by her side. The elder was a pretty girl. The younger was her brother, a small boy with auburn hair. The old mother died. Her cold body was buried by the parish, but, as none offered themselves to take charge of the two orphans, they left the place.

They went and went, over many a hill and dale, and had already covered a long distance when Jack felt burning thirst. They found in the road some turbid water in a rut, at the sight of which the thirsty little fellow shouted for joy. "My dear sister, I will drink from this rut." "Don't drink from it," said his thoughtful sister, "or you will turn into a cartwheel if you do." Jack sighed, and they went on their way. They found some bears' tracks in which some stale rainwater was putrifying. "My dear sister, I'm thirsty, allow me to drink of this rainwater." "If you drink, my dear brother, you will become a bear." The little fellow began to cry, but obeyed, and they went on. In the road they found some footprints of a wolf. Jack again implored his sister, with tears, and repeated his former request. "Don't drink, my dear Jack, or else you will become a wolf." Jack, although his tongue was parched with burning thirst, obeyed, and they continued their walk quite exhausted. They found the footmarks of a roebuck in the road. Water clear as crystal shone in them, that invited him to drink. Jack's feet gave way under him when he reached the water, and, in spite of all warning, he drank of it with avidity. His sister, seeing her fear realized, began to cry. The beautiful auburn locks of her brother suddenly turned to a soft greyish hair, and horns grew behind his ears. His legs and arms became the four legs of a roe deer, and the pretty little creature rubbed gently against his sister, who stroked him with her pretty hands. The little girl and her brother, the roebuck, continued their journey till at last they reached the king's palace, where the young monarch received them with smiles, and offered them a tidy little room. The little girl lived with her brother here, and, although she forbade him to speak before others, they would chat when left alone, their conversation turning mainly upon their deceased good mother, their journey, the handsome young king, and his frequent hunts. After several weeks the pretty girl received a royal splendid dress and was married to the young king.

The fame of their wedding travelled over seven countries. The loving couple lived contentedly together; the queen was pretty and good, and her husband was madly in love with her. The little deer kept continually by his sister's side: they ate from the same plate, and drank out of the same glass, and slept in the same room. But this happiness did not last long. There lived in the king's country an old witch, with iron teeth, who had a very ugly daughter, whose face was black, her eyes were yellow, her nose was full of warts, her teeth like hoes, her voice screeching, her waist crooked; and, besides all this, she was lame of one foot. It was the old witch's determination to make this creature the queen of the realm. As she was frustrated in her design she raved. In her fury she tore up bits of rocks, and dried up whole forests. She vowed death upon the poor orphan's head. And, in order to cheer up her ugly daughter's long forlorn hope, she prophesied the queen's death, and thus spoke: "Dear child, beloved Lucinda, would you like to be a queen? If so, go secretly into the king's palace, and when the king is out hunting, steal near the queen in her sleep, and cut off a large lock of her hair, and bring it to me. Mind where you step, and keep an eye on every movement of hers." Lucinda dressed herself in a cloak with grey and red stripes, and at dead of night she reached the king's palace, and without arousing suspicion stole into the queen's bedroom. She spread her cloak on the floor, so that she might not awake the sleeping queen with its rustling as she moved about, and at her mother's sign she approached the queen's bed on tiptoe, and cut off a beautiful lock with a rusty old knife; the little deer did not wake. In the morning, the witch wrapt the beautiful auburn lock in the lungs of a toad, and roasted it over the embers of some yew boughs which were cut on Christmas night. After a while, with the ointment thus made, the old witch rubbed Lucinda from head to foot, who became the next moment an exact likeness of the young queen. Now the old witch began to ponder how to do away with the young queen, and at last she hit upon a plan. There lived at court a miserly gatekeeper, whom she bribed with gold, and with his assistance, in the absence of the king, they broke into the queen's bedroom at night, and dragged away by force the poor innocent woman. The little deer woke at the noise, and followed the murderers at a distance.

In a secluded corner of the courtyard there was an old disused stone well, and in this well lived a huge whale. They threw the pretty queen to the bottom of this well, and in her now empty bed Lucinda was placed, whose outer appearance was not in the slightest different from that of the queen, so that when the king arrived at home he did not notice the awful fraud. The little deer henceforward spent all his days near the well, which circumstance did not escape the notice of the quick-eyed old witch. So she instructed her daughter to persuade her royal husband to have the deer killed, and in order to carry this out, she planned the following scheme. Lucinda shammed deadly illness, her mother having previously changed her red complexion to yellow; her husband sat every day and night by her bedside, while the little deer still spent all his time by the well. They could not find any medicine which could give the patient relief, when Lucinda, as planned beforehand, expressed a desire to have the deer's heart and liver cooked for her. Her husband was horrified on hearing this unexpected wish, and began to suspect his wife. He could not believe that she could wish to have her dear little animal, which she idolized, killed. But Lucinda would not give in, until at last the king, being very much concerned about his wife's recovery, allowed himself to be persuaded, and gave orders to one of his cooks to have the deer killed. The deer heard quite well what Lucinda wished and what the orders were, but kept silence, and, in order not to arouse suspicion, went back to its favourite place, the well, where, in its deep grief, it thus spoke down into the whale's dwelling:

> *My little sister, my little sister,*
> *You dear little sister,*
> *Come out of the well,*
> *Out of the whale's stomach,*
> *Because they are whetting the knife*
> *For my gentle breast,*
> *They are washing the basin*
> *For my beautiful red blood.*

When the cook, clasping a long knife, stole up to the little animal in order to drag it to the slaughterhouse, the deer repeated his mournful song, upon hearing which the cook got frightened and ran away and informed the king of what he had heard and seen. Thereupon the king determined to personally satisfy himself as to whether his tale was true. The little deer thereupon cried twice as mournfully as before, and amid tears sang out the same song as before.

The king now stepped forward from his hiding place, and the deer, upon being questioned, told him the story how the witch and the gatekeeper dragged his sister out of bed, and how they threw her into the well. As soon as the pretty animal finished its tale, the huge whale was dragged out from the bottom of the well. They slit open its stomach, and the real queen appeared, now seven times prettier than before; her husband himself assisted her and conducted her back to the palace in triumph.

Lucinda, her mother, and the gatekeeper were quartered, and their bodies exhibited at the four corners of the castle as a warning to everybody. The queen anointed her little brother with some ointment she had found in the whale's stomach, and he regained his old form. And so all three of them are alive to this very date, if they have not died since. May they get into an eggshell and be your guests tomorrow.

The Wonderful Frog

THERE WAS ONCE, I don't know where, a man who had three daughters. One day the father thus spoke to the eldest girl: "Go, my daughter, and fetch me some fresh water from the well." The girl went, but when she came to the well a huge frog called out to her from the bottom, that he would not allow her to draw water in her jug until she threw him down the gold ring on her finger. "Nothing else? Is that all you want?" replied the girl, "I won't give away my rings to such an ugly creature as you," and she returned as she came with the empty pitchers. So the father sent the second girl, and she fared as the first: the frog would not let her have any water, as she refused to throw down her gold ring. Her father gave his two elder daughters a good scolding, and then thus addressed the youngest: "You go, Betsie, my dear, you have always been a clever girl. I'm sure you will be able to get some water, and will not allow your father to suffer thirst. Go, shame your sisters!" Betsie picked up the pitchers and went, but the frog again refused the water unless she threw her ring down, but she, as she was very fond of her father, threw the ring in as demanded, and returned home with full pitchers to her father's great delight.

In the evening, as soon as darkness set in, the frog crawled out of the well, and thus commenced to shout in front of Betsie's father's door: "Father-in-law! Father-in-law! I should like something to eat." The man got angry, and called out to his daughters; "Give something in a broken plate to that ugly frog to gnaw." "Father-in-law! Father-in-law! This won't do for me, I want some roast meat on a tin plate," retorted the frog. "Give him something on a tin plate then, or else he will cast a spell on us," said the father. The frog began to eat heartily, and, having had enough, again commenced to croak: "Father-in-law! Father-in-law! I want something to drink." "Give him some slops in a broken pot," said the father. "Father-in-law! Father-in-law! I won't have this. I want some wine in a nice tumbler." "Give him some wine then," angrily called out the father. He guzzled up his wine and began again: "Father-in-law! Father-in-law! I would like to go to sleep." "Throw him some rags in a corner," was the reply. "Father-in-law! Father-in-law! I won't have that; I want a silk bed," croaked the frog. This was also given to him; but no sooner has he gone to bed than again he began to croak, "Father-in-law! Father-in-law! I want a girl, indeed." "Go, my daughter, and lie by the side of him," said the father to the eldest. "Father-in-law! father-in law! I don't want that, I want another." The father sent the second girl, but the frog again croaked: "Father-in-law! Father-in-law! I don't want that, Betsie is the girl I want." "Go, my Betsie," said the father, quite disheartened, "else this confounded monster will cast a spell on us." So Betsie went to bed with the frog, but her father thoughtfully left a lamp burning on the top of the oven; noticing which, the frog crawled out of bed and blew the lamp out.

The father lit it again, but the frog put it out as before, and so it happened a third time. The father saw that the frog would not yield, and was therefore obliged to leave his dear little Betsie in the dark by the side of the ugly frog, and felt great anxiety about her. In the morning, when the father and the two elder girls got up, they opened their eyes and mouths wide in astonishment, because the frog had disappeared, and by the side of Betsie they found a handsome Magyar lad, with auburn locks, in a beautiful costume, with gold braid and buttons and gold spurs on his boots. The handsome lad asked for Betsie's hand, and, having received the father's consent, they hastened to celebrate the wedding, so that christening might not follow the wedding too soon.

The two elder sisters looked with envious eyes on Betsie, as they also were very much smitten with the handsome lad. Betsie was very happy after, so happy that if anyone doubt it he can satisfy himself with his own eyes. If she is still alive, let him go and look for her, and try to find her in this big world.

The Girl with The Golden Hair

THERE WAS ONCE, I do not know where, in the world an old man who had twelve sons, the eldest of whom served the king for twenty-four years. One day the old man took it into his head that all his sons should get married, and they all were willing to comply with their father's wish, with the exception of the eldest son, who could not on any account be coaxed into matrimony. However the old man would not give in, and said, "Do you hear me, my son? The eldest of you must marry at the same time as the youngest. I want you all to get married at the same time."

So the old man had a pair of boots made for himself with iron soles and went in search of wives for his twelve sons. He wandered hither and thither over several countries until the iron soles of his boots were worn into holes. At last, however, he found at a house twelve girls, who, he thought, would do.

The eleven younger lads made great preparations and went to the fair to buy themselves saddle horses; but the eldest, who was serving the king, did not concern himself about anything, and turned out the king's horses to grass as usual. Among the animals there was a mare with a foal, and Jack – this was the name of the eldest lad – always bestowed the greatest care upon the mare. One day, as the whole stud were grazing in the fields, the mare neighed and said to the lad, "I say, Jack, I hear that you are thinking of getting married; your eleven brothers have already gone to the fair to purchase riding horses for the wedding; they are buying the finest animals they can get, but don't you go and purchase anything: there is a foal of mine that was foaled last year, go and beg the king to let you have it, you will have no cause to repent your choice. The king will try to palm off some other animal on you, but don't you take it. Choose the foal as I tell you."

So it happened Jack went upstairs and saw the king and spoke to him thus: "Most gracious Majesty! I have now served you for twenty-four years and should like to leave this place, because my eleven brothers are already on their way to get themselves wives. The tips of my moustache too reach already to my ears, the days fly fast, and it is high time for me to find a wife too. I should be much obliged if you would pay me my wages." "You are perfectly right, my dear son, Jack," replied the king, "it is high time that you too get married, and, as you have so faithfully served me, I will give orders for your wedding to be celebrated with the greatest pomp. Let me know your wishes! Would you like to have so much silver as you can carry, or would you prefer as much gold?" "Most gracious Majesty, I have only one desire, and that is to be allowed to take with me from your stud a certain foal that belongs to a certain mare that is with foal again this year." "Surely you don't want to make an exhibition of yourself on that wretched creature?" "Aye, but I do, Your Majesty, and I do not want anything else."

Our Jack was still fast asleep when his eleven brothers set out on the finest horses to fetch their girls. Jack did not get up till noon, at which hour the king ordered out a coach and six, together with a couple of outriders, and thus addressed the lad: "Well, Jack, my boy, I have no objection, you can take your foal, but don't reproach me hereafter." Jack thereupon had plenty to eat and drink, and even took out a bucketful of wine to his foal and made it drink the whole. He then took his goods and chattels and sat in the coach, but the king would not allow the foal to run along with the coach, and said, "Not that way, if I know it; put the ugly creature up on the box! I should feel ashamed if anybody saw the ugly brute running alongside my coach." So the foal was tied up to the box, and they set off till they reached the outskirts of the town. By this time the foal, which was in a most uncomfortable position, presented a most pitiful sight, for by rubbing against the box the whole of one of its sides had become raw. So they stopped, and it was taken down and placed on the ground. Jack got out, and, the coach having set out for home, he sat on the foal's back, his feet touching the ground. The foal gazed round to see whether anybody was looking on, and, not seeing a soul, it flew up high into the air and thus addressed the lad: "Well, my dear master, at what speed shall we proceed? Shall we go like the hurricane or like a flash of thought?" "As quick as you can, my dear horse," was his reply.

They flew along for a while, when the foal again spoke, asking: "Is your hat tied on, my dear master?"

"Yes, it is, my dear horse."

Again they flew along, and again the little foal said, "Well, my dear master, your hat that you have bought for your wedding is gone. You have lost it. We have left it some seven miles behind, but we will go back to fetch it; nobody has as yet picked it up." So they returned and picked up the hat, and the little foal again flew high up into the air. After proceeding for three hours they reached the inn where his brothers had decided to take up their night's lodgings. The other lads had started at dawn, he not till noon, after his midday meal, and still he left them behind. Having got within a short distance of the inn, the foal alighted on the ground with Jack, and addressed him in these words: "Well, my dear master, get off here and turn me out on to that heap of rubbish and weeds yonder, then walk into the inn and have plenty to eat and drink; your eleven younger brothers will also arrive here shortly." So Jack entered the inn, ordered a bottle of wine, made a hearty meal, and enjoyed himself heartily. He took out a bucketful of wine to his foal and gave it to drink. Time passed on… when, at last his brothers arrived. They were still at some distance when the youngest caught sight of the foal, and exclaimed: "Oh, look at that miserable screw! Surely it is our eldest brother's steed." "So it is! So it is!" exclaimed all the others, but at the same time they all stared at each other, and could not explain how it came to pass that, although they had started much earlier than their brother, they had been outdistanced by him, notwithstanding the fact that his animal could not be compared with their own horses. The brothers put their steeds into the stables and placed plenty of hay and corn before them, then they walked into the taproom and found Jack already enjoying himself.

"So you have got here, brother," they remarked. "As you behold, youngsters, though I had not left home when the clock struck twelve." "Certainly it is a mystery how you have got here on that thoroughbred of yours, a wolf could swallow the creature at a bite."

They sat down and ate and drank. So soon as it became dark, the lads went out to look after the horses.

"Well then, where will you put your horse overnight?" they inquired of the eldest.

"I will put it into the same stables with yours."

"You don't mean that, it will barely reach to the bellies of our horses, the stables are too big for that steed of yours."

But Jack took his foal into the stables and threw his cloak over its back. In the meantime his brothers had returned to the taproom and were holding council as to what was to be done with their eldest brother.

"What shall we do with him? What indeed? What can we do under the circumstances but kill him? It will never do to take him with us to the girls, they will laugh at us and drive us off in disgrace."

At this the foal began to speak, and said: "I say, dear master, tie me near the wall, your brothers will come to kill you, but don't do anything in the matter, leave it to me. Join them, eat and drink, and then come back and lie down at my feet, I will do the rest."

Jack did as he was told. Upon leaving the taproom he returned to the stables and lay down at the feet of his foal, and as the wine had made him a bit drowsy he soon fell asleep. Ere long his brothers arrived with their hatchet sticks which they had purchased for the wedding.

"Gee up, you jackass," they shouted, and all eleven were about to attack the poor little foal, when it kicked out with such force that it sent the youngest flying against the wall.

"Get up, dear master, they have come." Jack thereupon woke, and his little foal asked him, "What shall I do with them?"

"Oh! Knock them all against the wall."

The foal did as it was told, and the lads dropped about like crabapples. It collected them all into a heap, when Jack, seeing their condition, became frightened, so he hurriedly picked up a bucket, ran to the well, fetched some water and poured it over the eleven. They managed, with some difficulty, to get on to their feet and then showered reproaches upon him, complaining bitterly about his unbrotherly conduct in ordering his foal to handle them so roughly as it had done.

The eleven then left the inn without a moment's delay, and toiled along the whole night and the next day, until at last, on the following evening, they reached the home of the twelve girls. But to get in was not such an easy task, for the place was fenced round with strong iron rails, the gate was also very strong and made of iron, and the latch was so heavy that it took more than six powerful men to lift it. The eleven brothers made their horses prance about and bade them to kick against the latch, but all their manoeuvres were of no avail – they could not move the latch.

But what has become of Jack? Where did he tarry? His foal knew only too well where the girls could be found, and how they could be got at, so he did not budge from the inn until late in the afternoon, and spent his time eating and drinking. His brothers were still busily engaged with the latch, hammering at it and kicking, when at last, just when the people were lighting the candles at dusk, the brothers discovered Jack approaching high up in the air on his foal. As soon as he reached the gate he wheeled round, and the foal gave a tremendous kick at the latch, whereupon the gate, and with it a portion of the railing, heeled over into the dust. The landlady, a diabolical old witch, then came running to the gate with a lamp in her hand, and said: "I knew, Jack, that you had arrived, and I have come and opened the gate." This statement was of course not true.

The lads entered the house, where they found the twelve girls all standing in a row. With regard to the age of the maidens they corresponded to those of the lads, and when it came to choice, the eldest lad fell in love with the eldest girl, the youngest lad with the youngest maid, and so on, every lad with the girl of his own age. They sat down to supper, each girl by the side of her beau; they ate and drank, enjoyed themselves, and the kissing had no end. At last they exchanged handkerchiefs. As it was getting late, and the young folks became sleepy, they all retired to rest. Beds were prepared for all twenty-four in a huge room; on one side stood the beds for the girls, on the other those for the lads. Just then the mischievous old witch, who was the girls' mother, walked out of the house, and muttered to herself:

"Now I have got you all in my net, you wretched crew, we shall see which of you will leave this place alive!"

It so happened that Jack went out to look after his foal. He took a bucketful of wine with him and gave his animal a drink, whereupon the foal spoke to him thus:

"I say, dear master! We have come to an awful place; that old witch intends to kill you all. At the same time don't be frightened, but do what I am about to tell you. After everybody has gone to bed, come out again and lead us horses out from these stables, and tie twelve horses belonging to the old witch in our places. With regard to yourselves, place your hats on to the girls' heads, and the old witch will mistake the maids, and slay them in your stead. I will send such a deep slumber over them that even a noise seven times as loud as you will make cannot wake them."

In conformity with the advice thus received, Jack re-entered the bedchamber, placed the twelve men's hats on to the heads of the girls; he then exchanged the horses, and went back to bed. Soon after the old witch commenced to whet a huge knife, which sent forth a shower of vivid sparks. She then approached the beds, groped about, and as soon as she discovered a hat, snap! off went a head, and so she went on until she had cut off all the girls' heads. Then she left the house, fetched a broad axe, sharpened it and went into the stables. Snap! off came the head of the first horse, then the next, till she had killed all twelve.

The foal then stamped upon the ground, whereupon Jack went out, and was thus spoken to by his foal:

"Now then, dear master! Rouse up all your brothers, and tell them to saddle their horses! And let them get away from this place without a moment's delay. Don't let dawn overtake them here, or they are lost. You yourself can go back and finish your sleep."

Jack rushed in and with great difficulty roused them, and then informed them of the dangerous position they were in. After a great deal of trouble, they got up and left the place. Jack himself laid down and had a sound sleep. As soon as the first streaks of dawn appeared, the foal again stamped. Jack went out, sat upon it, and as they flew through the gate the foal gave the railing such a powerful kick that even the house tottered and fell. The old witch hereupon jumped up in great hurry, sat straddling an iron pole, and rode in pursuit of Jack.

"Stop Jack, you deceitful lad!" she shouted; "you have killed my twelve daughters, and destroyed my twelve horses. I am not sure whether you will be able to come again hither or not!"

"If I do, I shall be here; if not, then I shan't."

Poor Jack got weary of his life, not having been able to get himself a wife. He did not return to his native town, but went into the wide, wide world. As he and his foal were proceeding on their journey, the steed said to him: "Look, dear master! I have stepped on a hair of real gold; it is here under my hoof. It would bring ill luck if we picked it up, but it would equally be unlucky to leave it, so you had better take it with you." Jack picked up the golden hair, and re-mounted his foal, and continued his journey. After a while the foal again spoke, saying: "My dear master! Now I have stepped on a half horseshoe of pure gold; it is here under my hoof. It would be unlucky to take it with us, but we should not fare better if we left it, so you had better take it." Jack picked up the half horseshoe of pure gold, put it into his bag, and they again flew like lightning. They reached a town just as the evening bell rang, and stopped in front of an hostelry; Jack got off, walked in and asked the innkeeper:

"Well, my dear host, what is the news in this town?"

"Nothing else, my kinsman, but that the king's coachman, who drove his state coach, is lying on his deathbed; if you care for the situation, you had better take it."

So Jack at once made up his mind, and went to see the king – who was then still a bachelor – and was at once engaged by him to drive the state coach. He did not ask for any wages, but only stipulated that his foal should be allowed to feed with the coach horses from the same manger. To this the king agreed, and Jack at once proceeded to the stables. In the evening the other grooms (there were some fifty or sixty of them) raised a great cry, and all asked for candles from the woman who served out the stores. But Jack did not want any, so he did not ask for any, and still his horses were in better condition, and were better groomed than the rest. All the other grooms used a whole candle a head every night. This set the storekeeper woman thinking: she could not imagine how it could be that, whereas all the other men wanted a whole candle a head every blessed night, the man who drove the state coach did not want any, and still his horses looked a hundred times better than the others. She told the strange discovery to the king, who immediately sent for all the men with the exception of Jack.

"Well, my sons, tell me this: How is it that every one of you burns a whole candle every night, whereas my state-coachman has never asked for any, and still his horses look seven times better than yours?"

"Oh, your majesty, he has no need to ask for any; we could do without them, if we were in his position."

"How is that, explain yourselves."

"Because, sir, he does his work one morning by the light of a golden hair, and every other morning by the rays of half a horseshoe of pure gold."

The king dismissed the grooms, and the next day at dawn concealed himself, and watched Jack, and satisfied himself with his own eyes that his men had spoken the truth. So soon as he got back into his rooms, he sent for Jack, and addressed him thus:

"I say, my boy, you were working this morning by the light of a hair of real gold."

"That is not true, your majesty; where on earth could I get a hair of real gold?"

"Don't let us waste any words! I saw it with my own eyes this morning. If the girl to whom that golden hair belonged is not here by tomorrow morning you forfeit your life! I'll hang you!"

Poor Jack returned to the stables and wept like a child. "What is the matter?" inquired his foal. "Why do I see those tears? What makes you cry?"

"How could I help crying and weeping? The king has just sent for me and told me that if I can't produce the girl to whom the golden hair belonged he will hang me."

"This is indeed a very serious look-out, my dear master, because you must know that the old witch whose twelve girls we have slain has yet another most beautiful daughter. The girl has not yet been allowed to see daylight, she is always kept in a special room which she has never yet left, and in which six candles are kept burning day and night – that is the girl to whom that golden hair once belonged. But never mind, eat and drink to your heart's content, we will go and fetch her. But be cautious when you enter the house where the daughter of the old witch is guarded, because there are a dozen bells over the door, and they may betray you."

Jack therefore ate and drank, and took a bucketful of wine to his foal too, and gave it a drink. Then they started and went and went, until after a while they reached the dwelling of the old witch. Jack dismounted, cautiously approached the door, carefully muffled the dozen bells, and gently opened the door without making the slightest noise. And lo! Inside he beheld the girl with the golden tresses, such a wonderfully pretty creature the like of which he had not set his eyes upon before during all his eventful life. He stole up to her bedside on tiptoe, grasped the girl round the waist, and in another second was again out of the house, carrying her off with him. He ran as fast as he could and mounted his steed. The foal gave a parting kick to the house that made the roof tumble in, and the next moment was off, high up in the air like a swift bird. But the old witch was not slow either, the moment she was roused she mounted a long fir pole and tore after Jack like forked lightning.

"It is you, Jack, you good-for-nothing, deceitful fellow! My twelve daughters have perished by your hand, and now you carry off my thirteenth! You may have been here before, but I'll take care that you don't come again."

"If I do, I do; if I don't, I don't."

Jack went and went, and by dawn had already reached home. He conducted the girl into the king's presence, and lo! no sooner had the monarch caught sight of her than he rushed forward and embraced her, saying, "Oh, my darling, my pretty love, you are mine and I am yours!" But the girl would not utter a single word, not for the whole world. This made the king question her: "What is the matter, my love? Why are you so sad?"

"How can I help being sad? Nobody can have me until someone brings hither all my goods and chattels, my spinning wheel and distaff, nay, the very dust in my room."

The king at once sent for Jack.

"Well, my boy, if the golden-haired girl's goods and chattels, spinning wheel, distaff, and the very dust in her room, are not here by tomorrow morning, I will hang you."

Jack was very much downcast and began to cry. When he reached the stables his foal again asked him, "What's the matter with you, my dear master? Why all this sorrow?"

"How can I help weeping and crying, my dear horse; the king has sent for me and threatened to hang me if the golden-haired girl's goods and chattels, nay, the very dust of her room, be not here by tomorrow morning."

"Don't fret, my dear master, we will go and fetch them too. Get a tablecloth somewhere, and when you enter her room spread out the cloth on the floor and sweep all her paraphernalia into it."

Jack got ready and started on his errand. Within a short time he reached the dwelling of the old witch, entered the room, and spread out his cloth. But, would anybody believe it, the glare of the place very nearly blinded him; the very dust on the floor was pure gold. He swept everything he could find into the tablecloth, swung the bundle on his back, and ran out. Having got outside, the foal at his bidding gave the building a powerful kick that demolished its very foundations. This woke the old witch, who immediately mounted a red-hot broom and tore after him like a whirlwind.

"Confound you, deceitful Jack! After you have robbed me of all my thirteen daughters, you now come and steal the chattels of the youngest girl. I warrant that you won't return hither any more."

"If I do, I do; if I don't, I don't."

Jack went home with the luggage and handed it to the king.

"Well, my darling, my pretty love! Your wish is now fulfilled, and nothing can prevent you from becoming mine."

"You shall have me, but only on one condition. Somebody must go for my stud with golden hair, which is to be found beyond the Red Sea. Until all my horses are here nobody can have me."

The king again sent for Jack.

"Listen to this, my boy; the girl with the golden hair has a golden-haired stud beyond the Red Sea. If you don't go at once to fetch them, you forfeit your life."

Jack went downstairs in great trouble, bent over his foal, buried his face in his hands, and wept most bitterly, and as he sobbed and moaned the little foal asked, "What are you crying about now?" Jack told the foal what the king had ordered him to do, and what the punishment would be if the order were not obeyed.

"Don't weep, dear master, don't fret; the thing can be done if you follow my directions. Go upstairs to the king and beg of him twelve buffalo hides, twelve balls of twine, a grubbing hoe and an ordinary hoe, besides a stout awl to sew the buffalo hides together with."

Jack went to the king and declared himself willing to carry out his order if he would let him have these things, to which the king replied, "Go and take anything that you may require, there must be some sixty buffalo hides still left hanging in the loft."

Jack went up to the loft and took what he wanted; then he ate and drank, gave his foal a bucketful of wine, and set out in search of the horses with the golden hair.

He journeyed on till, after a short lapse of time, he reached the Red Sea, which he crossed on the back of his foal. As soon as they emerged from the water and gained the opposite shore, the foal said, "Look, my dear master; can you see the pear tree on that hill yonder? Let's go up on the hill, take your hoe and dig a hole big enough to hold me, and as soon as you have dug the hole sew the twelve buffalo hides together and wrap them round me, as it would not be advisable for me to get into the hole without them. As soon as I have got in, blow this whistle and the stallion will appear, and the moment you see it touching the buffalo skins, throw a halter over its head."

Jack tucked up his shirt sleeves, dug the hole, sewed the twelve buffalo hides on to the foal, and his steed got into the hole. Then he blew the whistle, and lo! a fine stallion, with golden hair, and almost entirely covered with golden froth, jumped out of the ground. It pranced about, and kicked out in all directions, whereupon Jack's foal said, "Now then, my dear master, throw that halter over its head and jump on its back." Jack did as he was told, and, no sooner was he on its back than the stallion gave a tremendous neigh that rent all the mountains asunder. At its call a vast number of golden-haired horses appeared; so many that Jack was not able to count them. The whole herd immediately took to their heels, and galloped off with the speed of lightning. The king had not yet finished dressing in the morning when the whole stud with golden hair stood arrayed in his courtyard. So soon as he caught sight of them he rushed off to the girl with the golden hair and exclaimed, "Well, my love, the golden horses are all here, and now you are mine." "Oh, no! I shan't be yours. I won't touch either food or drink until the lad who has fetched my animals milks the mares."

The king sent for Jack.

"I say, my boy, if you do not at once milk the mares, I'll play the hangman with you."

"How can I milk them, sir? Even as they are, I find it difficult to save myself from being trampled to death."

"Do not let us waste any words; it must be done!"

Jack returned to the stables, and looked very sad; he would not touch any food or drink. His foal again addressed him and asked, "Why all this sorrow, dear master?"

"How could I help being sad? The king has ordered me to milk the mares no matter what happens, whether I get over it dead or alive."

"Don't fret. Ask him to lend you the tub up in the loft, and milk the mares. They won't do you the least harm."

And so it happened. Jack fetched the tub and milked the mares. They stood all the time as quietly as the most patient milch cows. The king then said to the girl with the golden hair, "Well, my darling; your wish is fulfilled, and you are mine."

"I shan't be yours until the lad who milked the mares has bathed in the milk."

The king sent for Jack.

"Well, my boy, as you have milked the mares, you had better bathe in the milk."

"Gracious majesty! How could I do that? The milk is boiling hot, and throws up bubbles as high as a man."

"Don't talk; you have to bathe in the milk or you forfeit your life."

Jack went down and cried, and gave up all hope of life; he was sure of death on the gallows. His foal again spoke, and said, "Don't cry, dear master, but tell me what is the matter with you." Jack told him what he had to do under penalty of death.

"Don't fret, my dear master, but go to the king and ask his permission to allow you to lead me to the tub, and be present when you take your bath. I will draw out all the heat, and you can bathe in the milk without any fear."

So Jack went to the king, and said, "Well, gracious majesty, at least grant me the favour of allowing my foal to be present when I am having my bath, so that it may see me give up the ghost."

"I don't care if there be a hundred foals present."

Jack returned to the stables, led his foal to the tub, who began to sniff. At last it took a deep breath, and beckoned to Jack not to jump in yet. Then it continued drawing in its breath, and suddenly at a sign Jack jumped into the tub, and had his bath. When he finished and got out of the tub he was three times more handsome than before, although he was a very handsome lad then. When the king saw this he said to the lad, "Well, Jack, you see you would not have the bath at first. I'm going to have one myself." The king jumped in, but in the meantime the foal had sent all the heat into the milk back again, and the tyrant was scalded to death. The heat was so intense that nothing was left of his body except a few bits of bone, as big as my little finger, which were every now and then brought up by the bubbles. Jack lost not a moment, but rushed up to the girl with the golden hair, embraced and kissed her, and said, "Well, my pretty darling, love of my heart, you are now mine, and I am yours; not even the spade and the hoe shall separate us one from another." To which she replied: "Oh, my love, Jackie, for a long time this has been one of my fondest wishes, as I knew that you were a brave lad."

The wedding was celebrated with great pomp, that gave people something to talk about over seven countries. I, too, was present at the banquet, and kept on shouting, "Chef! Cook! Let me have a bone," till, at last, he did take up a bone and threw it at me. It hit me, and made my side ache ever since.

The Crow's Nest

THERE WAS ONCE IN THE WORLD a poor man who had a wife and two children, the elder a girl, the younger a boy. The poor man went out one day ploughing with two wretched little oxen, his only property; his wife remained at home to do the cooking. The girl, being the older of the two children, was often sent out on short errands. Upon the present occasion, too, she was away from the

house, her mother having sent her out to borrow a peel, the dough for the bread being very nearly spoilt for having been kept too long in the trough.

Availing herself of the girl's absence, the mother killed the poor little boy and hid him in a pot of stewed cabbage. By the time that the girl returned her dear little brother was half stewed. When the mess was quite done, the woman poured it into a smaller pot, placed the small pot into a sling, and sent the food by her daughter to her husband who was in the field. The man liked the dish very much, and asked the girl:

"What kind of meat is this? It is very nice."

"I believe, dear father, mother had to kill a small lamb last night, and no doubt she cooked it for you," replied the girl.

But somehow or other the girl learned the true state of things, and the news nearly broke her heart. She immediately went back to the field, gathered up the bones of her little brother, carefully wrapped them into a beautiful piece of new white linen and took them into the nearest forest, where she hid them in a hollow tree. Nobody can foretell what will happen, and so it came to pass that the bones did not remain very long in the hollow of the tree. Next spring a crow came and hatched them, and they became exactly such a boy as they were before. The boy would sometimes perch on the edge of the hollow, and sing to a beautiful tune the following words:

> *"My mother killed me,*
> *"My father ate me,*
> *"My sister gathered up my bones,*
> *"She wrapped them in clean white linen,*
> *"She placed them in a hollow tree,*
> *"And now, behold, I'm a young crow."*

Upon one occasion, just as he was singing this song, a man with a cloak strolled by.

"Go on, my son," he said, "repeat that pretty song for me! I live in a big village, and have travelled a good deal in my lifetime, but I have never heard such a pretty song."

So the boy again commenced to sing:

> "My mother killed me,
> "My father ate me,
> "My sister gathered up my bones,
> "She wrapped them in clean white linen,
> "She placed them in a hollow tree,
> "And now, behold, I'm a young crow."

The man with the cloak liked the song very much, and made the boy a present of his cloak. Then a man with a crutch-stick hobbled by. "Well, my boy," he said, "sing me that song again. I live in a big village, have travelled far, but have never heard such a pretty tune." And the boy again commenced to sing:

> "My mother killed me,
> "My father ate me,
> "My sister gathered up my bones,
> "She wrapped them in clean white linen,
> "She placed them in a hollow tree,
> "And now behold I'm a young crow."

The man with the crutch-stick, too, liked the song immensely, and gave the boy his crutch-stick. The next one to pass was a miller. He also asked the boy to repeat the pretty tune, and as the boy complied with his request the miller presented him with a millstone.

Then a sudden thought flashed across the boy's head and he flew to his father's house, settled on the roof, and commenced to sing:

> "My mother killed me,
> "My father ate me,
> "My sister gathered up my bones,
> "She wrapped them in clean white linen,
> "She placed them in a hollow tree,
> "And now behold I'm a young crow."

The woman was terrified, and said to her daughter, "Go and drive away that bird, I don't like its croaking." The girl went out and tried to drive away the bird, but instead of flying away the young crow continued to sing the same song, and threw down the cloak to his sister. The girl was much pleased with the present, ran into the house and exclaimed, "Look here what a nice present that ugly bird has given to me!"

"Very nice indeed; very nice indeed. I will go out too," said her father. So he went out, and the bird threw down to him the crutch-stick. The old man was highly delighted with the gift; he was getting very weak, and the crutch-stick came in useful to him as a support.

"Look here what a strong crutch-stick he has given to me! It will be a great help to me in my old age."

Then his mother jumped up from behind the oven and said, "I must go out too; if presents won't shower at least a few might drivel to me."

So she went out and looked up to the roof, and the boy gave her a present for which she had not bargained. He threw the millstone at her, which killed her on the spot.

Thus far goes our tale. Here it ends.